MAXIM JAKUBOWSKI was born in England but educated in France. Following a career in publishing, he opened London's famous MURDER ONE bookshop. He has published over 85 books, won the Anthony and Karel Awards and is a connoisseur of genre fiction in all its forms. His recent books include ten volumes in *The Mammoth Book of Erotica* series, as well as *The Mammoth Book of Pulp Fiction* and more recently *The Mammoth Book of Pulp Action*. Other well-received anthologies include: *London Noir*, three volumes of *Fresh Blood*, *Past Poisons*, *Chronicles of Crime* and *Murder Through the Ages*. A regular broadcaster, he is the crime columnist for the *Guardian*. His fiction includes *Life in the World of Women*, *It's you that I want to Kiss*, *Because She Thought She Loved Me*, *The State of Montana*, *On Tenderness Express*, *Confessions of a Romantic Pornographer* and *American Casanova*. He lives in London.

THE MAMMOTH BOOK OF

Best
New Erotica

Volume 5

Edited by Maxim Jakubowski

CARROLL & GRAF PUBLISHERS
New York

Carroll & Graf Publishers
An imprint of Avalon Publishing Group, Inc.
245 W. 17th Street
New York
NY 10011–5300

AVALON
publishing group incorporated

First published in the UK by Robinson,
an imprint of Constable & Robinson Ltd, 2006

First Carroll & Graf edition 2006

ISBN-13: 978-0-7394-6653-7
ISBN-10: 0-7394-6653-4

Printed in the U.S.A.

Contents

Contents

Contents

Acknowledgments

Introduction and selection © 2005 by Maxim Jakubowski

THE SALON by Martha Sterling, © 2004 by Martha Sterling. First appeared in *Ruthie's Club*. Reprinted by permission of the author.

ICELAND SUMMER by Bill Noble, © 2004 by Bill Noble. First appeared in *Clean Sheets*. Reprinted by permission of the author.

THE SCARLESS by Marcelle Perks, © 2004 by Marcelle Perks. First appeared in *Three-Way*, edited by Alison Tyler. Reprinted by permission of the author.

PERILOUS PENNY, PART TIME PORNOGRAPHER by Tara Alton, © 2004 by Tara Alton. First appeared in *Scarlet Letters*. Reprinted by permission of the author.

LONESOME LITTLE BLUE by O'Neil De Noux, © 2004 by O'Neil De Noux. First appeared in *The Big Book of Erotic Ghost Stories*, edited by Greg Wharton. Reprinted by permission of the author.

FOUR ON THE FLOOR by Alison Tyler, © 2004 by Alison Tyler. First appeared in *Clean Sheets*. Reprinted by permission of the author.

UNRAVELING THE THREADS OF AN ORDINARY LIFE by Amanda Earl, © 2004 by Amanda Earl. First appeared in *Erotica Readers & Writers Association*. Reprinted by permission of the author.

UTTERLY NUDE by Maxim Jakubowski, © 2004 by Maxim Jakubowski. First appeared in *Naked Erotica*, edited by Alison Tyler. Reprinted by permission of the author.

OUTSOURCING by Robert Buckley, © 2004 by Robert Buckley. First appeared in *Erotica Readers & Writers Association*. Reprinted by permission of the author.

FIVE STATES by Cheyenne Blue, © 2004 by Cheyenne Blue. First appeared in *Clean Sheets*. Reprinted by permission of the author.

UNDER MY THUMB by Thomas S. Roche, © 2004 by Thomas S. Roche. First appeared in *Naughty Stories From A to Z, Volume 3*, edited by Alison Tyler. Reprinted by permission of the author.

MY MOTHER'S CHILD by Marie Lyn, © 2004 by Marie Lyn. First appeared in *Clean Sheets*. Reprinted by permission of the author.

GIRL ON A SWING by J.Z. Sharpe, © 2004 by J.Z. Sharpe. First appeared in *Erotica Readers & Writers Association*. Reprinted by permission of the author.

NOT AT RISK by Joshua Hoobler, © 2004 by Joshua Hoobler. First appeared in *Suspect Thoughts*. Reprinted by permission of the author.

A STOUT LENGTH OF BIRCH by Lisette Ashton, © 2004 by Lisette Ashton. First appeared in *The Hot Spot*. Reprinted by permission of the author.

HIGHER POWER by Lisabet Sarai, © 2004 by Lisabet Sarai. First appeared in *Best S/M Erotica, volume 2*, edited by M. Christian. Reprinted by permission of the author.

UNORTHODOX GIGOLO by Misha Firer, © 2004 by Misha Firer. First appeared in *Scarlet Letters*. Reprinted by permission of the author.

ODALISQUE by Mitzi Szereto, © 2004 by Mitzi Szereto. First appeared in *Foreign Affairs*, edited by Mitzi Szereto. Reprinted by permission of the author.

THE PUSS HATER by Inna Spice, © 2004 by Inna Spice. First appeared in *Erotica Readers & Writers Association*. Reprinted by permission of the author.

PICTURE PERFECT by Donna George Storey, © 2004 by Donna George Storey. First appeared in *Taboo*, edited by Violet Blue. Reprinted by permission of the author.

DEATH POEMS by Mark Ramsden, © 2005 by Mark Ramsden. Reprinted by permission of the author.

IN THE STACKS by Kristina Wright, © 2004 by Kristina Wright. First appeared in *Master/Slave*, edited by N.T. Morley. Reprinted by permission of the author.

I WANT TO WATCH YOU DO IT by Mike Kimera, © 2004 by Mike Kimera. First appeared in *Clean Sheets*. Reprinted by permission of the author.

CHINCHILLA LACE by Cervo, © 2004 by Cervo. First appeared in *Erotica Readers & Writers Association*. Reprinted by permission of the author.

TURNING THE TABLES by Rachel Kramer Bussel, © 2004 by Rachel Kramer Bussel. First appeared in *Penthouse*. Reprinted by permission of the author.

EXCEPTIONS by J.D. Smith, © 2004 by J.D. Smith. First appeared in *Clean Sheets*. Reprinted by permission of the author.

WORSHIP by Elspeth Potter, © 2004 by Elspeth Potter. First appeared in *Best Women's Erotica 2004*, edited by Marcy Sheiner. Reprinted by permission of the author.

RESIGNATION by N.T. Morley, © 2004 by N.T. Morley. First appeared in *Naughty Stories From A to Z, volume 3*, edited by Alison Tyler. Reprinted by permission of the author.

GUIDED TOURS by Jolan Sulinski, © 2004 by Jolan Sulinski. First appeared in *Scarlet Letters*. Reprinted by permission of the author.

CRACKED BUTTERFLY by Teresa Lamai, © 2004 by Teresa Lamai. First appeared in *Clean Sheets*. Reprinted by permission of the author.

SECRETLY WISHING FOR RAIN by Claude Lalumière, © 2004 by Claude Lalumière. First appeared in *Fishnet*. Reprinted by permission of the author.

THE GIFT by Dahlia Schweitzer, © 2004 by Dahlia Schweitzer. First appeared in *The Mammoth Book of Women's Sexual Fantasies*, edited by Sonia Florens. Reprinted by permission of the author.

BELLS ON HER TOES by M. Christian, © 2004 by M. Christian. First appeared in *Naughty Fairy Tales From A to Z*, edited by Alison Tyler. Reprinted by permission of the author.

TWO OF CUPS by Elizabeth Margery, © 2004 by Elizabeth Margery. First appeared in *Clean Sheets*. Reprinted by permission of the author.

SCREEN PLAY by A.F. Waddell, © 2004 by A.F. Waddell. First appeared in slightly different format in *Erotica Readers*

& Writers Association. Reprinted by permission of the author.

THIRD PERSON SINGULAR by Richard V. Raiment, © 2004 by Richard V. Raiment. First appeared in *Clean Sheets*. Reprinted by permission of the author.

RICHARD'S SECRET by Saskia Walker, © 2004 by Saskia Walker. First appeared in *Taboo*, edited by Violet Blue. Reprinted by permission of the author.

MILEAGE by Tom Piccirilli, © 2004 by Tom Piccirilli. First appeared in *Down and Dirty, Volume 2*, edited by Alison Tyler. Reprinted by permission of the author.

PRIX FIXE by Riain Grey, © 2004 by Riain Grey. First appeared in *Clean Sheets*. Reprinted by permission of the author.

ZOE CLARK by Tara Alton, © 2004 by Tara Alton. First appeared in *Scarlet Letters*. Reprinted by permission of the author.

BEVERLY'S PASTIME by Sage Vivant, © 2004 by Sage Vivant. First appeared in *Wicked Words 9*, edited by Kerri Sharp. Reprinted by permission of the author.

THE SPACE BETWEEN by Helena Settimana, © 2004 by Helena Settimana. First appeared in *Three-Way*, edited by Alison Tyler. Reprinted by permission of the author.

THE HUMAN DRESS by O'Neil De Noux, © 2005 by O'Neil De Noux. Reprinted by permission of the author.

COINS FOR THE FERRYMAN by Robert Buckley, © 2004 by Robert Buckley. First appeared in *Erotica Readers & Writers Association*. Reprinted by permission of the author.

Introduction

Maxim Jakubowski

The years go by and still the fecund imagination of male and female writers of erotica continues to surprise and amaze me. This is the fifth instalment in our annual series in which I've attempted to select and present the best stories published worldwide during the course of the preceding calendar year; this in addition to five previous volumes in the series which paved the ground for our turning into a regular, annual event, as well as inspiring, dare I say it, an explosion in the quantity of original and reprint anthologies in our field which still sees no slowing down.

Yet again I was faced by a veritable mountain of submissions, originating in other collections, magazines, webzines and even e-books and I genuinely feel this volume genuinely represents some of the best writing in the genre. I am warmed by the fact that, once more, I am able to introduce a handful of brand new writers to our series. All of whom display a wicked imagination, sexy ideas and believable characters the reader can identify with.

Too many of the stories I have had to turn down, this time around, are sadly no more than mood pieces, climaxing with a sexual scene and the occasional taboo or unusual variation on a theme – some better written than others, some more psychologically credible than others. Or just wild fantasies with little grounding in reality, wish fulfilment episodes with often a touch of vulgarity which for me is a definite turn-off, or lyrical and meaningful odes to bodies and mating lacking in the art of storytelling, and aspiring desperately for the status of poetry and of course not getting anywhere near that level of inspiration.

So stories with men and women of flesh and articulate thoughts have been at a premium, even more so those with an added healthy sense of humour, as I perversely insist on thinking that a smile on one's lips when dealing with sex can often be a wonderful asset . . . Let's not always be so serious and earnest about what is after all one of mankind's oldest and favourite activities.

Alongside our Mammoth Erotica virgins, many of our most experienced and popular writers of erotica also make a welcome return to our pages, all tackling the thorny theme of sex between consenting adults in ever-more innovative ways which will have you frowning, wiping the sweat off your brow, smiling or even wide open-mouthed. Whoever thought one could conjure up so many situations and improvisations around the facts of life as we know it? But in fact, do we actually know it all? It seems we don't and I am confident that next year, I will have learned more from the world of erotica and I look forward to the continuing education.

Good erotic writing can be sexy, provocative, intelligent, even educational, but always fascinating.

Welcome one more time to the playing fields of the Gods . . .
Savour.

Maxim Jakubowski

The Salon

Martha Sterling

I never thought I'd go into one of those salons to make a quick buck, but there comes a time in everyone's life when all bets are off. It was that time for me. The hours of viewing at the videoport at home were starting to get on my nerves. I needed money to get the hell out of there, but Mom was out of the picture – gave all her money to some guy who looked like he just walked out of a wax museum. Dad, of course, would pass me a few if I asked him but I knew the price would be high – extended weekend visits with him and his henna-colored dog (yes, he does treat his dog's fur with henna) plus lectures on the coming destruction of the planet. No. Thank. You.

Besides, I had been feeling restless. That tension in the back of my neck was back again and I wanted it to go away. No point in going to the clinic since the pills they always gave me to release the muscle spasms were archaic, a throwback to the days of my grandmother when sleeping pills and tranquilizers were all the rage. Even if they are "newly engineered" "purer" and "safer," as they claim, it's still all the same – a blanket for the brain. I want access to the modern school of medicine, where they treat the cause, not the symptom. They zap your brain for about two minutes, I'm told, with electricity, and stimulate all sorts of reverse psychology that fights the anxiety. It has nothing to do with the electroshock therapy they used to do in the old days. Much more advanced than that. They use lasers. It's supposed to be brilliant, but still experimental. I saw a documentary short about it at the videoport in my doctor's waiting room. But the treatment's not open to the public yet, being practiced only by a few up at the Lehigh Medical Center at Yale or someplace like that.

And the salons are supposed to be really well run. A friend of mine (actually, a former friend) worked there for a time. She wasn't one of the personal service workers, just someone who handled the paperwork and check-in. She was a seasoned professional, and organized to a T, and I'm sure she did an A-1 job with the clientele. After we lost touch, I found out she had left the salon to work as the administrator of a cooperative farm in Birmingham, Alabama. I thought it was probably a good career move when I first heard about it but, now that I'm at the salon, I'm not so sure.

This salon job is turning out to be one hell of a trip – and not the type I would advise others to go on. It pays well, and my days are an endless siege of varied stimulation from all angles. Sometimes I leave exhausted but most of the time I'm light and airy and I flit around the streets like a moth. I have nothing more left to give by the time my shift is over, and the emptiness is cool and vast and weightless. The wet streets look slippery, but they are not, and I can move effortlessly while the wind cleanses me of my day's work.

If I can call it work. It's not work for me. I love it, and I live for it. And I live for that special person – I'll call him Jose, because I once thought I heard him exclaim *"¡Ai, caramba!"* when he was coming. Ever since then, he's been Jose for me. He comes in most weeks on Tuesdays and Thursdays, and he usually chooses the Full Anonymity wing, which is where I work. Because of the rules, I'd never seen him, but for some reason I always pictured him as having short, curly dark hair and big teeth. I pictured them shining as he sat and flossed at night.

The set-up at the salon is top-notch. The cleaning crew does a great job, spraying everything down practically constantly with that odorless anti-germ stuff. I don't think even the tiniest germ would have a chance in hell of surviving more than five minutes in that place. I haven't had so much as a cold since I started this job.

I think it was primarily because I mentioned my ex-friend's name that I got the job in the first place. That, and because I have such a terrifically large mouth and protruding jaw. I've always known it, and hated it, but now I feel kind of special because of it. When I was a kid, I heard that they could break someone's jaw and reconstruct their mouth to make it right, but no one especially wanted to do that for me, so I set out to break my jaw myself. I tried jumping off of the wall that jutted out beside our condo unit but, at the last second, I put my hand out to break my fall onto the pavement and ended up breaking my wrist instead. I made a few other half-assed tries, but most of them ended in a lot of pain, so I gave up.

But my mouth got me this job, which just goes to prove what I'm learning more as time goes on – everything has its time and purpose. What's a liability today may be my saving grace tomorrow, so don't ever say "Never." You just don't know.

At first, I was uncertain about the Anonymity Section of the salon, but the staff suggested it for me. They said it was often a good start for new people because there is no need to look anybody in the eye. Hell, you don't have to look at any part of them actually, except maybe their balls, but you can keep your eyes closed if you want.

The set-up here is ingenious. I'd like to get into the brain of the person who designed this place. Such creative brilliance. Such endless attention to detail. I'm in awe.

This is how it works: each service worker is assigned to a "Horse." The Horses are our specially designed units. Each one is adjusted to the particular body dimensions of the individual worker. They're called Horses because when a service worker lies on one she is on all fours, like a horse. But it's incredibly luxurious and comfortable. Every part of the Horse is padded with vasacloth, which makes it impossible to feel any friction or skin discomfort. And I love the way the middle of the Horse, the part that supports my entire abdomen, from hips to rib cage, prevents me from placing any actual weight on my knees or elbows. They rest on vasacloth surfaces, but they're really just dangling there, not holding me up. There are two holes in the torso support for my breasts to hang through freely. I'm told the person who designed the horse was a great mathematician and anatomist. She even designed it to prevent any backaches from lying in this position over a prolonged period.

An equally soft Face Bowl supports our heads. It has no middle so I can breathe freely but it holds up the weight of my head. When they fitted me for my face bowl, they had me lie on the horse and they adjusted it to the angle most comfortable for my neck. The technician was impatient, though, and she made me nervous, so I think the angle isn't quite right. I hope I don't get that technician again when I request an adjustment.

Once a service worker is comfortably on her Horse, she can press a button to have the Anonymity Partitions come down. One comes down from the ceiling and rests across her lower back, blocking any view of the front of her body from anybody who may come in behind her. The other is a cool, soft blanket that unrolls lightly over the front part of her body. The temperature is always kept at a strict 75 degrees.

These horses are arranged in a row. The effect is such that any customer who requests Rear View Anonymity will walk into a long room with a line of female backsides for him to survey. The Horses are designed to keep our knees dangling with a slight outward angle, so our cunts are open nicely. On my days off, I paid to come into the Rear View Room and I must say the effect is riveting. Some of the genitalia are wrinkled and pink, some are small, some are large, some have blonde hair, some dark. And the legs are both incredibly similar and various at the same time. They all look like female legs, and there is continuity in the way they line up along the side of the room, each on its knees. But at the same time, there are differences. Some are slender and angular, others meaty and muscular. And the color variations are enormous – every hue from dark chocolate to creamy vanilla.

The bottom view is not so much to my liking; it's the view of the hanging tits. Customers who enter this room see a long line of tits hanging from the enclosure where the women are encased. It sort of looks like a big box jutting out of the wall. A customer can reach out and fondle the tits as he walks along the edge of the enclosure. If he finds a set of udders he finds interesting, he can press a button and a cot emerges from underneath that box. He can then lie down beneath the tits, adjusting the height with an automatic button, so that he can suck, lick, and fondle to his liking.

It's particularly exciting for me as a service worker on busy days, because I may be chosen for rear and bottom view service at the same time. Of course, each customer doesn't know that the other is using me at the same time as another, which is kind of weird. I can have Jose behind me (which is where he always is) and any other Joe beneath me fondling my boobs. The double stimulation is great, but I find that my mouth waters when I get this double business. I can't seem to control the saliva, and my face bowl gets damp and unpleasant. I don't know what to do about that problem.

What I like about Jose is he likes to play. I have plenty of quick guys. You know, they come in, maybe stick a finger or two in with some lubricant on the ends, and then they thrust. I'm not saying that some of them aren't good; there is at least one customer a day who can go on for at least a half hour. But there's just no build-up there. No anticipation.

Jose's not like that. He takes full advantage of the hour he pays for in the Rear View Anonymity room. He starts with my feet, which are always sheathed in a colorful pair of thigh-high nylons and death-defying high-heeled shoes. First, he starts by kissing my toes lightly, as his hands travel up my legs. His mouth soon follows. Then he takes my buttocks and spreads me wide open. He starts to circle my anus with his tongue, never directly touching the hole. This always gets me moaning, and I know he can hear me. The face enclosures are not soundproof, although we're not supposed to communicate verbally, because that would ruin the secrecy.

After he's tickled me with his tongue a while, he starts to tug lightly on my pubic hairs. It's a little painful, but just a little.

It's somewhere on the threshold of pleasure and pain. So far, he still hasn't gone anywhere near my clit, and of course by now it's aching. And there's simply no way I can do anything about that – not with my hands clamped in the front half of the Horse – and so I have this excruciating, marvelous suffering while he does his thing.

It took me a few of his visits to work out that, at some point during all this, Jose pulls out his dick and starts jerking off big time. If I pay attention, sometimes I realize his mouth and only one hand are playing with me. Where's the other hand? He's down there whacking off good. I can hear him.

Sometimes he even just stands there for five or ten minutes moving his lubricated finger in and out of my ass while he whacks off. Eventually, he lays his head on top of my ass and shudders as he comes.

But Jose doesn't tire after he comes. No way. He keeps playing. I don't know how this guy learned how to control his dick so well, but he can bring it up again real fast after he comes. Maybe he's taking some of those new drugs, or maybe it's just training. It doesn't really matter.

Eventually, Jose makes use of the toys we keep in sterile solution at the entrance to the anonymity wing. It's not always the same. Last time, he just barely touched my clit with the edge of a tiny pulsating tool while he licked my anus. Just when I thought I couldn't hold off anymore, like I was going to have to come, he pulled it away from me. I yelled so loud, I think the other service women must have thought I was being hurt. But I didn't press the alarm bell or anything, so they realized it was pleasure, not pain.

Finally, each time when I'm certain I can't take it anymore, Jose presses the button to adjust the height of the floor so that he's positioned perfectly behind me, and then – slowly, centimeter by centimeter – he thrusts into me. I feel each segment of his cock as it enters me, and it is so slow. When he is fully inside me, he starts to pump with long hard steady strokes. I can hear him sucking in long fast breaths as he uses my wet, aching hole. Meanwhile, he usually keeps one finger in my anus to steady himself. I can feel the muscles in my ass holding on to his finger.

He pumps slowly, then quickly, then slow again, building and building. If I'm lucky, someone else is down below me gently sucking on my hanging tits. If everything happens right like that, it's as if Jose's life is being pumped right into my body and I'm completely open. I can't be open any further, and I'm finally alive. I don't know what time is at those moments – it ceases to exist.

Jose knows by now that, if he even so much as slightly touches my clit now, I will erupt into spasms of orgasm, so he waits until he's ready. When he is, he reaches around my hips and gently presses on my swollen clit. I immediately start to come in wave after wave as he bucks, and he screams as he squirts inside me.

He's very neat when he pulls out his cock, making ample use of the paper towels we provide. By now, I feel like I have been flying, and I feel like sleeping. Jose kisses my open asshole one last time before he dresses and leaves. I hear him shuffle to the door.

It's strictly forbidden to try and find out who one has serviced in The Anonymity Wing, but I just can't help but want to know. I could lose my job by trying and, like I said, this is a damn good job, especially when you consider the fringe benefits. But, when something as good as this happens to someone, there's this fear that maybe, just maybe, it will disappear and you won't be able to get it anymore. I'm not saying that other guys in the wing don't get me off – some have been damn decent – but this build up with Jose, it was unreal. Transported me to another dimension, if that doesn't sound too weird. What if he just stopped coming one day? That happens all the time with customers. How would I ever find him again?

And so, I broke the rules. I called in a few favors with the girl at the desk, made promises with part of my pay-check and found out that Jose's real name was Juan (I was damn close) and he was a waiter at the Fifth Deck, a swanky restaurant in the tourist district. It's not my typical restaurant, considering that the bill for a meal there would be almost a whole week's salary for me, but I decided it was worth it. Today I would be Juan's customer instead of the other way around!

The maître d' seemed surprised when I requested my table by the name of the waiter. I stated it simply: "I don't care where I sit, as long as Juan is my waiter," I said, and I winked.

I was trying to be sly or coy or something, but it went right over the guy's head. Either that or he was so over the hill and undersexed that he couldn't care less about whether I wanted to fuck Juan or not. He didn't even look at my breasts, even though I was wearing a sheer white blouse that clearly emphasized the outline of my nipples. What a prude.

But he escorted me to a table, and I felt my pulse start to rise. In a minute, I was going to meet the only man who had ever brought me to complete and utter ecstasy. This was the man who left me panting and satiated, and who made my body into a violin. Only he could play me. Finally, we would meet.

Juan's face was severe as he approached my table. He had thick black eyebrows, and they burrowed into the middle of his forehead. His hair was slicked back and shockingly long in the back, although tied neatly into a long ponytail. His lips were almost a candy-apple red, and I couldn't help thinking he had been sucking on some sort of lollypop recently. He was around thirty-five, and a little pudgy around the middle. He was neither more nor less appealing than I had expected. I'm not sure I would have made much of him if I happened to run into him elsewhere. He was simply a guy – perhaps a little darker and a little older than I normally like them – but not half bad.

Besides, this was the guy that fucked me right, wasn't it? I was prepared for almost anything. I didn't care. He was my magic. He was my instant turn-on. I wanted him, and I wanted him without the anonymity booth. I wanted to see him pull out his dick and whack himself on me. I wanted to see his face contort as he moaned in mounting tension. I had had enough of this hiding behind a partition.

I couldn't help smiling when he stood by the table. He had no idea who I was. He had fucked my cunt and my ass, fingered my clit, rested his head on my ass, and licked me all over, but he didn't know it. It was a hoot.

I pretended interest in the menu, but I'm not one for playing games for long, so I cut right to the performance. I knew that he had heard me moaning. I just knew he would recognize my voice, so I closed my eyes and imagined he was behind me fingering my ass. I imagined that he was licking my clit, like he had just the night before. I transported myself back to the booth. I felt my knees in the horse, and my legs spread apart, and I felt the liquid start to run down my inner thigh right there in the restaurant. And then I let out a long hard moan. I didn't hold back. I just moaned and moaned, and arched my back in the seat, for all to hear.

When I opened my eyes, Juan was gone. The other customers in the restaurant were staring at me, and the maître d' was shuffling nervously in the corner with another waiter. He was whispering, and both were looking my way.

I grabbed for my napkin to wipe my brow. I wasn't sure how long I had been moaning there. I started to come to my senses. I was moaning in a public restaurant. This stuff was supposed to stay in the salons. Absolutely no sex that is not regulated by management. I had broken the rule.

The whispering in the corner became more urgent. I looked around frantically for Juan. Surely, he had not deserted me in the midst of my ecstasy? Surely, he had recognized me for who I was and he would soon emerge from the kitchen to lead me from the restaurant? Surely, this man – who had opened my cunt in ways I had never dreamed of – had been dreaming of this moment as I had? Surely?

When Juan didn't appear, I grabbed for my purse and jumped to my feet. I was frantic now, humiliated and covered with a cold sweat.

"Where is Juan?" I shouted at the maître d'. "You! Tell me! Where did he go?"

I took a step towards him, and he took a step back. He was shocked, I could see. This was an unusual disturbance.

"Miss," he said calmly. "I have called the authorities. Please do not cause any more trouble."

I rushed for the door, and emerged into the damp night air. I wanted to get away from there fast. What was I thinking? Why did I come here? Of course, there could be no sex without monetary exchange. It was unthinkable. I needed to recover my senses.

I walked to the right, and rushed toward the waterfront. I think I had the vague notion of throwing myself off the bridge into the sea. I wanted to feel the cool water tugging me under and caressing my legs as Juan had done. I wanted the water to pull me down, down, down, and down further, until I was no more.

Then I saw him. He was standing under a lamp-post across the street staring at me. I started to yell and run towards him, but he swiftly ducked into an alleyway. I crossed the street and followed him in.

Instinctively, I knew to stop yelling. I knew that I needed to be quiet. Secrets cannot be shouted, only whispered. Secrets must stay secrets, because once they are out in the open air, the air becomes foul with reality.

Juan was leaning against a brick wall. The night was dark, and this alley was a simple path to the back entrance to a building. No one was coming or going at this hour. I could just make out the outline of Juan's black jacket. As I came closer to him, I could see that his pants were open and that he had his erect penis in his hand. His hand was moving up and down rhythmically as he penetrated me with his eyes.

I immediately kneeled before him and looked up at his dick as it rose above me. I rested my forehead against his leg, and let my tongue explore. I caressed the balls that had flopped against me and prayed to the shaft that had penetrated me with such slow precision. I felt my legs become weak with desire and I felt a pouring out of fluids between my legs. I rubbed his wet dick all over my face, bathing myself in my own saliva. Finally, I was touching what gave me such great pleasure.

After Juan came, he pulled his pants back up. I looked at his face again, and waited. Then he reached his hand down between my legs and slowly brought me to orgasm with the tip of his index finger.

I cried when I came. And then he smiled. It was the first smile I had seen on his worried face. And then he whispered in my ear, "See you at the salon."

Iceland Summer

Bill Noble

Midnight a hundred miles south of the Arctic Circle. Wind slammed the tiny tent, pressed it flat against his face for minutes at a stretch, then, relenting momentarily, let it spring up. Rain volleyed like grapeshot. The rain fly stuttered and whined but somehow held; the stakes he'd driven deep into muddy, gritty volcanic ash stayed anchored.

By first light, the violence had congealed to steady downpour. He struggled into clothes, dogged his raingear down, and crawled out into the weather to discover that his was the only tent still standing in the broad field. Dozens had been arrayed there at nightfall.

Head down, he splashed toward the park building. He shouldered its heavy doors open and found himself suddenly immersed in an explosion of warmth and light: a hundred sodden people crowded the park's lunchroom, clutching cups of cocoa in frog-wrinkled hands and gabbling in a dozen languages. Most of them had clearly spent the night here as refugees from the storm. A stench of wet wool filled the room. When he was finally able to reach the food counter, a steaming cup was thrust into his hands. A seat opened up, and he collapsed into it, hardly aware of the other person at the table. He took a first blessed scalding sip of chocolate.

Someone laughed, a tinkling cascade he sensed was aimed at him. He looked up, already half in retreat. An elf perched on the chair across from him, knees spraddled, head canted. The hood of her parka was thrown back, revealing a helmet of copper hair brushed forward to cup her face. She had a wide, mobile mouth and preternaturally huge brown eyes.

She spoke. He couldn't guess the language; his puzzlement must have shown because she leaned across to finger his dry sweater. Then she brought his hand to her breast to touch her bulky pullover. The wool was soaked, but her slender hand held fiery heat.

He had no idea what to say in the face of intimacy. "Uh, George," he said, because he had to say something, awkwardly pointing to himself, the blood rushing to his cheeks. "My name is George."

"Ah-ha," she repeated: "Jhoorj." And then she put a second warm hand over his. "Merete," she said. He flinched, but managed not to pull his hand away.

He pointed. "Merete?" Her head bobbed. Through the layers of wool, his imprisoned hand felt the unmistakable nub of her nipple.

The next day began under blue skies. The knife-edged volcanic ridges of Skaftafell National Park glowed emerald, crosslit by the early light. Tatters of cloud still clung to them. The campground was spread with gear and clothing, waiting for sun to reach the valley.

His tent was almost packed, his gear ready to hit the trail. Solitary and preoccupied in the midst of the bustle, he felt a touch – and of course, when he turned, it was the elf, hand on hip. The day before in the crowded lodge they had not been able to interpret a single word each other said beyond their names. George guessed she was Danish. Or maybe Dutch, though for a time he'd wondered if her strange vowels and convoluted consonants might be Portuguese. She leapt and swerved through her sentences; when she talked he was able to do nothing but watch her bright lips and pink, pink tongue. She'd worn a gold band on her delicate brown fingers and nodded when he tried to mime *husband*, but then she put his hand over her breast again and tossed her head.

Now she danced around him, waving toward the far reaches

of the valley, walking fingers along her forearm with one eyebrow arched into a question.

"You . . . want a hike?" he said. His first impulse was to
decline, to flee, but as her ring flashed he became conscious of
the ring missing from his own finger. A shadow passed over his
face as he remembered the brief happiness of that single year,
now half a dozen years distant.

"Hi-ee," she said, poking him to regain his attention.
"Hieek!" She scampered away, but returned in moments carrying a scuffed leather knapsack with brass buckles. She mimed
eating, waggling her eyebrows. He understood that she had
food, but beyond that his comprehension would not go. She had
the most beautiful tongue he'd ever seen.

"Jhoorj," she said, tugging at his hand, "Hieek!"

They sat crosslegged in the midst of the Baejarstadaskogur,
Iceland's only forest. Beneath pale birches, most scarcely a
dozen feet tall, the grass was starred with the blue and white of
Canterbury bells and sandwort.

He spread jerky and dried fruit on his parka, brought from
the States for his solitary summer. She had a small, tough loaf of
rye bread and at least three kinds of cheese. They talked and
chewed, and he began not to care that neither of them could
understand a word. She sat close, thigh pressed against his; the
contact warmed his whole body.

Their mutual incomprehension made it easy for his words
to pour out. He confessed he'd come to Iceland to be lonely,
shyly told her of his passion for wild places and his hunger
for solitude. And he spoke of his larger solitariness, its
longings and hesitations. He told her of the weeks alone
hiking the ffordlands and the desolate interior, encountering
swans and Arctic foxes and fumaroles and vast, distant
icebergs calved from Greenland. He spoke of the contrary
happiness his loneliness gave him. And the sadness. He told
her everything.

He had no idea what she told him. She stopped in mid-speech
when she caught him staring at her mouth, and then laughed

and put her warm hand on his thigh. Her tongue-tip traced the line of her upper lip once, and again.

Suddenly she kissed him. She proclaimed something remarkably like "Fender rumpus room!" and then sprang to her feet and pulled him up after her.

She peeled his sweater over his head. His heart began to race. "No," he said. "You mustn't."

She threw the sweater away, over her shoulder, and unbuttoned his shirt. It followed the sweater. "You're married," he protested.

She ignored his words, sniffed his undershirt and wrinkled her nose theatrically. She lifted it off him and tossed it, tangling it in the branches of a birch.

"I'm sorry—" he said. Falling to her knees, she tugged his boots off, and then his socks.

How could he stop her? She sang a strange small song with short lines and intricate, intertwined rhymes as she unzipped his pants. Murmuring, she pulled each leg of his pants down and off, did the same with his longshanked underwear, her lilting voice barely a whisper.

He was erect, of course. Wide-eyed. Frozen in place. Daintily, watching his face, she took thumb and forefinger and squeezed him until a single clear drop of fluid appeared. "Hah!" she said, as if she had proved something of great importance. And then she pecked him on the cheek.

She turned and went with a dancer's measured steps to the edge of the meadow, but spoke sternly and thrust a hand back toward him when he stumbled a step toward her. He stood, shivering, uncertain, while, facing away from him, she began a lazy, on-again-off-again disrobing, as if she might have forgotten his existence. Hot sun fell on his shoulders and warmed his rump; tendrils of cool Icelandic air tickled his scrotum and made each hair on his muscled legs stand up.

Naked, she turned to him, unreadable. Voids swam through his field of vision. His toes curled, cramped, into the moist turf. His jaw ached. Tiny-breasted, slender-hipped, she might have been no more than fourteen, but the smile lines and feral glow around her eyes hinted at thirty or forty. His cock jumped to the too-rapid tumble of his heart.

She spun away – and ran! Every muscle in his body tensed.

After twenty feet or so, she stopped and looked back at him, rooted next to his crumpled pants. She stamped the ground with her tiny foot. He took a tentative step toward her—

– and she ran!

His balls cramped. He lunged, but she was already scampering up the hillside, swerving among trees, the soles of her feet flashing at him.

He ran. Once he thought he'd lost her, till a stone thumped at his feet and he spun half round to glimpse her again. Minutes later he hurled himself panting up a stream bank, certain he was about to catch her, but as he reached the top she sprang out of the grass and shoved him. He toppled head-over-heels down the hill, tangled in her laughter.

He sprinted up a narrow defile, splashing in and out of a clear rivulet, careless of anything but pursuit, thoughtless of where he might have left his clothes. He rounded into a sun-flooded glade; there, a foot-wide cascade chuckled down the black cliff. She stood at the glade's center, chest heaving, slight shoulders bright with sweat, arms spread in welcome.

Headlong, he fell onto her body. Her nails raked him from buttocks to nape as he drove inside her.

She beat him with her heels as they fucked, grabbed his ears, bit his lip, and came. She came again, and then again, until he felt his own release boiling up – but just as a climactic roar was about to burst from his lips she threw him off and ran again.

Staggering to his feet, watery-kneed, he saw her a hundred feet away. She thrust her pelvis at him, displaying her engorged genitals, bright in the sun. He hurled himself after her.

They did this over and over. Each time he tried to hold her as he came; each time she somehow twisted herself from under him just before climax and leapt away, laughing.

At the end, though, she waited, motionless, back pressed against a slender tree. He charged at her, but she slowed him with her great liquid eyes, gentled him, took him tenderly and held him until his heart slowed. She stroked him. She kissed him open-mouthed and eased him closer against her body. When their kissing reached its deepest place, she twined one slender leg around his and brought him into her body. They moved bonelessly on each other, as if they were water. She climaxed around him in waves, sighing, holding his eyes with hers, and then led him higher, and higher still – calm, touching their whole length, breathing one breath – and higher yet, until with a long wordless note he emptied into her and she received him, coming with him once again, around him, all his solitude and hunger, all his fear, every locked-away yearning bursting out of him, flowering, as if the bright Arctic day were rising over the green land again and he was dissolving in its light.

Fourteen years.

How often had she sprung to mind? How many times had he let her go? Past is past, he told himself.

But one day, sitting at the computer in his Burlingame condo with San Francisco Bay twinkling in the middle distance, he typed her name. Of course, he cautioned himself, he was unlikely to find her. Names changed, people died . . .

It took an act of will to hit the enter key. In 0.31 seconds, the search engine noted, an email address appeared on his screen. He wrote a simple, conventional note, not thinking it appropriate to presume connection but simply recalling fondly their time in Iceland. He hoped she was well. It was a letter he might have written to a casual acquaintance. Two hours later, a reply popped into his inbox: a telephone number, with no other message whatever. It was a San Francisco number.

Three days later he had assembled the courage to dial it.

"Hallo. Merete here." She paused. "Hallo?"

"You speak English!"

A long silence. "Is this Jhoorj? Jhoorj Sutton, from Iceland. This must be."

"Yes, yes. When did you learn English?"

"Ah, dear Jhoorj, in school, in Copenhagen. When I was seven years old."

"But . . ."

"It would have made more magic, eh, if we had negotiated over sex, or told stories of our lives? Or you had worried all day at me about my husband?" She made a small, pleased sound. "I see from caller ID that you live somewhere close. When do you visit me?"

Her husband opened the door, a broad, well-dressed man on his way out. He offered a blunt-fingered, blond-furred hand to George, addressing him in that odd accent that betrays someone whose English has been learned late, on the Continent. "So, you are the famous George of Skaftafell! Merete recalls you most fondly. She is glad I was in Reykjavik those two days." He smiled. "I am afraid I am on my way to an evening meeting. I trust you to have a good visit." He bowed and made his way down the stairs. George was left standing in the doorway.

Merete sat in one of those extravagant, high-backed African chairs, one leg draped over its wicker arm. Behind her, ceiling to floor windows framed the sweep of the City and its spangled lights. Smile lines had deepened around her eyes and expressive mouth, and her copper hair was salted with gray, but she was still utterly elfin.

"Come, come," she said, patting the chair arm. "Would you like a drink? Juice?" He glimpsed her tongue. "Or would you prefer wine?"

Her smile was transparent, melting him. "Juice," he said, "or whatever you'll be drinking." She disappeared into the kitchen and reappeared moments later with two brimming glasses. He was still standing near the doorway.

"Bring that hassock and sit near me. I want to look at you. It's been a very long time." She touched his hand, gently, with her graceful fingers and he felt remembered heat. "You look well. Are you married? Have you been in good health? Have you ever been back to Iceland?"

He shook his head no, then yes, then no again.

She brought his hand to her breast, the fabric not bulky wool but silken. "I do not think you really want juice, do you, Jhoorj?

Come with me." She sprang from her chair and was across the room before the heat of her breast could fully register in his fingertips.

He followed, trembling inside.

Merete stopped in the bedroom door to take his arm. "You have barely said a word, Jhoorj. Perhaps it was better when I spoke only Danish."

She waited.

The melting had continued, washing something loose in him. His heart slowed; half surprised at himself, he took her hand and led her to the bed, where they lay side by side. He put a hand on her cheek and spoke in a low voice, stumbling over the first words. "You . . . you gave me a gift in Skaftafell. And you took something away." He brought her into his arms, pulling her closer until he felt her heart beating against his. "It wasn't the lovemaking, you know."

She giggled, and he looked first puzzled and then contrite. He smiled for the first time: "Lord knows, that was as magical as anything ever in my life. But no, it was the chase. Or catching you."

Solemnly: "You didn't catch me. I called you to me when I wanted you too much to tease any more."

"Then it was the chase. Letting myself want that much."

She nodded.

"You knew, didn't you?"

"My Jhoorj, you told me. You told me and told me when you thought I didn't understand. To make a man who had never been . . . who had never wanted, to make you want that much!"

"Are you living here?"

She shook her head. "We work for DanskeBank. We go back at the end of the month. So, since that time? Have you let yourself want?"

"No, not much. Not until now. And now we have just this little time. Like Iceland."

She watched, saying nothing.

"So I should practice wanting. And not being afraid."

Still she was silent.

He moved his hand from her cheek, slid it underneath the silk to hold her breast. Her breathing quickened, but no sound escaped.

He lifted her blouse, eyes looked with hers, and grasped her bra-covered nipple in his teeth. Still no sound.

"Stand up," he said. She stood.

He unbuttoned her blouse, his mouth twisting as he struggled with the tiny buttons. Trying to puzzle out the clasp of her bra his face reddened; he grabbed it suddenly in both fists and tore it apart, flung it into a corner of the room. She laughed aloud, her breath labored and shallow.

He flung her skirt away. He ripped her panties at the sides, jerked them from between her legs and dropped them at her feet.

"Go into the front room."

"Jhoorj, the windows," she objected. "All those houses just down the hill."

"I know. Go to the windows and put your hands on the glass. And wait for me. Without moving."

When he came to her, he pressed against her from behind, stirred by the familiar scent of her brown skin. She tilted her hips and he slipped immediately into her, both of them watching their faces reflected in the glass. In the night outside, people moved in bright-lit rooms, busy with dinnertime ritual, window after window multiplying into the distance.

She spread her legs to let him enter more deeply. With each thrust the window bowed and the reflection of their faces shrank and ballooned.

In moments her arms collapsed under the intensity of their coupling; her cheek and breasts pressed hard against the cold window. The two of them cried in counterpoint, she at each thrust, he with each momentary withdrawal.

In the yellow rectangle of light immediately below them a woman brought a birthday cake and set it twinkling in the center of a circle of friends. In the next window, a couple rose from their chairs to leave the image of Jennifer Aniston gesturing to an empty room. In another, a woman stood with a man's arms around her waist, swaying as she chatted on the phone.

Now each thrust lifted her clear of the floor. The window moaned in its frame.

"Turn!" he grated.

"What?" She was gasping, bewildered.

"Turn," he said, and pulled himself out of her. He spun her to face him and plunged in again. She knotted her legs around his waist as he slammed her back against the window.

He kissed face, mouth, neck, biting and licking. "Come with me!"

Her head snapped back and boomed against the glass. "I am," she said.

His thrusts accelerated. They grappled fingers into each other's hair to jerk their faces closer. His tongue raked the roof of her mouth. She bit his lip to draw blood, sucked it.

He slammed home in her with a guttural shout and went still, every muscle in his body locked and straining. With a rising wail, she began to come around him. He slammed deep again, and held. Her climax blurred into a series of contorted spasms centered on the root of his cock. He began to empty into her.

He slammed home a third time with such force it drove the air out of them both. With a *hisssssssss* the entire wall of safety glass shivered white and collapsed. The icefall of glass showered down. They teetered on the brink, eight stories up, braced, faces buried in each other's necks, each clutching the other to keep from tumbling outward.

He regained his balance as the seed ceased to pulse from his body; she settled against him, glittering shards still cascading from her hair and shoulders. He stepped back, his feet crunching in the snowdrift of glass.

She locked her hands with his and with a laugh threw her upper body backward, out into the cold night air. Their hands were slippery with sweat; it took all his strength to hold her. Tinkling fragments of glass still fell from them.

The woman clutching the phone stared up at them, pressed into her lover's embrace. The birthday party had drifted away from the table, out of view. Beyond the nearest houses lay the City, house after house, tower after splendid tower, as far as the jewelled hills across the Bay and further, beyond seeing. A net of longing and fulfillment glowed and sparked across the land, meetings and passings, losses and embracings in a ceaseless dance, uncounted, passionate and careless. Unnoticed in the heavens, the company of stars drifted west, eternal, empty of all desire.

The Scarless

Marcelle Perks

It was a big bed, something she could still appreciate. The plain white cotton sheet drained the heat from her exposed skin. The cameramen weren't ready yet and the longer she waited, the more the indent of her body pressed into the dampness. Yet she remained motionless, frozen to the spot. They always stressed that it was important to lie absolutely stiff, to "play dead." But they didn't want to see her soul dancing in her eyes, unlike the banal lingerie photographers who roved unfettered by their own demands and expected her to keep pace with their every turn and nuance. In cruel heels, she pranced for hours giving the camera what it wanted. Spreading her lips. Afterward, her face itched from semi-permanent smile lines that took all-night crying to rinse out, to return to the doll-blank face that was her own. Until the next shoot. Here, at least, her facial expression was underexposed, an outline for a figure, or a blur. Only the body with its signature of overstretched skin connected to the powerful lens; the burning studio lights; the strange rubber domwear of the extras. Although afterward she might have to cancel studio work for weeks until the wounds faded, it gave her a numbing lull. Her body was there, but she was not. The rabbit grin that constantly fretted between her mouth and eyes would be pushed back, temporarily plumped.

Soon they would start doing it. She couldn't see or smell or touch it, but the sense of it was a tendril of shame, an idea, like a germ, she couldn't allow to get hold of her. One of the extras was unpeeling his rubber trousers, by the sound of it, to unleash what was, undoubtedly, a large dick. Without faces or skin required for the males, they could afford to harvest the biggest dicks on the circuit, from those that in other departments had fallen from grace. Underneath the rubber, the flesh was allowed to sweat unchecked, corseted to superman proportions by the ten-thousand-dollar designer suits. Domwear for the corporate analysts and Wall Street kids who could afford to have it sitting in their vast closets while they imagined wearing it. The enormous metal tripods, stationed like stranded penises, straining now, overreaching themselves. *Click, click,* a flash of light. Something was being recorded while she didn't even recognize what position she was in. And then the whispers again, the uneasy *sss sss* seemingly both near and distant, the exact meaning falling just out of reach. These masks, sometimes even without eyeholes, rendered speech muddy, the actors drowning men trying to give their names out.

Without direction of how to carry that morning's expression, she was unsure her body could live up to scrutiny when she wasn't living in it. She wanted to look good still, even if she did not. Even as an anonymous actress under the replica nineteenth-century face mask, she was becoming precious, trying to work out which way the camera was working. Did they worry about not knowing when to stop or not wanting to stop? The men were like sticky, stretchy robots, hidden in the stretched synthetic hides, being the animals they wanted to be. Two of them perhaps, working at her now, through all the inches of identity-blurring rubber. Later she would never recognize them. The squealing burn, as familiar to her as the scent of her own front room, simply stunk, the worst part about the job. Underneath the rubber, the sweat formed grooves that wobbled as they worked. But the activities of its wearers was without tangible sensation, the rubber zipped mouth dry-fucking her a burlesque of her day work, its motions insincere, dry. The guy eating her tits had no teeth now to bite them, so she didn't have to be nice to him. With rubber men, it was the shape of their bones that defined them, and the sheets beneath her that felt like flesh, the lovers she should have had. The rubber creaked and shifted. Somewhere artificial lubricant was preparing the flesh, basting it for action. The crude dull dance of their ordinary lives, displaying them as puppets without faces, working without their needing to feel something. Until they stopped trying to be lovers and became rubber men with toys.

She didn't really want to be here now that her body was reacting back into consciousness, but she didn't want to spoil it either; in fact she wanted to go down the slide, all the way to another place where everything was different. Time, rather than uselessly ticking past her, was becoming precious, every second assuming a profound significance. Uncomfortable now, she thought that she enjoyed it, but even pleasure has its doubts. Her mind wandered as the army of arrested goose bumps jumped through her skin, and the dumb pink eight-inch dildo in her pussy was forced even higher, its sound a nasal swamp beat, mud squelching under paws, prodding unkindly the prickle of the rashly shaven lips. Specially bought pan foundation evened out the red first, then got messed up, like frosted underarm sweat, under the lights. In this line on your CV they wanted to read: *perfectly symmetrical pussy, no marks or pimples.* Flesh baby-button pink. She had done it yesterday, thinking this time might be the last, before she could let the hair grow, haltingly recover. But the agent had called today to beg her to do another photo session next week. Another retro Betty Boop chic shoot, with her ebony wig and own magic shoes the color of blood, and they had requested that she turn up clean shaved. She was getting into the fetish mainstream market as well these days. So her pussy lips, shaved by her lover of yesterday, the dark-haired bi dancer from Metro's, were being mauled by their own hair follicles. Skin the color of dull veal, delicate and unwavering under the brash lights, something not meant to be exposed. Unstopped, it might begin to burst, crease into blood orange, pulped. How will they know when it really hurts? The rubber men can't really see or feel what they are doing either.

Think, think about another place. The hotel where it all began. It was elegant, like her dreams, where she auditioned for the Northern Lights Contemporary Dance group at just eighteen. Twelve years of constant training, the whittled body eager, alive. She danced just like she knew she would, passionate and controlled, a wild animal available for hire. The movements were perfect, inspired, but her body rendered it false. The instrument was wrong. They didn't like her look. Recalling it, her feet are twitching now, unhurt, unneeded, inexplicably cold. In her later life, it was the inside of her body that would be performed with, cared for. She is walking back down to her audition again and now she can feel her feet are numb, pressing into the plush red carpet of the hotel. Every step destroying something that should have formed, little flowers pulped into a mash. Her feet no longer belong to her, she does not need them. She wants her ballet shoes, to cover them up, russet like in the Michael Powell film, *The Red Shoes*, the film of her teenage dreams, but they are lost. Her nubile, trained body can no longer respond and dance. Trudging over the sumptuous, plush carpet, she probably doesn't need the shoes to leap up, she goes along the intermittent corridor, the red carpet fading, murky, the walls jumping and dancing about, breaking up, the connection in her dream uncentered. She still believes she can make it, even though once you put the shoes on you have to dance until you die. Then she stops before a surprisingly workmanlike, steel utilitarian lift. Incongruous, that such a meat cart should be waiting here in this place that crushed her dreams. They had said her hips were overly luscious, breasts too firm. Perhaps her sex jutted too conspicuously from its leotard, her nose knelt too large in her face. She was eighteen, guys called her hot, and they could tell she had been fucked. The lift was also wrong, as fake as the yuppie elevator fuck set in *Fatal Attraction* that they only used to make it easier to film the pretend penetration long shots. Now the soles of her feet are sticking to the cold floor, she can hardly lift them, her body is so heavy. Even the square resistance of the buttons against her fingers in the lift seems massive, just pressing them hurts. The lift falls, ten years on, now she knows she will never be a dancer. Now she is back here, she doesn't want to go out. Don't think now, some things have to be blocked off, forgotten about, removed from the equation. The dancer's body has been remade, laid and spread like a vestal virgin again, red on black.

She shivered furtively, using a hidden reflex. It was important to remain expressionless, body dumb, limp. On the bed she was still, consumed with waiting, holding on to the edge of a prickling, mounting pain that, if she was to let go of it for a even second, would rise up and knock her down flat. And it wasn't possible to think of why she was here, how she could be doing this. The center of meaning had moved down from the head, the capital, now it was at the pressure points that her idea of existence was scrabbling. The lights seemed to be shining more brightly now, she could feel tears trickling down her face unseen, a faint tickle that mocked, compared and contrasted, with the biting torment that the straps were inflicting elsewhere. Yes they had done it tightly, constricting the blood flow as she had requested. And something has to give.

The pressure to cry out, go purple, thrash uncontrollably, say something, was mounting as if her very anguish was affecting the rules of gravity. Normal blood flow was being circumvented and she could hear the *tick tick* panic of her pulse stiffening and bludgeoning around the restraints. The blood surfing in pointless waves in the veins of her arms and legs, bulging thickly like a painful bladder as if she had woken up with four new genitalia strategically placed. And her own vagina dilating as if it might turn itself inside out, releasing a hidden trickle of heady juice that told of her excitement in restraint; of the pleasures to come. All the colors and shapes and distances of things were changing as she lay there responding witlessly to the squeeze and pressure. This was the start of when things started losing their meanings.

She had never felt more alive and receptive. Her body seemed both heavy and light, an oxymoron she couldn't explain, the very idea of herself slipping from memory consciousness. All the little trivial afterthoughts like, was her pussy still looking fresh? had vanished. That information was not filed, not found here. You know what you can feel. In this sensitive state it was like being born again, just assuming consciousness, waking up and discovering that the whole world was one big sensory masterpiece that you had created just for that moment. Pain was an art that could never be repeated, only rehearsed, each foray a different distance, another addition to the scar tissue. Idly she wondered how long she would be able to keep up regular modeling if she kept returning here.

And the knife, when it comes, is like a little bit of love all in once piece. The tip of it, held up to the light, gleams pretty, inches seemingly into infinity. The sharp end, symbol of horror movie posters, the part that does the damage, looks so wicked and long-drawn because the idea of it hurts. And the curl and snarl of the point gleams under the eye's scrutiny. But when it is whittled over the flesh, which is expectant and boiling in its own blood, the tip feels like a kiss, a little sting of attention. Blink away the thought of it and skin really parts so easily, incredible but easy, like Moses parting the Red Sea. So when the blood comes, the seeping of it soaking into the cloth is actually a relief. A slippery soothing milk to take out the pain. We bleed so we do not need to die.

Without her clothes she has mercifully lost part of her senses. Horizontal and bound, the world didn't feel right to her, or like the way it was. It was soothing to be so disconnected, untouchable, like a faulty electric machine taken out of service. Now they were perhaps cutting her, needling the skin, cameras crunched up tight to capture every single drop of blood. The cameramen not wanting to see it, but having to do it anyway. Special footage this, not normally available. It existed for a rarefied punter who realized he had special tastes that could be pandered to, paid for. By now she could think through most of the pain, anticipate and correct for it, toy mentally with what remained. A little game, a self-imposed mind fuck for her to wrestle with, no audience. What she felt, her own currency not exchangeable. And it was the pain, and the things that it brought, not the unexpectedly good pay, that attracted and repulsed her.

A job, like any other, except that what had started off as

something she couldn't even think about had become addictive, an acquired taste, a curious relief. Her body, that hunk of flesh, her life's work the controlled environment of its skin that she had spent so much time preparing this morning, was slowly being released from her care. The challenges: to get enough sun for it to glisten as a gold-textured surface, shiny, oiled, even, permanent, but never too much. Never to burn or malt. Or to get dry patches. Every day to feel just the right temperature floating in the bath, to scour every centimeter she could think of afterward with man-made bristles of a dry skin brush, savage-thoroughly, and then once again to reassure herself all of the circulation had been moved into life. Prodded. The oceans of buttermilk that have been applied, soaked-in overnight, rubbed off all over her sheets, every single piece of furniture tainted by it, reeking of decomposing grease, her body a man-made pet she can ill afford, and then all the effort, all the expense, only to wash it all off next morning, and the tedious process initiated again. Again and then again. And then the blockages, the buildup of dirty fat, slippery strings of goo, stinking fat and skin residue patties that clogged up the only orifices she relied on: the bath, the shower, the sink. The wooden floors dotted with greasy imprints, like the paws of some alien creature unaccustomed to human habits. The room deadened by the ghost of deodorants sprayed on in the past, sting of perfume catching you raw-boned in the throat, and over everything a dry residue of talcum powder, hovering, waiting to reattach itself to the skin. Even the washing machine reeling from the over-creaming, the careful measurement of the flesh, the smoothing, plucking, surfacing over the cracks.

In the straight world, without the brutal purity of pain, the women who, like Katje, were twenty-eight, youngish, were now often not young enough to face the haughty cameras; or back-stage, the nubile makeup assistants, whose average age, like soldiers preparing for war, was nineteen. The irony: just as you reached the point where you had trained enough; been in enough work to have the contacts, experience; reached the point where it could start to happen, along came the first alarming gray hair, gradual dipping of the breasts, a skin change. The professionals, if they could, dated pharmacists, befriended beauticians, worked at it harder, paid for surgery when they could find it, but they expected it. It was their job, they said to everybody. Annoyed boyfriends who couldn't grip why it took them so long to get somewhere; roommates sick of seeing half-dressed neurotics at any hour, doing something to themselves, stretching, scraping, taking something out of a bottle. Nothing had been given. Not ever. They had been doing everything specially as a way of life for so long that stopping now had to be learned again. Allowed. And it had always been work. Then as children, now.

Katje thinks back to a magazine feature she once read about a model who complained that her "normal" friends didn't understand how annoying it was not to be able to eat what she wanted. It's all right for them! But the girl next door, your friends, someone off the street, got it worse. Although in the course of everyday business they could cover up most of the piece, never had to think about spots on their bumcheeks or lighten a strip of pubic flesh, just in case, nevertheless in them throbbed the dirty desire. The desire simply to be adored. Their everyday bodies ached with it just as the models, the dancers, and the actors did, the desire unchanged, but without professional motivation. For them no tax deductible allowances for anything, and mostly hardly any time to keep it up. And other big issues that stood in the way that were always more important. It was the real women who often had the feeling that these bathroom rituals could never be enough. That the minute you started rubbing yourself dry after stepping out of the bath, the skin under your breasts was already leaking sweat. That even as you stood and blow-dried the freshly wet hair, you could feel heat perspiration breaking the barrier of the clean skin. The impossibility that you could ever feel you looked the way you were wanted to look.

And so many normal women had started off as princesses. The pretty ones, those who had emitted evocative poise in their first underage competitions, whooped and danced a-go-go, stammered posturing that was pedophiliac in all but name, metamorphosed into pressured baby flesh worked through a hundred stressed afternoons. The humbling-down local shows with filthy floors; tryouts; Proper School auditions for doll livestock; rigorous tests that began from as young as three, from as soon as the little girls could find their way to the bathroom to pee by themselves and therefore could be herded into halls, dumped in classes. Left to be prompted into positions, shouted at, stretched, blown up, cut down. By now, most of this talent have resigned themselves to their unaccomplishments with grace. Their hope folded away, but buffeted by the sense of a world where they can pay all their own bills. And this can hold them fast, give power in other means, but does not dwarf the desire. That seeps on as years tick past, unrelenting. And the women who are twenty-eight, but can no longer realize their idealized bodies, feel as keenly as a mother for a lost child the sense of missing in action, the emotional pull to recapture themselves as they were in their former picture-selves.

Uhaaaaghhhhhh. The knife is really wreaking it now, doing something bad. Right arm, top left, a contact point. She moves, tries to escape, even though they warned it would be worse if she reacted. She can imagine it now, pain blasting out raw energy, eco-power for the body system, the body's defenses springing into life even though it is mute. The body racked in nervousness. Her mind putting it into place, willing it. The glittering knife really another elaborate rubber toy, with a hidden reservoir of fake blood that the user can release with a series of mechanical clicks. The knife in the end as inconsequential as the heel of stiletto shoe, jagged edged, but destined only to skim the surface of the earth, never to force its way through. The pain real where, for what seems like hours but could be only minutes or seconds, time uncountable under the mask, the skin knits in the places it has been tied. The creases white-ringed, uncomfortable. Bondage giving always a throbbing and boiling pain. The jut of the fake blade sometimes had an edge nevertheless, even the droplets of the marketed blood, discernable, another wrench on the sensations. Katje's skin agonizing as if it were the real thing, the body's still desperation authentic somehow, even though the experience was not.

Cut to a long shot. Katje's body now arched, the legs raised, a bondage version of Marilyn Monroe in her first naked shoot. Naked, but for the mask, some rope. But still a dancer on the red sheets, unwieldy breasts thrust defiantly out from the extreme arch of the back, like a stilled limbo dancer ready to spring up, triumphantly. The hip bones rough cut, prominent. Splayed vagina as happy as a dog in mating season, its plump lips loud, one lip hanging, unconventionally lower than the other. Toby sees her pleasure is real, that the horror film mad bitch gets off on it, without telling anybody. She is too well formed to play a nubile virgin, over-muscular in parts from the various energetic training she endures to be a bimbo, but yes, she is interesting, he can use her. And he will. The punters from *Fetish Times* still get off on the fact that they can read her column as well as see her naked pictures in the same magazine. The fact that she is masked and anonymous just adding to the hype, her eclectic persona growing every month. Fans ringing with questions, other press even illegally running stills, passing it on. She remains anonymous. Someone Out There, a real person with a real job, who likes just to play a little for them.

For a moment Katje is fazed, orgasm high. It comes and goes all too quickly. She has to time it right because as soon as she's come, anything that can will chafe. Moment gone, now the comedown. The mask now sweated beyond use. The clutch of the rope at her wrists and ankles a child's game that seems sad and has gone on too long. Her bladder as usual, wanting to go. The need to satisfyingly piss, paramount. Above her, the two cameramen are talking intently about a missing light. The extras have vanished. She looks a real sight, tied up, anxiously waiting. The end bit, when all the sex acts have finished and she is herself again, is the hardest of all. Her breasts suddenly incongruous, difficult to manage without a bra. She's not really a porn actress, only allowing herself to be fucked by strangers' dildos, aping pain. Unusually shot retro bondage pics for punters who have tired of seeing it all. Who need a bit of safety, someone who won't kill them while they're getting off. As usual, the fantasy that she exists as one of those too beautiful to die. That she has to be tortured, finished off like a stray extra who wandered into a remake of *Last House on the Left*. The reality, that the dance lessons were sporadic. She had started gymnastics at fifteen, too late. That earlier she had been a dancer only in her mind, her Barbie doll had had the dresses, the dinky little shoes. And the self-conscious battle ever since to try to catch up with herself. Dancing most days, getting film extra roles, the odd fetish shoot only because she interviews the directors as a part-time journalist. That she is somehow in this world and behind it at the same time. She is everywhere and nowhere.

Now she's showered again, for the second or third time that day. Her skin is feeling too sore for another layer of body lotion. When she pissed it came with a little sting, today the guys were overzealous, but the sting-pain, though small, feels good, her body shudders deliciously at pain but she has to keep the skin undamaged for potential shoots, other work. The irony is that despite these fake gore photo shoots, she is unable, while still working as a model, to indulge in her predilections for hard CP and cutting. What was it that Brian Yuzna had been told while researching skin cutting for *Return of the Living Dead, Part III?* It's not the cutting of the skin that's the problem, it's dealing with the healing process afterward. . . . And her skin, on the outside at least, has to look patently undamaged.

In her street clothes she becomes a different person. You would never guess. And he doesn't either. Joachim, her occasional lover, once feted horror director, now reduced to hash ravings behind closed doors, doesn't want to hurt her, physically. He indulges in mental cruelty, belittling her with tales of his actress ex-girlfriends. And of course she's not famous, yet. That's his intention, but it excites her to hear about these other women. The dark pouty one who appeared in *The Witchwoman*. I knew she would make it. Lisa, the daughter of the famous Spanish director who has now started making her own movies. Joachim litters the house with hundreds of naked photos of Lisa and thinks she suffers when he talks so raptly about his ex. That she will feel jealous, deflated by comparison. But, mmmm, the delicious decadence of it. Just thinking about Joachim's treachery, her pussy juices are warming, tingling on her freshly shaved cunt lips. And they don't even have to touch each other to get excited, it's mainly masturbatory. Mind fucking leaves no traces. She walks toward his flat, taking pink, smooth strides, but inside her mind is singing.

Perilous Penny, Part Time Pornographer

Tara Alton

Christmas Cards

My sister stopped by today, not so much to see how I was doing, but rather to scope out which Christmas cards I'd gotten so far. She wanted to make sure that I hadn't received any more from our relatives than she did. I had to give her credit though. She waited an entire half hour before she mentioned my pile of unopened mail on the counter.

"You've got a whole pile of Christmas cards here," she said. "Why haven't you opened them yet?"

I shrugged. I hadn't had the time.

"May I?" she asked.

"Knock yourself out," I said.

I turned to pour us another glass of Peroni beer when I suddenly heard her choking. At first, I thought she was choking on a feta cheese stuffed olive from Dimitri's Italian Goods, but I realized she was horror struck by one of the cards she'd just opened.

Looking over her shoulder, I patted her on the back at the same time. It was from one of my publishers, featuring a woman's genitalia artistically perched on top a Christmas tree like a bizarre pink angel.

"Cool," I said. "I bet you didn't get this one."

Grabbing her camel hair coat and Coach purse, she stormed

out. Now she was going to be mad for six months. My sister considered my porn writing to be a short-lived hobby, like when I tried doing needlework or creating mosaics. She is certain I will get bored with it eventually. The only thing was that my needlework looked like a drunken hamster had attempted it, and my mosaics looked like someone had thrown up grout, broken glass and rocks. Believe it or not, I'm good with porn. People actually wanted to pay me money for what I've written. What better validation do you need than that? In addition, I wasn't going to get bored. I usually had sex on the brain anyway. Why not put it to good use?

My sister didn't see it this way. She hated the whole sordidness of it. To her *Showgirls* should have been rated XXX, and she never let her husband watch the Emmy pre-show because of the nipple factor on the red carpet.

The next time I see her I'm sure she will act as if everything was fine, but it will be in her eyes, a brittle little crack in what was left of our sisterhood.

Camel Toes

Today, I learned what a camel toe was. It's crotch cleavage, the distinct cleft between the legs when a woman wears her pants too tight. I had no idea this existed, that it had a name, or there were even a few Web sites devoted to it. See what you learn on the Internet by just following a few links?

Now, I find myself staring at women's crotches, in the drugstore, in the library and in the hardware store. It's fascinating. It's everywhere. In all shapes and sizes. Then at my favorite corner grocery store, I saw the mother of all camel toes. I didn't care that this blonde girl had mall hair or that she was wearing way too much makeup for daytime. It was her clothing. She was wearing a skintight black halter-top and the tightest pair of jeans I'd ever seen. She must have used pliers to zip them up. Her camel toe was so tight it looked painful. Just the thought of all that pressure down there made me want to go pee.

That was what I was thinking about when I was busted. The

head cashier caught me blatantly staring at another woman's crotch. How can I go back there now? Of course, it's the only place that carries my favorite no name sugar pops. My boyfriend, Michael, would never go get them for me. He hated the place. Moreover, the head cashier was always there, wearing her 70s frosted shag hairdo and dangling earrings like she existed in a time warp. I swore she never went home.

I can't believe I lost my no name sugar pops to a camel toe.

Love Notes

Michael thinks I'm cheating on him because he found a note with my handwriting in the laundry. Normally, this wouldn't be a big deal. I write a lot of notes, but this note was about a physical exam with Dr. Eric. I had written how much Dr. Eric turned me on with his swarthy dark looks and his warm hands on my legs.

I tried to explain to Michael that it was part of a story I was working on, but he wasn't convinced because I had recently gone to the doctors. Trying to clarify it further, I told him I was writing it from the point of view of the character, not me! It was hopeless. He just couldn't grasp the concept. So I gave up on the explanation and hoped to get the note back. I had defiantly written something sexy I needed.

"Where is the note?" I asked.

"I threw it away," he said.

"Why would you do that? Aren't you supposed to confront me with it?"

He looked as if it had never occurred to him.

"I was pissed so I threw it away," he said and stormed out of the room.

Once again, he was proving that some really good-looking guys aren't too bright.

When we first met, I thought he was a little too slick and cocky for me. We went to the same health club. I swam laps. He ran. We kept bumping into each other in the coed hot tub and steam room. Since I never considered him an option, I acted like myself for a change. Also, he had already seen me at my worst in my nasty old swimsuit. You have no idea how many swimsuits I've ruined because of the chlorine, so now I buy the ugliest, cheapest suit I can find because it's only going to last me a few months anyway. On top of that, he'd seen me with swimming goggles on, and that was just not a good look.

I figured he had to be talking to me because he was bored. Mostly to shock him and alleviate my own boredom, I told him about my part time porn career. He didn't seem too shocked, thus proving the boredom factor in his motivation to talk to me.

Imagine my surprise when he kissed me in the parking lot one night. He was a very good kisser, leaving me breathless. Then he told me he had been harboring a secret crush on me for months. I didn't believe him, but he convinced me with some more kissing. We moved in together six months later.

Girlfriends

After dealing with Michael, you can imagine my relief going to lunch with Jen, my one sane friend, although she was a little wild. She rented a big loft near the Eastern Market, and she goes to all the clubs on the weekends, where she likes to wear "fuck me" clothes and then acts surprised when men look at her.

We met at La Shish Kabob. I loved the Arabian Night atmosphere with the arched windows, brass chandeliers and fabric draped across the ceiling. The place was empty except for one other table. Of course we were seated close by them and there were kids, who amazingly were eating Happy Meals.

Over our freshly made pita bread, spicy salsa and mango smoothies, Jen started telling me in vivid and lengthy detail about the three way she had over the weekend. She had done it with two guys she was currently dating. Casually, she'd mentioned it to them as a fantasy she wanted to fulfill. To her amazement, they both agreed.

"Did they do each other?" I asked.

"No. Just me."

"So how did it happen?"

"I went and sat on the bed. Alex went into the bathroom and came out naked. It really broke the ice."

"Did it hurt?"

She shook her head.

"One hole or two?" I asked, eagerly.

The manager came over to us.

"I'm going to have to ask you to leave," he said. "There has been a complaint. Your topic of conversation is inappropriate for the restaurant."

We glanced over our shoulder at the family. The mother was glaring at us. Those kids were way too little to know what we were talking about.

"What if we change the topic?" I asked.

He shook his head.

"Can we at least get our food to go?" I asked.

I couldn't imagine leaving without our vegetarian platters with hummus, tabbouli, spinach pie and grape leaves.

"The manager says you have to leave. That is his sister."

"What about an order of the baklava?" I pleaded.

I had promised Michael I would bring him some back. I couldn't leave without it. This was the only place I knew that made their baklava with pistachios instead of walnuts, and they used an orange syrup instead of the usual lemon. Michael would flip if I didn't bring some home.

The waiter shook his head. After taking one more sip of smoothie each, we left.

Our lunch plans ruined, we stood in the parking lot, staring at one another. Jen didn't look happy with me, but it had been her fault as well. She was the one having the three ways. I promised to call her soon and we parted. I went home, where I had a peanut butter and jelly sandwich by myself.

Other Girlfriends

Lately, I'm not having too much luck with my friends. My other friend, Constance, was acting nuts. She claimed she was

into corsets, but she had never bought one. I caught her
complaining the other day that her bra was too tight. You
would have thought she would have liked that. She worked
at an upscale bed linen store with thousand count sheets and
wrought iron beds, and yet she chowed down on little greasy
hamburgers at places truck drivers would stop.

Constance thought I wanted her, because I took a scrap of our
conversation in a dressing room and inserted it into a story
about two women doing it in a similar dressing room. What
happened was this. We were trying on lingerie in a dressing
room together because the place was so crowded during a sale.
Constance mentioned that she had been checking out girls
recently. I didn't pay her much attention because she was
always saying stuff like that, but nothing ever came of it.

In my story, I had the two girls in the dressing room hook up
after the confession with admiring glances of long limbs, lots of
lace and garters. In real life, I had been trying on a yellow
rubber duck design nightshirt, and Constance had been trying
on a boring white slip.

I was so excited about seeing the story published on this
classy erotica Web site that I sent her a link to the story online,
totally forgetting where the inspiration for the story came from.

Now she kept leaving me voice mails, asking me to get
together for lunch and lingerie shopping.

Cats Under the Bed

A few days later, I finally finished the Dr. Eric story. It was
truly a masterpiece of sexual degradation, and it made me so
horny I had to masturbate.

Michael's cat wanted some attention. He's had this cat ever
since he was a little kid, and now she's like seventeen years
old. I gave her points for lasting this long, but sometimes she
was a pest. She had the most unimaginative name in the
world, "Kitty." I've thought about upgrading her name,
but Michael won't hear it, so sometimes I've added adjectives
like "Pretty Kitty." Michael just rolled his eyes. Sometimes, I

think it was more important what his cat thought of me than his parents.

I tried to pacify her with a couple quick pets and hoped she would go away. I was not going to do it front of her. Rolling over onto my other side for some privacy, I accidentally knocked her off the bed. The sensitive little snot head shot under the bed like I had struck her with a broom.

That was when Michael came home and found me trying to coax her out.

"Why is Kitty under the bed?" he asked.

I shrugged. "Who knows? Maybe a breeze blew on her and she took it the wrong way."

Sizing me up on the bed, he raised and an eyebrow. "You look sexy lying there," he said. He took off his shirt, his signal that he wanted to do it. He's never been big on foreplay. It's more like "let's kiss" and "let's do it." But since I was already sort of warmed up, I nodded.

I did feel a little guilty about the masturbating thing so to make up for it I initiated butt play with a dildo. This was something he wanted to do to me for a long time. Thank goodness, he didn't ask me, "why now." Then I would have to explain I needed the details for another story.

It was a little uncomfortable at first, but toward the end, I got into it, good enough to have a mind-blowing orgasm and then pass out.

When I woke up, I couldn't find the dildo. The little pink plastic butt fucker was gone.

Please don't let Kitty be using it as a cat toy, I thought. Michael was still sleeping. Quietly, I got out of bed and bent over to look for it on the floor when suddenly I farted. The dildo shot out of my ass.

Young Women

After I recovered from the dildo incident, an editor called me. He couldn't use the story I had submitted to him, but he liked my style of writing. He wanted to me to write these 200 word

blurbs for beneath some photos for another one of his magazines. I happily agreed.

The photos came by overnight mail. I pulled them out their
envelope and raised an eyebrow. These young women looked
very young, maybe a day or two past eighteen at the most. I kept
thinking about myself at that age. Did I want horny men
looking at my crotch?

I had the worst time making up the scenarios, but I did the
best I could and sent them off. The editor didn't like them. He
said I tried to cram too much story into a small space. He
wanted a single scene.

Michael once said he had read a lot of these magazines when
he was younger. Wanting his advice, I visited him in the
bathroom as he was taking a shower. I sat on the toilet seat,
explaining my frustration.

"What's the deal with these girls?" he asked.

"Well one girl is a babysitter who finds a pair of naughty
panties and whacks off with them. The other girl is trying to
seduce older men at a pool."

"So say this," Michael said.

And he launched into the raunchiest word festival I've ever
heard come out of his mouth. Maybe the hot water was doing
something to his brain. I hadn't expected him to come up with
something this quick. I had a pencil tucked behind my ear, but
no paper, so I used the inside of a tampon box.

Watching him in the shower, I thought he looked sexy right
now. I should hop inside the shower with him, but I wanted to
get these words down. I ran to my desk, but I felt like I was
leaving something important behind.

Deadlines

My computer locked up this morning. Michael had already left
for work. I told the editor I would have the scenarios to him by
this morning. Since I can't email them to him, I decided to fax
them from work.

At work though, under the fluorescent lights, I was concerned my copy wasn't dark enough for our crappy fax machine, so I made a darker copy first. Thank god, it went through the fax the first time, but as I got back to my desk, I realized the last page of my original draft was missing. Of course, it was the page with the big orgasm scene with the babysitter.

Panicking, I ran back to the copy machine to find it gone. I glanced down. It was in the trashcan, ripped neatly in half. Oh no. Someone found it. Looking around the room for the culprit, I realized my boss was staring at me by the postage machine, an eyebrow raised. I swallowed.

"Oh my Lord," I said. "Who would write such filthy disgusting stuff? I'm so glad someone ripped it up."

With that said, I headed back to my desk, feeling like I had betrayed myself.

Constance Again

After work, I came home to find Constance's car in the driveway. What was she doing here? I went inside and heard voices coming from the kitchen. At first, it looked like a normal scene. One of my girlfriends had stopped by for a visit and my boyfriend was sitting at the kitchen counter talking to her, but then I saw Michael's face. It was drained of color. What on earth could make him look like this? Had something happened to Kitty?

"Your girlfriend wants to do a three way," he announced.

"What?" I asked, stunned.

"Your girlfriend came over here, and she said she wants to have sex with me and you, because she has a crush on you, and it might be easier if I was there. Apparently in some story you posted online you communicated to her that you felt that way too."

"I didn't post it. It was published," I said.

Michael rolled his eyes.

"What the hell is going on?" he demanded.

"Are you crazy?" I asked her.

Acting embarrassed, Constance crossed her arms over her chest and looked at the floor.

"So, Penny, what happened in a lingerie dressing room?" Michael asked.

"That was a couple months ago. Remember when I brought home the rubber ducky nightshirt."

"You went to a lingerie store and came home with that?" A color was coming back to his face. It was red.

"Constance," I said to her, like a parent might to a naughty child. "I told you that was a story. It's not real life. I just put a lost dildo up the ass in a gay story, and I'm not a gay man."

"You put the dildo up the butt thing into a story?" Michael asked. "That was personal."

"But Jen said you were really into three ways," she said.

Oh, God.

"When did she say this?" I asked.

"We've been seeing each other. Meeting for shopping and lunch."

"You guys hate each other."

Constance shrugged. I tried to compose myself, but I couldn't believe they were seeing each other behind my back.

"Why does Jen think you're into three ways?" Michael asked me.

"She did one the other weekend and she was telling me the details at La Shish Kabob. We were kicked out for inappropriate conversation."

"That's why no baklava," he announced, like a private detective figuring out a twist in the crime.

I looked at Constance.

"Look, Constance," I said as gently as possible. "I like you as one of my friends, but I do not want to have a three way with you or any other way, as a matter of fact."

"Nor do I," Michael said.

"I never want to see either of you again, as long as I live," she shouted.

In a torrent of tears, she ran from the kitchen. A moment later, we heard the front door slam.

Michael leveled his gaze on me. It was so cold it gave me a chill.

"I got an invitation to go out tonight with the guys, and I wasn't going to go because I wanted to spend time with you," he said. "But I think I'm going now."

Once he was gone, I sat there fuming, desperately needing a bowl of my no name sugar pops to calm myself down, but since I didn't have them, I ate two Snickers Bars and drank two cans of Coke. Then I left Jen a message, thanking her for destroying my relationship with Constance and maybe my relationship with Michael as well. I finished with "Don't bother calling me again."

House Parties

Michael had never been this mad at me before. There had been no cuddles, kisses, or jokes all week. That weekend, we were invited to a barbecue at Josh's house. He was Michael's best friend. I wasn't sure if I should go or not.

"Do you still want me to go?" I asked, the day of the party.

"Why wouldn't I?" he asked.

I was a little worried about how he would act, but as soon as we got there, he started acting like himself again. I started to relax for the first time in days.

All the other girls went into the kitchen to check on the food, but I stayed by Michael. He was in such a good mood I didn't want to leave him. Besides, I didn't click with these girls. All they talked about what was an acceptable carat size for an engagement ring. After listening to them for the past half hour, I actually missed Jen and Constance.

We were in Josh's sports room, or what I liked to call the Male Bonding Room. There were a lot of sports memorabilia, an actual bar and a huge sectional sofa. Plus, Josh collected celebrity autographs.

The guys started talking about all the stupid stunts they've pulled over the years. Then the conversation led to the times when they used to visit strip clubs. I didn't mind. They've talked about stuff like this before in front of me because they know I write porn.

Suddenly, I realized they weren't talking about the far away past. They were talking about the other night, and how this stripper sucked this gum out of one their mouths, chewed it and spit it back in. Michael was cracking up and blushing, saying how after it happened he'd accidentally swallowed the gum.

I got a chill. That's where he went the other night when he was mad at me. My boyfriend was sharing gum with a half-naked girl. I felt nauseous.

"Why didn't you tell me about this?" I asked.

I tried to control the tone of voice, but it came out like cold water on barking dogs. Everyone froze. His smile faded.

"I told you I went out," he said.

"You didn't tell me this," I shrieked.

Immediately, everyone filed out of the room but us.

"I would never cheat on you," I said. "How would you like it if I got it on with Josh?"

He looked pale.

"Well, you stop writing porn, and I'll stop the strippers," he said.

"Michael, you knew I wrote porn when you met me. You're like a girl who hooks up with a guy who races bikes and yet the moment they are together, she wants him to get rid of the bikes."

"But I'm so sick of your exploiting our personal business," he said. "Sometimes you just don't think."

I hesitated.

"Think about it, Penny," he said. "A lot of this shit happens because you don't use your head."

I opened my mouth to say something more, but he interrupted me.

"Think," he said.

So, I thought about it. Could I avoid some of these perils of writing porn if I used my head? My sister probably wouldn't be mad at me if she hadn't opened my Christmas cards. Michael would have gotten his baklava if I had monitored my conversation with Jen in front of those kids at La Shish Kabob. Constance wouldn't have wanted to do a three way if I hadn't sent her the link to that story.

"I think you might be right," I said. "I do need to start using my head when I write porn."

As soon as I said it, all this fog in my brain started to clear. It was like all the porn neurons were confusing my common sense neurons.

Michael looked relieved.

"I'm sorry, too, for everything," he said.

To show me he meant it, he gave me a sweet, tender, probing kiss like he had the first time he kissed me, the kind that took my breath away and made me fall in love with him, but immediately I started categorizing the details. This kiss would be perfect for this new story idea. The way his mouth was pressed against mine, the way his tongue traced my teeth.

Stop it, Penny, I told myself. If Michael didn't want me to use our personal details in stories than I wouldn't.

Breaking the kiss, I let him lift me up in his arms to give me a big squeeze. That's when I saw it. Over his shoulder. A newly framed autographed photo on the wall. The picture was from a strip club with all the guys, including Michael, and sitting on his lap was the headliner.

And guess who she was? Camel Toe Girl.

I was definitely putting this kiss in a story.

Lonesome Little Blue

O'Neil De Noux

[*For Debb*]

Sitting in a high-back chair in the lobby of the Klamath Hotel, Sam Hyde waited for a woman he hadn't seen in seventeen years. His eyes were focused on the front door, so he could see her the moment she arrived. He crossed his left leg and involuntarily ran his fingers down the crease of his gray dress pants. He fidgeted with the knot of the wide flowered tie he'd picked up in New Orleans a month ago, in anticipation of this very moment, or was it Hong Kong? For some reason he couldn't remember.

He glanced at the Rolex on his right wrist. It was four minutes until six. Looking back at the front door, he noticed how dark it was outside. Beyond the door, a man in a gray sweat suit was scraping snow off the sidewalk, piling it on the curb. Although it seemed cool in the quiet lobby, Sam felt perspiration working its way down his back. Tiny beads of sweat also collected along his forehead. He wiped his brow with his fingers and let out a nervous sigh.

He promised himself he wouldn't be nervous. He'd planned on being in control, being cool when she stepped in and their eyes met. He wanted to be the successful man he'd become since leaving Grayville seventeen years ago. He reminded himself of his successes in business and with women, but it was no use. This was the woman he'd never forgotten. In fact, he had trouble thinking of any of the other women.

Since the first crush he'd felt for her in junior high, she'd never left his mind for more than a few days. No matter where he'd traveled, his mind always returned to the flatland of his youth, to the small Kansas town nestled between the Big Blue and Little Blue Rivers just south of the Nebraska border, to stuffy classrooms and the memory of her skirt bouncing against the back of her thighs as she walked down the hall in front of him.

Checking the time again, he saw it was one minute until six now. He focused on the door and tried to swallow, only his throat was desert dry. He readjusted himself in his seat and had to pull his feet quickly out of the way of an elderly man in a large bear overcoat who almost stepped on Sam. The old man didn't even seem to see him, as he shuffled across the lobby.

"Old age is hell," Sam thought.

Tyler Sproul rounded the corner at that very moment and walked around the man shoveling snow off the sidewalk. Moving purposefully in her high heels over the slick sidewalk, she sucked in a deep breath of brisk air as she approached the front door of the old Klamath Hotel. She wondered what Sam would look like at thirty-five. She wondered what he'd think of her now.

Entering through the revolving door, Tyler stopped just inside the doorway and looked around. The old hotel smelled musty, stuffy from forced-air heat. Tyler felt her face flush in the sudden warmth just as she saw Sam. He smiled at her as he rose from his chair. She felt her breath catch as she recognized that same smile from high school, the smile he'd flashed her way after winning the state swimming title, all those years ago.

She noticed a streak of silver along the temples of Sam's dark hair, and a deep tan on his exquisite face, and those light blue eyes that looked like the morning sky on a bright summer day. He still had his swimmer's physique, tall and lean. He also had a moustache now.

Sam studied her as he crossed the lobby on legs that felt suddenly weak. Her hair was shorter but still reddish brown, parted down the center now. She was still slender, with her legs still long and shapely. She was wearing a burgundy dress and a gold topcoat that she removed as he arrived.

Stopping in front of her, Sam looked into her green eyes. He saw something in them that made him smile even wider. His most vivid memory of Tyler was the liveliness of her green eyes, the youthful sparkle in them. He realized he had been most worried about her eyes, rather than what she looked like now as a woman. He wanted her eyes to be lively, more than anything.

Tyler felt a swell of emotion crawling up her throat, felt a stiffness in her back, a salty wetness in her eyes. She blinked. She thought he was about to say something, but when he opened his mouth his lips began to shake, so he closed it and just stared at her with those warm blue eyes.

He found himself studying every detail of her face. It was still the face from his dreams; only there were lines now, on her cheeks where she smiled and smaller lines next to her eyes. She still had that triangular face, the pointy chin, the nearly perfect nose, those well-formed lips he'd never tasted. He found himself staring at her lower lip, which was fuller than her upper lip.

Tyler always loved the small cleft in the center of Sam's chin. She found herself looking at his moustache, his wide dark mustache that looked so soft. And when she looked up at his eyes, she saw they were now damp.

No longer a girl, Tyler had become a truly beautiful woman. And when she smiled it was the same smile of that young girl from the halls of his dreams. Tyler had the warmest, nicest, most beautiful smile Sam had ever seen . . . ever. He could see the wetness in *her* eyes now. She blinked again at him.

They both let out a nervous sigh. Sam reached his hand out, and she took it and squeezed it.

The palm of his hand felt moist.

"How about that steak I promised?" His voice was scratchy and he cleared his throat immediately and smiled again.

She nodded, biting her lower lip, blinking her eyes once more to keep the wetness from rolling down her cheeks.

★   ★   ★

She ached for him to touch her. All evening she wanted to feel his touch on her skin. Now, in his hotel room, on the second floor of the old Klamath, two days before Christmas of her thirty-fifth year, with the plates from their steak dinner still sitting on the small table against the window, Tyler felt Sam's arms wrapping around her. She pulled herself to him. She let out an involuntary sigh and tightly shut her eyes.

Sam felt all the evening's tension slip away as he hugged her, as she snuggled her cheek against his, as she pressed her breasts against his chest, her legs against his legs. She was finally in his arms. This girl he had dreamed of since junior high was there with him, holding him, and this was no dream. He kissed her gently on her cheek.

Tyler brushed her lips across Sam's face until her lips found his. He kissed her back, softly at first, his lips parting until their tongues found each other. His kiss remained soft as his hands moved from the small of her back down to her rear. He squeezed her ass, pressing her against him, his crotch digging into hers.

Still kissing, Sam worked her dress up with his fingers until his hands were on her panties, rubbing across the cool slickness of her silky panties. The fingers of his right hand slipped under the elastic, and he felt the naked flesh of her ass.

Tyler's hands rose to his head to run her fingers through his hair. Lifting her right knee, she wrapped her leg around his waist, feeling his crotch moving slowly against hers, feeling a flush of dampness growing between her legs. The stiffness of his erection pushed against her.

Sam moved a hand up and unzipped her dress down to her waist. He sank his hand down into her panties from the top this time. He squeezed her ass.

Tyler pulled her right leg down. Breathing heavily, she pushed his jacket off, loosened his tie, pulled it off, and unbuttoned his shirt. She unbuckled his belt and opened his pants.

Their lips parted momentarily when Sam pulled her dress off. He took a second to look at her as she stood in front of him, running her hands through her short hair. Her chest rose with her heavy breathing. He watched her bare breasts rise, their delicate roundness, the pointy nipples. She was wearing white panties, thin enough for him to see the dark hair between her legs. Her stockings were held up by lacy elastic bands at the top, an inch or so from her crotch. He bent over and removed her heels and began pulling her stockings down.

He kissed his way up her legs, alternating from one to the other as his hands returned to kneading her ass. He traced his tongue up her thighs. He lightly kissed the front of her panties and moved up to her navel. He tongued her navel and stood, moving his hands to her breasts now to squeeze them softly, to run his finger over her nipples.

Tyler was breathing much heavier now. When Sam moved his mouth to hers, she yanked off his shirt and tossed it. Then she worked his pants down and off. She knelt in front of him, took off his loafers and each sock. Craning her neck up, she tucked her fingers into the waistband of his jockey shorts and pulled them down. Sam's erection was straight up, thick and swollen, surrounded by hair as dark as the thick hair on his head.

She ran her fingers over the delicate hairs between his navel and the base of his dick. She circled his dick with the fingers of her left hand, letting her right hand caress his balls. She kissed the tip of his dick softly, then licked her way down, along the warm shaft that led to his pubic bush and then back up to the hypersensitive membranes at the tip.

Tyler moved her head back and forth flicking her tongue along the underside of his dick. Sam moaned deeply. Tyler's hands grabbed his ass now as he pumped her mouth.

Sam felt the passion rising quickly in his thighs and pulled her up to kiss her again. He shoved his hands into her panties and pushed them down. She lifted her legs to step out of them. Grabbing her ass again, he pulled her to him. She wrapped her arms around his neck and opened her legs as Sam rubbed the length of his dick against the front of her pussy, against her silky, wet pubic hair.

Moving to the bed, Tyler climbed on backward. Sam moved over her. He paused as she lay back. He looked at her body, at her soft breasts and hard nipples, at the flatness of her belly, at her reddish pubic hair and the pink slit of her pussy. He kissed her pubic hair, ran his tongue through its silkiness to the top of her slit.

"Oh," Tyler sighed.

Sam looked up at her face. Her eyes were closed as she moved her hips slowly. Her face looked so lovely. He licked her pussy, inserted his tongue into her, and began to rub his tongue against her. He flicked his tongue in quick movements, and then pressed it hard and rubbed it against her.

Tyler began to make crying sounds. She reached down and pulled his hair, pulled his lips up to hers. When he kissed her, she grabbed his dick. Tyler guided Sam's dick to the opening of her pussy. She pulled her knees up to allow him to enter her smoothly. She felt his thick, hard dick sinking into her, filling her, causing shudders of passion to pulse through her body.

Pumping her, working his dick in her, Sam kissed her neck and throat and around to the soft spot beneath her right ear. Tyler let out deep cries with each pump, her voice husky and sexy as she cried, "Oh, yes. Oh, yes. Oh! Ohhhhhh!"

Tyler was near tears as she felt herself shudder in climax. Sam's balls continued bouncing against her ass. She grabbed his shoulders and felt the tightness of his lean body as he made love with her, as he screwed her, as he fucked her, as he sent her through a second climax, a much deeper one, one that caused her to cry out louder.

Sam worked his dick feverishly now as he felt his semen spurting into Tyler, losing the years of unfulfilled passion, the years of dreaming of doing this with her.

"Oh, *darling*," he cried.

He held her close after, cuddling with her. She snuggled against his chest and felt herself winding down slowly. Later, when she craned up her neck, she saw he was looking at her and kissed him. Their kissing led to a long, slow second lovemaking.

They took small naps between making love, sleeping wrapped

in each other's arms. After, they fell into a deep sleep, still snuggled together, beneath the sheets.

Some time before the gray dawn, Tyler woke. Still in Sam's arms, she blinked away the sleep from her eyes and watched him sleep. He looked so much younger asleep, more like the eighteen-year-old of her memories than the man who'd just loved her all night. His mouth was slightly open and his moustache was messed up, his thick hair disheveled.

The room was still scented with the faint odor of their steaks. Nuzzling close to him, she smelled the mustiness of their sex, the sweet smell of his semen mixed with the distinctive scent of her juices.

Tyler remembered how they'd made love the first time, on the banks of the Little Blue, on a bed of cool grass, the green scent of woods around them. It was a freak winter, a Christmas Eve with temperatures in the high sixties. It was their first Christmas together. They were nineteen.

She felt a sudden sadness because Sam wouldn't remember their first time, just as he wouldn't remember this time.

Tyler put barrettes in her hair, high on the sides of her head. In the early morning light, her hair showed streaks of blond. Sam watched her as they sat eating a late breakfast next to the frosty window in his hotel room, *their* hotel room. He noticed how her hands never seemed to keep still, how they darted around as she spoke and ate and lifted her coffee cup to her pretty lips.

The room was filled with the smell of fresh muffins and steamy coffee and pancakes. Tyler ate two chocolate chip pancakes, covered with whipped cream. Sam had blueberry pancakes with cane syrup.

Sam liked the warm look on Tyler's face that morning, that look of a woman who's just been loved, that lecherous glint in her eye when their eyes met and she smiled at him. He knew his face must look the same, satisfied and warmed from all the intimacy.

"Remember the time your gym shorts split?" he asked.

Tyler covered her mouth and laughed. He'd caught her with

a mouthful of pancake. He liked the way she laughed, especially after she swallowed and really laughed, deep and satisfying, no "tee hee" like a shy schoolgirl. She was a shy schoolgirl the first time he saw her panties back in junior high when her gym shorts split.

It was at a basketball game. Tyler, her hair in a double ponytail, was the team's ace player at stealing the ball. Sam had gone to the girl's basketball game just to see her play. It was in the school cafeteria, instead of the gym, and Sam sat in a chair near to where the team sat.

He first noticed her gym shorts were split when she ran past him. He saw a light-colored streak along the rear of her blue team shorts. He had been looking at her butt as she moved away from him, just as he'd followed her hips down the halls.

"Tell me about it again," Tyler said, moving her hand up to her right ear to toy with one of her earrings. She had three earrings in her right ear and four in her left, all delicate gold hoops.

"It wasn't until your second pass that I was sure I was seeing your panties. I remember how excited I became."

"Got erect?"

"Immediately." Sam smiled. "Had to adjust myself in my seat." He felt a faint longing in his loins again as he replayed the first erection she'd given him.

"Then you stole the ball from a girl and ran right near me and stopped to dribble a second. It was then I could see your panties clearly, those light multicolored panties. Looked like satin. I remember the split was right down the center of your shorts, big enough to see both cheeks."

"Ouuu," Tyler said in a deep flirtatious tone.

"Then you came and stood right in front of me. Your hands on your knees, bent at the waist. Pointing your ass right at me." Sam snickered. "I was mesmerized."

Tyler liked the sound of that. Too bad they were so young back then.

"I remember looking around after you moved on. I saw one of our teachers, our math teacher, Mr. Cotton. He was also watching you, looking at your panties too."

"Everyone saw," Tyler said. "After our coach told me about it, I asked why she didn't warn me. She said I was playing so well . . ."

"Yeah," Sam agreed. "I remember a couple of boys, older boys, whispering and pointing at you as you passed. They were getting a big kick out of seeing your panties."

Tyler rolled her eyes and laughed that deep laugh again.

"That bothered me, those guys looking."

"Oh?" She was teasing now.

Sam glanced out the window at the snowy scene outside. "I remember the slickness of your panties and how I wondered what it would be like to touch you there."

"Ouu."

Sam had no problem remembering the game. The memory was so vivid. He was bothered though, trying to remember what he'd done yesterday and the day before that. Over dinner the previous evening, he felt frustrated when he tried to tell Tyler about his life, about his successes and his business dealings. He was confused. "Probably the anticipation," he told himself.

Tyler narrowed her eyes and said, "Remember the fire drill in high school?"

The fire drill was his most erotic memory from high school, even more than Mary Jane, the girl he lost his virginity to in a Chevy after a swim meet.

"I had a real crush on *you* by then," Tyler said.

Sam felt suddenly sad. His voice sounded hollow. "I didn't know."

"I know you didn't."

It was a chilly day in December when the fire drill caught Sam and the rest of the boys in his gym class in the showers. An excitable coach came in and hustled the boys out into the gym. There was a fire in the cafeteria. Sam grabbed a towel, wrapped it around his waist, and went out to discover that the girls, also in towels, were standing outside of their shower room.

For the next few minutes, both classes stood in close proximity, wrapped in towels while their gym instructors rushed off to check the status of the fire. Outside, the rest of the student body was assembled in the snow.

Sam remembered the growing erection beneath his towel as he checked out each and every girl. All of them were naked beneath those towels. *Naked!* He remembered the tension, so thick in the quiet gym that he felt hot even though it was goose-bump chilly. Everyone looked at one another in complete silence. He remembered Tyler. He had never seen so much of her long legs. Her towel, like most of the girls, barely covered her from her armpits to just below the cheeks of her ass. It was *so* sexy.

He remembered her smile. When the coaches came back in and barked their orders for them to go back into their respective showers, Tyler's eyes met his and she smiled at him, warmly, a hint of naughtiness in the lively green of her eyes.

She looked at him with a similar look as he poured her a fresh cup of coffee. Staring at her face as she reached for her coffee and took a sip, he realized just how much he adored that face.

The Little Blue River was partially frozen with clumps of snowy ice along its banks, and mini-icebergs lodged in its shallow stream. Sam led the way down to the edge of the bank, Tyler's gloved hand in his. Wrapped in their overcoats, the couple stood on the bank, arms around each other's waists.

Tyler turned to watch Sam's face as he gazed at the river. She leaned forward and kissed his cheek. It was cold. He pulled her closer. Their breath came out frosty and mixed in the frigid air.

"I just wanted to see the river again," Sam explained. He could feel Tyler trembling. He looked at the icy water for another long moment before pulling Tyler away from the bank, and walking with her back through the trees and across Pawnee Park toward their hotel.

They snuggled as they moved, which slowed them, but felt so good. Sam always wanted to walk with the woman he loved across Pawnee Park. He'd dreamed of it. Only, in his dreams it was always summer and Tyler was in a light dress.

Tyler had a similar dream, a dream of walking arm-in-arm

with the man she loved through the park. In her dream it was always autumn and they would stroll through the crisp red and yellow leaves. They would even kick the leaves, like high schoolers. Now, as they approached Washington Avenue to cross to get back to the hotel, Tyler noticed that the leaves that weren't covered in snow were soggy and black.

Pausing before they crossed the street, Sam looked back in the direction of the river. He let out a long frosty sigh.

"It's lonely, isn't it?"

"What is?"

"The river. It's such a lonely river."

Tyler felt an immediate heartache. They had made love for the first time on that very bank they had just stood on, all those years ago. She reached up, placed her hand on Sam's chin and turned his face to her. She looked in his eyes and could tell: he had no idea. Of course . . . he was right. The Little Blue was the loneliest place on Earth. Sam leaned forward and they kissed.

She felt her eyes watering up again. "No," she told herself. She wouldn't let it happen yet. She would fight it. Tucking her arms around Sam's arm, she walked with him across the street.

There wasn't enough time to get depressed. Later, there would be plenty of time, plenty of time for that.

They had a quiet dinner in their hotel room. Tyler had changed into the new dress she had bought after Thanksgiving, a gold strapless that fitted around her breasts and then full below the waist. She knew it would accentuate her coloring perfectly. She was thinking Sam never looked better in his light gray suit and a blood red tie.

He loved her sculptured shoulders, the fine lines of her neck, the way she smiled at him. She had never looked more beautiful than that evening, in that strapless dress, her hair fluffed out and curled, the soft makeup above her eyes, the deep brownish-red lipstick.

As they dined on veal and baked potato and rich Burgundy wine, Tyler felt it again, that wave of emptiness, that sinking feeling in her heart. "I won't let it happen," she told herself. "Not now."

But it happened anyway. It came to her while they made love. Like a rush, it filled her heart with a hollowness, surging into her throat, bringing the tears.

Sam stopped in the middle and asked, "What is it, babe?" She couldn't stop crying.

"Oh, darling." He held her tightly and kissed her eyes and her cheeks and her lips. She kissed him back and finally stopped crying, but only after a long time.

A blizzard surged across the Kansas plains from the west and stuck Grayville shortly after dawn Christmas morning. Tyler was already awake, staring at the ceiling, holding on to her man as he slept next to her. She had her right arm under his neck and her left leg draped over his body. After a while, she looked at the window to see the snow slamming against the pane. She almost smiled. Snowed-in for Christmas with her man. What could be better?

Later, as they sat up in bed cross-legged and naked, facing one another, they exchanged gifts. Sam gave her a gold necklace with a ruby pendant. Tyler gave him a lapel pin, an Egyptian scarab she'd had copied from the Treasures of King Tutankhamen. On the back she'd inscribed: All My Love Forever.

Turning on the radio, Sam found a slow song so they could dance. Still naked, the couple embraced and moved slowly to the haunting voice of Marvin Gaye. Tyler felt her excitement growing with their bodies pressed together, moving with one another.

In the middle of the second song, by Nat King Cole, Tyler felt her nerves acting up again, felt the depression pouring in on her. She fought it. She fought it hard and told herself she was with her man for Christmas. She was *with* her man for Christmas. She was *with* her man for Christmas!

But she knew. Tomorrow, he would be gone.

It came to Sam as soon as he woke. He had to go. He lay there for a while, Tyler pressed against him, her breath falling on his neck. He tried to concentrate on *why*. Why did he have to go? He couldn't figure it out. There was something he had to do, something important. He had to go. That's all he knew.

He tried to fight it. Told himself he wasn't going anywhere. He would stay with Tyler. But he knew, as sure as he knew the love in his heart for this woman was real, that he had to go.

Pulling the covers back, Sam looked at Tyler as she lay on her belly next to him, facing away from him, her right leg curled up. Her creamy skin looked so beautiful in the morning light. He watched her, studying the lines and curves of her sleek body. He reached over and ran his hand along the small of her back, over her ass and around to her breasts. She felt warm. When Tyler woke with a start, he kissed her and smiled at her.

As soon as he told her, she blinked her damp eyes and said hoarsely, "I know."

They made love once again. They made lingering love in their bed on the second floor of the old Klamath. Sam caressed Tyler as he'd never caressed anyone in his life. He was certain of that. He kissed her as if the world centered on that kiss. He filled her with his semen until there was no semen left. He loved her so much his heart ached.

Tyler felt it. She felt every scintillating emotion. She felt . . . loved.

Banks of snow from the blizzard had been shoveled away from the railroad tracks, piled into little white hills. The air wasn't as crisp that morning. The sun was bright in a sky the color of Sam's eyes. Tyler looked at her man and saw tears in those eyes, which caused her throat to tighten once again. She tried her best to keep from crying.

Sam put his hands on her shoulders and blinked his tears away. She could see his bottom lip quivering as he struggled to speak. She kissed his lips. As soon as she pulled away, he said, "I love you."

She nodded, her eyes blurred now.

"I love you so much, babe," he said in a voice filled with emotion.

She told him she loved him too. Her throat was so tight she could barely speak.

Sam took in a deep breath and said, "I don't know why I'm crying. I'll be back."

"I know." She barely got it out.

Sam kissed her. She kissed him back like it was the last kiss of her life.

The train whistle blew again reminding them it was time. They kissed once more and Sam slowly pulled away. The train began moving. Sam stepped up on the platform and brushed his hand across the scarab pin on the lapel of his overcoat.

Tyler mouthed the words, "I love you."

He mouthed them back.

Smiling at his love, he caught sight of the station sign over her head and repeated what he'd told her a few minutes earlier. "I still don't understand why my name's up there."

Tyler wiped her tears away and said, "I love you. Oh, how I love you."

She watched until Sam's image blended against the train and all she could make out in the distance was the blueness of his overcoat. She continued to watch until the train was a speck on the horizon and long after it was gone.

Sam watched the Grayville station shrink behind. The frigid air washed over him, chilling him deeply, tearing against the heartache pounding in his chest. When the station and his hometown were gone over the horizon, Sam stepped back into the train. He made it just inside the door before a piercing jolt of white-hot pain jammed his chest, took away his breath, and doubled him over. Faintly, as he sank to the floor, he felt a familiar agony, a long excruciating familiar agony.

Turning slowly, Tyler looked at the station sign and said the words aloud, "Sam Hyde Station." She had to sit for a moment, on the bench. She buried her face in her hands and let it out, let it all out.

In the living room of her small red brick home on the south side of Grayville, Tyler Sproul sat cross-legged in front of her fireplace. Wearing only a nightshirt, she had pulled the shirt down over her knees to fend off the chill in the air. Next to her left knee was a glass of white wine. In front of her were the memories of a lifetime. She opened her high school yearbook and found her own picture first, a young face that seemed a little heavy. Smiling in her graduation picture, Tyler's hair was long and curled. She'd worn a black-and-white-striped sweater over a light blue turtleneck pullover.

She turned back the pages until she found him. There, between a boy named Hudson and a girl named Indihar was Samuel Dennis Hyde. His hair was styled in a Beatles haircut, a slight smile on his lean face. He was wearing a blue button-collar shirt. Beneath his name was listed: "Senior Most Likely to Win an Olympic Medal." Tyler read the credits below: "State Swimming Champion 100 Meter Freestyle and 400 Meter Freestyle; District Champion in 9 events; Letters in Swimming (4 years); Key Club; Young Democrats Club."

Thumbing through the pages she found the only other photos of Sam, both taken at swim meets. In one, he wore his two gold medals from his state championships. He had the same slight smile on his face. The other had Sam diving at the beginning of a race. He wore a striped bathing suit.

Closing the yearbook, Tyler opened a tan leather scrapbook. She moved the fingers of her left hand across the news articles as she read each again. Delicately, she turned the pages and continued reading each and every article in which Sam Hyde was mentioned in *The Grayville Gazette*. She read about each of his triumphs and stared at more pictures of Sam, grainy black-and-white photos yellowed with age.

She stopped and studied one particular picture. It was the only photo in which both of them appeared. In it, Sam was receiving a district champion medal. Off to his right and slightly behind was Tyler's beaming face. She was in her cheerleader outfit, a pom-pom in her hand.

She turned the page and felt her breath slip away slowly, as it always did when she read the article: "Olympic Hopeful Drowns in Little Blue." She didn't realize she was holding her breath until she finished the article and let out a deep sobbing sigh. She put her hand over her mouth and took in a deep breath. She fought back the tears and turned the page.

Sam's graduation picture was used in his obituary.

She turned the page to a later article, which featured the same photograph. Beneath it was a line Tyler had underlined years ago. "Originally thought to have drowned, a medical exam revealed Mr. Hyde succumbed to a congenital heart defect."

Tyler shut her eyes to keep in the tears. Her mind continued working, flashing memories of a funeral in the rain, of touching his coffin before it sank into the earth, of that first heart-wrenching phone call the following Christmas Eve from a voice she'd known, a voice she'd cherished. She remembered crying and not believing, then dressing up and going to the Klamath anyway. She remembered Sam's smiling face and all the Christmases after.

She opened her eyes and turned the last page. She didn't bother reading the last article, the one about how the train station was named for Sam Hyde. She closed the book and reached for her wine.

Her hand was shaking so she was barely able to get the glass to her lips. She couldn't drink, and had trouble putting it down without spilling it. Closing her eyes once again, she took in another deep breath and tried to fight the sadness. But it was no use. She thought of all the lonesome nights ahead until he would call again. The tears came. She caught her breath and, for a moment, tried to think of what Sam would look like at thirty-six.

Four on the Floor

Alison Tyler

We weren't very nice about it. That was the surprising part. I expected the cliché of scented oils and gilded candlelight and slippery limbs entwined. But how we acted afterwards was unforeseen. Alone together, reliving the night, Sam and I were truly cruel. Here I was, operating under a false impression for so many years: you see, I always thought I was a nice girl.

Others reminiscing over the experience might focus on the way Sheila's gray-blue eyes lit up when I pressed my mouth to her freshly shaved pussy, or the look on her husband Richard's craggy but handsome face as he started to slowly stroke his long, uncut cock. But not this girl. The best part of the evening for me was the laughter with Sam afterwards, giggling all the way home about the freaks we'd spent the evening with. The freaks we'd just fucked.

They were decades older than us, and richer by far, and they'd run a charming ad at the back of the Pink Section of the *SF Chronicle*. Filled with dizzy anticipation, we met for drinks, to check out the chemistry.

Sizing up potential fuck partners is a heady business. Nobody else in the trendy after-work bar knew that we were responding to a personal. Not the cute curly-haired bartender. Not the female executives lined up against the wall like pretty maids all in a row. The thought of what we were actually there for made me giddy with excitement, and desire showed rather brightly in my dark eyes.

The woman said I was pretty. Her husband agreed with an

anxious nod. All evening long, they looked at me rather than Sam, and I knew why. Sam is tough. He has short, razor-cut hair and a gingery goatee. If you met him in a back alley, you'd offer him your wallet in a heartbeat. You'd beg him to take it, the way I beg him to take things from me every night.

The couple didn't understand Sam. So they talked to me instead.

"So pretty," the woman repeated. "Like Snow White."

I grinned and drank my Cosmo, then licked my cherry-glossed lips in the sexiest manner I could manage, leaving the tip of my tongue in the corner of my mouth for a second too long. Iridescent sparkles lit up my long dark hair. Multi-colored body glitter decorated my pale skin. I wore serpentine black leather pants and a white baby-T with the word SINNER screaming across the chest in deep scarlet. There was an unspoken emphasis on how young I was in comparison to the woman. She was holding firm in her mid-forties, while I was just barely getting used to being in my early twenties. Her entire attitude was both calculating and clearly at ease, obvious in the way she held court in our booth, in the way she ordered from the waiter without even looking up.

"Two Kettle-One Martinis, another Cosmo, another Pilsner."

I was her opposite, bouncy and ready, a playful puppy tugging a leash. More than that, I was bold from how much they wanted us, and we from how much I wanted Sam. When he put one firm hand on my thigh under the table, I nearly swooned against him. We'd be ripping our clothes off each other in hours.

After drinking away the evening, we made a real date with the rich couple for the following weekend, a date at their place, where they promised to show us their sunken hot tub, wrap-around deck, and panoramic view of the city. In cultured voices, they bragged to us about the gold records from his music-producing days and her collection of antique Viennese perfume bottles accumulated with the assistance of Ebay. But though I listened politely, I didn't care about their money or what it could buy. All I wanted was all Sam wanted, which was simple: four on the floor.

We had done the act already, nearly a year before, with a lower class duo Sam found for us on the internet. The woman was thirty-eight, the man twenty-six. They'd been together for two years and had wanted to sample another couple as a way of enhancing their already wild sex life. After dinner at a local pizzeria and two bottles of cheap red wine, Pamela and I retreated to the ladies' room to show each other our tattoos. Hers was a dazzling fuchsia strawberry poised right below her bikini line. When she lifted her white dress. I saw that not only was she pantyless, but that she'd been very recently spanked. She blushed becomingly as I admired her glowing red cheeks, where lines from Andy's belt still glowed in stark relief against her coppery skin.

"He gave me what-for in the parking lot," she confessed. "Told me that he wanted me to behave during dinner."

"What would he think of this?" I asked, stroking her still-warm ass with the open palm of my hand.

"I think he'd approve." She grinned.

I gave her a light slap on her tender skin, and she turned around and caught me in a quick embrace, lifting my dress slowly so that she could see my own ink.

Teasingly, I turned to show her the cherries on my lower back, then pulled down my bikini to reveal the blue rose riding on my hip. She traced my designs with the tips of her fingers, and I felt as if I were falling. Her touch was so light, so gentle, and in moments we started French-kissing, right there in the women's room at Formico's. I could imagine what the men were doing: speaking macho to one another, sports and the recent war, while growing harder and harder as they waited for us to return to the red-and-white checked table.

Sam and I followed the duo to their Redwood City apartment and into their tiny living room, overshadowed by a huge-screen TV and a brown faux-leather sofa. Pamela had her tongue in my asshole before my navy blue sleeveless dress was all the way off, and my mouth was on Andy's mammoth cock before he could kick off his battered black motorcycle boots.

The TV stayed on the whole time we were there. Muted, but on. We had crazy sex right on the caramel-colored shag rug in front of it, while heavy metal bands played for us in silence. It was like doing it on stage with Guns & Roses. Surreal, but not a turn-off.

I remember a lot of wetness – her mouth, his mouth, her pussy. I remember Sam leaning against the wood-paneled wall at one point in the evening and watching, just watching the three of us entwined, the TV-glow flickering over us, my slim body stretched out between our new lovers. I felt beloved as their fingers stroked me, as they took turns tasting me, splitting my legs as wide as possible and getting in between. I held my arms over my head and Sam bent down and gripped my wrists tight while Pamela licked at me like a pussycat at a saucer of milk.

Scenes flowed through the night, lubricated by our red-wine daze, and we moved easily from one position to another. Pamela bent on her knees at Sam's feet and brought her mouth to his cock. I worked Andy, bobbing up and down, and after he came for the first time, I moved over to Pamela's side so we could take turns drinking from Sam. I was reeling with the wonder of it. The illusion that anything was possible. Any position, any desire.

"You like that?" Andy asked when I returned to his side, pointing to Pamela as she sucked off my husband. "You like watching?"

I nodded.

"What else do you like?"

"I like that you spanked her," I confessed in a soft voice.

"Ah," he smiled. "So you're a bad girl, too."

My blush told him all he needed to know; soon I was upended over his sturdy lap, and the erotic clapping sounds of a bare-ass spanking rang through the room. Andy punished me to perfection, not letting up when I started to cry and squirm, making me earn the pleasure that flooded through me. Sam filled Pamela's mouth while watching another man tan my hide.

Andy was a true sadist, which I could appreciate. He had a pair of shiny orange-handled pliers which he used like a magician on his girlfriend's teacup tits. She didn't cry or scream – she moaned. He twisted the pliers harder, and her green eyes took on a vibrant glow, as if she'd found some deep hidden secret within herself, and that secret gave her power. Andy told us how he liked to spank her with his hand or belt or paddle. Sometimes he used a wooden ruler. Sometimes he used whatever was nearby.

He told us detailed stories of how he fucked her up the ass, how he made her bend over and part her cheeks for him, holding herself open as wide as possible and begging him for it. He liked to lube her up good, and then pour a handful of K-Y into his fist and pump his cock once or twice before taking her. The size of his cock in her backdoor would often make her cry, but it was a good sort of cry, he explained. Pain and pleasure were entwined in everything they did. Andy's stories made me more excited, and we kept up our games all night long, screwing on stage with the long-haired boys in the bands.

Sam and I had fun with that couple, and we didn't laugh afterwards. We fucked. Not like bunnies, which are cute and soft and sweet. We fucked like us. Hard and raw and all the time. Sam's large hand slapped down on my ass, connecting over and over as he relived the night. "You little cock slut," he said, his voice gravelly and low. "Your mouth was all hungry for him. You couldn't get enough." I would be red and sore after our sessions, and I relished every mark, every pale plum-colored bruise, every memory. The night was fuel for a year's worth of fantasies.

We got precisely what we wanted. We never saw them again. The woman called and called after our one-night stand. She emailed that she was in love with me, that she was desperate to see me. But Sam and I didn't want love. We wanted something much less involved but much more momentarily intense: four on the floor.

★   ★   ★

With Sheila and Richard, we got a great deal more than we bargained for. A gourmet dinner – delivered by a local party service – that dragged on for hours. A tour of their two-story house and their walk-in closets. Close-up views of their his-and-hers Armanis.

These appearance-obsessed people were the ones we were about to have sex with. I had a difficult time picturing it. Yes, she was attractive, although "cool" was a better word. Yes, I liked how distinguished he looked in his open-necked crisp white shirt and pressed khakis with the ironed crease down the center. He was so different from Sam with his faded Levis and dangling silver wallet chain. But they were trying to win us over, and somehow that made me feel hard and bristly inside.

Didn't stop us from getting busy, though and peeling our clothes off. Richard didn't fuck me. He sat nearby and stroked my sleek dark hair out of my eyes and said he wanted to watch. Sheila had on a black velvet catsuit, and she stripped it off in one practiced move and was naked, her platinum hair rippling over her shoulders, her body gleaming chestnut in the candlelight. She stood for a moment, holding the pose, waiting for applause or flashbulbs.

Sam took his cue from Richard, backing away, watching while Sheila courted me. Sheila had obviously done this before. She strode to my side and helped to undress me. She cooed admiringly as she undid my bra and pulled it free, as she slid my dove-gray satin panties down my thighs. Her fingers inspected me all over, as if she was checking to see that a purchase she'd made was acceptable.

She kissed wetly into the hollow of my neck and caressed my breasts with her long, delicate fingers, tweaking my rosy nipples just so to make them erect. Then she spread me out on the luxurious multi-colored living room rug and started to kiss along the basin of my belly. I had a second to wonder why it is that menages never take place in beds before I sighed and arched my back, parted my legs for her, closed my eyes. She turned her body, lowered herself on me, let me taste her.

Everything about her body felt cool, like polished foil. Her skin. Her lips. Her tangy juices when they flooded out to meet my tongue. We sixty-nined for the men, and for a moment I was won over. I was fine, alert and happy. With my mouth on the older woman's pussy and my hands stroking her perfect silky body, I lost myself in momentary bliss. She was exotically perfumed, a scent I didn't recognize but knew must have been imported from Europe. She even tasted expensive. But sex levels out any playing field. I might only have been able to afford CoverGirl dime-store cosmetics rather than Neiman-Marcus special blends, but I could find her swollen clit, and that's all that mattered. I teased it out from between her perfectly shaved pussy lips. I sucked hard, and then used my tongue to trace a ring around the rosy.

When I felt Sam's eyes on me, I turned my head to look at him. He gave me a wink, as if to let me know that he approved, and then he nodded forward with his head for me to continue. I could already hear his voice in my head, "You liked your mouth all glossy with pussy juices, didn't you, girl? You liked the way she tasted, all slippery and wet?"

But then Sheila started to direct, positioning my body on all fours, before grabbing a carved wooden box from under the coffee table and pulling out a variety of sex toys. This wasn't like Andy lifting his pliers off the oval-shaped coffee table, an unexpected turn-on. This was planned; I could tell. We had been carefully chosen to star in a pre-written fantasy of Sheila's. A fantasy in which she was the star and I was her assistant, her underling, her protégé. And even as she buckled on the thick, pink strap-on, I felt myself withdraw.

Still, we fucked.

She took me from behind, held tightly onto my long black hair and rode me. Her manicured fingertips gripped firmly near the base of my scalp, holding me in place. Sam stared into my eyes as I was pounded by this icy woman, and then he came close, his cock out, and placed the very head on my full bottom lip.

I heard Sheila hiss something – Sam was taking charge and she didn't like it. But she also didn't know Sam. Sam would have none of her noise. He fucked my mouth fiercely while she fucked my cunt, while Richard, silent and somewhere off inside himself, tugged on his dick and watched us all.

Sheila had oils that she spread on me with the finesse of a masseuse, and soon we were drippy and glistening in the golden light. She had sturdy metal nipple clamps and assorted colorful dildos, vibrating devices and butt plugs. She arrayed her collection and went to work. And Sam let it all happen. This was far different and far less spontaneous than our experience with Pamela and Andy, but we'd use it. We'd go with it. There were four of us, after all, and we were there.

I came when she oiled me between my rear cheeks and slowly slipped in a petal-pink butt plug, her knowing fingers working between my thighs to tickle my clit as she filled my ass.

I came again when Sam jacked himself hard and let loose in my mouth, filling me up with his cream as Sheila fucked me from behind.

I jammed my own fingers between my legs, working my clit to come a final time when Richard, so distant, lowered his head and shuddered, his body wracked with tremors as he climaxed a white fountain up onto his hard belly.

But in the car at 2 a.m., on the way home, still reeking of imported essential oils, still throbbing from the poundings I'd taken, I started to giggle. And then Sam started to laugh out loud, shaking his head as he drove the empty highway.

"Crazy."

"So much Armani," he snorted.

"And gold records."

"And cigars."

"And their view."

"And their money."

And we didn't see them again, even though they called for weeks afterwards. Even though they fell a little bit in love with us, as had Pamela and Andy. Because Sam and I weren't looking for love. We had plenty of that. We were looking for one thing only. And somehow I was sure that we'd find it again once I placed a personal ad of our own:

> *Happily married twosome seeks similar couple for debauchery. For intensity. For four on the floor.*

Unraveling The Threads Of An Ordinary Life

Amanda Earl

I am an excitable person who only understands life lyrically, musically, in whom feelings are much stronger as reason. I am so thirsty for the marvelous that only the marvelous has power over me. Anything I cannot transform into something marvelous, I let go. Reality doesn't impress me. I only believe in intoxication, in ecstasy, and when ordinary life shackles me, I escape, one way or another. No more walls. – July 7, 1934 from *Incest* by Anais Nin

After class that first day, the day it all began, he'd called her over to his desk and asked her to walk with him to his car while they continued the talk about Anais Nin's writing. Actually he didn't really ask, he told her. And she obeyed. She admired him so much as a professor. He was erudite, intelligent and very attractive with his black hair, tinged with silver, tailored suits, and black leather shoes.

His car was a Jaguar XK with a robust V8 engine. He asked her to join him for a drink so they could discuss Nin further and she found herself agreeing. It wasn't forbidden to associate with faculty, just frowned upon.

In the car, she felt like the professor was inspecting her as his eyes lingered over her tight black skirt and thin braless blouse. Yes, perhaps it was a bit over the top, but heck, one of the reasons she was taking university classes was to meet men. She hadn't thought about professors as possible candidates for bedding, but he certainly turned her on.

"You like to dress like a slut, don't you, Clare?"

This surprised her. She blushed and slouched down on the buttery black leather seat.

"Hey, if you don't like my outfit, or my company, why don't we just forget about the drink?" This wasn't any way to talk to a professor, but he'd called her a slut.

"I didn't say that I didn't like your clothing, Clare. To the contrary, I find it very alluring. Do you think being a slut is something to be ashamed of?"

Clare sat up a little taller in her seat.

"That's it, girl, show me those long legs."

Clare found herself complying, strangely proud of her body. She used to hide it behind layers of clothes, but she'd lost weight, rather a lot of weight. The curves remained, but now she was much fitter and trimmer, and she loved to show it off. And her professor was right, she did wear those clothes to be a slut, to find a man, men to fuck. She smiled up at him, feeling as if a weight had been lifted off her shoulders.

"You know, you're right. Why deny it? I am a slut."

"That's a good girl. And what are sluts good for, Clare?"

Clare's cunt got wet as she listened to David, his voice sliding lower, the car mesmerizing her with its sensual rocking motion and the gentle purr of the engine.

"Being used, sir?"

"That's right, Clare. You are such a quick learner." David stopped the car in front of a hotel surrounded by rolling hills and farms. Clare looked around. She hadn't been paying attention to the drive at all from Concordia University in Montreal. They were now up in the Eastern Townships, a beautiful area of Quebec. She was rather surprised. This man was very presumptuous, and yet, she was also curious and turned on by his presumption.

"Now that we both know you are a slut, girl. Let's enjoy it, shall we?" He grabbed Clare's arm and walked her into the hotel.

"Saint-John, checking in," he said to the front desk clerk. "You've got the usual room, Professor Saint-John. Here's your key."

He just marched Clare into the elevator, and she said nothing. Her cunt was moist, her breasts tingled and she felt so sexy and powerful, being able to get a man to want her like this, to command her. In the elevator, David unzipped his pants.

"What does a slut do, girl? Show me."

Clare looked at the massive cock, poking its head out of the open fly of the professor's pants, and she knew. She knew exactly what a slut does. She got down on her knees and took it in her hand, held it reverently and then said, "She worships it, sir."

"Yessssss," said David as she lavished adulation over his cock with her tongue, then took the head into her mouth and sucked it down, feeling the hardness thicken, filling her. He continued to stroke for a while inside the willing wetness of her mouth.

"Up now, girl. I have so much more to teach you," he said as the elevator slowed down. Clare rose and he allowed his erection to subside a bit before zipping up his pants. The doors opened to an empty hallway.

"One day you will crawl down this hallway for me, girl, and you won't care who sees."

Clare tried to visualize his words. Her body responded, nipples turning upward toward his hands, legs spread for his touch, her cunt moist and ready. But the idea seemed hard to imagine intellectually, and yet . . .

"Are you willing to come into this hotel room with me? Are you ready to let yourself go? To surrender control to me? Because once we enter this room, I will expect you to do so. If you don't I will be a stern master. I will punish you for it."

Clare's lower lip trembled as they paused outside the door. "Uh . . . I'm not sure, sir. I'm, uh, well, I'm nervous about it. I don't know what you expect. I don't know if I can comply." A tear rolled down her eye. "I don't think I'm ready."

"One day you will be my little slut. One day you'll beg for me to strap you down onto a bed, to cover your ass and back with

long red lashes. I know this. But for now, you've shown honesty
and courage, and even a bit of trust towards me. That's enough.
Let's go have that drink."

"What?" Her whole body shuddered and she expelled the
breath she'd been holding on to. "You mean you aren't going to
. . . uh, we aren't going to . . . have . . . um . . . sex?"

"What I have to teach you is so much more than sex. Now
come along."

Clare was quiet as they rode down the elevator. He did not
force her to do anything else. The silence should have been
awkward, but it wasn't. Her curiosity and arousal alleviated the
awkwardness.

That night David chatted with her about literature, asked
about her taste in music, wine, art, and travel, but the subject of
power did not come up again. Clare found herself enjoying the
evening very much and relaxing. Professor David Saint-John
was a master at everything, including charming conversation.

He escorted her back to her apartment, a hole in the wall near
the University of Montreal that she liked to think of as Bohemian. She used to live in her own house but, now that she was a
full-time student again, she'd needed the cash, so she'd down-
scaled. It was very late, but she invited him in.

"Not this time, Clare." He took her hand lightly in his and
looked in to her eyes. "You have slender wrists, Clare. Imagine
them bound with cuffs and chains, my slut. See you Monday.
Have a stimulating weekend."

Clare spent a restless night, tossing and turning and using her
vibrator. The image of kneeling below him as he stroked her
head, the memory of the taste of his precum, and the word
"slut" culminated in a massive orgasm. She had never really
thought about sex in terms of control and surrender. Mostly it
served to relieve a temporary itch, and she always hoped that it
would provide intimacy, but none of her relationships with men
had done that so far. There was always something missing.
Perhaps this was it.

Her workload at the university was heavy, so she spent the
weekend working on papers, researching in the library and

reading. She stayed up late with her collection of Nin books, reading until the early hours of the morning.

On Monday morning, she lingered over her toilette, shaving her pussy, legs and arm pits smooth and dabbing jasmine on her erogenous zones: the valley of her neck, behind her knees, around her areolas. She gazed at her face in the mirror. Was she pretty enough? Was she young enough to hold a man like David's attention? She had lived such an ordinary life; what could he possibly see in her? She realized that she'd been in hibernation all her life. Maybe she didn't want to sleep any more.

She couldn't concentrate in any of her classes that day. David's class started at three pm; it was her final class of the day. She wondered if he would like her dress. She'd chosen her most sophisticated black dress with abalone buttons all the way down the front, almost to the floor. But she'd left the buttons undone from mid-thigh down, hoping to give him a flash of her long legs. She imagined undressing for him, unbuttoning the buttons with clumsy fingers as she trembled with excitement. Would he punish her if she took too long or had trouble undoing the buttons? Maybe he'd lash her with a whip, unraveling the black threads of her ordinary life.

She sat through the entire class, not saying anything, not raising her hand. His voice crackled against her skin like fire. She watched his hands poised on his thighs as he sat on the desk and remembered how they held her head. His suit pants were the same ones he'd worn on Friday, the ones she'd knelt before and unzipped. She thought of crawling over to the desk on her hands and knees and opening her mouth to suck his cock, to take his come down her throat.

"Clare!" she heard suddenly. The sternness of his voice brought her out of her reverie. "Please see me after class." The other students tittered.

She trembled nervously, fidgeting with her papers and pen while she waited for the slow tick of the clock to turn over to five pm. At the end of class, an attractive, well-endowed blonde lingered by the professor's desk. Clare felt that David was stretching the conversation with the young student just to torment his willing slut. Finally the blonde left and they were alone.

"Close the door. Quickly." Claire drew a sharp breath and rushed to close the door, her long black dress rustling against her naked legs.

"My slut has been daydreaming today. What about?"

Clare blushed and hesitated and then answered truthfully. "About Friday, sir, and everything we talked about."

"Is that it?"

"Uh, no. I also thought of undressing for you. Undoing my buttons at your command."

"Good girl. You have such a natural instinct to obey, don't you?"

"I don't know, but I thought about what would happen if I took too long. Would you punish me?"

Clare took shallow breaths as the professor moved gracefully toward her, like a leopard to his prey. "Do you think you deserve punishment, my little slut?"

"Yes, I do, sir."

"What for?"

"For not paying attention to you, sir."

"That's right, smart girl. Now come here and bend over my desk."

Clare wobbled on unsteady legs to his desk and pressed herself over the solid wood desk.

"I don't need you to unbutton your slut dress, girl." He yanked it up above her breasts and the buttons went flying off, abalone shining in the light from the blinds, which were closed against the late afternoon sunshine.

Clare cried out. "I'll make you crawl for those buttons later, girl. And you'd better find every single one."

He placed his hand on her finely shaped ass cheeks and caressed the soft curves of her naked bottom. "So soft and unmarked, girl. I think it's time you were spanked."

Clare felt a draft of air move over her body as he lifted his hand and slapped it hard against her ass. She drew a sharp breath and let out a tiny squeal.

"Do you deserve to be punished, slut?"

"Yes, sir."

"Then stop your squirming and take your punishment." With that he began to cover her ass with sharp stinging slaps, alternating with circular caresses. Clare held herself still and quiet from then on, but couldn't help the juices from overflowing her aroused cunt and trickling down her leg. She felt his fingers trace the come along the inside of her thighs.

"Well, girl, you are wet. I'm going to enjoy taking you. Making you mine." His hand resumed spanking her ass. "Next time, I'm going to cane you, like the bad little school girl you are."

Clare moaned as the thought of being punished like a naughty schoolgirl aroused her body and her mind. She felt his fingers enter her sopping sex.

"You are wet, girl. What kind of a slut gets aroused by a spanking?" He plunged his fingers in and out of her, but she forced herself not to move. It was difficult, but she did it, biting down hard on her lip to keep from screaming. Her ass was hot and sore from the strong hand, which had smacked, cupped and then caressed her flaming buttocks. She'd never had a spanking before. And she wanted it. Wanted him to keep going. But he stopped. Removed his fingers from her cunt.

"Get up, girl. Are you ready to crawl for those buttons?"

"Yes sir," Clare said breathlessly.

"Get on the floor, on your hands and knees, my slut. Pick up every one with your mouth and deposit them at my feet."

Clare lowered herself to the floor, her open dress causing her to feel cold tile against her nipples and cunt. She raised herself onto her hands and knees and crawled along.

"Spread your legs open when you crawl. I want to see those cunt lips, slut."

She spread her legs and awkwardly crawled to the first button, trying hard to retrieve it with her tongue, which was parched and dry from her deep breaths of desire and frustration.

"Bend lower, girl. Use those teeth." The button was large

and flat, and eventually she managed to secure it with her teeth and keep it between her lips as she crawled back to the professor's feet.

"Now drop it, girl." She allowed the button to drop and it bounced, landing quite far away from the professor's black leather shoes. "No, slut, that's too far. Go back for it and put it at my feet."

Clare moaned in frustration but would not give up. She retrieved the button, the floor beginning to wear on her knees and hands. Her body was sore at the end, but she managed to find all of the buttons and place them at his feet.

The professor brought out a plastic bag.

"Now open the bag, girl."

She sat at his feet, looking up at him warily. What was he going to make her do now?

She snapped open the bag and pulled out a beautiful silk dress, gasping at its beauty.

"I'll take your black dress and get the buttons sewn on by another one of my slaves. This is your reward for being so obedient and truthful, girl. Now put yourself together so we can show you off. Dinner is at 7:00 pm. I expect you to be ready."

"Thank you, sir." The dress fit perfectly, and Clare went in to the women's washroom to fix her makeup and calm herself.

Once again that night the two spent a pleasurable dinner and afterward, David drove her home, but once again did not enter her apartment.

He did not contact her the rest of the week, and by Friday she was feeling insecure and angry. Maybe she deserved an ordinary life. In an ordinary life, men kissed her but she never felt intimate with them like she did with David. Men came into her apartment and fucked her, but David never did. They'd never even had sex. She was confused and frustrated.

In Friday's class she made sure to pay attention. After class, he didn't call her over and she marched past him. She was walking quickly through the parking lot when suddenly she heard his voice, not loud just strong: "Clare, stop."

She did not stop at first. The parking lot was empty. She

didn't know what to do. She wanted what he did to her, but she wanted more, and he wouldn't give it to her. She knew that if she ignored him, their relationship, or whatever it was, would be over. She would be back to occasional sex with unmemorable men. Back to her ordinary life.

She stopped. He got into his car and drove over to her. "Get in."

She entered the car and fastened her seat belt. Not sure what to say. He just drove on until they reached a hotel in downtown Montreal. "It's up to you, Clare. We can go into the hotel where I have a room for the night. You can let me control your body. You can let me into your mind. Allow me to unleash your deepest fantasies. I can tie you down and whip you, or you can leave now."

Clare thought of the spanking and how good it felt. She thought of how freeing it felt when he held her head as his penis took her mouth. She wanted him to take her again. She needed more than an ordinary life.

"Yes, sir. Please take me."

The two rode up the elevator and she assumed her position at his feet.

Utterly Nude

Maxim Jakubowski

He'd always been attracted, sometimes fascinated by the smooth hairless crotches of women. Not just the fact that some women wished to shave their sexual parts, or more likely in the pursuit of fashion, wax them. What also exercised his imagination were the deep-set motivations behind the decision to reveal their cunts so openly, to regress to a state of far from innocent childhood, unprotected by a bush of curls or a minor forest of imitation barbed wire in all shades of colors and textures. Quite often, he had convinced a lover to allow him to trim her pubic hair and, on one occasion, to actually allow him to shave her fully. The experience itself had proven most erotic and the ensuing fucking had acquired an extra dimension. It was summer and the South of France and, the next day, he had half jokingly suggested she refrain from wearing her thong under her short skirt when they went out dining and she had playfully agreed. A memory that lingered with him much longer than the intensity of their love-making. But she had drawn the line at returning to that nude beach some miles away from the port where they were staying with her cunt in full naked display. He had failed to persuade her to do so, and his innocent request had visibly irritated her. It would seem that a hairless cunt was a private matter that should only be witnessed by a lover of long standing. By coincidence or otherwise, this was to be their last trip together.

His next mistress was already shaven. Had been so for years, long before he emerged on her scene. It seems the practice was widespread amongst young women in Germany and, having noted the fact during endless telephone conversations and e-mail exchanges, this was one aspect of hers that had immediately attracted him to her in the first place. And her jovial willingness to sleep with him. Undressing her for the first time, in a hotel room in Frankfurt that smelled of illicit sex already, proved an exhilarating experience, but also a sort of anti-climax as he finally unveiled the silky smoothness of her cunt, and the red gash of her sexual parting in a wet state of readiness. The thought briefly occurred to him that it would have been so much more exciting to have witnessed her passage from hairiness to utter nudity himself. Maybe it wasn't the state of nakedness of a mons veneris that did these strange things to him, but the very act of revelation, the passage from hirsute parts to billiard-ball shininess. He hadn't had much time to reflect on things though with her, as he quickly discovered the ever so slightly masochistic streak that illuminated the young woman's sexuality, as she greedily invited him to twist her nipples between the vice of her abandoned hairpins once he had set her dark auburn hair loose.

"Yes," she had moaned, begging for the pain.

He had soon forgotten the initial ecstatic vision of her smooth cunt as further excesses quickly suggested themselves to him, none of which she rejected during the course of a long night of sheer, mutual madness.

But the fascination remained. Encouraged, exacerbated, provoked, kept alive by the torrent of images of exposed, naked cunts he kept on coming across in magazines, books and even movies (European ones by Peter Greenaway, Julio Medem, Mike Figgis and others . . .).

So, it was no surprise that one summer whilst on holiday on a small Caribbean island, his enfevered mind should spin an unlikely variation on the theme. This was not a place where nudity was tolerated on beaches, despite the idyllic setting that so effortlessly evoked the Garden of Eden and its bucolic innocence. Even topless displays of female pulchritude were few and far between here. The heat over his first few days at the resort had proven oppressive, steamy, sticky, with no relief in sight. On previous trips here, he had been close to the hurricane season and there had always been a gentle wind rising over the ocean from mid to late morning to cool one's body down. By lunchtime, every day, he was sweating profusely and his trunks or shorts stuck aggressively to his skin, the friction between the material and his flesh annoying and increasingly unpleasant. Dredging up instant nostalgia and longing for those nude beaches in France he had frequented some years back.

Maybe he should shave. Like a woman. It might feel cooler, he thought. And then remembered how some past conquest had once mentioned how unpleasant it could become when the hair inevitably grew back, the skin irritable and prone to bursting out in unseemly bumps. He would choose cream. It should be safe if women used it under their arms, he reckoned. He located some in the hotel's lobby shop and deciphered the instructions in Spanish as best he could . . .

Straight from the tube he squeezed out the thick white paste that smelled of almond oil in parallel trails across his thick, dark curls and flattened and liberally spread the viscous substance until his bush was fully obscured and covered. The label said to leave it soak in for five minutes, although to take care not to rub it in and especially not to exceed ten minutes. He kept an eye on his watch. Then, with the help of the green plastic spatula supplied in the depilating cream's pack, he began gently rubbing the drying cream away. It worked. The hair was coming off with a minimum of effort. He sat on the edge of the bath tub, his legs spread open and began to systematically scrape away the dead vegetation surrounding his now half-erect penis until the whole area looked uncannily bare, the paler than pale skin a mighty contrast with the onset of a deep tan across the rest of his body. After rinsing the newly depilated zone with some warm water, he passed his fingers over the whole area and found it surprisingly, pleasantly silky. Which conjured instant memories of the cunts of the women he had caressed lustfully during the course of recent sexual encounters. His hand moved down to his cock, and he was taken back by the fact that some stray, almost spiky hairs still adorned the lower reaches of the thickening trunk of his member. His fingers lowered and swept across his testicles and again became aware of the sprinkling of hairs that coated them. Out came the cream again and he covered his balls all the way down to his perineum, as well as the stem of his cock. Soon, he was totally bare, all the way from his lower stomach area to his anal opening.

It felt good. Curiously arousing and it proved difficult during those few first days of total nudity not to touch and finger himself constantly. As if the skin above his jutting cock had acquired a new, sensual texture and the taut sack of his balls invited the tentative contact of errant fingertips as he explored the newly uncovered territory. He imagined how a woman's tongue would taste him, lick him and again came hard in the wink of an eye.

At regular intervals, he would examine his genitals in the mirror of the bathroom, or the half mirror that the hotel provided in the bedroom. He became an inveterate voyeur of his own parts, finding new subtleties in the ever-changing shades of white and pale brown in the virgin skin that dominated his cock, the reddish hue of his heavy balls. Actually, his cock now appeared longer, thicker, bigger, not that he'd ever had grounds for complaint previously. There was a nagging desire to expose himself, to surprise others, to reveal to the world at large how utter his nudity now was. He even began to dispense with underwear altogether, dangling loose under his trousers and shorts in the resort's large dining room that overlooked the sea, joyous with the secret knowledge of his uncommon state under the already thin material. It was definitely most arousing. One morning, he even deliberately left the room around five in the morning and walked a few miles up the beach to an area he had once spotted, far from the hotels and beach guards, and swam naked. More than naked. The lapping of the water against his parts was joyous, liberating, even stronger than the feeling he had experienced the first time he had swam on a nude beach, albeit with his previous abundance of pubic hair. It wasn't just the sexual effect of his newly acquired nudity but a weird sense of possibilities that engulfed his brain.

He thought he now understood why some women depilated their sexual areas. He sympathized. Empathized. This was more than mere hygiene or practicality. To the extent that the compulsive desire to present himself in total submission, in all his childlike nudity, began to dominate his dreams. Surely there was no greater sense of vulnerability to be displayed thus, so shorn of all protection, sexually available to all comers and potential users. For the first time, he was beginning to understand better the mind frame of submissive women, all those doughty heroines from O to the legions of abused women from the Roquelaure tales of Anne Rice and her cohorts of more recent followers. He could close his eyes and silently yearn to be tied to some pole or tree, legs held apart by a spreader bar, ridiculous cock dangling in the forest breeze, while men of all shapes, sizes and sexual persuasions could liberally gaze at him, touch his parts, weigh his melancholy nudity in the palm of their hands, poke his holes, gently slap his butt cheeks, examine his teeth as he lay waiting to be auctioned. Yes, knowing how unprotected he was down there literally made him feel like a sexual slave in waiting. He did have a roaring imagination, he surely did.

Back in Europe, he would often wake at night from savage dreams of exotic, novelistic adventures full of rape and heavy use by Masters. His lust raged at the idea of such ravishment and in each scene or sequence that his fever lust conjured, there were also beautiful women watching as he was being defiled, all with Mona Lisa smiles, some clothed in sheer silk, others in progressive stages of deshabillé, calmly appreciating the sheer art his torturers exercised as they took merciless advantage of his now so prominent cock and shiny balls, and induced endless after endless erections until he felt he was about to burst, as each toy, object or alien penis dug its painful way into his innards, stretching him more than he ever thought possible, deep-throating him until he gagged, and all because his shaven parts betrayed his abject condition as a sexual slave available to all, obedient, displayed, ripe for defilement.

He even went so far as advertising himself in veiled terms as a sub for use when he ventured onto Internet chat rooms, hoping for takers and resolute enough to follow through should someone local and reasonably dominant actually take him up on the offer. But no one did; all they sought were female subs, no doubt similarly shaven. His sisters in arms.

And, at four or so in the morning when the dreams came to their spectacular climax (you couldn't call them nightmares after all), he would invariably be untied, his collar straightened and a chain attached to it and he was led, so naked and proud, to a stone table where the spread-eagled body of the most beautiful young blonde he had ever dreamed of was on public display to the leering gaze of a growing crowd, and, as a reward for having survived his own ordeal, he would be summoned to mount her, required to perform, take her virginity. And always he would note that she also had been depilated, her cunt lips gaping open like flowers and the skin surrounding her gash slippery like glass, smooth as a window pane, and when their flesh made contact, it would be like an electric shock. Nakedness touching nudity, as obscene as two skeletons mating, the nee plus ultra of performance art. At which stage, he usually woke up, his cock hard and raging and ready to spill, like the lone tree in a defoliated forest.

But the first time after the Caribbean holiday that he took a woman to bed, she barely noticed the uncommon hairlessness of his crotch, didn't even remark upon it. Which not only brought him down to earth but also made him temporarily impotent. They parted in embarrassment. Anyway, he reflected, following her departure, she had just been trimmed and the conjugation of his cock and her cunt would have certainly lacked the obligatory magic. From here onwards, he swore to himself, he would only have sex with women who were similarly, utterly nude. Somehow, it became a clever, subtle question he would manage to introduce into the proceedings of seduction from an early stage. Some minded and went their own way; others were coy, some intrigued, partly offended by his outrageous and indecent curiosity about the state of their parts. He was not a totally hopeless case and still practiced the art of courting with a modicum of elegance and intelligence and did not find it impossible to convince an attractive woman to go to bed with him, but he invariably became the one to surprise and disappoint them shortly after their answers to his one track enquiries always seemed to reveal their uselessness to him. It was not so much that he didn't feel capable of convincing them, once lovers or in a bedroom, naked, lustful, to allow him to shave them; no, he wanted them to come to him in a natural state of nudity below from the outset, like Venus arising from the shell, their cunt more naked than naked ready for his kiss, his tongue, the heat of his lips. He had no wish for preliminaries, or hard work. Once together, they must both shed their clothing and witness their bare areas meeting, like waves lapping the shore, like a pagan ritual.

But somehow all the women he came across socially or attempted to weave into the fabric of his life now guarded the sanctity of their pubic hair like dragons, and bristled at his unkind suggestion they should do away with their heavenly bush.

So, instead, he masturbated a lot, familiarizing himself even better with the new texture and feel of his own cock and balls. Altogether a pitiful state of affairs for a man who had now reached the stage where he was actually turning women away. And the fact he so often would not take advantage of their proffered charms – he would never say exactly why – only spurred them to attack him with more zest. Never had he been more popular with women, and never had he not fucked anyone for such a long period of sexual drought. If only they knew, he thought, as he perused a room full of beauty and talent. But then he couldn't just drop his trousers here and now and expose himself and reveal his secret. Or should he?

But he was a patient man. One day, she would arrive, he was convinced, and at the very moment that bare cock and bare cunt would meet, as the mushroom tip of his thick purple cock would at last breach her opening and plunge deep into her pinkness, then their sex flesh would finally meet with a vengeance.

Smoothness to smoothness, silk against silk, electrons against electrons, blissful innocence against total vulnerability. And everything would explode in an orgy of momentous pleasure, like an atomic bomb exploding. Like the end of the world.

Until then, he would wait, he reckoned. And stay chaste, and shaven.

Outsourcing

Robert Buckley

He grasped his coat below the collar and shivered against the raw dampness that seeped into his bones.

This was too much, the third time in two weeks that she had failed to pick him up on time. No more. From now on he would order up a company limo. But for the moment, he needed a ride. He loathed riding in cabs, but he had little selection in the matter. Besides, the homeless were coming out and beginning to pick through the remains of the day in the financial district.

A red checkered vehicle pulled around the corner and came toward him. He stepped off the curb and waved it down. He winced as he opened the rear door, but at least it was warm inside. He slid onto the seat, laying his briefcase beside him.

"Do you speak English?" he inquired.

"All my life," the driver replied, eying him laconically in the rearview mirror.

"You're white," he said.

"Yup, been white all my life too."

"I didn't think there were any white cab drivers left."

"It's not my preferred line of work, just something to tide me over. But since you think it's such a novelty, maybe I should levy a surcharge."

"I can see that a smart-alecky attitude still goes with the job," he huffed.

"Look, mister, I got to make a living. We can chat all night in one spot if you want, but I'm gonna flick the meter anyway. Or would you rather tell me where to?"

"Can you drive beyond the city?"

"Yup, but after a while we get into flatrate zones."

"I'm going to Manchester-by-the-Sea."

"Uh-huh. That'll be thirty-six bucks flat."

"Very well – get moving."

The driver pulled away, making his way to the tunnel that would bring them north of the city. His passenger sniffed, pinching his face into a scowl.

"I don't like cabs," he said. "They smell."

"Hmm, you think so?"

"Yes, they smell of the people who rode in them – unwashed."

"You should have been in the cab I drove a couple of days ago – it smelled like pussy. I didn't mind."

"Are you serious?"

"Yup, someone was well and truly fucked in the backseat before I got it. Damn, made me randy all day."

"That's disgusting."

The driver shrugged.

They just entered the tunnel when the passenger asked, "Did you say you were between positions?"

"Huh? Oh, yeah. I lost my regular job seven weeks ago. It was outsourced."

"I see. Well, you'll just have to adapt. It's an evolving world, you know."

"Evolving? Outsourced? Do you remember when they called it 'downsizing'? It seems every decade or so they come up with another euphemism for tossing people out on the street."

"My company outsources," he said with a hint of satisfaction. "It's a global economy – workers in this country – in the entire developed world – will just have to adapt and evolve along with it."

"Really? I suppose we're supposed to evolve into a Third World workforce."

"Labor is a commodity, young man. Those are cold hard facts, but facts nonetheless. Adapt or perish."

The driver rolled his eyes. "I have two degrees, and I haven't even paid off the student loans on the first one. Am I supposed to go into debt to get another – to adapt?"

His passenger sniffed again. "It smells like stale popcorn back here."

"What are you, some top-suite executive?"

"Yes – yes, I am."

"So, if you hate cabs so much, what are you flagging one down on the street for?"

"My wife was supposed to pick me up. I don't know what's happened to her. I can assure you, this is the last cab I'll ride in if I can help it."

"Maybe you just missed her. What does she drive?"

"A Jaguar."

"Hmm, seems I recall seeing a Jag in the area a few times last week – not tonight, though. Oh, well, sit back and enjoy the ride."

"Not likely."

"Really, mister, a lot of strange and wonderful things happen in cabs."

"I can believe the 'strange' part."

The driver chuckled. "Well, yeah. Like for instance, remember I told you about the cab I drove all day that smelled of pussy."

"Yes." He winced.

"The reason it smelled that way is because the night before I drove it, my pal, Raul, was at the wheel."

"Oh? Does he rape his passengers?"

"Ha! That's funny. No, sir. It was Raul who was nearly raped. See, he had picked up this woman in the financial district – a handsome babe she was. She had a buck too. Anyway, as soon as she got in the cab she started coming on to Raul, talking dirty to him. At one point she says – now get this: 'Give me some of that greasy spic cock.'"

"Sounds like she had issues."

"Issues? Man, she had issues soaking her pants, is what she had. So Raul fucked her in the backseat. She took him every possible way she could. Finished up with an inspired ass-fuck."

"Driver, you really don't need to share this with me."

"Oh, I beg your pardon, sir. I thought you might be interested. You see, she was obviously a well-to-do woman. Who knows, she might live in Manchester-by-the-Sea."

"Driver, I really am getting irritated. There is a number here that I can call to complain, in case you've forgotten."

"Sorry, sir. I really did think you'd be interested. I'll shut up."

The passenger nodded. He was silent for a few miles, then he peered at the driver in the rearview.

"Why did you think I'd be interested – in the woman, I mean?"

"Huh? Oh, it's just – well she was something of an enigma, that is until she came on to me."

"You?"

"Yes, sir. I was getting to that. You see, this chick has been showing up off and on in the same area for about a month now. She parks, then trolls for cock. She isn't fooling anyone. And it isn't just cabbies she picks on, I've spotted her pick up guys stumbling out of bars, any guy who looks a little rough and ragged. You see, I figured she had some sort of self-humiliation thing going – some women are really into that."

"Like I said, she must have some serious issues. I think she needs help. I hope, for her sake, her family finds out and gets it for her."

"That's a nice thought, sir, but that isn't what she's about."

"Oh?"

"No," the driver said. "People who are into humiliation – well, they get off on their own degradation. Picture a soccer mom allowing herself to be fucked by some greasy slob. She's thinking, 'Oh, I'm so pure and wholesome, and this dirty beast is defiling me with his dirty cock.' But she loves it – see what I'm saying?"

"Hmm, are you some kind of psychologist or something?"

"Amateur – but you get my meaning."

"Yes, driver – degradation, fresh scrubbed soccer mom allowing herself to be violated." He tried to sound bored.

"Exactly – hey you're a lot sharper than a lot of the execs I run into."

"You're very close to having a complaint lodged against you and your company, young man."

"Sorry – you still want to hear about the woman, right?" Feigning exasperation, he sighed. "Go ahead."

"Well, you see, she wasn't into degradation – not her own anyway. She was just looking for a stud. She liked them rough and dirty, but she made no bones about it, she was in charge."

"How do you mean?"

"When she fucked Raul, for instance. She called him everything: lousy spic, grease ball, taco fucker. Told him he was a dirty, greasy mongrel, and how she was privileging him by letting him fuck her rich, white suburban ass."

"Issues."

"Maybe. Now, Raul, he doesn't give a shit. He's getting his balls drained, and she can call him anything she wants for all he cares."

"Well, no one's cheated if everyone's satisfied," his passenger sniffed.

"Hey, that's good. I have to remember that." The driver laughed, a sharp hard laugh.

"Now," he continued. "This same crazy bitch came on to me just the other night. She waved me down and told me to drive to the waterfront. We parked in a lot and left the meter running.

"This babe – well, she might have been in her early fifties, but she took good care of herself. Nothing sagged – I'm saying she had a body as taut as a 20-year-old girl. She was rich, you know? And she looked like she'd paid top dollar all her life to keep her body in pristine condition. She smelled good too – expensive."

"And?"

"Hold on, I have to tell it right. Anyway, she says, 'It's your lucky night.' And she kneels on the seat and lifts her skirt up. She's got no panties on, and she pats one cheek and says, 'You get to fuck this fine piece of ass.'

"So, I say, 'Yes, ma'am' and I climb in back to oblige her.

Then she hands me a jar of some nice-smelling cream and says, 'Grease my asshole', and I say 'Yes, ma'am'.

"So I'm sliding my finger in and out of her back door and she's snarling: 'That's right, grease me up good, I want your whole cock in my bowels.'"

"Did – did you?" his passenger said, his voice hoarse.

"Mister, I pushed my pole through her pucker hole in one thrust – no stopping, right up to my balls. Then I began to pound her, and she started talking real dirty. She says, 'Yeah, come on, shitfucker – you filthy lout . . . fuck me.'

"So I decided to give her as good as she's dishing out, and I say, 'What's up, princess? Can't your old man get it up for you?'

"Just then she gets real squirrelly. She says, 'You dirty pile of shit – my husband makes more in a day than you will your entire, pathetic life. Now shut the fuck up and fuck me, that's all I want from you, you fucking insect.'"

The passenger chuckled.

The driver eyed him through the rearview. "Yeah, she thought it was funny too – right up until the second I pulled out of her ass and shoved her through the door."

"You did what?"

"Threw her out. Damn, you should have seen her face. There she was crawling around the pavement on all fours. Her stockings were torn, her clothes all muddy, ''cause she fell right into a puddle."

"What – what did she do?"

"Glared at me. She said, 'You prick, I'll have you charged with rape.'

"And I said, 'Go ahead, you twisted bitch. And I'll tell the cops how you've been slumming for meat – I'm sure the pudgy Honduran driver you fucked yesterday will back me up, and if he doesn't do the trick, then those truckers you sucked off in the alley beside Cabot's Bar and Grill.'"

"What – what did she say?"

"You kidding? She didn't know whether to shit or go blind. Her jaw dropped to the pavement where her knees were. I shut the door and drove away laughing, but not before I took my fare from her purse and tossed it out the window."

"Hmm, that's quite a story, young man."

"You don't believe me?"

"It seems preposterous that a woman of the caliber you describe would risk her position, her marriage so recklessly. It's an insightful fantasy, though."

The passenger directed the driver off the highway and through the rustic, tree-lined streets of the town. They passed a row of mansions, set well back from the road, then the passenger directed him to turn into a crescent drive. The cab stopped in front of a huge brick house, just behind a dark, green Jaguar.

The passenger got out and counted out $36 exactly. "I hope you didn't think that fairytale you told would earn you a tip."

"People with money don't generally tip well," the driver said.

"In that case, here's a dollar for your imagination – that's about what it's worth."

The driver grinned. "You know, mister, I was thinking – what you said about a woman like that not wanting to risk her marriage and such."

"Yes, what of it?"

"I don't think she looked at it that way. See, I figure she really wasn't getting satisfied at home. – You know what I think she was doing?"

"What?"

"Outsourcing."

The man glared.

"And I just realized another thing – she drove a green Jag – just . . . like . . . that."

The driver grinned and pulled away. "Have a nice night, sir."

He left him standing in his driveway – shaking.

Five States

Cheyenne Blue

"Arizona?" said my mother. "Watch out for the pricks."
I think she meant the cacti.

I was young and crazy, living on the beach in Mexico with
Jonno. Hippies, I guess you would call us, running ragged and
barefoot over the burning white sand, living on shellfish and
marijuana, sex and sunlight. Our canvas tent was set amid the
swaying eucalyptus that fringed the beach, set back from time
and tides, a discreet distance from the village of dark-eyed
Mexicans who studied our movements. Jonno said they were
envious; I guess that was one explanation for the silent faces
that watched us fucking on the shore and heard the gasps of
satiation that we offered to the moonlit night. They never
intruded, merely watched. I sensed their vicarious pleasure
and often the thought of those fish-net roughened hands stroking their cocks to climax would send me spiraling to my own
completion.
Free spirits, Jonno called us. We drifted through the villages,
buying nopales, frijoles, and cheap tequila with the money we
earned from selling strings of shell beads to the few American
tourists who ventured our way. Free spirits, tied to no corporate
world, no nine-to-five and, as I found out eventually, to anybody.
I saw Jonno fucking Rosa from the village one sun-dappled
afternoon. The sun burned through the swaying eucalyptus,
painting his golden body with a sunshadow collage of leaves and

seagulls' wings. Rosa was small and plump, curved belly arcing toward the ground as Jonno pounded her from behind.

I watched. I couldn't not. Hell, it was exciting, even as my heart was shattering. I confronted him later, when it was just us spooned together in our canvas world, just him and me and the night rush of waves on the shore.

"Free spirits, Moni," he said. "I have only myself to give. To share my body only with you would be selfish. I'm not like that."

Yeah, right.

I left him the next day, bumming a ride to the Arizona border with a fisherman who was carrying shellfish and his daughter to a better life in the United States. I walked across the border at Nogales into Arizona, carrying only a daypack containing a change of panties, a bottle of tequila, and a ten dollar note. Once in America, I stuck out my thumb on I–19.

A family in a shiny sports utility picked me up almost immediately.

"Where to?" The white-shirted husband looked like he was regretting the decision to stop, even before I climbed aboard.

"Canada," I said.

He looked uncomfortable. "We can take you as far as Tucson."

"Whatever." I settled into the leather upholstery. Silent children watched me over their handheld computer games.

"What's your name?" A small pale-eyed girl with a sullen mouth asked me.

"Rosa," I replied.

She returned to her game, and no one said a word to me until they dropped me off on the outskirts of Tucson in the hot July night.

My next lift took me to Sedona. Ah, Sedona, with its tapestry of new age and new money. My ride was a pony-tailed businessman from Phoenix, who was spending a weekend in Sedona "discovering his inner self." I didn't like to tell him that he could do it on a beach in Mexico, high as a kite on dope and tequila, for a fraction of the price.

He talked about his karma and his katra and his cat for all that I was listening. I put my hand on his thigh. Underneath the smooth suit he was jagged with tension. He had probably fantasized about someone like me.

We fucked at the site of an energy vortex, deep in the red rock country surrounding Sedona. The ground was hard; dusty and unyielding and the red ants ran over my thigh as I flexed and pulled him into me, let him pound my slick walls. My pussy stretched to accommodate the shape of an unfamiliar cock. Jonno had been long and solid; slightly curved in arousal and full of the jutting prominence and swagger of the young. My businessman was more assured; confident in his ability to please me. The pungent sharp smell of sage was in my nose, the tickle of impending hayfever blending with the esoteric promise of ritual and knowledge.

Sacred sex? He seemed to think so.

I didn't care; I pulled him to me, forcing his head to my breast, encouraging his mouth to open on my nipple with guttural grunts. He bit down, hard, and I pinched his buttocks with my fingers, drawing his surging cock deeper into me. He came in short, hard spurts, and I welcomed his stickiness, his seed upon my thighs.

Take that, Jonno. My thoughts were hard and vicious, just like the cock exploring my inner depths, diving and delving into sticky heat.

We washed afterwards in a natural spring. The water sprang from the loins of the earth. His cock sprang from his loins too, but I wasn't interested any more. I was still engorged and dilated from his fierce fucking earlier and right now the knowledge that he wanted me again was all I needed.

I didn't let him have me again; instead we dressed and I teased his twitching cock with hot fingers, letting him think that any moment now I was going to rip off my pants and let him back into me. He drove me north, up Oak Creek Canyon, and I left him without a backward glance, left him gaping in astonishment, his cock tenting his pants like a teepee.

"What's your name?" He called the words after me into the
stillness of the desert highway.

"Lileth," I called back over my shoulder. I don't know why;
it just seemed to fit.

I hitched up my shorts, feeling the seam bite deep into my
engorged sex, pulled down my top so that my breasts were
barely covered, and stuck out a thumb.

Somewhere in the banging and heat of the vortex, I had
decided that I would fuck one man in every state to Canada, and
only one. So it was easy to resist the backpackers who picked me
up next. They must have smelt my scent; the pungent smell of
sex must have been rolling off my body in waves, blending
seamlessly with sagebrush, pine, and dust. I made them drop
me at the Utah border; a new state and I didn't want to waste
my opportunities.

Hah! I should be so lucky. Utah passed in a blur of minivans,
disconsolate housewives, teenagers with babies on their hips
and a wave of pale skin. I stopped for a beer in a silent, deserted
bar and met Jorge, a trucker of eastern European descent.
Sturdy and thickset, his short stubby cock matched his short
stubby body. He grasped my hips and pounded me with short
fat strokes, crying a name that wasn't mine at the moment of
climax.

He left me unsatisfied, but my resolution wouldn't let me
assuage the ache in Utah. Nevada was closest, so I headed west.
Jorge dropped me on the state line.

"My fey and silent brown-eyed one," he mumbled into my
hair. "So beautiful, so willing and I don't even know your
name."

I told him the name he had called at the moment of his
orgasm and watched his eyes widen in fascinated horror.

I walked for a while in Nevada; miles along the heat-hazed
bitumen, feeling the bite of sun on my exposed shoulders. The
road was a shimmering ribbon, evaporating into the horizon. I
heard the sounds of small and wild things; the click of the
crickets, the buzz of a rattler, the loud rasp of the sagebrush
against my legs.

I heard the pickup long before I saw it; old, a diesel with a missing beat in the thrum of the engine. I stuck out a thumb without looking behind and heard it slow and shudder to a halt.

"Lift, ma'am?" The drawl was mischievous, as if the owner knew my intent before he picked me up. Maybe he did; the shorts were stuck to my ass in the heat and trickles of sweat ran in rivulets down my back, sheening the strip of skin between shorts and top.

My Nevada fuck had arrived. I smiled my acceptance of his offer, climbing up in such a way that he caught a glimpse of smooth bronze thigh and a flash of brown pussy hair up the leg of my shorts.

Fifty miles down the road he swerved the pickup onto the hard shoulder and cut the engine. My hand explored the contours of muscled thigh and the bulge of his groin that swelled beneath my hand. He leaned over the gear stick to kiss me, thrusting a heated tongue in and out of my mouth in mimicry of what I knew would come later.

I left the truck and pulled my top off, exposing my breasts to the burn of the sun. His mouth was on them immediately, suckling in that strange way that men have, as if they gain sustenance. Maybe they do. He pushed me down, into the dust and the small sharp stones right there on the hard shoulder. His lips moved down my stomach, unzipping my shorts with indecent haste and sending a probing finger down inside my panties then up into the liquid heat of my sex.

Even though I had washed, I wondered if he was feeling the slippery ropes of Utah semen as he probed inside me. His fingers skated over my clit and delved inside. I lifted my hips and let him pull the shorts away from me. I ran my own fingers over his sides, soft and strangely vulnerable in contrast to the hard, muscled chest that loomed above and the jutting urgency of what was below. My hands fondled his stomach, down to his sex, feeling the lift and contract of his testicles as I kneaded their exposed vulnerability.

He devoured me with his mouth, lifting my hips to meet him; sucking and slurping with abandon on my sex. I came for the first time when he rolled his tongue around my clit, flicking it at lightning speed. I came for the second time when he pushed his thick dark cock into me and started thrusting; pushing down on me, grinding my ass into the dust and seeds that littered the desert floor.

He didn't last long but it was long enough. He lay on top of me, covering me like a blanket, his cock softening inside me. His come was slick on my thighs. His mouth moved against my neck.

The whine of passing cars intruded, but although we were barely hidden by the carelessly parked pickup, we didn't stir for long moments.

He lifted himself off and out of me. "Where to?"

"Idaho," I said.

He wanted to fuck again and so did I, in spite of my resolution. His turgid, pulsating penis was good, better than the indifferent Utah fuck, more real than the Arizona prick. As we drove north through the long plains of sage and creosote bush, passing purple-topped mountains and salt pans, I fondled his prick; exploring its hardening contours with my hand, delving into his pants to wipe the moisture from the slotted tip.

We compromised, he and I. At the bullet-ridden border sign on a deserted dusty road, he pushed me up against the roughened trunk of a juniper and drove himself into me; sloppy wet in the spend of our previous encounter. I came quickly, contracting around him, drawing him into me. One leg in Nevada, one leg in Idaho.

As he did up his pants he asked my name. "Sedona," I replied. It just seemed to fit.

In Idaho I had a slow and not-so-meaningful encounter with a churchman on his way home, slow driving through the forest in his battered old sedan. He was elderly and it was a pity fuck. I felt magnanimous enough to give him that. He called me "Ruth" and I didn't care enough to ask why, but I let him take me home and feed me overcooked meat and soggy vegetables. I slept in his daughter's bed, surrounded by teddy bears and the stench of damp and decay.

Washington State was cold, even for July. The forests of damp-barked trees stretched out in military rows, dripping lichen and dank, dark water. It took me a while to get a lift, thumb outstretched on the back roads that I preferred. A woman picked me up, the first of the journey. She was stout and olive, dressed in a touque and fleece pants. She reminded me of a pit-bull; all hard-eyed hackles and defense. She was going to save trees in one of the national forests outside of Seattle, she said.

She invited me along; I caught the flicker of interest in her eyes, but I was too tired to play the coy games of seduction that women need so I refused.

"Is it a man?" she asked me in frank curiosity.

I told her about Jonno, and the beaches, and the men I had used on this trip.

"Found your Washington fuck yet?" Her inquiry was blunt and to the point, like her sharp-featured face.

I shook my head and she smiled in satisfaction.

"Come and meet my brother."

It felt almost like prostitution; being led off to sleep with a stranger, but the border was close and I liked the idea of the decision being taken out of my hands.

Her brother was a lean, earnest man, shambling and skinny. He lived in a cabin on the edge of the woods, a hermit-like existence that had me hunting furtively for evidence of gun-powder and ransom letters. He was the sort of man who would cut you into small pieces and put you in his freezer. Liver for supper on Monday, shanks on Tuesday.

His sweet and tender lovemaking caught me unawares. I had expected a quick and desperate copulation, a quiet fitting together of sticky body parts, but the prolonged and crawling sex he gave me made me long for more. His morning beard rasped my skin as he kissed me without haste, sweeping his tongue into my mouth, fitting his lips to mine with great deliberation.

He undressed me with care, moving his mouth over my breast, suckling my nipple as his fingers crawled with agonizing slowness down, over the planes of my belly, tripping lightly along the top of my cotton panties. I was sobbing with the need of him when his mouth followed the path of his meandering fingers. If I had known his name I would have been grunting it at that moment.

He pulled my panties away from my body, parted my thighs and rested his head between. He studied me with great care, parting my sex with a gentle finger. I knew he would see me reddened and swollen from the not-so-sacred sex of the past few days, but he made no comment, simply slipped two fingers into me, swirling them around, stretching me open.

He put his mouth to me and I gasped with the suddenness of it. His long tongue lapped me like a puppy, stiffening to jab inside, then gentling to soothe my rawness. I came with an incoherent shout, my back arching up from the bed in a bowstring of tension, convulsing again and again against his mouth. He quieted me with stroking hands, gentling me like a skittish colt, then drove me up once more from my plateau into a second climax.

I was gasping like a landed fish when he moved up and over me, pushing in his penis, long and slender. I could scarcely feel him at first, but then he started to move, circular motions that changed the angle with each thrust so that he stroked my inner walls with every slight movement. I was so wet that there wasn't any friction. I tightened myself in counter to his strokes and reached between us to stroke his balls. They were small and hard, like marbles, tight up against his body. His lean and muscular butt tightened each time he pushed inside me.

He went on and on, showing no sign of coming. I came enough for both of us, pushing my clit against his narrow, hollow pelvis, wrapping myself around him, stroking his balls with wet fingers, spreading my moisture over him until he was as messy as I.

It must have been an hour later when his sister banged on the door. "You ready?" she hollered through the leaning timber frame. "Come now and I'll give you a lift to the border."

He lifted himself off and out of me; his penis was still hard, wet and sticky. He hadn't come. Without a word he stood over me and brought himself off with three hard strokes. His spend dropped down onto my belly, landing in great gobs in my pubic hair, already dark and matted with my juice. He turned and left through the other door, walking naked out of the house into the forest without a word.

He never asked my name.

I rang Jonno from Vancouver, and found him at the bar where we used to drink. "Are you coming back, Moni?" he asked. "I miss you."

I smiled into the payphone. "I think I will."

"Take the coach," he urged.

"No." Anyone watching me would have recognized my grin for what it was; feral and predatory. "I want to hitch."

"Texas?" said my mother. "Watch out for the longhorns."

I think she meant the cattle.

Under My Thumb

Thomas S. Roche

Spider was horny when he walked into the hotel room – he was always horny after a gig. But it wasn't like he planned to do anything about it – at least, not right away. He had a 3 a.m. "dinner" date with Sierra Verdi from *Darkness Calls* magazine, who, in creaking from her usual reticence the last time he was in town, reviewed Spider's show by saying that "Spider is the only guy in creation besides Billy Bob Thornton whom I would gladly fuck for a dime and a cappuccino."

Spider had a pocket full of dimes, and Daddy's All-Night on Castro had the best espresso drinks of anywhere in town.

He'd already stripped off his sweat-soaked muscle shirt when he hit the lights. For a second, he thought Sierra had jumped the gun on him; in fact, he wondered if maybe she'd waived the cash fee and ordered room service. He'd never actually seen Sierra outside of her photo accompanying her column, and of course hair colors changed as quickly as sexual orientations in the land of rock and roll, so the possibility that Sierra had picked his lock – so to speak – was not dispelled by the fact that it was not a curvy thirty-something brunette but a slim twenty-something blonde stretched out on the hotel bed wearing only leopard-print underwear and a pair of handcuffs.

But the gag – that *definitely* wasn't Sierra's style.

Spider walked over and sat on the edge of the hotel bed. The chick was young, maybe even younger than mid-twenties, and had a longish mane of platinum-blonde hair scattered across the crisp hotel pillows. Her teacup breasts were clutched in a tight push-up bra in pink-and-silver leopard print with black lace at the top, and her cute little ass was cupped in a matching pair of panties. She lay on her side, twisted slightly so that he could see both ass and tits. Obviously she knew her ass was her best feature, but it received stern competition from the tits, which spilled lushly over the tops of her bra cups.

She was pretty. Her features were delicate, those of a perky rock-and-roll starlet effecting the pierced-and-primped look. She definitely wasn't aping the sexy honorary femme-dyke punk style that Sierra sported. Truth be told, the latter was Spider's preference, but the girl on his bed certainly wasn't in danger of getting kicked out.

The girl's big blue eyes blinked up at him cheerfully; only the oversized gag preventing her from showing a broad smile.

Spider rooted under the bed and found the girl's clothes: skimpy black jean shorts, high boots, and a crop top. Tucked into the shorts was a small key-ring, a packet of lube and a tiny leather clutch purse. He tossed the lube on the bed, unsnapped the girl's wallet and took out her I.D. The I.D. looked reasonably convincing – she was twenty-two, well within the legal range. Still, he put his hand on the girl's hip, turned her to her side, and unlocked the handcuffs. She wriggled slightly, resisting his attempts to free her and keeping her wrists pressed together behind her back. She whimpered in protest as he unbuckled the gag. It was one of those ring gags like Spider had occasionally seen on bondage websites – allowing full access while preventing effective protest. Though she whined a little, the girl didn't say a word.

She was so petite that it wasn't hard to wrestle her into a sitting position against the hotel headboard, even though she kept trying to rub her ass up against Spider's crotch. She uttered little protests as he did, though, plainly preferring her prone position. But Spider wasn't taking any shit. He turned her around and sat on the bed, opposite her, cross-legged, not even caring that his heavy boots were still on.

"Hi," the girl said with a smile. She had a pierced tongue and he could see the faint glint of nipple rings, too, through the pink leopard-print fabric and black lace.

Spider looked at her I.D. "Kimberly," he said. "Welcome to my nightmare."

"Ugh," said the girl. "Nobody calls me that. My name's China."

"All right. Listen, I'm going to take a shower."

"I like you dirty."

Spider slapped the girl's thigh, making her jump a little.

"My dear China," he said. "You'll have me clean, if you have me at all. Of course, if you've got second thoughts or the E has started to wear off—"

"I had *one* rum-and-coke," she protested petulantly.

Spider slapped her thigh again.

"Be quiet. If you've got second thoughts, there's the door."

China sat there watching as Spider unbuckled his belt and pulled off his motorcycle boots. He stripped off his stretch jeans as he walked into the bathroom, well aware that China's eyes were burning an invitation into his ass.

The hot water felt good. He heard the doorknob jiggling and was glad he'd locked it. Showers were one of the few things in the world, to Spider, that were not sexy. He lathered himself up and washed the sweat from his body, brushed his teeth but didn't shave. When he walked out of the bathroom, China was handcuffed and gagged again, spread out on her belly having discarded the bra and panties. Her legs were spread wide. Her head was turned to the side; she looked up at him with love in her eyes.

He could see that her pussy was both shaved and pierced – four rings through each of her lips. A similar ring glinted from her clit. Her ass was lifted slightly, invitingly revealing her pink asshole between her smooth, well-toned cheeks.

Spider glanced at the bedside clock. It was already two-thirty, and he didn't want to keep Sierra waiting after the months of email flirtation they'd enjoyed. A ten-minute cab ride left . . . just enough time for a quick tryst with a groupie. It's not like he and Sierra had any kind of agreement – on the contrary, it was an expected value of the rock 'n' roll world that double-dipping was customary.

He let the white hotel towel drop to the floor, and China's eyes zeroed in on his cock, standing hard and ready from his body.

"You realize you're about to be used and discarded," said Spider.

"Yes, please," came China's muffled reply from behind the ring gag. She lifted her ass higher into the air, displaying both her pussy and her ass for Spider's hungry eyes.

He climbed onto the bed and took hold of China's hair. She wriggled slightly to get into the right position as he guided her face to his cock and slid his cockhead through the ring gag. Her tongue immediately began working along the underside. He would have liked to see what those lips could do, but the sparkle in China's eyes as he fed her his cock was more than enough. He eased his cock deeper into her mouth and with a smooth, expert gesture she opened her throat wide and pushed herself onto him, swallowing Spider's cock all the way down to his balls.

Her muscles contracted against him as he began to ease his hips back and forth, fucking her throat. He heard a whimper of pleasure deep in China's throat – without a hint of a gag. This was a well-trained groupie, he decided. He ran his hand down to her handcuffed wrists and savored the feeling of having her in bondage, then slowly drew his fingertips up her back, making China's naked body shiver. He grasped her hair tightly and began to fuck China's pretty face.

He could see the moist hint of water in her eyes as his big cock savaged even her well-subdued gag reflex. Leaning heavily over her, Spider reached down and pressed his hand between her legs, feeling that she was even wetter than he'd anticipated. When he touched her clit, her whole naked body shivered, and she lifted her ass high as if to invite him in.

As he fucked China's face, Spider lifted his hand and gave her a hard, merciless spank on her pretty butt. That made her wriggle and whimper as he plumbed her throat. Spider spanked her again and a low moan shivered through his cockhead,

Thomas S. Roche

trapped in China's breast by the cock filling her throat. He spanked her harder, making her lift her ass to beg for more as her round cheeks pinkened.

God, she looked glorious spread out on the bed like that. Her throat felt so good around his cock, bobbing up and down as she gasped for air between thrusts. But he knew time was short, and he wanted all there was to have of her.

Spider grasped China's hair firmly and pulled her face off his cock. Her eyes flashed hungrily as she held her lips, forced open by the ring gag, just an inch from his glistening head. Then he grabbed her handcuffed wrists and pulled her up on the bed, forcing her face into a pillow.

Her ass lifted to reach him, her hips pivoting to accept his cockhead between her pierced pussy lips. She groaned as he entered her, and from the first inch of her cunt Spider realized that he was still underestimating how wet this little groupie was. He drove deep into her, his cockhead striking her cervix with a firm thrust, and a tiny squeal erupted from China's forced-open mouth. He grasped her hair more firmly as he started to fuck her.

Her pussy was tighter than tight. He ground deep into her, feeling the press of her swelling G-spot as his cockhead reached the perfect depth within her. Still holding her hair with one hand, he slipped the thumb of his other hand into her pussy, moistening it as he pulled his cock out for an instant. Then he was back inside her, thrusting deep into her cunt, and another squeal escaped her mouth as he forced his pussy-slick thumb into China's asshole. He seized the little packet of lube he'd taken out of her shorts and ripped it open with his teeth. He drizzled lube between her round cheeks, sliding his thumb in and out to slick up China's asshole. Tight at first, it opened and relaxed as he matched the thrusts of his thumb to the pounding of his cock. China barely seemed to know what was happening as he pulled his thumb and cock out at the same time, position-ing his cockhead between her cheeks.

Still using China's hair, he forced her face to the side so he could look into her eyes. As he entered her ass, he saw them go wide at first, then, heard her low moan, unmistakably a sound of ecstasy, as he forced his cock slowly into the young groupie's ass. China pushed her ass up against him, meeting his thrust and begging him to enter her ass all the way.

Spider felt China's asshole enveloping his cock. He leaned hard against her body and reached under to feel her clit. It was rock hard, its metal ring standing fully at attention. Spider toyed with it as he took China's ass, each thrust bringing him closer to completion. Spider leaned down heavily and forcefully grasped her hair. He pressed his mouth against China's, loving the feel of its softness against her, the fact that her mouth was forced wide open and there was no more way she could resist the hard thrust of his tongue than she could resist the thrust of his cock up her ass. China began to moan wildly when Spider pulled his mouth off of hers. Her moans rose in volume. Spider pulled the buckle of the gag and tugged it out of her mouth, forcing her face to the side so he could kiss her, hard. As his tongue left her mouth again, Spider heard her moaning "Fuck me . . . fuck my ass . . . please . . . harder . . . fuck my ass harder . . . come in my ass . . ."

Spider obliged, pounding China mercilessly as she shoved her ass up into the air to present it for his use. Abandoning her clit, he reached under her and felt the firm, small mounds of her naked breasts, pinching her pierced nipples as he fucked her harder. Then he felt her body go rigid, heard her moans turn to wails, heard her struggle to get out the sobbing words "I'm coming" as he drove faster and faster into her tight asshole – and he felt the clutch, the rhythmic muscle spasms through China's ass that spelled the intense orgasm of a groupie who'd trained for her moment in the spotlight. The grip of China's no doubt Kegel-enhanced climax drove Spider right over the edge, and he came hard in China's ass as she pushed her body up against him, begging for his come.

When he'd finished, he rested there atop her and listened to the whimpering sounds of China's post-orgasmic bliss. He looked at the clock.

He slid out of her, off of her. He found the key chain again and unlocked China's handcuffs, then slapped her once more on the ass, playfully, lightly this time.

"I've got a date," he said.

"I know," said China enigmatically, shooting him a mischievous smile.

Spider went into the bathroom and locked the door again, but this time China didn't try to make her way in. When he came out, the scent of China's body scrubbed from his, he discovered her curled up in bed, the covers pulled over her naked body.

"I'll be back in an hour," said Spider. "I'll probably have company, so please don't be here. I'm calling housekeeping to change the sheets."

"I'll do it," said China, picking up the phone.

Spider listened to her sweet-talking the housekeeping staff as he got dressed. He wondered if the girl was a hotel groupie, too. "Call me a cab, will you?" he asked, and she did, obediently, without hesitation. Spider felt a strange sense of satisfaction about that.

When he was dressed the way he figured Sierra would expect him – stretch jeans, tight T-shirt, high boots and a leather jacket – Spider looked at China, the outline of her body still fetching despite the bulky covers.

"Gone," he said warily. "In an hour. All right?"

She nodded.

"Steal anything, and my goons will track you down and break your legs."

"I love it when you talk dirty," she said.

The cab was waiting downstairs.

Sierra was already there, sipping an Evian as he slipped into the diner booth. The place was practically empty. She looked even cuter than her picture – dark hair, full features, and thick, kissable lips. She was wearing a tight black dress that revealed the top of her bra with her legendary breasts spilling out. The bra showed black lace, and underneath it pink and silver leopard print. Spider puzzled over that.

"Sierra? It's nice to meet you," he said, shaking her hand. "Sorry I'm late."

"No problem," she said with a knowing smile. "Did you get my gift basket?"

Spider felt a momentary stab of guilt – he hadn't even bothered to check for gift baskets. He hoped Sierra wasn't the easily offended type; she didn't seem like it. Still, she seemed even less like the type to send him a bunch of tropical fruit and a bottle of cheap champagne.

"I don't think so," he said.

"You didn't? I was sure it'd be there when you finished the show. About five-two, blonde, pink-and-silver leopard-print underwear?"

"Excuse me?"

"Nice tight pussy, teacup tits, gag, and handcuffs?"

After ten years as a rock 'n' roll star, corrupting the morals of America's youth and driving the world inexorably toward Sodom, Spider just then discovered he could still blush.

"Looks like I got it after all," he said. "It was a lot better than a basket of pomegranates."

"Don't get me wrong," smiled Sierra. "She was just warming you up for me. And, for the record, I can live without the cappuccino."

"They've got decaf," said Spider.

"If I'm not mistaken, China'll have room service waiting."

Spider looked into Sierra's dark eyes for a moment, chuckled and took out a roll of dimes.

"Oh, please," said Sierra Verdi, breaking the roll open and fishing out a single dime. "No need to overpay."

The two of them left four dollars and ninety cents on the table – nice tip for an Evian. Luckily, Spider's cab was still parked outside.

My Mother's Child

Marie Lyn

I was conceived twenty-three years ago in the walk-in refrigerator of Jonathan's Family Restaurant in Dayton, Ohio. My mother was a server. My father was a customer; a wiry, eager college kid who guzzled his coffee and focused lustfully at the tanned, freckled breasts of his red-haired waitress. "He didn't *look* like a stud," my mother laughs. When she laughs again, her whole body laughs, those ample breasts still rounded and dotted with amber freckles, still welcoming.

When my mother tells this story, she describes herself as a beauty of pin-up girl proportions, a Betty Page with the rosy cheeks of a fairy princess. She's half Aphrodite, half Marilyn Monroe. She tells how he left a generous tip and how she waited for him at the kitchen door, next to the bathrooms. When he emerged from the men's room she grabbed him, shuffled him through the back entrance and into the cold, frosty depths of the walk-in refrigerator. "I thought he'd be shocked! But it was like he knew all along, you know?" Then she'll close her eyes, pause, remember. "He wanted to be sure I wanted it too, and then – Bam! Oh God," she sighs. "Just bam! Bam bam bam." She laughs at her words.

He was more than eager, she says, kissing her like a husband just returned from war, like he'd just come from the dessert and her mouth contained his first drink of water. The timid kid turned into a firecracker, hands all over her, fumbling the zipper of her skirt, pushing it down. She helped him, pulling down her nylons as he kissed her neck. When she was naked enough he shoved her ass against shelves of ground beef, her head by the boxes of lemons and limes. The smell of citrus, she tells me, still brings her back.

In the story, my father is the possessor of a tremendous uncut cock which he thrusts into her, pulsing in and out of her deep, wet, throbbing hole. They fuck for "some time" (that's how she tells the story – as if the exact time of the fucking is the one part of the tale that's too much for my tender ears – and this is one of many things I don't understand about my mother). Then he pulls out, falls to his knees and sticks his tongue into the bush of curly red hair that surrounds her clit. After he brings her to orgasm, she turns and lets him pummel her from behind. Her head is almost entirely submerged in a pile of lemons when he comes.

That was the beginning of me. My mother was fired and she never saw my father again.

Does this surprise you? That a daughter should know so much about her mother's sex life, that a daughter should be privy to the intimate details of her mother's fuck? My mother doesn't keep secrets. I didn't realize until high school that no one else's mother talked about "getting wet" or "zipless fucks". No one else's mother decorated the living room with Mel Ramos nudes (I still dream about pale women making love to ketchup bottles, to gigantic cigars). So it was only natural that I'd grow up feeling different from the other girls in my class. Instead, I was close to the oversexed boys who knew about the same things I did, boys educated via porn and older brothers. I did my best to further their education with invitations to feel my new breasts or with open-season kissing practice.

And it's only natural that, when I grew up into the red-haired vixen my mother had once been, I'd end up in a similar place. I have my mother's hair, her breasts and her complexion, but my father's skinny limbs. I radiate sex. My mother passed sex on to me like other mothers pass on manners. So why wouldn't I repeat the sins of my mother?

I'm twenty-three, fresh out of college, where I've fucked my way through the core curriculum and written a glorious thesis on Dorothy Parker. I'm living outside of Chicago. I'm engaged to Carter, a wonderful, forgiving man, a law student at Northwestern who wakes me up before his 7 a.m. torts lectures for lazy, delicious morning sex. I wake up five hours later tingling and wet. He makes me feel all kinds of new things, like the desire to be faithful.

I work at Goldie's Steakhouse, an easy job that got me through college. I cling to this job like some girls cling to families, boyfriends: the one part of my life that stays the same. I'm waiting for a journalism job to fall into my lap.

I step out to the back dock of Goldie's, carrying a mug of merlot and my cell phone. My mother's on the phone, delivering a diatribe on menopause, interrupting herself periodically to exclaim, "Oh! Hot Flash!" like a DJ announcing a new dance.

"Where are you?" she asks suddenly.

"Umm – at work?"

"At work? Jesus – you have tables, honey? Don't talk to me if you have tables."

"No, I'm done for the night, I just have my sidework." I sit down and extend my legs. With my right hand I roll my nylons off, revealing the sun-desperate legs underneath. I've shaved my legs this morning. I'd been waiting for Carter to complain about the hair, but he hadn't, and before long I couldn't take it anymore. I lathered up, slid the razor up and down each leg and delicately around my pussy. I love feeling smooth. I'm constantly amazed by my body, by how smooth my skin is. The night manager has gone home, and I'm free to be bare-legged, and I like the way the night cold feels against my naked limbs.

"Are you smoking?"

"What? Why? I haven't smoked since high school. Are *you* smoking?"

"You've had a lot of stress lately," my mother says. "I don't want you to hurt the baby."

"Mom, I'm fine," I take a long drink of wine. "And I'm not fucking pregnant! Lay off already."

"You could be."

"Mom, I have a fifteen-minute break. Anything else you'd like to talk about?"

"I want a grandchild," she says softly.

"I must have the wrong number. What happened to the 'don't settle down' lecture? The 'men are only good for one thing'? The 'if he can't make you come, get rid of the bastard'? She sighs, mourning herself. "I guess it's menopause."

I wiggle my toes, watching the light from our outdoor lamp that bounces like stars against my cotton-candy-pink toenails. And then something moves in the parking lot.

A man. A single man. A rarity at this corny family place, he emerges from a white Lexus. He steps out like a politician on a small-town tour, taking a quick look in his mirror, touching up his hair with a wet thumb, preparing to encounter the citizens.

"My God, Mom, my prince has arrived."

"Huh?" I imagine her at the kitchen table, fanning herself with a page of the Trib. "Carter's there?"

"No! When have I ever called Carter a prince? Whatever – I'm kidding – Look, I gotta go fill the barbecue sauce bottles."

"Okay, okay," my Mom sighs. "Take a pregnancy test."

"Mother! I'll be fine. Don't start planning a baby shower, okay? I'm not even married!"

Silence on the other end of the line. I'm holding my breath, realizing what I've said. "I love you," she says, finally.

"I love you, too."

My eyes follow the prince as he walks, moving in and out of the slivers of light cast across the parking lot. It's like a cartoon: with each flicker of illumination he looks more like a superhero, approaching me in a series of comic book panels, growing more handsome, and larger, with each new image.

The dregs of my wine sting like pine needles in my throat. I almost float, free of gravity and logic, back inside the restaurant. I float like that to the guy's table, where he's just settling in. On closer inspection he's kind-looking, gentle and blue-eyed. His jaw is broad; his nose almost hooks, but in a good way. I avoid the looks of the other servers – they know Carter – and set up my napkin-folding station next to him. I stretch my legs under the table, resting my feet on the chair next to him. I leave my shoes on the floor.

He looks up as if I was his dinner companion. "So," he smiles, "what's good here?" His voice is soft, like a boy whispering in class. He stares intently at me afterwards. I like it; it makes him hard to figure out. He's removed his jacket and rolled up the sleeves of his white shirt, loosened the collar, draped his tie over his chair.

"Get a burger."

"I don't eat red meat." He's offhand, as if the information's inconsequential.

"Well, you've come to the wrong place." I laugh, folding a checkered napkin into a neat pattern.

He lets his eyes meet mine, then chuckles and looks back down at the menu. "You must have something."

The night closing waitress arrives, interrupting our triumphant love scene. She goes through the menu with pointy red fingernails, discussing each dish with gusto, as if this was a real restaurant worth talking about.

"So, you work here?" he says when she's gone.

"No, I just think this shirt looks good on me. And I enjoy folding napkins. It's kind of a hobby." *So is fucking cute strangers.*

He shakes his head, as if he's saying, *You're gonna make me work for this, aren't you?*

I slide over in the booth so I'm sitting across from him. I don't give a fuck, really, about getting fired, because I've worked at this place for so long I practically have tenure, and besides, I'm doing my best to provide one-hundred-per-cent guest satisfaction.

He looks like a soccer coach, or a grown-up frat boy who still writes checks to his alma mater's philanthropic fund knowing every cent of his charitable tax-write-off will most likely pay for kegs. Does this make it easier – his goodness? Does it make me feel, as my cunt ripens and swells, like I'm not a cheater? Maybe. It feels like it's past time to remove my damp panties, but I can't do it alone.

Under the table, I stick my foot between his legs. He just raises his eyebrows, smiles that charming smile again, and leans back. I move my toes up and around the bulge in his pants, tracing his cock.

His salad arrives, and I set my foot down.

"I'll be right back." I slide out of the booth, my panties wet and warm. I feel like my juices are purging fidelity, all the life I've been trying so hard to want.

I do my sidework. Then I walk over as he's paying his bill.

"How was everything?" I ask.

He just signs his credit-card slip and stands up. He motions for me to follow him, and so I do, out to the parking lot, and I run towards his car to see if he'll try to catch me.

He comes after me. I am leaning against the car, still panting. He takes my hipbone in broad hands and lifts me onto the hood of his car. The car is wet from a sprinkle of rain, but I don't care. I can't imagine any rainstorm wetter than my pussy. My pussy: it opens up like a fire-eater's throat preparing for the plunge of the torch and the sweet, salient ecstasy of penetration.

"I saw you," he whispers. His hands glide through my hair, his eager lips plant kisses up and down my neck, biting and sucking and licking.

"Where?"

He bites my earlobe, and I gasp. He traces the rim of my ear with his tongue before answering, his breath so hot that his words feel like sex. "Outside, taking off your tights. I saw you. You were sitting under the light."

"I thought you were hungry."

"I was," he says, and he demonstrates by biting my neck. I scoot forward to feel the pulse of his cock against my panties.

"But I was lost." He reaches up under my shirt, fingertips grazing my stomach, and lifts my shirt over my head.

"I needed directions." He slides his hand between bra and breast, rubbing one nipple and then the other. They're as erect as earring studs and I want so badly for him to suck them.

"But then I got hungry." He unsnaps my bra and it falls to the dingy pavement, and I don't care. I love the feel of my bare buds against his chest. I love knowing that I'm almost naked and he's altogether clothed, because it makes me feel vulnerable, ethereal, lusty and alive.

I feel taken, and even with my feminist morals I love to fantasize about being dominated. I'm a waitress hungry for tips, outside on the hood of a car, pussy dripping like the gently falling rain. Her seducer, in a dry-clean-only suit, drives his pelvis into her like he's trying to push through his pants and all the way through her body.

I unbutton his shirt, and he throws his head up to the sky like he's eating rain. His body bursts from his shirt: Clark Kent turning into Superman. We're beautiful. We're a pornographic Hallmark card. We're two kids necking in the high-school parking lot.

He looks at me for a few silent seconds with his unbelievably tender eyes – the eyes of a boy, not a lusty, swashbuckling lover. I think of how he *is* that kind of lover. Our bare chests smack together. He kisses me. I'm waking up from a coma of fidelity, Sleeping Beauty resurrected by impassioned lips.

I clasp my thighs around his legs, pulling my knees towards each other and drawing his package up to my stormy cunt. It's raining harder, and my hair is sticking to my neck.

He wraps his mouth around my right nipple, its erect tip.

"Bite it," I whisper, and he looks up half-smiling like I've just confessed all my sins, all my secret desires. *So you're like that, are you?*

And then he bites down so hard I scream. The pain is followed by a deep rush of pleasure, a tingling down my spine to my pussy.

I take him by the shoulders and pull him up, and he looks at me like a teenage boy about to take my virginity – *Are you sure I'm the one? Are you ready?*

I smile coyly and pull his head towards mine. As we kiss I undo his belt and let his pants drop to his knees.

I reach inside his shorts, where his cock is hardening and shifting, and he laughs quietly as I stroke his balls with my nails. They're smooth and bare, his balls, just like my cunt – and thinking of my baby-bare pussy makes me crave his dick even more.

I push down his boxers, which fall in a ring around his feet. We must look ridiculous, I think, but then I stop thinking altogether, stroking the underside of his shaft, grabbing hold of it with both hands . . . and I notice that it takes both hands to hold his cock, and I'm already imagining how it will feel slipping between the walls of my cunt, filling me, all of me.

His legs slide between mine. He starts playing the skin of my thighs like a piano. I pull at his cock like tugging on a rope. It's uncut and generous; he rubs its head up and down and across my clit and I gasp every time, thinking he's about to enter me. He's biting his lip, looking up at me like a kid, and I can't help but pull him towards me and kiss him in a fit of tenderness – which is when he plunges himself inside me.

The first thing I think is, *This isn't Carter's penis.* It presses against the muscles of my cunt, which seem to have forgotten everything but the shape of Carter, and now they retract as this foreign cock intrudes, staking its claim.

I feel like he could fuck right through me. He grabs my ass with his hands and pounds. He clenches his face, his arms bulge, he squeezes me, tighter and tighter, and I feel like he hasn't done this in a long time. My stagnant fidelity and his. I want to know if he's thinking of someone else – a wife, a girlfriend – but I don't want to ask, so I just surrender to the pulsing. A thousand nerves up and down my insides fire like a pinball game where every shot wins.

I want to feel his tongue lap against my clit. I want to come all over his mouth. So I set my hands on his hips and grind his thrusting to a halt, wind him down like a toy out of batteries, and he looks concerned.

"Let's get in the car," I tell him. "I want you to eat me out." I say it sweetly, demurely, like a girl asking him for a walk to school.

He shuffles to retrieve his keys and opens the trunk door. I crawl in and start to pull off my skirt. He reaches over my body to lower the back seat so I can lie out flat, ready and waiting.

"I'm gonna come inside you," he says, "and then I'm gonna go down on you when you're wet with my come." He hesitates, needing my approval. So I give it to him: I flip onto my stomach so he can take me from behind.

He fucks me. He fucks me like I need to be fucked. He fucks me like I deserve it. And then his body jerks. It vibrates. He wraps his arms around me tight with his orgasm.

He pulls out with his juice still dripping down my legs and gives me the most amazing eating out I've ever had. He plants kisses up and down the insides of my thighs, up to my pussy and back down the other leg until I'm mad with desire. His tongue flicks my clit and then he puts his mouth tight over my cunt and slaps his tongue back and forth until I scream and climax.

He pulls back and wipes his mouth with his hand, and I giggle. He shrugs in unwarranted apology. Rain spatters against the roof and along the windows. I feel like we've just made love in a car wash.

We lie naked, his cheek against my breast, which makes him seem so much younger than he did at first.

All at once, I realize this: I'll never make love to a stranger again. I'll never feel anyone's manhood inside me except Carter's, from now on.

I'll get a "real job", I'll grow up, I'll build a house and a life with a man who tosses and turns in his sleep and always seems to be riding the fantastical in his dreams. Carter is hopeful; he makes love earnestly. He wants to find a million new ways to pleasure me. He wants to understand, claim, and seduce every nerve on my skin. He wants to fill me and spill me over like popping the cork of champagne.

I don't feel guilty. I feel like my mother for one last moment.

She never wanted to settle down. For her, the world was a sea of cock primed for fucking, a thousand ways to fill the same hole. I had felt that same need and this man beside me in the back of a car had filled it. My last zipless fuck. Devotion washes over me, an emotional orgasm; all my aimless desire seems to focus, to narrow onto Carter. I close my eyes and fill myself with him.

"I should go home," I say to this sweet man, supplicant across my naked body.

"I should go, too," he says.

We slide off one another and pick up our clothes, silent. My body is tingly. We share a laugh as he opens the back hatch of the car and we climb out, and standing in the rain, he holds me for a moment. I hold him more. Tighter. I smell him. I kiss him, and smile at his adorable face, his potential. For a moment I'm jealous of the woman who has this man as her Carter.

"Thank you," I say.

"Don't mention it," he replies. And then he grins shyly. "Thank you."

I almost stumble to my car, and I drive home feeling woozy. Carter is asleep in our warm bed, dreaming, and I join him there.

One week later, the doctor tells me that I'm pregnant. She tells me that I've been pregnant for a month, and I'm relieved; it's Carter's baby. But it still excites me to think that that new almost-person was already there when that man was inside me.

Time passes.

Sometimes I rewind my life so that all my sexual encounters blur together in one long movie in my head, grainy and flickering, sloppily edited; a quick scene in the dark, and another, and another. Whose arm, whose leg? My lips tracing the line of whose jaw, searching for a mouth to kiss. The squeak of a bedframe, the quiet of a mattress on the floor, the blare of the horn when my back bumps somebody's steering wheel. A rainbow of panties, all beautiful, some lost in someone else's room, someone's car, in the recesses of somebody's couch. A slow-motion gang bang, spliced and reassembled for my pleasure.

And now I have a daughter. She's beautiful and precocious, just like me.

She asks me questions and I reveal everything to her, slowly and carefully. At night, the three of us watch the news together. She crawls onto Carter and he holds her near like a lover, and she fits there, just right.

In fact, it all fits, just right.

Girl on a Swing

J.Z. Sharpe

Inspired by
"The Swing" (1766)
Jean-Honoré Fragonard (French, 1732–1806)

I can see the painting from my place in the cloakroom. It's so lovely. When I'm alone, I can't stop staring at it. I want to find its secret. I'm quite sure there is a message in there for me, hidden in the branches intertwined at the top of the canvas, or perhaps in the fluttering skirts of the woman on the swing, the painting's focal point.

I don't dare go any closer. If Madam Cleo finds me anyplace but where I belong, there will be consequences. She threatens to take me to her office, slam the door behind her, and throw me over her knee. With my panties around my ankles, I'll be spanked until my bottom smarts. Just thinking about it makes me squirm.

So why do I smile as well?

"Madeleine?"

I snap back to reality. Mr Bach is here, one of our regulars. I take his coat from him and hang it with the others, brushing its cashmere softness against my face as I put it on the rack. It carries his scent, a woodsy aroma with a hint of leather, like none I've ever known. Sometimes I spend the entire evening pressed against it, wishing that I belonged to this man, a treasured possession just like this coat. I hand him a brass tag with a number on it, although he won't really need it when he comes to claim the coat again. Believe me, I will know which one to give him.

He takes the tag from me and slips it into his pocket. His dark eyes twinkle. "Thank you, Madeleine. How are you this evening?"

"I'm well, thank you, sir." I'm always careful to address every guest as "sir" or "ma'am". Failure to do that would also be cause for one of Cleo's spankings, or so I'm told.

"You look lost in thought."

"Just daydreaming, sir."

He laughs. "Well, I hope they are pretty dreams, my dear." Then he turns and goes down the hall toward the red door, where the secrets of the house wait for him.

I don't know much about those secrets, myself. I've only worked here for three weeks. When I came to New York to go to graduate school, I knew I would need a job, but what could I do? I tried waiting on tables like my roommates, but after dropping three trays in one night and creating massive amounts of broken glassware, I knew it wasn't for me. I can't type very well; cash registers bore me. What was left? Would I be forced to stand on the sidewalk in the rain, handing out flyers to people who would only throw them away?

Then I stumbled across an advertisement for a "discreet attendant" in a private club, and now here I am, taking coats and being polite to people who travel in circles quite different from mine. Madam Cleo hired me on the spot, thank heaven. "You can keep a secret, can't you?" she said that first night, after she dressed me in my uniform, a stiff black dress, black stockings, and heels so high, I felt ready to topple over without warning. She answered her own question as she pinned my hair atop my head. "Of course you can. And you will."

But the secrets, behind that red door . . . the cries, the shouts, sometimes the sound of a cracking whip. I have seen Madam's cabinets where she hangs the "toys", although she won't let me look for very long. All I get is a glimpse, and the rest is up to my imagination.

My eyes wander to the painting again. The girl on the swing

wears a pink dress with skirts that billow around her; that particular shade, I must confess, reminds me how much I hate that color. It's the color of weakness, of mushy overchewed bubble gum, of pretty girls who are just so damn perfect. She doesn't look happy to be in that dress; indeed, on that swing she looks a little out of her element. A man on the ground below points with glee; he looks at her legs and those private places revealed by the swing's movement. Then back she'll go, toward the man in the shadows behind her.

I squint, trying to see that second man. He is half-hidden by darkness, holding ropes that control the girl's motion. He looks older, wiser, more diabolical. Why does he look slightly familiar? The answer comes to me immediately, and I shudder and close my eyes. He reminds me of Mr Bach.

The door from the street opens again and a group comes in, one member accompanied by several guests, probably from out of town. I take their coats and smile, but am relieved when they disappear behind the door, greeted by Madam Cleo herself. My eyes meet hers; "Behave!" they seem to say. I look away as the door closes quietly.

And so the evening goes, here at Madam Cleo's house . . .

I have only had one boyfriend. Yes, at my age, I should have more of a track record – after all, I'm already in graduate school! Schoolwork kept me busy, and I went to college close to home in Massachusetts, where my parents could keep an eye on me. When I met Peter, they reluctantly let me go out with him, and only because he was the son of one of my father's best business associates. I guess they figured he was safe.

Little did they know! "I like your ass," Peter would say, running his hand down my backside in admiration. "I'd like to see it naked." So we hid in his father's toolshed, where he ordered me to grab one of the low rafters and with my feet barely touching the floor, my jeans and panties would be yanked to my knees. Now he could admire me by the glow of a kerosene lamp. "Oh, yes," I heard him whisper. "Madeleine, please let me mark you."

"Mark me?" I swallowed. What did he want?

"Yes, with my belt."

I shook my head. What a sick thing to ask! I let go of the rafter and landed on the floor with a thud. "No!" I shouted. "Are you out of your mind? Let me out of here!"

We broke up the next day.

Yet I couldn't stop thinking about Peter. I shouldn't have broken up with him, he was the only boyfriend I'd probably ever have. My girlfriends had a steady stream of guys, one right after the other. Was I destined to attend parties alone for the rest of my life? Worst of all, the scene in the toolshed played over and over in my fantasies. What if I'd allowed Peter to do what he wanted? Would it really have been so bad? How was being "marked" any different from wearing a guy's ring or some other symbol of endearment?

One night, out of curiosity, I went to my closet and took out a belt, not as wide and harsh as the one Peter wore that night, but the nearest I could come to it. Naked, I knelt on my bed and gritting my teeth, I began to thrash at my backside. Yes, it hurt, I won't deny it! But it was not like any other pain I'd ever known, not like menstrual cramps or getting a tooth pulled. It had a certain – what's the word I want? – deliciousness to it. I stopped after ten good swats.

Later, sitting in front of the TV with my parents, I could still feel it. I should have let him, I told myself. If I had, we'd still be together.

Even to this day, I relive those moments in the shed, re-arranging them to suit myself. Sometimes Peter uses a small paddle, sometimes he ties my hands to the rafter so I don't have to hold on so hard. Sometimes it's not Peter at all, but someone else – more often than not, it's Mr Bach. He strips me naked and when he finishes, he holds me in his arms, where I cry with relief and love into the fine fabric of his coat.

I have to get a better look at that painting. I just have to.

The tiny clock on the cloakroom shelf, next to the jar where I keep my tips, reads 10:15. The lull usually begins right about now. This is when I bring out my schoolwork, knowing that I'll probably have a good hour or two before anyone wants to retrieve a coat. A new arrival at this hour would be rare. I take out my literature notes, but somehow, I can't seem to get interested. My handwriting swirls before my eyes and makes no sense to me. With a sigh, I close my book and rub them with the back of my hand.

The painting beckons. So many details, so many secrets. One peek, close up, couldn't hurt. I'll be right here; if someone comes looking for me, I'll see them first.

With my ears attuned to any approaching voices or footsteps, I walk down the hall to where the painting hangs. I take a place before it with my hands behind my back, raise my eyes to its top, then let them scan, falling like a leaf toward the bottom. So much to absorb on the way! Such fine detail in the leaves, the trunk of the trees. The stone cherubs have as much expression on their faces as the humans. The woman flies through the air, bright, brave, one shoe lost, hurtling toward the ground. The suitor before her smiles, eager to touch. But he never gets a chance, because the man in the shadows pulls her back. Her hidden lover never allows her to fly too high.

Fingers surround my wrists, holding them together at the base of my spine. "So, do you like the painting?" a voice whispers in my ear. "I sold it to your boss, you know."

No need to turn around. No need to look. I recognize his scent.

"I'll tell you a secret," Mr Bach says. "It's a forgery." I gasp. "But don't tell Cleo. She thinks it's the real thing."

I try to wriggle free. "I – I think I better get back to work."

He has other ideas. "Study the woman for a moment, my dear Madeleine. Look at her face. She's not smiling, is she? In fact, she looks a little scared, a little hesitant. Do you think she desires the man at her feet? Or is it the man in the shadows who's her true love?"

"Please, Mr Bach, I need to get back to the cloakroom."

"Oh, I'm sure Cleo won't mind if you take a little time for an art appreciation lesson."

"No, she won't like it. She won't like it at all. I'm not supposed to leave my post."

He laughs. " 'I'm not supposed to leave my post!' " he says, imitating me. "Such a good girl you are, Madeleine! So obedient! Such a prize! Come with me, my dear. Let's go back to the cloakroom."

Not letting go of my hands, he returns me to the tiny room where his coat hangs with all the others, a black shadow hidden among the rest. I open the half-door and slip inside but, when I try to close it, I discover Mr Bach has followed me. He closes the door and latches it, then does the same for the upper portion, effectively closing us off from the rest of the world.

I shake my head. "No, please, Mr Bach! What if Madam Cleo comes out and finds me in here with you? She'll punish me!"

"Has she ever punished you before?" His dark eyes meet mine in the dim light of the tiny room as he brushes a bit of hair away from my face.

"No, not yet."

"Then how do you know what she would do?"

"She's told me. She's described it for me."

"Tell me more," he says, drawing me closer and placing a gentle kiss on my forehead. "What would she do if you disobeyed her?"

"She – she would take me to her office. I've only been in there a couple times, to get my paycheck, and she never lets me stay very long. She has all those cabinets? The tall black ones where she keeps what look like – like whips?"

He nods. "Yes, my dear, those are whips. Among other things." Then he kisses me again, on the cheek this time. "What else did she say she would do?"

"Well, she said she would pull down my panties and take me over her knee, and give me the spanking of my life, hard enough that I won't be able to sit. Hard enough for me to remember for a long, long time. That's what she says."

"Does this frighten you, my dear?" I start to nod, then I switch directions and shake my head no, an action which makes him laugh out loud. "Ah, your indecisiveness is so charming! Tell me – have you ever been spanked before?"

"Of course, when I was a girl."

"But as an adult?" His smile warms my face. "You know, it's different when you're all grown up. Quite different indeed." He nods toward the folding chair where I am allowed to sit briefly during the slower periods. "Would you like me to show you?"

Without waiting for my answer, Mr Bach takes a seat and beckons to me. I approach with caution, still holding my hands behind my back. He looks up at me; even in the scant light, I can tell that I have become an object of great fascination. For a moment, we just stare at each other. Then he puts one arm around my waist and in one swift movement, pulls me across his knees. I yelp.

"Shh!" he cries. "I can see you're going to need to be silenced." Cool air brushes my derrière as he pulls off my panties and twists them into a compact little ball which is then crammed into my mouth. "Now, on to the business at hand."

I hold my breath. The first blow is coming, I just have no idea when. He surprises me with a caress instead, down one cheek and up the other, his palm tracing large circles around the contours of my flesh. I sigh – how good it feels! No one has ever touched me like this. I want more, but all too soon, he lifts his hand away.

And then – smack! I startle, but his arm holds me fast against his knee. Again – smack! Smack! Three more times he lets loose, stinging first the left side, then the right. "Equal treatment!" he says. "We wouldn't want one pretty globe to be jealous of the other, now would we?" Back and forth he goes, until the pain begins to melt into a curious warmth. I feel moisture gathering in that secret place between my thighs. Once again, I want more, I need more. I squirm against his gabardine slacks, unable to help myself, the mix of pain and pleasure is that delicious.

The loud thump of a fist against the closed door demands my immediate attention. "Madeleine! What are you doing? Come out here immediately! You have people here who want their coats!"

But Mr Bach chuckles, and gives me two more slaps in quick succession, right-left. "Madeleine is a little preoccupied, Cleo. Tell them to come back tomorrow for their damn coats."

"Maximilian Bach!" The door flies open and Madam Cleo is standing outside, four feet and ten inches of rage. "What are you doing?"

"Come on, darling Cleo. Surely you don't expect to leave a tasty creature like this one out here in the cloakroom, do you? She surpasses anything else you have to offer."

"Don't touch her!" Madam Cleo grabs my arm with unexpected force and yanks me to my feet, grabbing the panties from my mouth and throwing them in Mr Bach's face. "I have a house full of fine merchandise, and this is the thanks I get!"

"Fine merchandise? Maybe at one time, Cleo, but not lately. I have been sorely disappointed for quite some time now. In fact, I was thinking about going elsewhere – until you placed this tempting creature in your cloakroom. This one has spark, passion, she's ready to learn and to be properly trained. A refreshing change from the jaded sluts you've been pushing on me."

"How dare you!" The tiny room echoes with the sound of Cleo's slap across his face.

Time seems to come to a halt, as it often does in moments like this. My stomach quivers and I suddenly realize that I have forgotten to breathe. Mr Bach rises to his feet, taking his time, coming up slowly until he towers over Madam Cleo. Without taking his eyes from hers, he speaks to me. "Madeleine, get my coat."

I do as I am told, drawing in his scent one last time, so I will never forget it.

"Now, get your own," he says. "That is, if you would like to come with me."

"If you do, you're fired," Madam Cleo growls through her teeth.

So, it is up to me.

I pause. My coat hangs at the end of the rack, a threadbare trench coat I've had since high school. I'd been saving for a better one, a faux fur that I'd seen in a second-hand shop on the way home. If I go, that coat is nothing but a broken dream.

Or is it? I look at Mr. Bach, and he smiles. "Get your coat, Madeleine. You will not regret it." He touches my cheek. "I know what you need."

I melt inside. I can't put on that coat fast enough.

As Madam Cleo hustles us past a cluster of customers who are no doubt baffled by all this brouhaha and just want their own damn coats, I take one last look at the painting. A forgery, if Mr Bach is to be believed, with the real one hanging in a museum somewhere – but does it matter? The man in the shadows looks back at me, holding the ropes that control the swing. Go, he seems to say. And remember – the girl in pink, she could not fly without me.

I take Mr. Bach's hand and we walk into the cold, cold night. The ropes pull me back, deep into the shadows. I know I will be happy there.

Not at Risk

Joshua Hoobler

I've got six hours of VHS tape with women getting their asses fucked. I've pieced together all the anal scenes from forty or so different pornographic films. At four bucks a rental that's one hundred sixty dollars, or one percent of my annual net income. But that's an underestimate, as I've had to rent more than forty videos since many don't contain gaping scenes. See, it's not sufficient that the woman's ass be vigorously penetrated, no, the penis or vibrator or dildo (no cucumbers – I can't stand the mixing of food and sex) must be fully withdrawn while someone (the woman herself, the third or fourth or fifth partner in the scene) spreads her ass cheeks apart as wide as possible – hopefully the penetrating object is plunged back in and withdrawn again repeatedly – this allows the anus (or is it the sphincter at this point?) to remain dilated or, in common pornographic parlance, to gape. It depends on the scene and the angle and the lighting, but ideally it should appear like a small cavern with a red mouth between two fleshy mounds.

On Sunday mornings I wake up early, have my regular bowel movement, wipe thoroughly, take the enema bag out from the bathroom cabinet, fill it with warm water, hang it on the towel rack, grab the Astroglide, slip on some latex gloves, lube up my asshole and commence upon a series of two quart enemas. From what I've read, the industry standard is two enemas prior to an anal scene, the first to clear away the big stuff and the second to clear away the soupy remnants. It takes me at least three and sometimes up to five to get to where the toilet water is as clear when I'm done as it was when I sat down. I don't know if I'm particularly foul or maybe it's just that many women in the porn industry are anorexic and/or speed freaks and subsequently don't have as much to clear away.

After the final enema I take a long bath. It takes my ass a couple of hours to recover from all that water rushing out. The filling up is actually the easy part – once one becomes accustomed to it – in fact, after five enemas I'm sometimes so chapped I have to kiss-off the rest of my routine. Typically, I do household chores at this time.

When my ass feels ready I tack sheets up over the Venetian blinds, strip, switch on the afore-mentioned video tape, grab the blue duffle bag from the closet and set it on the bed. In the duffle bag is: another bottle of Astroglide; another box of latex gloves (at this stage they're not for the sake of cleanliness, as by now I'm quite clean, but to avoid any rough edges on my fingernails); two smooth vibrators, the first is small and silver, maybe seven inches long but narrow, I use it to get comfortable having something in my ass after thoroughly lubing myself up with the latex gloves and more Astroglide, the second is a larger gold vibrator that I use to really break myself in; lastly there's a large black strap-on dildo with a harness.

I fasten the strap-on to a long piece of rope tied around the edge of the bed. I set a folding mirror on the bed above the dildo, place a towel on the floor underneath it, get on all fours, back myself up onto the dildo and rock back and forth, pulling it out and pushing it back in spreading my ass cheeks with my hands. My face is half against the floor but I can look back over my shoulder and stare up at the reflection of my gaping asshole.

Michelle would spank me before shoving the gold vibrator up my ass. She'd coo in my ear while pulling my hair, "What a dirty little boy." When I was ready to come she'd cup her hand over the end of my dick and catch my come and smear it on my face or make me lick it up, whichever I wanted. I was the bottom, but I was in charge. Afterwards she'd hold me while I cried into her neck and asked if she thought I was sick or not a real man. She'd say she didn't think I was sick and that only a real man could expose himself like that – until she couldn't take it any more: instead of giving those soothing answers she finally started crying, started saying she couldn't do it any more, saying she felt like an accessory: unnecessary to my pleasure.

Rocking against the bed. *I'm sorry.* Lube trickling out of my ass and down the back of my balls. *No, I'm sorry.* It hurts. I want it to hurt. To put me so in the moment that I cease to be, become egoless, until I'm nothing but the rush, no more conscious than the big black dildo eight inches up my ass. *I just wanted to make you happy.* Mouth dry and sticky. *I thought you liked it.* The scene on the video cuts to two women, I'm too fixated on the reflection in the folding mirror to look at the television. *How could I like it? What does it do for me?* But I know the scene: the dark-haired woman is on a gynecological table, her feet in the stirrups while the blonde, dressed as a nurse, pushes and pulls on a butt plug in the patient's ass. The butt plug is connected to one of those bulbs used on blood pressure gauges, this allows the size of the butt plug to be expanded after having been securely inserted in the anal cavity. *I'm sorry.* The look on the dark haired woman's face is extreme: her eyes wide, she alternates between wailing and sputtering obscenities through clenched teeth. *It's only when we're done, and I'm holding you, telling you it's OK.* The blonde is working hard, sweating even, the nipples on her large fake breasts point straight ahead without so much as a jiggle. *It's not OK, is it?* And I'm thinking how lucky they are, how desired, how literally thousands of men have jerked off staring at them, wanting them, hating them. *What am I supposed to say?* And I want to know do they hate themselves as much as I hate myself? *You don't even need me to be here.* Do they look at themselves and feel shame or is it just another day on the set, giving the public what they want, providing a community service. *I'm so sorry. God, I'm so sorry. I do need you.* An article of trade is more than I want to be. *I can't do this any more. I've got to get out of here, I'm sorry.* I want nothing, blankness, emptiness. *No. please.*

★   ★   ★

If I want to come I have to take one of my hands off my ass and start jerking off. I grind up against the bed as hard as I can, pushing the dildo as deep as it will go, then start making short violent thrusts. My prostate is positively bruised. It only takes a minute. My back and shoulders go cold, my vision blurs and my heart skips or jumps or seizes or does whatever the fuck it does. My ass clenches around the dildo and a spasm shoots semen onto a towel.

I stay right there for a few moments. Slowly pull myself off the dildo, sometimes some air escapes, not with the bubbling sound of gas but more like its being let out of a tire. I ease myself down on the towel and feel the come stick to my belly. My legs are shaky and my ass is sore. It will be a few minutes before I can stand. I rest my forehead and the bridge of my nose on the carpet. With my eyes closed I let out a self-pitying sigh.

A Stout Length of Birch

Lisette Ashton

"I know lots of ghost stories, I could keep you awake until dawn recounting some of the bizarre tales I've heard. But if we're all ready for bed, I'll just tell you this one. Mind you, it's rather a special story because it happened here, in this house. And it's not actually a ghost story. The word 'story' implies that it's a made-up tale or that it didn't really happen. But this one most certainly did happen – and there's proof."

Serena shivered nervously. She glanced at Charlotte and saw her sister was studying Parnell with the same dreamy smile that she had worn throughout their meal.

"I already feel spooked," Charlotte whispered.

Parnell smiled, adjusted his spectacles with a gesture that looked embarrassed, then cleared his throat. "It's difficult to tie the story down to an exact time period but since this house was built around the 1840s, and the incident happened shortly after that, it's safe to say it was the early Victorian era. The grounds stretched for miles around, and the owner was making fortunes from his thriving investments in the railways. He had a beautiful wife, two lovely daughters and a host of staff that included a gamekeeper for his pheasant."

"Barbaric," Serena whispered.

Seeming uncomfortable beneath her criticism, Parnell shrugged apologetically. "It was the two daughters who caused the problem. They'd both spent some years away from the house, enjoying an education in one of the few private schools that catered for the fairer sex. When they came back to the house they grew a little bored. The eldest daughter had seen the gamekeeper thrashing the bushes, trying to startle the pheasant with a stout length of birch. She watched him do that for three months before she came to a decision. She wanted him to try thrashing her."

"Parnell," their host growled. "Is this another of your bloody spanky stories?"

"It's all true," Parnell protested. "I got most of these details from one of the daughter's diaries. I was asked to research the legend for the local historical society."

Serena could see something flash between their host and Parnell but she couldn't work out what it was. The meal had been sumptuous and entertaining and had proved the ideal end to their weekend break but she didn't want it to end with an argument. Her expectations were building to something far greater than that. Sensing their host might be trying to shield her and her sister from an unseemly tale, she said, "I don't mind if it's a ghost story or a spanky story. I just want to hear it then get off to bed."

Her words were the encouragement Parnell needed. He cast a final glance at their host, then continued. "It was all in her diaries afterwards but by the time anyone else read those it was too late for the gamekeeper. The eldest daughter had something of a penchant for discipline, although no one knows what started her on the habit. Her earlier diaries are filled with graphic entries about some mystery man using a tawse on her. It's impossible to say if this is the recounting of genuine incidents, or simply detailing gratuitous fantasies. Whichever it is, it seems that she had an avaricious appetite for chastisement."

"Parnell!" their host warned.

Serena frowned at him. Parnell's story had touched a nerve and she wanted to hear more. No, she thought quickly, that wasn't quite right. She didn't want to hear more – she *needed* to hear more. "Please," she broke in. "Please let him finish."

Grudgingly, their host nodded assent.

Parnell went on. "The younger daughter wasn't as enthusiastic but she was known to go along with whatever her sister suggested. The pair of them went to the gamekeeper and asked him to thrash them with his stout length of birch."

"I can't believe that," Charlotte interrupted. "Even nowadays, no one would dare to do that, would they?"

Parnell grinned at her and Serena noticed his smile was always that tiniest bit broader when he spoke to Charlotte. She catalogued this observation, sure that she would be able to use it to her advantage later on.

"We all have a mindset about the propriety of the Victorian age," Parnell explained. "But we have to remember that the Victorians were only people, pretty similar to ourselves. They had appetites and desires much like those we have today and, whilst it would have been difficult for a young Victorian woman to state her needs so directly, it wouldn't have been beyond her. As the gamekeeper was in her father's employ, she would have probably seen it as little more than another instruction for one of the staff."

Serena decided it was a plausible theory. She could see that Charlotte was coming to the same conclusion, although it was difficult to read all her sister's thoughts whilst she gazed at Parnell. Charlotte's inane grin was the perfect reflection for Parnell's broad smile.

"Just because it wasn't the done thing, that didn't mean it wasn't done."

Charlotte nodded and Parnell continued.

"Of course, the gamekeeper refused at first but the eldest daughter was insistent. One diary entry says that she had been watching him thrash for pheasant and, '*was stricken by a delicious fever like I had never known.*' She described her fever more fully but it doesn't take the Rosetta Stone to translate what she really meant. Nowadays we wouldn't say she 'had a fever,' we'd just say, 'she had the hots'."

Serena smiled at this and in the same instant saw their host frown.

Telling his story, Parnell seemed oblivious to all of them except Charlotte. "They asked him on three occasions and the gamekeeper refused as many times. The final time, the eldest daughter blackmailed him. She said if he didn't do it, they'd thrash one another and tell their father that the gamekeeper was responsible. They detailed the repercussions he would suffer and the poor man was left with no option. He had to do as they asked."

"That is so manipulative."

Serena glanced up and saw their host's wife had made this declaration.

Their host squeezed her hand and winked. "It's so manipulative, and so unlike a woman," he intoned sardonically.

She gave his arm a playful punch and turned her attention back to Parnell. "What happened?"

Charlotte nodded, encouraging Parnell to continue. "Yes, what happened?"

As Serena had known he would, Parnell responded to her sister's question. "The gamekeeper did as the girls asked and he acted on their specific instructions. They wanted him to thrash them, using his stout length of birch. They wanted him to do it beneath a full moon, under the oak tree in front of the house. The eldest daughter seems to have had some exact idea in her mind but her diaries don't explain where it came from. Perhaps she had read it in a book, or maybe she just heard it in a story. That's one aspect that we're never going to know. However, the diaries do detail the thrill she got and I can remember that part verbatim."

He swallowed and closed his eyes before reiterating the memorised passage. " '*His first blow was like a bee sting and his second was worse. It was the precise sensation that my body craved but it didn't assuage my fever. It made my blood begin to boil and nowhere was that more apparent than inside my womanliness.*'

"As I said," Parnell grinned, "she had the hots."

Serena watched him wink at Charlotte and was surprised to see her sister return the surreptitious gesture. Beneath the table, Serena gave Charlotte a warning kick on the shin.

"At the beginning, they'd asked him to give each girl six of the best but, as it turned out, that wasn't enough to satisfy either of them. When the six were done, they wanted more and the thrashing went on for a good hour. It might have continued into the morning but unfortunately they were discovered."

"My God!" Charlotte exclaimed.

Serena was intrigued. "Who caught them?"

"They were caught by the owner of the house. Returning from his gentleman's club he was outraged and demanded an explanation but no one could give him that. Both daughters knew it would presage their downfall if they told him the truth. I suppose they were right – it was the Victorian age and if the two young ladies had said they were being willingly thrashed it would have caused a sensational scandal. The gamekeeper tried saying he hadn't done anything, but he had a piece of birch in his hands and the daughters had striped and reddened backsides to prove that something had gone on. With that sort of evidence against him, the gamekeeper eventually fell silent. He stayed silent until they hung him an hour later."

"My God!" Charlotte gasped again. "How could he have been tried and sentenced so quickly?"

Parnell shook his head. "Vigilante justice wasn't common back then, but it did happen. The house owner was influential enough to be forgiven for such judicial decisions and, at the end of the day, the gamekeeper's job was only another staff vacancy."

"That's terrible," Charlotte told him.

"The strange thing is, the gamekeeper actually had an alibi as to why he wasn't there. One of the housemaids saw him outside the kitchens, whilst the thrashing was meant to be happening. She spoke to him and although he didn't tell her his reasons, he did tell her that he was looking for a stout length of birch. They talked for a short while and the conversation ended just before the owner returned. According to the housemaid, the gamekeeper didn't have the time to thrash either of them. However, she only spoke up whilst the gamekeeper was still swinging from his rope."

"If he didn't do it, then who did?"

Parnell shrugged. "I think the gamekeeper must have done it. There was no one else in the vicinity to carry it out and the eldest daughter is uncommonly open and frank about everything like that in her diaries."

"But you said there was proof," Serena reminded him.

"There's proof that something happened," Parnell agreed. "And not just because of what's written in her diaries. After the incident, the family tried to put it behind them but the gamekeeper wouldn't allow that. The first sounds started on the night of the next full moon."

Serena swallowed. Her skin had turned to gooseflesh and she could feel the prickle of every stiffening hair on her body. It was a surprisingly arousing sensation and she tried to ignore its pleasant tingle by concentrating on Parnell's words.

"The sounds were loud enough to wake the entire household. According to the diaries they were the most bone-chilling sounds anyone has ever heard. From the front of the house, beginning at the base of the oak tree, there came the sound of a birch slicing through air. It's not a loud sound, try swinging a length of birch yourself and you'll hear, but on this occasion, it shrieked through the night. Every month after that, as soon as the moon turned full, the sound recurred. Even then, people were sceptical enough to doubt that it could be a ghost but there has never been any other explanation. The sound would come on windless nights and whenever any brave soul went to investigate, they never found any earthly reason for what they had heard. All they ever found, unusual to find beneath an oak in itself, was a stout length of birch, propped against the base of the tree."

Serena shivered.

"The family tolerated it for six months and then they left."

Parnell's voice had turned matter-of-fact and Serena guessed he had reached the end of his tale. That realisation did nothing to calm the nervous prickle that thrilled along her spine. An idea was forming in the back of her mind and, as much as she tried to push it away, it stubbornly remained and grew more appealing.

"The owner realised he'd done wrong by the gamekeeper and

they say the sound haunted him to the end of his days. More than anyone else, he firmly believed the noise was caused by the gamekeeper, perpetually carrying out the final duty that he had been given – the task he had been hung for performing."

Thick silence cloaked the room. Beneath the monotonous tick of the grandfather clock, Serena could hear the deepening pitch of her own excited breath.

"The sounds are still meant to occur now and again but in this age of insulation and double-glazing you'd have to be outside to hear it," Parnell told them. "All you have to do is wait for the night of the full moon, stand beneath the oak tree, and they say you can hear every slice of the birch descending." He adjusted his glasses again and glanced at the grandfather clock. "They also say that if you go out there just after midnight, propped against the oak tree, you'll find a stout length of birch."

Serena could hear her heart pounding.

"And with that said," Parnell told them. "I'm going to excuse myself and get some much needed sleep."

There was a murmur of goodnights as Parnell made his way out of the room. Serena feigned a theatrical yawn and said, "I think I should turn in now." She kicked Charlotte's leg beneath the table and, for the benefit of their hosts, glanced at her with an expression of polite enquiry. "Are you ready to retire, sis?"

"Apparently," Charlotte replied.

Ignoring her questioning frown, Serena said goodnight to their hosts and escorted her sister from the room. "What do you think?" Serena asked, as soon as they had reached the stairs. "What do you think?"

"I think you should stop kicking my leg when we're at dinner parties," Charlotte replied. "I thought you'd broken that habit when you were six. I'm going to have a bruise now."

"I don't mean about my kicking you," Serena hissed, not bothering to disguise her impatience. "I'm talking about Parnell's story. Did it give you any ideas?"

Charlotte shrugged. "It made me question the dubious mentality of our hosts and their guests. Or did you mean something other than that?"

Wearily, Serena shook her head. They mounted the stairs quickly and she pushed her sister into the shared bedroom before daring to raise her voice above a whisper.

"I want to try it."

Charlotte rolled her eyes. "Have you been mixing travel sickness pills and alcohol again?"

"I mean it. I want to try it."

Charlotte shook her head. "No way."

"Didn't the idea excite you? Didn't it give you a thrill just thinking about it?"

"No," Charlotte said firmly. She frowned and then asked, "What idea?"

"The idea of being spanked beneath a full moon. Doesn't the thought send your pulse racing?"

Charlotte shook her head. "No." She looked as though she was trying to make her denial sincere but Serena could see something shining in her sister's eyes.

"Well, the thought sends my pulse racing," she decided. "Look." She was standing by the window with the curtains pulled back. With an accusing finger, she pointed at the full moon. It stood brilliant silver against the night's blackness.

Charlotte glanced at it, then looked away. "You're crazy," she whispered.

"It's a full moon," Serena told her. "Perhaps you can't see it, but I know exactly why the eldest daughter wanted to be spanked in such a way. Can't you imagine the excitement of being chastised in a situation like that? Can't you picture the thrill of a full moon and the chilling sound of a sweeping birch? Can't you imagine the sensation of having that stout length of birch landing against your buttocks?"

"I'm going to bed, Serena," Charlotte said coldly. She began picking at the buttons on the front of her blouse. "Try not to wake me if you have any more grotesque fantasies."

Serena stepped towards her and grabbed her wrist.

"What are you doing?"

"You're coming with me. We'll ask Parnell if he can oblige us both."

Charlotte shook her head. "No way."

"You two have been giving one another eyes all weekend," Serena reminded her. "He'll do it if you ask."

"He won't do it for me, because I won't ask," Charlotte said simply. "No way, sister. No."

Serena glared at her. "Please," she started. "I really want to try this. I don't know why, but it feels important to me."

"No way." She glared up from the bed with an adamant expression thinning her lips.

Serena snatched her hand away and turned her back. Slumping her shoulders into a sulk, she growled, "I should have expected as much. You never do anything for me, do you?"

It was a calculated posture, and her words were equally well-planned.

Charlotte sighed heavily, "This isn't fair, Serena. You always say things like that and we both know they're not true. I do loads of things for you."

Serena listened attentively, waiting for Charlotte's next words. In the punishing silence, she heard Charlotte sigh again before deciding to relent.

"I'm not happy about it, but if you really want us to do it . . ."

Before she could finish the sentence, Serena had snatched at her hand and started tugging her out of the bedroom in search of Parnell.

Afterwards Serena realised that Parnell had refused three times before consenting to do as they asked. She had stated her desires boldly at first and he had refused with the same frank tone. She had tried pleading with him – saying that she knew he would get a lot out of the chastisement – but he had still said no. It was only when Charlotte asked that he grudgingly agreed.

"Just stand there," he told them. "Backsides out, bending forward with your hands against the oak." He used a stiff, authoritative voice and Serena could feel her knees beginning to weaken as she listened to him. Her anticipation for this moment had grown from a tingling interest in the dining hall to an unquenchable need beneath the tree. The night was clement with only the mildest breeze to tease her hair as it fell over her face. She glanced at her sister and hissed, "Isn't this exciting?"

"No talking," Parnell growled.

His tone defied argument and Serena fell silent and straightened into a submissive pose.

"Neither of you will speak whilst I'm doing this, or I'll simply stop. None of us are going to say another word until we're finished."

Serena nodded and from the corner of her eye she saw that Charlotte was giving the same eager assent. Intuitively, Parnell seemed to have guessed that she wanted silence for this little ceremony. Any talking throughout their punishment would have lessened her picture of how things were going to develop.

"I'm going to prepare you both, then I'll find myself a length of birch and begin."

Serena drew a heavy breath, surprised by the quickening of her excitement. She heard his footsteps squash the grass as he approached and she felt the caress of his trouser leg against her backside. The sensation evoked a ripple of pleasure she had difficulty concealing.

Without a word, he reached for her skirt and unfastened the button at the waistband. The sound of the drawing zipper was deafening in the still night but the noise was almost drowned out beneath the hammering pulse in her temples. His hands were cool, but not unbearable and she didn't flinch as he tugged the skirt away from her body. However, it was impossible to remain properly still when he reached for her panties.

Ignoring her unspoken protest, Parnell eased his thumbs beneath the band over her hips and pulled the garment down.

She could feel the fabric pulling away from her buttocks and knew she was being exposed. The thought sent her body's need spiralling upwards. As her breathing deepened, she wondered if he was able to discern just how excited she was. Admittedly, in spite of the full moon, it was still a dark night but she felt sure that he would be able to see her wetness or sense the perfume of her arousal. Aware that those thoughts were driving her wild with anticipation, she gripped the oak tree harder. Deliberately, she tried not to register the caress of her panties as he tugged them down her legs.

"You look ready to be thrashed," he said, drawing his hand against one cheek.

Serena blushed, surprised by her response to him. The palm of his hand cupped one buttock whilst the tips of his fingers fell close to her sex. She knew he wasn't touching her accidentally and felt sure she could feel his fingers combing through the curls above her sex. The sensation was subtle but it fired a heat that left her sweating. She squeezed her thighs together and was surprised by the thrill of pleasure that rippled through her body.

When he moved away, she knew he had gone to tend to her sister. She heard Charlotte's shocked gasp as Parnell began to undress her but the sound tapered off to a sigh of whispered permission. They were bending for him with their hips touching and Serena could feel the after-echo of each movement vibrating from her sister. She felt the tug of the skirt as it was removed and, as a second-hand experience, she enjoyed the caress of Charlotte's panties being tugged away.

"Why are you wanting to go through with this?" Charlotte whispered.

Serena shrugged. "I don't know. I just need to do it," she replied honestly.

"I suppose I can understand that." Charlotte agreed.

In the darkness, Serena could hear the smile in her sister's voice and knew the moment's excitement had touched her as well.

"No more talking." Parnell's brisk voice sliced through the air.

Charlotte made a surprised sound and Serena wondered if he was touching her as he spoke. She wouldn't have put it past him and if he was, she wondered how he had managed to contain himself for so long. The attraction between him and her sister had been obvious from the first day of the weekend.

"No more talking," he repeated.

Charlotte purred by way of response and Serena contemplated glancing over her shoulder to see what they were doing. Tiny shivers were emanating from the hip against hers and she realised the tremors were caused by Charlotte's growing excitement. Under other circumstances she might have thought there was something perverse about experiencing the shadows of her sister's arousal but on this evening it didn't seem inappropriate.

She tried to shut the thought from her mind, surprised by the intense reaction it evoked. Her pulse was pounding so loudly she felt certain she was going to be driven mad by its deafening throb.

Charlotte's tremors continued to quicken and Serena could feel her own excitement building. She swallowed thickly and moved her hip more forcibly against her sister's pleasurable shivers.

"I'll go and find some birch," Parnell whispered.

Serena thought she heard the whisper of a kiss before hearing his shoes against the grass.

As soon as she felt sure Parnell was out of earshot, she pushed her face close to her sister's. "He wants you badly," she murmured,

Charlotte's reply was a husky whisper. "He can have me badly," she grinned. "He's already got me more excited than I would have believed."

Ignoring the weight of envy that nestled in her stomach, Serena opened her mouth to say something encouraging about her sister's good fortune.

The whistle of a birch sliced through her thoughts.

She didn't bother wondering how Parnell had managed to get back to them so quickly. Her backside was aflame with the sudden sting of wood against her exposed cheeks.

Charlotte started to say something but her reply was cut off by a second whistle. Instead of speaking, she released a grunt of discomfort. The sound was almost lost by the snap of wood striking flesh.

"He didn't want us speaking," Serena reminded her sister. "Not another word, remember."

Charlotte nodded and as she moved her head, Serena could see she was squeezing her eyes against the threat of tears. She empathised with her sister's anguish and then forgot about her when the second blow struck her exposed cheeks. The birch landed across both buttocks, inspiring a fury of pleasurable pain.

The length of wood rose and fell with the monotony of the ticking grandfather clock. The stripes were delivered in a punishingly slow tempo, with one blow for her, then another for Charlotte. Each descent managed to find a new target and she was surprised by the thoroughness of the punishment. A dozen stripes had landed against her and it didn't feel as though the same piece of skin had been touched twice. The moons of her arse cheeks felt hot and red and she found herself flinching from the birch's descent before the length had landed.

The wood whistled loudly as it fell, its shriek presaging a blistering eruption that was too intense to be wholly painful.

As each blow landed, Serena realised that their burden was being distributed evenly. The birch struck her arse and, whilst she was still trying to adjust herself to its bitter kiss, she heard it fall against her sister. When she believed she had almost come to terms with the intensity of the last blow, the next one fell more firmly.

It was the experience she had known it would be and then some more. The combination of moonlight, punishment and sexual excitement were forbidden thrills that worked as catalysts for one another. The harsh pain of each impact barely registered beneath the spreading warmth of her arousal. With every alternate blow, when Charlotte was enduring the birch, Serena found herself anticipating the next stinging assault. The combination of sensation left her feeling giddy and wanton.

Charlotte was breathing deeply, each exhalation coming in a laboured gasp. Serena thought she could feel the sensation through their touching hips, then wondered if she was the one who was causing it. The heat of her backside was furious but peculiarly warming. Her arse felt burned by the wood but it was not an unpleasant sensation. Remembering the quote that

Parnell had given from the diaries, she realised that someone had already described exactly how she felt.

"It made my blood begin to boil and nowhere was that more apparent than inside my womanliness."

The words echoed through her mind as though they were being whispered in her ear. The need between her legs was euphoric and she knew she couldn't resist it for another moment. Squeezing her thighs together, Serena snatched one hand from the tree and pushed it against herself.

A shockwave of pleasure rushed through her body. She had been told not to make a sound but beneath the stimulation of so much pleasure it was a command that she could no longer obey. She screamed her elation into the night as the orgasm battered its way through her. Every nerve-ending was pulled taut by the shrill climax that hurtled through her. The eruption was so strong she felt sure she was leaving the impressions of her fingernails in the oak's rough bark.

When the ripples of joy began to subside, she realised the birching had stopped. In a way it was a saddening thought and she wondered if there would be any chance of continuing with the game once she had been given the opportunity to apply some sorely needed cold cream. She blinked her gaze free from the misty haze of her pleasure and wondered if she dared to turn and thank her tormentor. It was only a passing thought, almost drowned out by the fading echo of her guttural sighs.

"Right, ladies."

Parnell's voice had a grin to it that Serena could hear through the ringing in her ears. She heard his footsteps treading grass as he came closer, and she listened as he tested his strip of birch through the air.

"Now I've found a piece of wood, we can begin."

"Begin?" Serena repeated doubtfully. She glanced at Charlotte but her sister's face was obscured by shadows from the overhanging oak tree. She wondered how Parnell could use the word "begin" after what he had just done for them.

"Yes, begin," Parnell repeated. There was a disappointed

frown in his voice when he asked, "or have you changed your minds?"

She glanced back over her shoulder and studied his face, trying to see if he was teasing. To listen to him, it sounded as though he hadn't even been there when they got their backsides thrashed.

But he had to have been there, she thought wildly. Rising panic was tightening her chest and making her forget all the punishingly pleasurable sensations that she had just endured. Glancing down at the reddened cheeks of her arse, she knew that he had to have been there and from the corner of her eye, she saw the proof that confirmed that thought. Propped against the base of the oak tree, looking as though it had only just been left there, Serena could see a stout length of birch.

Higher Power

Lisabet Sarai

The ad was a long shot, but I was getting desperate. It had been nearly two months since I'd had a gig. One more month of waitressing, I had sworn to myself, that's all I'll endure before I give up and go back to Pittsburgh. Live theater, soap operas, commercials, music videos, I'd consider anything but porn as a step toward my goal. Still, this listing in the Chronicle's classified section was definitely on the fringe.

"Wanted. Attractive female magician's assistant. Regular work, excellent remuneration. Will train."

I'm generally considered pretty, but my auburn curls and freckle-dusted nose are more likely to cast me as the girl next door than the exotic femme fatale. Still, it was worth a try. I dialed the number from the ad.

"Hello."

One word only, but spoken in a voice so rich and melodious that I was temporarily speechless and astonished.

"Hello, is anyone there?"

Flustered, I collected myself and my thoughts. "Yes, hello. My name is Myra O'Toole. I'm calling about your advertisement, for an assistant."

There was silence at the other end of the line, as if he was trying to gauge my personality from my speech. "Myra," he said finally. "Thank you for calling." His voice was truly marvelous, washing over me like a Bach cantata, filling me with light. Socially, though, he seemed awkward, not knowing what to say next.

"Is the position still open?"

"Yes, it is. I haven't found the right woman yet."

"Well, would you like me to come and audition for you?"

"Yes, I'd like that very much. Would this afternoon be convenient for you? Around four?"

"That would be perfect."

He gave me an address in the Mission district, an easy bus ride. As I hung up, excitement was singing through me. I had a premonition that I'd get the job.

I arrived ten minutes early, but I rang the bell anyway. The building was one of those middle-class Victorians on Dolores Street that have been converted into flats. It had been defaced with vinyl siding and wrought iron security bars, but the curved windows fronting the street were intact. His apartment was on the second floor.

He was not what I expected. Well over six feet tall, he was a massive presence, more than a little overweight. From his voice, I had imagined someone slender, elegant, and considerably more mature. He seemed to be in his early thirties, a scant half-dozen years older than I. He wore a Jefferson Starship T-shirt and jeans. His thick, coarse black hair had a tendency to fall into his eyes.

Those brilliant black eyes held me transfixed. They searched my face; they searched my soul. They interrogated me, asking questions that I sensed but could not articulate. Standing on his threshold in my neat skirt and sweater set, clutching my folder of head shots, I suddenly felt stark naked.

His silent scrutiny seemed endless. Finally I could bear it no longer. I held out my hand. "I'm Myra O'Toole. I've come about the job."

Slowly, as if waking from a trance, he grasped my hand. His hot skin made me wonder if he had a fever. "Myra. Welcome. Thank you for coming. Please, come inside." That voice. I could not resist it. I followed him down a shadowy corridor, into what must have been the front room.

If his appearance did not exactly jibe with my idea of a magician, his flat certainly did. The windows were all draped in heavy black velvet. Candles provided the only light, dozens of them, tapers stuck in bottles and squat votives burning in glass dishes. There were books everywhere, not only on the shelves that lined the walls, but in piles on the chairs and in the corners. I noted other oddities, too: an antique model of the solar system, a stuffed owl on the marble mantelpiece, a grimacing mask fashioned of beads and feathers. There was a faint, strange odor. I thought that I recognized sage, and perhaps sandalwood.

He gestured for me to sit in a tattered Victorian-era arm chair and settled his bulk into its mate. There was another long silence, during which I squirmed under his appraising gaze. At last he spoke.

"I am Magister Aleister."

"Like Aleister Crowley?"

"A distant relative, I've been told. And you are Myra O'Toole." He leaned forward, his lips parted to reveal sharp white teeth. "Tell me something of yourself, Myra. Where are you from? Are you married? What prompted you to answer my advertisement?"

"I'm an actress." I held out my portfolio to him, but he ignored it. "I thought that working as a magician's assistant might – broaden my perspective."

He did not speak, expecting more.

Despite my best efforts, a bit of my frustration and despair crept into my voice. "I need the work."

He nodded, silently inviting me to continue.

"I came to San Francisco from Pittsburgh nine months ago to live with my boyfriend. He's a poet."

"And?" Magister Aleister prompted. I hesitated, not wanting to get into the sordid story of Dylan's drinking problem.

"It didn't work out."

"So, you are currently on your own?"

I nodded, wondering what possible relevance this question had to the job. Almost as if he could read my thoughts, he answered my mental question. "This position will demand a great deal of you. We will be working intensively on your training. Day and night. Thus, it would be best if you had no encumbrances, no competing claims on your time and energy."

This made sense. I almost relished the thought of work so encompassing that it could make me forget about Dylan.

Brilliantly talented, irredeemably bohemian Dylan. Unshed tears gathered in my throat as I recalled our all-night conversations and our funky passion. The way he had showed up at my door that first night, with his torn dungarees, droopy moustache and bottle of Stolichnaya. When he came to the City to seek his fortune, I followed like a moth to a flame, though New York or Los Angeles would have been more logical places to pursue my theatrical ambitions.

After a few months, his dingy basement apartment in the Tenderloin had begun to feel like a prison. He was my jailor, sitting up until five a.m., writing, chain-smoking and guzzling cheap vodka, while I tossed alone in our bed. Finally, I left to save myself, knowing that I could not salvage him.

I swallowed my regrets and turned my attention back to the magician. He still watched me as if he would strip away my masks and lay me bare. Suddenly, he reached out and with one blunt finger touched the little gold cross hanging around my neck.

"Are you a believer?" he asked. Memories shot through me: my childhood awe as I knelt under the cathedral arches; my first communion, colored light through the windows staining my bride-like finery; my mother dying of cancer, asking for my prayers.

"I'm not sure," I replied. "I used to be, but now . . ."

"And what about magic?" he asked with that ironic half-smile on his full lips. "Do you believe in magic?"

My heartbeat inexplicably quickened. "I don't know that, either."

"There is much in common between religion and magic. Both are grounded in faith and love. The essence is a trust in things unseen." I thought this a peculiar observation from a practicing conjuror. Surely the essence of magic was manipulating expectations and perceptions. Show business. "I have something to show you," he continued.

He removed the dusty velvet cloth shrouding what turned out to be a combination television and VCR. It must have already had a tape loaded; as soon as he hit the button, it began to play. "Watch closely," he said.

It was a recording of one of his performances. At first, I did not recognize him. He was clad all in black, with glittering rhinestones at his collar and cuffs. He moved with a grace and economy that negated his bulk. There was no sound.

He offered a few deft sleight of hand tricks as warm up. Then he was joined by his assistant, a slender, raven-haired Latin beauty wearing a scarlet evening gown. How could I compare? I wondered. As if he heard my thoughts, he commented. "Rox-anne. Exquisite, isn't she?"

"What happened to her, that you need a new assistant?"

His face darkened. "She suffered an unfortunate – accident."

Roxanne lay down on her back on a trestle table. The magician draped her with purple satin. He passed his hands over her, clearly speaking some incantation. The draped figure began to rise, until it hovered level with his chest. The mage then removed the table.

The illusion of levitation, I thought. Cleverly concealed wires.

But then the scenario began to veer from the standard. Magister Aleister whisked the drapery off Roxanne's prone body. He picked up a full-length oval mirror and held it above the immobile figure, moving it up and down her body in a manner that would have effectively interrupted any possible attachment of cables from above. I could see her reflection in the glass, and faintly, a misting from her breath. Her eyes were closed. Then he crouched and moved the mirror underneath her, as if to prove that she was not supported from below. He released the mirror, and it hovered below her form, halfway between her body and the stage.

The mage now made some passes over his assistant, his hands elegant and evocative. Her body began to rotate. First, she floated in a lazy circle around the vertical axis, her head and feet changing places. Then, very slowly, she rolled over, so that she was facing downward, once more face to face with the mirror. The video was clear; again, I could see the marks of her breathing.

I was impressed. I could not understand how such a trick could be accomplished. What arrangement of wires or hidden frames could provide so many degrees of freedom? The next trick, however, amazed and horrified me.

The magician gestured and Roxanne floated to a standing position, her crystal slippers barely touching the ground. Her eyes were still closed. He did not wake her from her trance. Instead, he pulled from the wings a framework of wrought iron, rather like an oversized bird cage. It was hinged along one side. He opened it, pulled it around Roxanne's body, and snapped it shut, then applied a padlock to the latch. I could almost hear the clang of metal on metal.

A heavy cable slithered down toward the stage from above. He fastened it to a loop on top of the cage, and gave an almost imperceptible signal. The cage, with Roxanne within, rose about a foot off the floor.

Now what? I wondered, as he disappeared offstage again. He returned with a rack of swords.

He was talking during the entire performance, though I could not read his lips well enough to determine what he was saying. He chose one of the blades and swished it through the air in a swashbuckling manner. Then he appeared to plunge it between the bars of the cage and through Roxanne's body.

She did not flinch. She did not move. Aleister seized another sword, circled behind her, and impaled her from back to front. I could see the tip of the blade emerging from her body, just below her breasts. There was no blood.

I did not want to watch the rest of this performance; the illusion was too perfect, too disturbing. But I could not look away. The magician skewered her with a half a dozen more blades. He spun the cage in a circle so that the audience could see Roxanne from every angle. Unlike the usual sword gambit, there was no opaque box within which the assistant could hide or contort her body to avoid the sharp instruments. Everything was clearly, awfully visible.

Finally, Aleister removed the blades, with great care, in the opposite of the order in which he had inserted them. He lowered the cage to the ground, and clapped his hands once. Roxanne's eyes flew open, and her lips curved in an enigmatic smile. Aleister unlocked the cage and handed her out of it as if it were a royal coach. They bowed deeply, in synchrony. Then the tape went blank.

My heart was pounding uncomfortably hard. The magician re-covered the television, then turned to me. "Well?" he asked, fixing me again with those unnerving eyes.

I took a deep breath and tried to meet his gaze. "That's – unbelievable. Remarkable. Not to mention very creepy."

"Convincing, isn't it? Makes you wonder what kind of power I really have." There was an edge to his politeness, the slightest hint of arrogance in his well-tempered voice. He smiled in a way that I suddenly saw as seductive. "Do you still want to audition?"

Curiosity and fear, wonder and terror, warred in me. I stared at my hands, distinctly uncomfortable. Then I had a vision of myself in that red dress, smiling at the audience, basking in thunderous applause. I almost felt the heat of his hand in mine. I looked up at him and tried to sound brave. "Of course."

"Excellent. Come with me, then." He opened a set of French doors, and gestured for me to precede him. When I saw what the room contained, however, I faltered.

No one can live in San Francisco for more than a few months without becoming somewhat familiar with the trappings of sadomasochism. The room that confronted me was obviously furnished as a dungeon. I noticed wooden frames fitted with steel rings, chains affixed to the ceiling, a wide variety of whips and paddles neatly mounted on the far wall. I also recognized the trestle table and iron cage from the video; I suspected that the rack of swords was somewhere about, also.

"Go on, Myra," urged the voice behind me. "Don't be afraid. I won't hurt you." Hardly realizing what I was doing, seduced by his voice, I entered. He followed close behind, and fastened the draped glass doors shut. "Sit, please," he said, pointing to a high-backed wooden chair in the center of the room. I felt paralyzed by fear and suspicion, yet I found myself obeying him. As I seated myself, I noted the leather straps fixed to the massive arms.

He stood before me, surveying me frankly. "This may seem unorthodox," he said, "but in order to determine if you are right for this part, I need to bind your wrists and ankles. May I do this?"

I was silent. Inside, I churned with mingled terror and excitement.

He leaned forward so that he could look deep into my eyes. "Trust me, Myra. No harm will come to you, and you may discover something wonderful."

Slowly, I nodded my assent. It seemed that I could not refuse this strange man. My practical side screamed, danger, beware, but as should be obvious from the fact that I was here in San Francisco at all, from the fact that I was in this musty flat in this bondage chair, skewered by his fabulous, knowing eyes, I often ignore my practical side. For better or worse.

"Remove your sweater, please." I did so, shivering a little in my silk shell, though the September afternoon was warm. His hot fingers brushed my skin as he fastened the bonds. Goosebumps traveled up my arms.

He knelt in front of the chair. Next I felt him nudging my ankles apart and circling them with leather. This time, when he touched me, there was a stirring in my sex. Despite my nervous uncertainty, this peculiar, awkward, powerful man aroused me. I blushed at this realization. As if he sensed the blood rushing to my cheeks, he looked up at me from underneath that dark mop of hair, and gave me a smile that turned my limbs to rubber.

He turned away for a moment, then returned with a leather blindfold. "This will help you to concentrate," he said. I nodded, not daring to speak. I blushed again at my reaction to his brief touch as he slipped the blind over my head. Everything turned velvety black, black as his curtains and his eyes.

Now there was nothing but darkness, darkness and his luminous voice.

"Myra, I want you to relax and trust me. Listen to me. Focus on me. Let me fill your consciousness, until you know nothing but me." As he spoke, I thought I felt his fingers, dancing lightly over my body. Yet I could tell from the sound that he was standing several feet away. He began to chant in some language that I did not recognize. His musical voice rose and fell in a soothing rhythm. I felt a stirring of air around me. Little by little, the tension leached from my body. Warmth flowed in like honey to take its place, thick and sweet, coalescing into a dampness between my thighs. I could not understand what he was saying, but his intonations gradually took shape in my mind, whorls and eddies of vibrant color that held me spellbound. I hardly realized it when his incantation ended. Then I smelled sulfur and heard the snap of a match bursting into flame. My fear flared in response.

"Myra," he said softly. I could tell that he was closer now, right beside the chair. "Trust me. There will be no pain." I felt intense heat against the skin of my forearm, smelled paraffin and singed hair. Yet he spoke truly. I felt no pain, only exquisite warmth that began in my extremities and raced toward that swelling center below my belly, which seemed to have become the center of the universe.

"I choose you," he intoned. "I anoint you. I consecrate you to my service." With each phrase, he sprinkled burning wax onto my skin as if it was holy water. I smelled the incense of my childhood, and felt the ancient awe. Yet at the same time my whole self hummed with lust. I was aware that the evidence of my desire leaked from me, staining my business clothing and scenting the air. I did not care. Shame had left me. I hung on to his voice, rising and falling, eagerly awaiting the next blissful, fiery benediction.

Complete bliss. That was what I felt. Then suddenly, there was a giddiness, a disorientation. My body was moving, floating upward. A shard of terror threatened to rend my joy, but his voice knit up the fabric of my concentration. "I choose you, I anoint you. Trust me. Yield to me. I am the One, the One you seek, the One you crave."

I was suspended in his net of words. I understood with new wonder that my body hung unsupported in the air, mysteriously buoyant. I was literally flying. I could still feel the embrace of leather on my wrists and ankles, yet somehow, irrationally, I knew that I hovered several feet above the seat.

Suddenly I comprehended the reality of his power. This was no illusion, no hypnotic suggestion. I knew, with total conviction, that magic truly lived in this man's voice. "Yield to me," he said softly, and touched me between the eyes with one delicate finger. A fireball of an orgasm seized and consumed me. I swear that I smelled burned flesh as I convulsed blindly in the air.

The next thing I knew, I was crying. He was brushing my hair back from my face and speaking some soothing nonsense. I looked into his eyes, excitement flooding through me. "It's real, isn't it? The tricks, the magic? The power?"

He smiled enigmatically. "As real as your submission. As powerful as your concentration." He handed me a glass of water, and my skin tingled at his brief touch. "In any case, Myra, you've got the job." There was mischief in his eyes. "That is, if you want it."

I did not have to answer. He knew my thoughts.

"We'll start work tomorrow. I think that tonight you will need some rest. You will call me 'Master'. And to honor this occasion, I believe that you should have a new name. I will call you 'Ariel'. Does that please you?"

I smiled through my tears. "Yes, Master."

The training was as rigorous as he had claimed. Sometimes he would bind me; sometimes he would beat me. As long as I yielded totally to him, shut everything but him from my ken, I felt no pain, no matter how he abused my body. Sometimes I would climax during our sessions, though he never touched me in any carnal way. Always I shivered with arousal in his presence.

We practised the levitation sequence, but he never brought out the rack of swords. When I questioned him about this, he smiled his secret smile. "I do not want to dull your edge, sweet Ariel. I need you to be afraid, when I cage you and pierce you with my blades. Your terror feeds my power. Or more correctly, the strength of your trust, overcoming your terror."

He saw the worry in my face. "Trust me, Ariel, and all will be well. 'There is no fear in love, but perfect love casts out fear.'" I recognized the verse, a dim memory from catechism class. The Gospel of John. What an unlikely soul to be quoting scripture!

Finally, the night of our debut arrived. My hands were bloodless and cold as I waited in the wings for my cue. When I saw my Master, resplendent in his costume, however, everything drained from me but total devotion. That night I heard him dually, his physical voice and his voice in my mind, equally real. In fact he was my only reality. I did not hear the clank of the cage enclosing me or the click of the padlock. I was deaf to the gasps and applause from audience. Each time he threaded a sword through my flesh, he whispered in my mind that it was his cock, penetrating to my core, and that was what I felt: a hot, hard penis piercing my loins. Each time he pulled a blade from my body, I shuddered in a silent climax.

When we stood together and bowed, energy surged between us. That night, he made love to me for the first time, and I understood that up until now, I had only felt the shadow of his power.

The weeks flew by in a blur of pleasure and exhaustion. I gave up my apartment and moved into the Dolores Street flat. We performed four nights a week, to packed houses. A bewhiskered German came by to discuss a European tour.

I was happier and more fulfilled than I had ever been. All the ghosts of my past seemed to have dissolved in the brightness of my Master's presence. Little by little, though, I sensed some restlessness in him, some urge to explore new frontiers, to push past our current limits. One day, he called me to the dungeon.

"I want you to see our new piece of apparatus," he said, pointing to a roughly rectangular object about his height, draped in the same purple satin he used in our levitation sequence. With a flourish, he whisked off the cover. Despite myself, I gasped in horror.

A wooden frame constructed of thick beams. A rack near the bottom, pierced with a circular hole, stained a rusty brown. A silvery steel blade suspended from a pulley, glittering in the candlelight. A guillotine.

My Master seemed to take some pleasure in my terror. "Lovely, isn't it? Finely engineered, and guaranteed to make our audience squirm in their seats."

"Surely you don't intend to use this in our act? To use this on me?" Much as I loved and trusted him, the thought chilled me.

"Ariel, it is just another blade. You know that the swords do not harm you. Why should you fear this instrument?" He gathered me in his burly arms, and I melted, as always. "Trust me, lovely Ariel. You are dearer to me than my own life. I will not let you come to any harm." How could I refuse him? Or refute him? I had experienced firsthand the potency of his will.

Still, that night, I was not as much at ease, at first, as I usually am. Then, while my Master spoke to the audience, expounding on the history of the guillotine and its legendary effectiveness, I heard him in my mind, reassuring me, commanding me, filling me with his glory. As he positioned my head in the stocks, I heard him singing, a lovely melody without words that turned my flesh to rippling water. Yes, I cried with the remnants of my mind. Yes, yes!

I did not feel the blade slicing my vertebrae. There was only the dappled light of his smile, the peace of a summer breeze, the delicious sensation of his caresses. I heard him call out to me: "Ariel!"

"Yes, Master. What is your will?"

"Tell me how you feel, Ariel."

I could feel his arms, cradling me, cherishing me. "I feel perfect, Master. Perfectly whole in my love for you."

Suddenly, there was a bolt of darkness in the summer sky.

"Myra!" The name was familiar, someone I had known once. The voice was familiar, and full of angst. Then my unconscious betrayed me. I smelled vodka and intoxicating sweat. Dylan! All the pain of our relationship poured into me, the longing and the frustration, the always-foiled closeness. Then the stink of a hospital reached my nostrils, antiseptic and vomit; my mother's face swam before me, skin stretched tight over her bones, sad gentle eyes. Next in the parade was my father, flushed, disheveled, snoring off his drunk on the living room sofa.

"Myra!" cried Dylan's voice again, loud against the murmurs of the audience, and then the physical pain engulfed me, and I forgot my memories. Every nerve screamed with the anguish. My flesh was being ripped apart. I was burning at the stake, my skin blistering, my bones cracking and crumbling to ash. Poison was racing through my veins, leaving agony in its wake.

Dimly, I felt wetness and knew it was my own blood. Everything became dim. I was slipping quickly into death, and knew this well enough to know the terror of that final moment.

Then the voice, quiet, sure, strong, deep in my soul. "There is no fear in love, but perfect love casts out fear." Master! I reached out to him with my last ounce of strength, and mercifully, the pain ebbed, faded away into darkness.

His power saved me, his power and my trust. I am grateful. I lie here, watching the sun sparkle on Sausalito Bay, breathing the floral scents, waiting for my Master to return. It does not matter that I cannot move, paralyzed by my moment of doubt. My Master knit together my bones, but so far, we have not succeeded in mending my nervous system.

He has renounced performing in order to concentrate on healing me. He blames himself, his arrogance and his pride, for my injuries. I smile quietly and try to soothe away his guilt. We spend time each day on rituals, exercises and ordeals. When he lays his hands on me, I sense his caress and it inflames me as always. Is this sensation born of my mind of my re-enlivening flesh?

I do not care, not really. My Master loves me and cares for me. He raises me up with his power. He takes me to places where I have never been. He nestles in my heart. Nay, he is my heart. I know that the next time that I meet death I will yield gracefully and without pain, for my Master is with me, now and always.

Unorthodox Gigolo

Misha Firer

1

Rabbi Klum chuckled and belched behind his rugged beard. He put down his silver fork without excusing himself and spoke to David in his sweet lisping voice. "Having a wife doesn't necessarily bind you to practising monogamy. It's a popular misconception, of a dangerous kind I would say."

David, a young man of twenty-five nodded reluctantly: "You may consider me naïve, but I know so little about this matter."

The rabbi looked intently at David's father Abel, a generous contributor to the reconstruction of the synagogue, well-known and respected for organizing charities for the various needs of the Syrian-Jewish community. He was sitting quietly, consuming macrobiotic food. Abel caught the Rabbi's penetrating look and held it without blinking, until the rabbi turned back to David. "You must get married, young man. We're talking about a deadline." Then he added promptly, "You are going to be like King Solomon, given a choice of the most beautiful brides in the community. All virgins. You shall be the first and the last man in one of those girls' lives."

The rabbi turned to Abel for paternal affirmation of his sales pitch. Abel was concentrating on the food. David looked at his father and wondered, "If the eyes are really a window to the soul, what is that cryptic, dull message in those black eyes meant to represent?"

A middle-aged waitress scurried to their table. Her smile was as broad as it was fake. Seeing her prostitute herself before his father's money only heightened David's annoyance. "What else would you like?" she asked in a heavy Middle-Eastern accent.

The rabbi inspected his guests' plates, "I'll have another pasta primavera." Father and son were brooding, deep in their private stormy thoughts.

"Sure," the waitress exclaimed, "not a problem."

David inspected the waitress's body, hipless, large-breasted, chunks of fat dribbling over the bra band on her back, pock-marked face, and greedy eyes.

The rabbi anticipated the arrival of another delicious meal. "David," he said, "let me explain your role in this world." The rabbi's eyes darted towards Abel, but the latter was picking at his food nonchalantly, immersed in a chewing meditation. The rabbi continued in a whisper, "Life is a business enterprise. So is marriage. There are rules that you have to follow but, trust me, this system that has lasted for more than three thousand years was designed specifically for male convenience. As a man, you can only benefit from it."

David nodded tentatively. He finished his frittata and began to diddle with a spare fork. The rabbi continued, "After getting married, you will start making money. It won't be a challenge either. Your father's business is profitable as never before. You will work hard and bring all the money home to your wife and if she says a word you shut her up and the Torah will be on your side. Your wife will do nothing but have children and take care of them. She won't work, and," the rabbi looked mischievously at David, "never will she be unfaithful to you. She knows that if you catch her once, she will be excommunicated. That has not happened in this community for two generations. Women are smart; when they know what they have to lose, they restrain themselves from rash, emotionally impulsive actions. You, on the other hand, can have any woman you want outside the Syrian-Jewish community."

The pasta primavera was placed in front of the rabbi. Already he was grinning, anticipating its familiar pleasure. With his eyes on the plate the rabbi said, "This system was made by men and caters to men's needs. Don't you forget it."

Silence reigned over the table. David was tearing the soft tissue of a napkin with the glittering tines of a fork. The rabbi was shoveling pasta into his yellow-toothed mouth. Abel stared through the window at passing cars. "Look," David began uneasily, "I can't marry a woman I don't love."

"Love?" The rabbi cringed, as if punched in the face. Theatrically he threw a fork down and exclaimed, "An idiotic notion of feudal Christians commodified by post-industrial pop culture." Then he realized that he was not lecturing his yeshiva students, caught himself, changed tactics, retreated back to familiar territory. "If not for Shakespearean fairy tales, Christians wouldn't even consider getting married. Their priests and politicians had to trick them into marriage by inventing the concept of romantic love. Don't tell me you believe in all that romantic bunk?"

"You can't deny the existence of love between man and woman," David said.

The rabbi was good at polemics. He would counter every contradiction with another one of his own. "When you get married you will love your wife, no less than those supposedly-in-love, married Christians do. G-d—" Abel looked at the rabbi in wonder. The rabbi rarely spoke of G-d in casual discussions but when he did it was always in connection to a very important issue, "always wanted man and woman to be together, rather than wandering the world in search of 'true love'. That's not only ridiculous, it's sinful."

"But in the Torah one can find many an example," David began.

"You compare your case to the Torah?"

"No, but . . ."

Abel raised his hand, silencing the two quarreling men. His rigid body language conveyed that he would accept no compromises. He said calmly, emotionlessly, "For three thousand years this system has worked, David. You will not change the rules of the game on a whim just because you have some idiotic secular notions. You will be married by the end of the year. You have seven months to find a bride. Rabbi Klum will help you. Otherwise you will be stripped of your inheritance and be free to wander the world in search of your true love."

David jumped to his feet, "I'll do whatever suits me without following your outdated codes of behavior," he exclaimed, bolting for the door.

His father stared after him as he departed.

"Oh, America, what do you do to our sons?" the rabbi asked piously of the electric lights on the ceiling.

David was seated in the barber's chair, examining his looks in the mirror. At times he thought those good looks were all that he had. Izzy Michel, the hair-designer and proprietor, spoke to him from behind, trimming his wavy hair, carving an even crater on the top of the head to accommodate his black yarmulke.

"Have you found a bride yet?" Izzy was a good guy, but all the complimentary rumor-spreading services he provided deserved vindication. David thought, "Whatever I tell him now will spread throughout the two thousand plus members of the Syrian-Jewish community of Brooklyn, New York. But what the hell, let 'em all know."

"I'm not going to get married."

"What?" Izzy Michel gasped and then he burst out in shameless laughter, "And what do you think you are going to do?"

David looked at Izzy gaunt but trendy figure in the wall mirror. "Nothing."

"What do you mean, 'nothing'? How are you going to make a living after your dad kicks you out of his three-story villa on Ocean Parkway?"

"Don't know."

"You got no education, no profession. What can you do? Work for minimum wage and live in a basement?"

"I really don't know, Izzy."

"Why not do what they want you to do? You can't lose."

"The rabbi and my dad keep telling me that. Unfortunately, I see things differently."

"Whatever light you see marriage in, staying a bachelor you'll have to face a grim reality that has no future for you. Unless—"

"I know what you are going to say."

Izzy Michel finished trimming the top of David's head.

There was a good-looking woman sitting in the barber chair next to David's. She was in her early thirties, but mooning into the mirror like a teenager. David knew her vaguely – she was the wife of one of his father's many friends. She fidgeted on the chair, clad in a long skin-tight skirt and top that overexposed her breasts in an unorthodox fashion. David remembered Rabbi Klum's words about Syrian wives' total fidelity. She caught David's glance and rewarded him with a big iridescent smile full of whitened teeth and glossed lips, preparing to speak to a promising bachelor.

"Dave, have you met my daughter Julia? She's sixteen."

Julia? Oh yes, a silly little girl with Dumbo ears. She had flirted shamelessly with David at the opening of his father's new pickle factory. This marriage could easily be brokered without the rabbi's help. His father's money would pave the way.

"Yes."

"She's a good girl, Dave. She adores children."

The mother's attention span was a second long. Not waiting for an answer, she turned to her cell phone and spoke quickly to someone or another, "I'm going to order a salmon wrap next. Then I take the kids to the movies. My schedule is packed. Can you imagine, I have absolutely no free time? Tomorrow? Appointments with two doctors, working out, Julia's birthday preparations, my facial."

Izzy Michel whispered in David's ear, "These J.A.Ps only pretend to be busy to hide the fact that they don't have anything to do all day long."

It was then that David had the revelation. He was thrilled by the sheer chutzpah of it. One moment he was looking at his image in the mirror, the next he disappeared into it. He was on the threshold of overthrowing a three-thousand-year-old system, which the rabbis claimed to be the greatest in the history of the human race. "How many Syrian women pass through your business each day?" David asked.

"Well, all of them come here sooner or later. I'm damn lucky to have their lucrative business."

"But you wouldn't mind making even more money, would you?" David winked slyly at Izzy's reflection.

Izzy Michel placed the scissors on the counter and began to brush off David's shoulders, sweeping cut hair onto the floor. A Mexican woman with a broom was approaching from the far corner.

"Look, nothing illegal, David. I'm not taking part in anything that's not kosher."

"What about being a go-between?"

"Maybe."

Turning to the matchmaking mother on the right, David said, "I would really love to meet your daughter Julia. I haven't stopped thinking about her since the last time I saw her."

She raised her heavily made up eyes, "What did you just say, David?"

"I said I want to meet your daughter, Julia."

Syrian-Jewish houses occupy thirty square blocks, stretching from West 1st to East 19th Street, and from Avenue M to Avenue X. They are some of the most expensive prices in Brooklyn, created by a low-key community of very rich people. Just two blocks away, across McDonald Avenue, you enter a different neighborhood where Russian, Arab, and Chinese immigrants live side by side in the mutual harmony of complete ignorance of each other's way but with the common goal of the American Dream, where house prices drop by roughly a half.

David crossed McDonald Avenue with the rampaging silver train above and rented a one-bedroom apartment with a queen-sized bed. The success of his future enterprise relied heavily on Izzy Michel's oratorical skills, which Izzy honed to perfection

talking to women round the clock on the job. His staff would
help to provide alibis for missing wives.

The first problem was to escape the persistent eyes of curious
friends. Syrian women formed a spy circle. Everyone spied on
someone else and then spread her accumulated data to the
others. At times there would be up to a dozen women spying
on the suspicious activities of one wayward wife. Rabbi Klum
endorsed these clandestine activities, striking fear into the
hearts and souls of those who yearned to transgress, coercing
them to abandon their sinful thoughts and sublimate their
desires through jogging, shopping, or gossiping.

Of course it was a matter of Judaic law that prohibited a
husband from having sex with his wife a week before menstrua-
tion, a week after, while she was pregnant, during holidays,
while he was on a work assignment or after having visited his
mistress.

2

David's customers would park in front of an old brick building,
walk through Izzy's place, head towards the manicurist, vanish
through the back door into a prearranged taxi. David would be
waiting just a few blocks away in his new apartment.

The door stood ajar and Bat Sheba lightly shoved it open. She
timidly walked into the candle-lit room. David, clad only in
Calvin Klein boxers, was seated on the armchair, looking at her
intently. She stood still for a second and then automatically
began to turn to exit the twilit room as quickly as possible.
David raised his hand and said, "The dichotomy between the
physical and the spiritual doesn't exist. Judaic law was originally designed to curb human excess, until finally it has curbed
human nature. I am here to set you free."

Bat Sheba stood still. Slowly she lowered her eyes and stared
at the appetizing bulk between David's legs.

"To resolve the crisis of denied pleasure within the religious
community of Syrian women, this house was opened. For the
first time in three thousand years you will get the kind of sex

that you have been lacking. Not for the purpose of procreation, but for the sheer pleasure of it. You will not be betraying your husband, but rather the system that enslaves you both."

Bat Sheba came closer – David's words and a growing bulge beckoned to her – life-long restraint abandoned. "Come undone, Bat Sheba."

"What if Schwaki finds out?"

"He never will. It will be our secret, Bat Sheba. Izzy Michel who sent you here has no idea what this is all about. There are only two people in the whole world who know. You and me."

Her eyes were shining. She touched her breasts and slid her arms down. She came closer and embraced David. She had entirely lost control over her decision-making.

Sublimation knows many tactics and techniques. Linda's was a mainstream, widely acclaimed, obsessive profusion of diets. She tried them all, she went from "plump" to "super-skinny", and eventually cut her daily ration to five pieces of grilled tofu and two glasses of filtered water. Her limbs shook from malnutrition, her skin was ashen, her hipbones protruded far beyond normal, and her mind raged with vivid hallucinations. In order to choke her sexual hunger, she suppressed it with hunger for food. She would pick up her tofu from a kosher vegetarian café on the way to David's bed, where her activities required some extra nourishment.

Once when her order was delayed, David called her cell phone to ask why she was late. "Either come right now or not until tomorrow." He knew Syrian women tended to always come late, and he wanted to train all of them to keep to his schedule.

Linda steered madly through the neurotic traffic of New York. When she arrived, she began to see monsters in David's little bedroom. They were naked men dancing around a hellish pyre, fallen angels eating fire and disgorging yellow flames upon the heads of female apparitions. Anti-rabbis blessed the copulating bodies, packing their souls into crocodile-skin bags and sending them to purgatory via UPS. Corporate backers were

Misha Firer

advertising and selling contraception. Unlicensed doctors treated venereal diseases.

"Are you OK, Linda?" David asked from the bed.

Linda was shivering violently.

"I'm hungry, Dave. My husband and I are going to Hawaii
this week."

"Where's your husband now?"

"Probably with some Gentile hooker."

Making love like it was the last time in her life, she screamed
so loudly, bottles of beer were exploding in the apartment
below. She was insatiable. In her taste for loving she was
gluttonous. Three thousand years of tradition was being shattered one thrust at a time.

The next day she sent her friend, Vivian.

Vivian was a dragon woman. She didn't have to carry a gun, it
was in-built into her retina. She took it for granted that she
would be the ruler in David's kingdom.

"I've seen you before. You are Syrian, aren't you? Why aren't
you wearing a yarmulke?"

David patted the mattress, "Sit down and count out your
money. It's $300 for the first time. I'm sure your friend has
already told you."

Her eyes exuded acid, it dripped on the carpet and burned
dime-size holes in it. "What will your mother say when she
finds out?"

David spoke gravely, imitating his father's intonation, "Remember, there is no way back once you've started. You will
notice changes occurring in your perception of the world on a
daily basis. You will see things that you have been taking for
granted in a totally different light."

"What do you mean?"

"You have four children, right? You have to remember that
you will be excommunicated if you are found out."

Vivian was a big woman. Like her skinny friend, she had tried
many diets with no success, however her plumpness was
healthy and natural. To protect her self-esteem from the Syrian

women's smirking ridicule, she built up a virtual combat wall. She made her husband buy her a SUV the size of a tank. She drove it around her twenty-block perimeter with the spite of an adder, the spirit of a tiger. Vivian exercised totalitarian control over her family, as she did with all who served her, from waiters to nannies. She was in this world to command and to be obeyed. That was her line of defense against derisive attacks about her weight. This tactic seemed to work everywhere except in David's kingdom.

"Get undressed, unless you want to have sex in your clothes," David said.

Vivian fidgeted on the bed uneasily looking at the unorthodox gigolo.

"Get undressed," David repeated.

"You know what, forget it. I'm going home," Vivian bluffed arrogantly and jumped to her feet.

"Too late," David said with a gentle smile.

Vivian blushed. Her eyes downcast, acid-free, softened up. She was a boss no more. David stood up, shedding his clothes on the move, and approached.

Rent-A-Romeo's customized Juliet was sitting at the family table congratulating herself on her community-acclaimed success at dancing and singing. David pretended to listen carefully and squeezed out smiles here and there, praising his chosen bride. His Father couldn't help but be content, despite David's conviction that his father had never been content about anything in his entire life. Of course the patriarch had to mask his true character at moments of common celebration. Thinking about his clandestine business activities, David concluded that the capitalist acorn never manages to fall far from the tree.

Suddenly Julia spoke with ambition, as if mimicking some pop song, "Dave, I'm not like those girls [yeah, right, but then who ARE you like], not vulgarized, digitized, cashed in. I have a heart and soul and I treasure them above all else. I'm not just another plaything to use, abuse, and discard. I believe in G-d. I adore children [wasn't that what her mom said? How touching!]

and I will always adore my husband and be faithful to him. I will look at no other man and will desire no other man [how can she be so sure?]. I'll be your only one. I'll be everything to you, lover, housewife, partner, friend, mother of your children. I want you to love me for who I am, and in return I will be everything to you, your whole world."

Julia finished her speech and turned back to her food. Silence reigned over the table occupied by David, his parents, and Julia, the center of all attention. Abel hmmed theatrically. No one budged, mulling over Julia's outspokenness. Abel had to take this awkward situation into his own hands armed with the commonest of platitudes, "David is so lucky to have you as a bride (at which Julia blushed and nodded) and you will be the best wife this community has ever known."

David rose to leave. Abel spoke to him, "Where are you going?"

"I have some urgent business to attend to."

David's mother complained, "This is so impolite."

"I know," David said bluntly and promptly excused himself, in order not to complicate matters further. As he was opening the door he heard Julia say, "I love you, David."

For the first time in many days, David couldn't find words to give a sensible reply.

Ruth was hyperactive. She caught that special New York insanity from her peers. She had to be in many places at the same time to manage all her commitments. She tried hard to stretch space and time, believing them to be of elastic nature, using white and black magic, a Ferrari twelve-valve engine, her long legs, and a cell phone. She could afford to spend no more than ten minutes at a time in David's secret apartment.

Ruth was constantly on the move. The only problem was that she never had a purpose; she jetted chaotically, screaming, gesticulating, rushing the servers to be quick with her orders so that she could keep moving. She was quicker and lighter than a proton of helium circling around its nucleus, only Ruth didn't recognize what rules she obeyed nor the center she gravitated around. Even her household was a mere waystation in her hectic agenda. She wrote down a schedule for the day, but as time progressed, she invented more tasks than she could possibly fit in.

She was the busiest woman in North America. She was always behind schedule, always late. Her mind raced ahead of her legs, trapping her in cycle of useless motion. Frustration was her perpetual condition, her permanent state of being.

She would storm into the second-story apartment, get undressed and jump on David. While making love she would look at her watch, planning her next step, or rather figuring out how to balance several errands, striving to squeeze them into narrow frames of limited time. So now even her orgasm became one of many tasks of the day. She even managed to calculate the time required to reach her climax. Ten minutes sufficed. She would throw her money on the bed and run away, without saying goodbye, already late to her next arbitrary destination.

Rene wanted to fuck. Immediately upon entering David's enterprise, she began to vaporize her husband's hard-earned money – as David liked to say, "one thrust at a time". It felt damn good to her but she never had an orgasm. David had a big-time customer in Rene. Whenever she had a chance, she snuck out of the house on East 4th and Avenue U and headed her silver Mercedes straight towards David.

Rene, like an adolescent, experienced every act of intercourse as a brand-new adventure. She liked to try out new things, new positions. She had seemed to know of only one or two prior to her magical discovery of love outside her husband's three-story palace.

She would have done it all day and all night if not for her responsibilities at home. Once, she begged David to come along on her family's vacation in Florida. She asked him for many other perilous favors and she always paid with new hundred-dollar bills.

3

In his study, Rabbi Klum offered a chair to a yarmulked David. All around him was the graveyard of ancient Jewish knowledge. The past buried itself in written history prescribing codes of moral behavior.

Rabbi Klum held a Torah in his hands, an amulet against worldly evils. David envied him his naivete. How easily this religious man could twist reality, automatically adopt the system of his parents, take it for granted, believe in it to the depth of his soul.

David thought, "Rebels will always be rebels. It's in our blood."

Torah has answers for absolutely everything. All pain is explained and justified, taken out of context, put under the sanctified prism of the Divine. A simple application of twenty-two letters can vanquish existential doubts, reanimate the spirit, make everything right. Like a bottomless well, the Holy Scripture provides assistance in times of trouble, explanations to the most complex personal paradoxes, promises of never-ending life.

Torah is the world's greatest psychologist; it has cures for every neurosis to afflict humankind. Dismissing rabbis' assurances that it was written by G-d, David pondered the idea that the authors might have been a band of talented and very bright human beings. They never asked to enter this world and wandered around in a blind attempt to figure out their place in it. They were as lost and bewildered as David. Frustrated, they tried to grasp and throw their arms around a Higher Being. Their ultimate failure can be traced throughout the Torah – something rabbis choose not to address.

A primary mission of Torah was to protect man from man. That was what the Ten Commandments were all about. But now, generations later, the Chosen People have gotten themselves lost in linguistic interpretations encumbered by outdated laws that strictly prohibit almost all expressions of man's nature. David was born into an over-civilized community of fear-stricken, super-isolated people of G-d's choice.

Rabbi Klum interrupted David's internal philosophizing, "You made the right choice. Julia is a good girl. She will make you a good wife." David nodded thoughtfully.

Rabbi Klum continued uneasily, "I heard about . . . that woman business of yours."

David stared at the rabbi, stunned, "How did you know about my business?"

Rabbi Klum shrugged his wide shoulders, "Women talk; that's their nature. Women never stop talking. You must know that."

David looked away at the shelf full of Hebrew and Aramaic tomes.

"Your secret will rest with me, David. I have just one thing to ask of you, to repay me for the favor I'm doing you."

"Why do you think I owe you a favor?"

Now it was the rabbi's turn to look at David in amazement. "Because if it gets out you will be excommunicated."

"And who says that's not the reason I've been doing it in the first place?"

The rabbi smirked, thought for a second and said calmly, "Look, David, you are not a threat to the integrity of our community. Even if you were discovered, it wouldn't change our traditions. Our community is like a dynamic swamp. If you try to move too much you'll get submerged. You have to move carefully, according to the rules. If you go public, we'll drown you. Eventually no one will be on your side – not your father, nor Julia, nor your lady friends. In the end, you'll have to go live with the Gentiles, but even they won't be interested in your story. It will die with you and your rebellion will perish unnoticed."

"How can you be so sure?"

"Because it has happened before to no avail. We are bigger than life. We are untouchable. Our actions are justified by G-d Himself. And that's why I can be so sure."

Rabbi Klum took David by the hand, "I want to be your friend, David. It's politics. It's money. I want you to understand the truth of your situation. Either you do it our way, or you're out. You want your freedom? Here's your free choice. The favor I need you to do is to terminate your illicit enterprise immediately. Excuse me David, but I have to go to pray now. Hope to see you soon. Shalom."

The rabbi hurried into the sanctuary to don his talith and enter a directive trance to inch closer to the Divine Being.

David tossed his yarmulke away and headed for the street.

Odalisque

Mitzi Szereto

So how's Dubai? friends ask over the phone. Dubai. How can one possibly describe this mixed-up parcel of sand that's part Arab, part British, part Indian, with some Lebanese, Malaysians and Iranians thrown in for added spice? Have I left anyone out? I'm sure that I have.

Hot and sandy, I say. I don't say it's a sand beneath which nothing grows . . . except perhaps, fundamentalism. How long will it be? I wonder. How long will the freedom last in decadent Dubai? In the neighboring emirate of Sharjah a man and woman can't hold hands in public, nor can a woman wear short sleeves. They can get great rugs, though. The winds of change blow close, I fear.

I don't tell my callers about the smell of Arabic perfume that has made a permanent home in my nostrils. Oudh, amber, sandalwood, rose. These are the scents that fill my nose, seep into my skin and the skins of everyone around me. Arab perfume is a great equalizer among men and women; there are no His and Hers sections at the perfume counter. Eventually they stop asking about Dubai. Stop ringing to see how I am. Leaving me on my own, a foreigner in a foreign land. Forgotten by the West.

Citizen of the world, that's what I am. What would my American friends think if they saw me now – a woman caught between two cultures? Their only reference points being harems, white slavery, religious fanatics. They know so little about this part of the globe. Only what they see on the news – the extremists, the haters of the West. The *Death To America* coalition. They would not know this beautiful Arab man on the prayer mat, his long limbs bent in supplication as a muezzin calls out the afternoon prayer through a loudspeaker hitched to a minaret, his smell of oudh, amber, sandalwood, rose teasing me, making me desire.

They would think I'm not safe here. Yet I am probably safer than on the street of any American city or town. (Crime is low in the United Arab Emirates; Sharia law makes a powerful deterrent.) They do not hear the lively Arab music coming through the open windows of taxicabs. They do not see burka walking alongside tank top, both of which have breasts bouncing beneath them. They do not taste the salt on the air blowing in from the Gulf. I hear and see and taste all of these things. I love them all.

Especially his prominent nose. We are in the land of prominent noses. Ah . . . but that is a superficial thing to say. An American thing to say. The cliché springs to mind of big noses and big—. No. I won't even go there. Dubai may be a lot of things. A cliché isn't one of them.

We met over the pastry table at Spinney's supermarket in the Mankhool district – the Spinney's with the Filipina hooker who hangs around outside the glass doors day and night, her skin-tight pants splitting her crotch, her painted face devoid of expression. Perhaps she isn't a hooker at all, but only looks like one. No matter how many times I go to buy my groceries, she's there. Alone. Standing. Waiting, her mobile pinched between her long painted fingernails. Just as the Latino hustler in his tight black T-shirt and jeans is always there on my way home, cruising up and down past the hotels, day and night. Though mostly at night when it's cooler. After all, it can get up to 120 degrees Fahrenheit in the summer, and Gulf winters aren't exactly Zurich either. I've often wondered who his clients are – wealthy Arabs for whom homosexuality might be punishable by death, or lonely sunburned Englishmen working for the big tax-free bucks in Dubai. Probably a bit of both.

They have a pork counter at Spinney's for the foreigners, the heathens, though I've yet to see anyone make a purchase. It's expensive to buy pork in a Muslim country. Not sure I'd want to either. You tend to get away from the taste of pig flesh until it becomes a distant and unmissed memory on the tongue. Booze – well, that's another matter. You can always get booze. Westerners wouldn't come here if they couldn't. Not the Brits, anyway. When I was still the new kid on the block, I asked the waitress at a Chinese restaurant if the dumplings in the won ton soup had pork in them, concerned as I was for the spiritual well-being of my Muslim dinner companions. They're chicken, she said. Of course. What else could it be?

Meanwhile, back at Spinney's. I was in the process of selecting some baklava to have with my meal that evening. This is very important business, I should add – food in general being an important business in the Middle East. I was dying to pop a piece into my mouth right that minute, but it was Ramadan and the sun was still shining. Not that I would have been led away in handcuffs, but the consumption of food or drink during Ramadan is frowned upon. Everything goes on behind closed doors – stuff your face as much as you want, but not in public, please. Unless you're at a hotel, where Islam vanishes the moment you step inside the refrigerated lobby. Even a drink of water on the street is prohibited, though you might see overheated English tourists going about with a plastic bottle of mineral water, their faces running the gamut from lilac to pink to lobster-red. The same English tourists whose ultimate calamity in life is the absence of liquor for the holy month. It's the major topic of conversation – hear an English accent and you can guarantee it'll be complaining about the lack of booze. They'd have happily gone without food and sex for the month, providing they could get a drink. Abstention isn't so hard once you get used to it. You can get used to a lot of things in Dubai.

In my modern air-conditioned apartment in Mankhool it took some getting used to the cold water taps running hot. The water boils beneath the desert sand, and a cold-water wash in the washing machine comes out hot, shrinking all those beefy cotton T-shirts you brought with you from home. The water in

the toilet bowl simmers when you sit down to take a pee, the
heat from the tank radiating warmth better than the radiators in
my old New York apartment. It's hot here. Too hot. The sun's
always there, burning into you, judging you like those lamps the
cops shine in suspects' faces in those old black-and-white
Hollywood movies. Where were you on the night of—? Did
you murder—? Movies where women were *dames, tomatas.*
God, how I miss those movies! We get plenty on television
here, but they're nearly all Bollywood films. Or rather *fil-ums.*
Lots of slender women singing in high-pitched voices, lots of
slim men with smoldering dark eyes and flashing white teeth.
Sometimes I'm not sure what country I'm in. I see as many saris
on the streets as dishdashas.

He wore a dishdasha. My partner in crime at the baklava
table, that is. Pristine white against smooth flesh bronzed from
generations of Arab blood and unrelenting sunshine. You see a
lot of dishdashas here, especially in the swanky lobbies and
restaurants of the *Bladerunner* city center hotels. Conducting
business. Dubai is all business. All money. Slippery with oil. If
you don't hold on tight, the dirham will slip out from between
your fingers.

He must have seen the hunger in my eyes as I perused the
staggering variety of pastries laid out on the large table –
honeyed and walnutted and pistachioed sacrifices to those
who'd spent the day fasting. Yes, there's plenty of temptation
here. When he looked at me, he too, had hunger in his eyes, and
it wasn't for the trays of sweets. I felt that familiar little tickle of
desire between my thighs as my face heated up from his gaze – a
heat which shot all the way down to my toes. The eyes beneath
his ghutra were as black as his neatly trimmed beard and
mustache – in fact, as black as the agal that held this head
covering in place, and they seemed to darken as they studied
me, burrowed into me. I'd later learn from resident foreigners
that this is called *The Look.* They're a horny bunch round here,
my English friend in Abu Dhabi told me. I should have taken
that as a warning, though it was surely not meant as such.

He kept a villa at the beach. A villa bought with oil that he lived in all by himself. Massive tiled rooms, ceiling fans, hand-carved furniture, hand-women silk rugs. The constant hum of the air conditioner in the background. Servants came and went unseen, discreet as a tampon. The place was within walking distance to the Jumeirah Beach Hotel, where we often had dinner. I'm glad it was walking distance, since I hated getting into a car with him. He drove his Range Rover (not a Merc – the police drive Mercs!) through the streets like a madman. Though so did everyone else, cutting in and out of traffic, running up the bumper in front, flinging arms to and fro in exasperation at the sluggish traffic. All this while maintaining a steady stream of Arabic obscenities. There are probably more men in the Middle East whose mothers mated with dogs than anywhere else in the world.

He was distantly related to the Maktoum family, the rulers of Dubai since the early 1800s. Although nearly everyone who's wealthy seems to be related to them in one way or another. He always smelled of sandalwood and rose – of that Arab perfume worn by men and women. He liked to take the little wand from the ornate glass bottle and dab the oil onto me, onto my wrists, behind my ears and knees, the crook of my elbows, in that snug place where inner thigh joins the flesh of my sex. He'd whisper to me that I smelled better than any perfume as his fingers smoothed the amber-colored liquid into my skin, rubbing it in until it was no longer oily. He liked to dab a bit of perfume onto my clitoris, which he'd take a lot of time over, rubbing in circular motions and causing it to heat up from his touch and from the oil itself, not stopping until he had me squealing and shaking with orgasm. I had no protection from his fingers, since I'd taken to removing my pubic hair shortly after our affair began. Not to be the trendy American sporting a Brazilian (which always looks to me like a cunt smoking a cigar), but because of Islamic codes of cleanliness. They make a lot of sense, when you think about it. Besides, he asked me to. How could I refuse? How could I refuse *anything* he asked of me?

In the afternoons after we made love, I'd remain lying in his bed as the call to prayer started up again – a Muslim rave blasting from the loudspeakers at the Jumeirah Mosque, which has a Starbucks across from it. Get in a few prayers, then nip next door for a no-foam double latte. Islam keeps you busy, I'll say that much for it. With wake-up calls at five a.m. you've no need for an alarm clock. He would spread his prayer mat over the cool floor tiles and kneel upon it, still naked and dripping from me, as he began bowing toward Mecca. I suspected his lack of attire might not have been entirely respectful, but who was I to point this out to a good Muslim? I remained still, silent, not even wanting my breath to disrupt him from his link with Allah. Because there are some lines you just don't cross. Not even in Dubai.

When he finished, he'd look up and see me reclining on my side, nude. Like the famous painting, he'd say. The Odalisque. I am his Odalisque.

With lovemaking and praying out of the way, we'd indulge in an afternoon snack. He'd order me to stay in bed while he prepared something in his cavernous kitchen. I didn't argue. I was still glowing from his flesh, his saliva, the heat simmering over the sandy earth beyond the high walls surrounding his villa. He'd return a short while later carrying a hammered gold tray containing plates of grapes, black olives, labneh, feta and hallumi cheese, and cucumbers, along with some Lebanese sweets. We mustn't forget the sweets! He'd hand-feed me bits of cheese, followed by bits of cucumber, following it up with a spoonful of thick yogurty labneh that stung my tongue with its tanginess. Sometimes he tipped the spoon, and a blob landed on my belly. A perfect mountain of creamy desert snow. He bent down to lick it away, his dark head moving lower as his tongue searched out places where the labneh could not have possibly gone, the silky black hairs from his beard and mustache tickling the insides of my thighs, which I'd thoughtfully parted for him. He opened me up with his thumbs, taking his dessert where he found it, the sweets he'd brought into bed with us now forgotten.

Do we have a future? I asked.

Inshaallah, he answered. If Allah is willing.

We'd go dancing – the Kasbar or even the Planetarium, where we'd rub up against each other like two cats in heat. Exotic desert cats. Music thundering in our ears, lights flashing, no one watching and everyone watching. Maybe go hear some jazz at Issimo. Sit outside at a shisha joint sharing a pipe, arguing good-naturedly about whether we should try strawberry or green apple next time. The smooth smoke slipping down our throats in the warm night air. Just as he had slipped down my throat only moments before, his elixir as sweet as the tobacco.

He took me shopping, buying me the latest clothes the European designers had to offer. He took me to the gold souk in Deira, where he had me try on gold headdresses. I was blinded by gold – everywhere where I looked it glittered at me, showing off its extravagant beauty. I didn't wear a headscarf, so he had to fit the dangly strands over my hair, which fortunately is straight and rests neatly against my skull. He whispered that he wanted to drape my naked body with strands of gold, place gold rings on my fingers and toes, then burn frankincense and myrrh in homage to me. As he said this, his tongue tickled my earlobe and I shivered, remembering where it had been only that morning. How deeply it had penetrated before he replaced it with his penis, taking me from behind. The Arabic way, he called it. Arabic birth control, more like. Not that I complained. He made it into an art form. I couldn't bend over far enough for him, spread myself wide enough for him. Anything. Just ask. Just take. I am your desert houri.

I could tell that the old merchant with his clicking worry beads didn't approve of us, but since the headdress cost about forty grand in American money, he wasn't about to complain. You can't be serious, I'd said, smiling, my mind calculating dirham into dollar. I wouldn't be so gauche as to mention cost, but the thought of wearing something this expensive made my bowels knot up. Thieves would chop off your head in the States to steal something like this. Hell, people were killed for only a few dollars back home. And they say the Middle East is dangerous. Maybe the State Department should reevaluate its warnings to Americans traveling abroad and instead issue warnings that they aren't safe at home.

In the end he didn't buy it for me. Maybe it was stupid, but I graciously talked him out of it, squeezing his hand affectionately as the Abra ferried us across Dubai Creek to Bur Dubai. I thought it would make me feel like a kept woman if I accepted a gift like this. Now I realize how shortsighted that was. How stupid. At least I would've been left with something in the end. I could have always tried to sell it back to the man at the gold souk or one of the other merchants. Even if I'd only got half its value, it would have been enough. But I had my pride. An Odalisque has her pride.

Of course he played golf. What self-respecting Emirati doesn't? Several times a week he met up with friends for a round or two. He never asked if I wanted to join in. Not that I'd have wanted to, though it might have been nice to be invited, especially since I'd already met most of his golfing buddies. He did take me to the camel races though. He owned several camels and more often than not they won. I'd sit miserably beside him under an oversized umbrella, sweltering in the desert heat as camels loped along the track, their sun-blackened jockeys hitting them with sticks to urge them quicker and quicker toward the finish line. If it happened that his camel was gaining the lead, he'd lean in close to me, his fingers stealing beneath my gauzy skirt, heading toward their own finish line. My thighs would be slippery with perspiration, but I couldn't open them, since we were quite visible sitting alongside the track. I could hear his breath laboring with the excitement of the race and perhaps with the excitement of touching me, his fingers working my clitoris, thrusting inside me, swimming in a pool of my sweat and my own excitement from what he was doing to me. The farther ahead his camel reached, the quicker his fingers moved and I'd climax just as his camel passed the finish line. I could see that his thighs had begun to jerk beneath his dishdasha, making me suspect that he, too, had come. Though whether it was from winning the race or from touching me I could never be certain.

For Eid he took me to a beauty salon to get my hands decorated with henna. Beautiful intricate designs that put any ring or bracelet to shame. Graceful floral and vine patterns that performed a sinuous dance all the way down to my fingertips. He got off on the sight of my henna-painted hand pumping him to orgasm. He even made me wear a shaila. Nothing else, just this stern black headscarf as my hands – which he'd tied together with the agal from his ghutra – worked him to a frothy conclusion. My friend in Abu Dhabi had neglected to tell me the Emiratis were a kinky bunch as well.

The henna faded. And so did his desire for me.

He tired of his Western woman. His Odalisque. I suppose it was a matter of practicality. It was time for him to get married. To an Arab woman. To have Arab children. I wasn't the former, I couldn't offer him the latter. There was no argument. Just tears. Mine.

They said they'd cheer me up – take me out for a night on the town. Dubai has a swinging nightlife, if you know where to look. They were just some guys who'd come around to visit sometime, whom we'd meet for dinner, share a shisha with. Golfing buddies, camel racing cohorts. His friends. My friends. Or so I thought. *Salaam Ale-Koum* they'd always greet me, and I'd *Walaikum-asalaam* them right back. Young Arab men with dishdashas and black beards and mustaches. Going to a night-club filled with rich Arabs – the Kasbar, maybe. At least that's where I figured we were going. Instead they took me some-where I'd never been.

To a house off Sheikh Zayed Road. A villa like the one I'd spent so many days and nights in, simultaneously shivering and sweating with desire and pleasure, my sighs a fusion of English and Arabic as I reached toward my black-eyed love. They seemed surprised when I pushed their hands away, slapped off their offending fingers. I'd slept with their friend – why wouldn't I sleep with them? They didn't know I was an Odalisque. Their dark scowls burned me as they put me in a taxi, threw some dirham at the driver, who smirked knowingly, making me feel like the Filipina hooker from Spinney's. He'd driven whores home from a job before. The sun was already high over the tree-barren city, judging me although I'd done nothing to be judged for.

I wanted to tell him about his so-called friends, but I knew he wouldn't be interested. He was gone from me now. I even thought of taking revenge, maybe saying things had happened that hadn't really happened just to show them I wouldn't be disrespected like that. But I'd heard how women were treated, even when they were telling the truth. *Adulterous behavior* they call it.

Here no one's interested in the truth. Not a woman's truth, a Western woman. A former Odalisque. It's all about power and money, where you're from, what you have dangling between your legs. Guess it's not that different from America, when you think about it.

The Puss Hater

Inna Spice

I once did a very bad thing in the name of Love. Love has always been a bitch to me and I thought I could fool it.

I always took the romantic stuff very seriously, getting to know the guys before allowing a first kiss, becoming friends before being lovers. I built up rose-coloured and scented scenes in my head of how Mr Right and I would be so happy just sharing a dinner in a fancy restaurant and playing footsie under the long starched tablecloth. But every time a prospective Mr Right appeared in sight, things went terribly wrong. So I kind of gave up my hazy dreaming and went for a fun-of-the-moment thing.

I met Lenny at a Valentine's bash in a club. I was twenty-eight at the time and single, as I have been for most of my life. My friend Jenni brought her boyfriend, and he in turn brought a couple of friends. I knew everyone else; we were all at the same drama school. I was drinking as if it were my last chance and flying across the dance floor imagining I had wings. I didn't pay any particular attention to the new guys since I'd given up on meeting a potential husband or even getting laid. We hadn't been properly introduced as I got to the club late, fought my way in through the pushing crowd by the door, got a drink and tried to spot a familiar face on the dance floor. Jenni was already twirling around with half-a-dozen guys, and so I joined them. We danced like crazy, blood pumping at our temples and ecstasy filling our hearts.

After an hour or two of hot dancing I had to pee – the fact, which I announced shamelessly in the hope that someone would direct me to the bathroom. Suddenly, I heard a whoosh and everything went blurry below me, as my very gentle dance partner scooped me up in his arms and carried me, still swaying to the music, to the john. By the entrance he put me down and beaming from ear to ear said, "I am Leonard. Lenny to my friends."

"Suzie. Thanks for the ride," I grinned. "Got to go . . ."

When I returned to the floor, Leonard had got a table, drinks and ice cream sundaes. We savoured the treats and the buzz, chatting away till two o'clock in the morning. He pulled up my socks for me and retied my boots before we left the club. He hugged me tight as we walked to the subway station. In the dim lights of the train he held me, staring deep into my eyes as if trying to hook up my soul. He got me safe to my door, gently kissed me good night and left his phone number in the palm of my hand. I think I was too drunk to appreciate all his sweetness.

However, the next day I called the number. We went for a coffee and walked along the river. He was exciting in his simplicity; he told me stories of his childhood, of the plays he'd written, and I felt as if I had known him all my life.

His mother, he said, was obsessed with animals. She had a collection of nearly two dozen pets: eight dogs of different breeds, four cats, five finches, a parrot, a guinea pig, a couple of rabbits, a ferret and a porcupine – all in her one-bedroom apartment.

I always liked animals, but in reasonable numbers. When I was little, I used to bring stray cats home, saving them from freezing to death in the winter, but we had never kept more than two cats at a time.

Lenny had a cat too. Only one, so that was a relief. I met it the first time we came to his place to have sex. We had been dating for several weeks then and his affectionate talk and arousing kisses made me want to know him better.

The temperature dropped drastically, making it the coldest day of the winter. It had snowed the night before, and the trees looked like huge white monsters out of some marvelous magical fairytale. Our walk didn't last long – we had to sneak into a coffee shop and fuel up with liquored hot chocolate to defrost our toes and fingers. I told Lenny that I had a craving to curl up with a hot water bottle. He said he had something much better to offer at his place.

Red-cheeked from the frost and anticipation, we stumbled through the knee-deep snow towards his small cosy residence.

As soon as we opened the door, an all-black, sleek, very serious-looking creature with enormous yellow eyes came out to greet us "Meow."

"Meet Lenny Junior!" Lenny laughed.

"Lenny Jr., this is she, my cat-woman I told you so much about."

I said hello and stretched my hand out for him to sniff. He pushed his little brown nose into my palm and affectionately rubbed it all over my hand, his tail standing tall and still. He was kind of handsome and so far he liked me.

"Now it is my turn, Junior," Lenny wrapped his arms around me and rubbed his cheek into mine. His chocolate breath was hot. We stood there licking each other's lips, sucking tongues, nibbling ears and stroking every inch of the exposed skin. His breath mixed with the puffy fur collar of my coat tickled like crazy, sending electric waves from my neck to my butt. I giggled. He pulled my coat off, dropping it on the cat.

"Meeeooooow!"

"We better hide," I whispered. Lenny led me into his dark bedroom leaving the door open a crack. He lit a few candles the room filled with a warm wonderful glow and the seductive aroma of spices. He complemented the sensation by caressing my neck, moving my long hair out of my face and barely brushing my eye lids with his sensual lips. He took a long while kissing my face all over, making me hot and wet; I yearned to feel his hands squeezing my breasts.

He was in no hurry, and I impatiently tugged on his shirt, pulling it up and sliding my hands to his nipples as a hint. His chest was smooth and muscular – I wanted to press it to mine, to melt into him, to devour him with my pussy.

I dug my fingers into his hair, long, soft and wavy. I reveled in his fingers and lips upon my skin. He slowly slid my dress off my shoulders – I wore a stretchy low-cut dress – and pulled it down to my waist. His fingers caressed my breasts, brushing my tickly hard nipples. He sucked on each one, smacking his lips in delight. He breathed on my belly and stuck his tongue into my navel, while sliding my dress down my dancing hips. I had worn stay-up stockings and no underwear. His warm heavenly palms caressed my buttocks, cupping them, squeezing. I moaned as my pubic area became madly ticklish.

He fingered my clit, pinching it gently, and then slid three fingers deep inside moving them around, causing me to whimper and shiver. He kissed my mouth and pushed his fingers in harder. I cried out and bit into his shoulder, pulling him close, wanting to be crushed by his weight. He slowly pulled his fingers out and hugged me. I felt a light tickle on my cheek; I thought it was Lenny's hair and pushed my face into it as a cold, wet, leathery curious snout snuggled into me.

"Oh goodness! What's he doing here?"

Lenny laughed "He is my buddy, he wants to know why I like you so much . . . Here Junior . . ."

He shoved his fingers that had just explored my insides to the cat's nose.

"What are you doing, Len?"

"It's all right, Suzie. He likes you."

Sure as hell he did. He rubbed and nuzzled Lenny's fingers and then he started to lick them, slurping as if they were dipped into some catnip.

"You're crazy, both of you!"

"Suzie, it's just a joke. He misses me, I am never home, and he's such a cuddly thing. He needs attention. Come here, babe."

He pulled me closer again and kissed my lips. I melted. I wanted to make him feel as good as he made me. The cat jumped off and disappeared under the bed – not that I liked his presence in the room, but I wanted to please Lenny.

*   *   *

After that, we fucked quite regularly, sometimes at his place, more often sleeping over at mine. We were great together. His every touch was a turn-on, every position he chose I loved. Even when I was tired or moody, all he needed to do was give me a lick and I became slippery, itchy and throbbing for him.

The only thing I couldn't stand was . . . yes, Lenny Junior. Why, he even had his name! He was all over us whenever we came home or in orgasm. He meowed and purred, he walked on top of us and stuffed his muzzle into our faces; but Lenny adored him. He cuddled and squeezed him, patted, carried him around in his arm while preparing our food. The little black devil possessed the very heart I was trying to win.

But each of the few times that we slept over at his apartment, the cat came and sat on Lenny's chest, while we were still in bed, and Lenny smiled wholeheartedly, and rubbed behind his ears.

"Good morning, Lenny-buddy," he would say in a voice full of tenderness I hadn't heard before. I honestly wished he talked like that to me. If I could only make him love me as much.

When I spoke to Jenni, she complained of her obsession with her boyfriend. She said he flirted too much with his customers. He ran a coffee shop and had to be polite and friendly, I told her. But she sat and watched him for hours, her frustrations boiling up until she could no longer bear it, and then she screamed and made a fool of herself in the middle of his shop. Well, I told her, at least she was reasonably jealous of the female coffee-lovers – I, however, was jealous of a PET. A little furry thing, that most wouldn't even give a second thought to, drove me absolutely insane. I hated Lenny Junior's guts. I loathed his smart, observing yellow eyes. I despised his murmuring voice. I was repulsed by his black hair that I occasionally found on my white sweaters. But I tried to tolerate him for Lenny's sake.

In the spring, Lenny came to my house, beaming as bright as the sun outside, with a rose-bouquet he could barely hold in both arms. I felt ecstatic as well. He looked so fresh, happy and sexy in his cream-coloured suit. He said he wanted us to move in together.

I embraced him and kissed his face, grateful that he wanted to be with me. But the cat issue bothered me and I didn't know how to tell him. I said I wasn't sure we were ready but I was willing to try and stay at his place for a week.

The first couple of days went relatively well; I had to lock Junior in a closet only once. It was a weekday and Lenny had to be at work early. My class didn't start till eleven that day and I slept in. After I got out of the shower, the freaking cat sat on a dresser and watched me dress. I tried to brush my discomfort off and laughed, telling him I might just strip for his pleasure. He tilted his head as if in contemplation and then he nodded. Wickedly, I jumped at him, grabbed the scruff of his neck in one hand, his hind legs in the other and threw him into my closet, quickly shutting the doors. I let him out before I left for school. No one had to know about my little rage.

That evening we went out for pizza. Lenny was sweet as usual and smirked calling me his "real girlfriend". We came home feeling happy and excited like newlyweds.

We hopped and danced around the living room wiggling our hips and swinging our arms like little wild children; we tickled and hugged, making our way to the bedroom. Lenny gently thrust me on the bed, grabbed my sleeves and pulled them up, quickly slipping the sweater over my head. I wore no bra and my little tits jumped as my arm swayed around him. He suckled on my hard nipple while pinching the other one with his fingers. I threw my head backwards and caressed his muscled back and his gorgeous buttocks. I slid down, unzipped and pulled his pants to his knees. Surprise – he wore nothing underneath and his massive cock was wiggling right in my face.

"You are adopting my undergarmentless habits," I whispered and slowly licked his musky hot cock. I sucked it into my mouth and squeezed my cheeks, stroking it hard with my tongue. Never a great cock-sucker, I stopped before I was ready to gag and pulled myself up, kissing his half-open mouth.

He turned me around and pushed me down on my fours, my ass sticking up high, pussy swollen in readiness to take him. He fucked me hard, forcing his thick dick deeper with every push; it seemed he was determined to pierce me through all the way to my throat. He pumped in and out, squeezing my ass with one hand, slimy juices flowing down my thighs, my pussy squirming and queefing like a hungry bitch. Moaning, I turned my head around to look at Lenny's face and noticed . . . in the doorway sat a black silhouette, quiet and serious, its studying eyes sparkling gold. I swear I saw him grin.

"Your cat, Lenny!" I hissed as he pulled out and squirted his hot come over my back. I fell asleep feeling I had to get rid of him to have my boyfriend all to myself.

The next morning I let the cat outside, hoping he would get lost. But he came back in an hour and scratched at the door. Then I took him for a ride in a taxi to the other end of the city, and let him out by some small veterinary clinic.

I told Lenny he sneaked out while I was checking the mail. He, being very distraught, placed an ad in a newspaper, announcing quite a handsome reward for the finder.

They say pets can smell their home from hundreds of kilometers away. How was I supposed to know that this black little beast had extraordinary abilities? He showed up on our doorstep in five days.

As if in a snowball fight, I fought the furry balls that someone pitched at me. They came at me in all directions at incredible speed, bruising my arms and legs, raising blue swollen bumps on my head. I felt horribly sweaty and hot as I threw off my blanket. Suddenly something gently tickled my bum.

"Oh, Lenny, just a little more sleep . . . please . . ."

I turned around to smack him.

"Jesus! Fuckhead! Get lost!" I yelled at the sniffing cat. He ran away as fast as a cannon ball. And Lenny ran in from the bathroom, confused and worried about my nightmares.

"Lenny, I can't do this!" I wailed.

He held me tight, stroked my back, told me he loved me and that I had to get more sleep. He said he was going to shut the bedroom door before he left for work.

★   ★   ★

There was a bridge over our river. Tall pines on each end made it a quiet, secluded place. A few metres down, the river turned to a waterfall – high, rocky and loud – where I would come to watch and listen to every time I felt disturbed or distressed. I walked there that day in search of my peace again. Only this time, I carried a bag – one of those old fashioned net bags like the one my mom used to carry potatoes in, or beach towels. No one had used it for years, and it sat losing its colour hidden in my closet.

My mom would not have been proud of me had she known my plan: the bag contained the cat. The beast moved about and squirmed, making pathetic little squeaks, but I wrapped it in a newspaper and a garbage bag too.

I looked over the railing and heard the river calling me in. How liberating would it be to sail down and crush all the annoying troubles, I thought. To rid myself of the mess in my head. Forever. I took a deep breath, closed my eyes and threw the bag in. I swear I did it in the name of Love.

For weeks, Lenny was devastated as if he'd lost a child. I tried to comfort him with my presence, thinking up various activities for us to do. Reluctantly, he came along but the sadness in his eyes was too hard for me to bear. Finally, I had suggested we get a finch. But he wanted the whiskers.

It is August 19 and my birthday. I never work on my birthday, I never go to school or see people I don't like. I celebrate with my best friends and a ton of presents. I go out, I go wild, I get laid. As usual, this is the plan for tonight, except I want to lay Lenny. I cuddle up in the sheets, listening to noises from the kitchen Lenny must be making my birthday breakfast. I hear his shuffling steps and spoons chiming on the tray. His lips stretch in his usual sunny smile. His chest hair is secretly peeking at me from under his robe.

"Good morning, my birthday girl . . ." His voice sounds so loving. "I got you a present!"

He sets the tray on the bed beside me and shuffles away. I sip champagne and watch him come back with a medium-sized pink box tied with lots of ribbon. He hands it to me but, somehow, I'm not eager to open it.

"C'mon, I think you'll love it."

He picks up his glass ready for a toast. I undo the ribbons and lift up the lid, out pops a white, fuzzy, blue-eyed kitten wearing a red collar with silver bells and a beautiful solitaire diamond ring.

"Suzie, will you marry me?"

I heard Karma never forgets.

Picture Perfect

Donna George Storey

I didn't mean to shave it all off. At first I was trying for a whimsical heart shape, but I couldn't seem to get the curves even. Then I sculpted a fur patch like those models in men's magazines, but it looked too much like Hitler's mustache. In the end I went all the way – the Greek statue look. It's harder than you think to get yourself all smooth down there. I stood with one leg propped up on the side of the tub, studying my cunt like exam notes. I'd never looked at myself so carefully down there before. What surprised me was the color – the deep, almost shocking pink of the inner lips. The skin looked so sensitive and dewy, I was scared to get close with that nasty razor, so I left a little fringe. There was no room for mistakes.

I called Brian at work to tell him about my art project.

"Hey, Kira." I knew someone was in his office by his offhand tone, but I went ahead and told him anyway.

"I just shaved my pussy."

There was a pause.

"Oh, is that so? Listen, honey, I'm in the middle of a meeting right now. I'll call you back when I can. Okay?" Only a wife would have picked up the faint tremor in his voice.

Unfortunately, Brian was a model employee – not the type who would stand up in front of the boss and announce, "Sorry, I have to go. My wife just shaved her pussy." It would probably be hours before he could get home. That left a whole afternoon alone, just me and my bald snatch.

I went over to the full-length mirror. My heart was pounding. I hadn't felt this naughty since I was a teenager doing "homework" up in my bedroom with my panties around one ankle and a pillow pushed between my legs, ear cocked for the sound of my mother's footsteps in the hall. Which was silly because I was alone in my own house and all I was doing was looking at myself, my new self: the white triangle of smooth skin, the fold of tender pink flesh now visible between the lips. There was an indentation at the top of the slit, as if someone had pressed a finger into it. I had an overwhelming urge to play with myself. Just an appetizer before I jumped Brian's bones tonight. I touched a tentative finger to my clit. I was already wet.

The phone rang.

"I'm taking the afternoon off," Brian told me. His voice was husky. "I'll be home in twenty minutes. Don't you dare touch that shaved pussy of yours until I get there."

When I hung up, I had to laugh. My husband knew me well. Very well.

There were no *hi-honey* kisses or *how-was-your-day*; the moment Brian got through the door, he pushed me back on the sofa and yanked open my robe. He made a little sound in his throat, half gasp, half moan.

"Wow, you really did a job on it."

I smiled. "Didn't you believe me?"

He gaped, eyes glowing. *Pussy power* – suddenly the words took on fresh meaning. Gently he nudged my thighs apart. I shivered. He bent down. I thought – and hoped – he was going to kiss me there.

"You didn't get all the hair off."

"Hey, it's a tricky job."

He frowned. "Don't move."

He left me lying on the sofa with my legs spread like a virgin sacrifice. My pussy was getting chilly, but my breath was coming fast and I had that naughty teenage feeling again, arousal so sharp it was almost pain.

Brian returned with a towel, a canister of shaving cream and a razor. He'd changed into his bathrobe, which did nothing to hide his bobbing erection. He came back again with a basin of water, which he set carefully on the coffee table. The last trip brought the video camera and tripod.

I felt a contraction low in my belly.

"Spread your legs wider."

I caught my breath, but obeyed.

He patted a dab of shaving cream between my legs. The coolness made me squirm.

"Lie still."

He was acting awfully bossy, but I didn't want any slipups. I held my thighs to keep them from shaking.

"Relax, Kira," Brian said, more kindly. Guys are always saying that when they're about to mess around with your private parts. Still Brian did have plenty of experience with shaving, so I closed my eyes and took a deep breath. The room was quiet, except for the scraping sound of the razor and the occasional swish of water. At last he rinsed me with a washcloth, smiling as I wriggled under his vigorous assault.

He leaned close to examine his work.

"Picture perfect," he declared.

Five minutes later, I was sitting naked in our armchair, watching my own twat, larger than life on our new plasma TV screen. My legs were modestly pressed together, but Brian had me lounge back so you could see the slit, shorn of its covering. He knelt, pointing the camera straight at me.

"Did you get turned on when you were shaving?" His tone was soothing now, like a friendly interviewer on a weekly news magazine.

"Yes," I admitted in a small voice.

"Did you masturbate?"

"No." A few flicks didn't count, right?

"You wanted to, though."

I swallowed.

Brian clicked his tongue. "Why don't you do it now? Don't you want to know if it feels different when it's shaved?"

My cheeks burned, but I ignored the question and turned to the screen. "It sure looks different."

"Yeah. It really does look like lips. The skin gets pinker here and pouts." He reached over and pinched the edges.

I bit back a moan.

"We could put lipstick on it. Deep red like a forties movie star."

"No, that's too weird," I said and immediately regretted it. Why was I being such a prude? After all, I'd started this with my little experiment in the tub. Suddenly bold, I glided my middle finger up and down along the groove. "This is an easier way to make it redder."

Brian grinned. "Yes, indeed. Let's get the full view." The camera zoomed in expectantly.

I hesitated. I'd played with myself in front of Brian before, but now a stranger was in the room with us, a stranger with a round, staring eye. "Go ahead, honey. I know you're turned on. Your chest is all flushed." I inched my thighs open, glancing at the TV. To my embarrassment I was already quite ruddy down there and shiny-slick with pussy juice. The fleshy folds and hole filled up the screen. My finger, laboring at my clit, looked strangely small.

"Does it feel different?" Brian was back to being the cordial journalist.

"A little."

"Tell me."

"The mound is really smooth, like satin."

"Is it more sensitive?"

"Yes, I think so. The outer lips are tingling. Or maybe I'm just noticing it more." I looked up at him. "What's with all the questions? You sound like you're interviewing my pussy for a dirty documentary."

Brian laughed. "What if I was?"

"Now wait a minute." I sat up and snapped my legs together.

He turned the camera to my face. A frowning twin gazed back at me from the TV.

Brian, on the other hand, was still smiling. "What if there was a guy in the city, a dot-com billionaire, who collects videos of married ladies pleasuring themselves?"

My pulse jumped. "You're joking, right?"

"For his eyes only, discretion guaranteed. He pays well for it."

"Oh, yeah? How much?"

"Three grand for a genuine orgasm. That won't be a problem for you. We might get even more because you're all shaved down there. Just think, Kira, we could go on a nice vacation for a few very pleasant minutes of work." I moaned and covered my face with my hands.

"Don't worry. I'll edit this part out. He specifically requested no faces. Just sweet pussy."

Would my own husband really sell some rich voyeur a movie of me masturbating? I never thought he had it in him. And I never thought I'd find the idea so fiercely arousing. Funny all the things you discover when you shave your pussy.

Brian put the camera on standby. His eyes twinkled. "Jake and Ashley did it."

"No way."

"Lie back. I'll tell you about it."

There I was with my pussy on the screen again, a sprawled-leg Aphrodite, her naughty parts tinted dark rose.

"Ashley let Jake talk her into this?"

"Better than that. She went with him to drop it off. The guy tacks on a bonus if the lady and her husband join him for a drink."

I pictured Brian's best friend's wife, with her spiky blonde hair and lip ring, swishing up the stairs of a mansion in a black party dress and heels. That wasn't so hard to believe. "What was the rich guy like? I bet he was a creep."

"Jake said he was the perfect gentleman. Fortyish. Friendly. He served them a glass of champagne and hors d'oeuvres made by his personal chef. They chatted a bit, then left with an envelope of cash. Easiest money they ever made."

"I don't think I could meet him." So why did I see myself walking up those same mansion steps, Brian at my side, video in hand? I wasn't as wild as Ashley. I'd have on something prim: a lace blouse, a velvet choker with a cameo, a long skirt. I'd wear my hair up and keep my eyes down, blushing under his billion-dollar gaze. The perfect lady. That rich guy would get a boner the size of Florida just looking at me.

"Jake said the guy only did one thing that crossed the line. When they were leaving he took Ashley's right hand and kissed it like he was a baron or something."

"What's wrong with kissing her hand?" I had a weakness for old-fashioned manners.

"Well, it's the hand she uses to masturbate, of course. Like you're doing right now."

Without my realizing it, my hand had wandered back down between my legs. I jerked it away.

Brian laughed. Holding the camera steady, he reached up and guided my fingers back to my pussy. "Don't be bashful, honey. He wants to watch you do it. So do I."

And the truth was, I wanted them to see, the two pairs of eyes floating before me, Brian's the greenish-gray of a northern sea, the rich guy's golden and glittering.

"Where does he watch it? In his home theater?" Under the veil of my lashes I studied the screen. My labia jiggled lewdly as my finger strummed on. That's what the rich guy would see as he sat on his leather couch in his silk dressing gown. A wine-colored gown, the same color as his swollen dick. He'd pull it out and stroke it as he watched.

"A home theater, yes," Brian said softly. "State of the art."

"Why are you doing this? Don't you care if your wife shows her cunt to some horny billionaire?" The words came in gasps.

"The joke's on him. We'll take his money and get a suite in the fanciest hotel in town and fuck all night." Brian sounded winded, too, as if he'd just finished a run. Then I realized he was jerking off.

"I'm not a whore." I was half-sobbing, from shame and pleasure.

"Of course you're not, honey. You're a nice, pretty married lady. That's what he wants. Someone he'd glimpse at the gourmet grocery store or the espresso bar, buying a nonfat decaf cappuccino. I see guys staring at you. If only they knew the truth about my sweet-faced angel. If only they knew you want it so bad you shave your pussy and let men take pictures of it."

Sounds were coming out of my throat, sounds I'd never made before, high-pitched whines and animal moans.

"You're the hottest thing he's ever seen, but no matter how much he pays he can never have the real you."

"Oh, god, I'm gonna come," I whimpered.

A hand closed around my wrist and wrenched it away.

"He'll pay an extra thousand if you come while we fuck."

"Did – Ashley do it?" I panted. I knew what the answer would be.

"Jake said she had the best orgasm of her life."

Brian hurriedly fixed the camera to the tripod, adjusted the height, then lifted me to my feet and took my place on the chair.

"Face the camera," he said.

My knees were as soft as melted caramel, but by gripping the arms of the chair I managed to position myself properly. On the screen Brian's penis reared up, my smooth snatch hovering above.

"Sit on it."

I lowered myself onto him with a sigh. Then I was up again, a woman who couldn't make up her mind. Up or down? It was there in full color: Brian's rod plunging in and out, his balls dangling beneath like a small pink pillow. "Now turn around and ride me."

In a daze I straddled him, my knees digging into the cushion. Just last week, we'd done it this way on the sofa. We pretended it was prom night and we were sneaking a midnight quickie while my parents snored in the bedroom upstairs.

"Do you like to fuck with a shaved twat?"

"Yes," I confessed. "I like to rub my bare lips on you." Which was exactly what I was doing, lingering on the downstroke to grind my exposed clit against the rough hairs at the base of his cock.

"You're so wet. That rich guy can hear it. Your hungry lips gobbling up my cock."

Brian began to twist my nipples between his fingers.

"It's an extra five hundred if you show him your asshole."

I grunted assent and bucked harder. In that position, the rich guy could see it anyway.

Then he whispered in my ear, "And another five hundred if you let me touch it."

I froze mid-thrust. "Please, Brian, don't," I whispered back. I didn't want the rich guy to hear. We'd recently discovered that when Brian diddles my butt crack when we fuck, it feels like a second clit. I loved it, but I was embarrassed and wanted it to be our secret. Brian knew he could make me blush just talking about it.

"Why not, baby? Because he'll know you're a bad girl who comes when I play with your pretty ass?"

"Please," I begged. My asshole, however, seemed to have other ideas, the brazen little show-off, pushing itself out, all plumped and ticklish.

"Please what, Kira? I know you want it, but I won't touch it until you say yes."

"Please," I gasped. "Yes."

"That's a good girl. Nice and polite."

Good girl, bad girl, I wasn't sure what I was, but it didn't matter. My torso rippled like a column of heat between his hands, one tweaking my nipple, the other going to town on my quivering bottom. Our bodies made rude noises, swampy, squishy sounds — or was it the rich guy whacking off? He probably used a special custom-made lotion to make his dick all slippery. He'd be close to the end now, pumping his fist faster and faster, his single nether eye weeping a tear of delight. He'd gotten everything he wanted. The cool lady in the gourmet grocery store was unzipped and undone, a bitch in heat, writhing shamelessly on her husband's cock for his viewing pleasure.

But I had one little surprise left for him.

"What if you spank it? Is that another thousand?"

"Two thousand." I could tell Brian was close, too.

"I want him to see it. Spank my naughty asshole," I yelled, so the rich guy could hear.

The first slap sent a jolt straight through me that quickly dissolved into pleasure, foamy fingers of a wave creeping into the hollows of my body.

"Again."

Smack.

Each blow hammered me deeper onto Brian's cock. I pushed my ass out to take the next one, to show that rich guy I could do it. He was so turned on, I could feel his eyes burning into my back through the screen. But it wasn't just him. There were others watching – my parents, my tenth-grade science teacher, the postal clerk who sneaks glances at my tits, a Supreme Court Justice or two – dozens of them, their faces twisted into masks of shock and fascination. And beneath, in the shadows, hands were stroking hard-ons or shoved into panties, damp and fragrant with arousal. They liked it, all of them, and I was watching them as they watched me in an endless circle of revelation and desire.

"I'm . . . gonna . . . come."

"Come for him. Now!" Brian bellowed. The last slaps fell like firecrackers snapping, and I jerked my hips to their rhythm as my climax tore through my belly. With the chair springs squeaking like crazy and Brian grunting, *fuck your shaved pussy, fuck it*, that rich guy got himself quite a show.

I'd say it was worth every penny.

Afterward, I pulled Brian down to the carpet with me. Our profiles filled the screen. He'd seen me and I'd seen him and we fit so well together and I loved him more than anything. I told him that. Or maybe I just kissed him, a deep soul kiss that lasted a long, long time.

The rich guy got that part for free.

Death Poems

Mark Ramsden

"Japanese monks compose a poem on the day of their deaths," said Madame Petra. "Words they want to be remembered by."

Madame Petra. The big blonde. The vast blue eyes. The soppy red heart. We were at her place, a pleasant space tucked in, up?, the East End of London. It's more or less where the prostate gland is in a gentleman's anus, if we are using the London Underground district line analogy. As I believe we should. Lube in at Liverpool Street, ease gently, very gently, up the Hackney Road, and find pleasure gland in Bethnal Green, Tower Hamlets. Which may not be green or a hamlet any more but is adequately supplied with tower blocks.

"That makes the City of London, the financial district, the World's Anus?" she said.

"Am I mistaken?"

"Not necessarily."

It was full moon in Taurus. Late Autumn with a cruel wind rustling the leaves. We were sprawled inside on the chocolate leather sofa, Petra's ample warmth wrapped in her courtesan's kimono.

Small red paper lanterns cast a glow. She riffled the pages of her blue sky book.

" 'Autumn driftwood. My day here is done.' "

It would be good to accept death as easily as the poet did.

When I remembered to take vitamin B with ketamine I sometimes experienced blissful near-death experiences. As opposed to the often harrowing K-trips produced by coffee, stress, running around town without adequate fuel or water. The best method of release seems to be drifting gently downstream on a straw mat, head dipping backwards into the warm water. Although it might not be awkward for scribbling down any last minute pearls of wisdom, of course.

"I was thinking of what people say at the moment of orgasm, the little death," I said. "Maybe there should be a little book of those."

"Doesn't matter as long as you say the right name, really."

Yes.

Saying the wrong one in a moment of ecstatic transcendence can be tricky. It can change your whole life.

For ever.

It may alter your profile, blacken an eye or two. But don't take any advice from me. I just spent a weekend trying to get up a lovely post-op transsexual's derrière when the only thing post-op transsexuals want – reasonably enough – is to be treated like a lady. And this wish should certainly be granted after the lengthy ordeal they have been through on their long, difficult journey. We did satisfy each other eventually but it's sometimes embarrassing how much of an obsession anal sex can become. It's hardly the Holy Grail, that renowned vaginal cup. It's closer to a dance with My Lord Lucifer – not that you need adolescent bogey men when you have reached a state of mellow grace in your forties.

Madame Petra liked to be listened to. Shame we are a couple who both like to talk too much. Although we are now learning to pause, in the twilight of our youth. We are both still pretending middle age isn't happening – despite my glasses and her various ailments. We still stay up all weekend every now and again. Which is easier now the chemistry students have shared their homework with the DJs and the club owners.

I always thought the best times were private parties, most especially ones where there were only two guests. Where pleasure eventually mellows into an absence of strife. Chasing evermore frenetic highs can be a good way of checking out for good. I had so many near-death experiences with Ketamine that eternity will come as no surprise to me. Not after all those chats with St Peter, work experience as an angel and experiencing the interdependency of all matter and energy beyond life and death. You used to have to meditate to get to those places. Fifty years in a Zen monastery. Now it costs about ten quid and a train to Peckham.

"Some of these sound like you," she said, flicking through the book of Death Poems. 'Fifty years. More than enough for me!' "

"I suppose if you just spent fifty years on a mountain top eating cold white rice that's probably an adequate sufficiency."

I was hoping she wouldn't put another Rock Hudson – Doris Day movie on; she was hoping for some protestation of eternal love. Maybe that's why there was extra warmth in the pussycat smile. There was a time when we could make each other literally groan and moan with gratitude. "Thank you! Thank you! Thank you!" we said, where other people would say "Oh God! Oh God! Oh God!" Not much of a poem. But heartfelt. However.

What goes up must come down. And the many extremely bitter "this time it's final" tussles sometimes lasted for months at a time. E-mails that would sizzle Charles Manson's hair off. Vitriolic phone calls. Letters written in bile, baked in blood, then soaked in cat piss. It wasn't nice. Not nice at all.

Time eventually heals and there came a day when they started to tentatively take steps to start again. Four or five slumber sprawls into the peace process we were on the queen-size chocolate leather sofa, small black cups of aromatic green tea at hand. Various other aromatic herbs were being ingested as we discussed recent club depravity.

"I saw a Domme make her sub beg for release while being stuffed over a trestle in a club," I said.

"Did he ask nicely?"

"It was a woman. All that 'Please may I come, Mistress'. It was really horny. It was Mistress Mayhem. And Mitzi. And the biggest strap-on I have ever seen."

In cold, damp weather I can still feel her strap-on – a

multicoloured totem pole we named after an Amazonian lesbian tennis player. This particular item was not penis-shaped – therefore the weapon of choice for those who did not wish to be associated with men in any way whatsoever. She was the second women I had seen who put a smaller strap on and said, "I wish it was bigger." Tell me about it.

So we got the top of the range, if a thing's worth doing, it's worth overdoing. Back then our rule was no penetration by penis, to honour my primary partner, my dear beloved ex-wife. Perhaps it's why our energy kept building. It's harder to come, sex lasts much longer, you are forced to be more inventive.

Actually all we ever needed was the scent of her breath or body, some lewd game that fired us up and small amounts of herbal inhibition-suppressants. That and not being chained together by marriage. ("They met, they fell in love and then tragedy struck . . . they got married . . .")

Our preliminary fumble was certainly working right now.

"Look at *you!*" she said, speaking as if to compliment a child or a pet. Even feminists eventually discovered you get more out of a man with a compliment. Jolly good! And it only took them about twenty years . . .

"It's not Viagra, is it?"

"Your blue eyes are the only blue pills I need."

She smiled. "You're a poet."

Certainly poor enough to be one. That's why you have to be charming to get past women's insatiable desire for money. And their immediate perception that you don't have any.

"I don't need V when I'm not on MDMA. Or dead drunk," I said, unwisely. It was true, but reminded her that all men care about is their dicks and not their partner's emotional and physical well-being. Not to mention whatever that oxytocin nonsense is again, that hormone produced by – what's the word we often forget when wrapped up in this stuff? Love! Of course. How silly of me . . . A type of love that is easy to reference because it isn't a sentence of death – thirty years of shared family, money, health and property worries. Married love? Don't make me laugh . . .

Marriage becomes a prison pretty quickly. But at least it's an open jail. As for the transfer to death row that the divorced suffer, the solitary confinement where penniless bachelors wait to die alone . . . the place where I live. Maybe that open jail wasn't too bad after all. If only men didn't keep searching while women kept on nesting. If I ever meet Mother Nature I'm going to . . . what can you do? She always wins . . .

There may be short poems about divorce but I would rather write or read about actual death than spend any more time mired in bitterness, revenge and greed. Except to say: eroticism is a pitiless mistress. She doesn't like mortgage and marriage. She likes mad dashes across town in the middle of the night and secret e-mails and guilt and terror and beauty and the inevitability of divorce. Even if you can see it coming three years ahead, as I could, there was still no stopping it.

And then the questionable stream of silly (male) sluts I resorted to when Venus slammed the door shut, the transgender caravanserai: beautiful creatures, exotic blooms. Extremely exhilarating. For a while . . . until all that chitter chatter and tranny prattle starts to pall. Like those snake oil books: "How to keep your marriage hot." "Making Love to the same person forever." They might sell. Diet books *sell*. Doesn't make them *true*.

Maybe I have been drawn to mysticism recently because that is all there is left. Space, silence, asceticism.

The Zen of
no
thing.
Sweet Fuck All is all I have left.

In these circumstances it's a miracle I can persuade anyone to perform any sort of lewd, libidinous service. She backs her soft, insistent undercarriage into me.

Thank you, Lord. Such abundance. Rolling rump. Humping haunches. It's always good to slip a thumb in her as she backs towards me, hear her sigh as she bends forward to enable a gentle stir of the honey pot. Once she had that clit bar put in there's no real excuse any more for not giving her a proper tweak or twiddle. You can't plead ignorance of where it is any more . . . certainly not when most people are shaved these days. The clean pucker of her anus winks seductively. Demanding to be kissed and teased gently open with the tip of the tongue.

Madame Petra certainly has one of the plumpest and juiciest rumps, firm yet tender, a big heart-sized bum that wobbles when spanked, sizzles up nicely when flogged and spreads willingly when stroked.

Her pelvis rotates as slowly and pleasingly as a bossa nova, the circular motion that makes the world go round, the dance that fires up the men and fills up the women.

It would be tempting to heat her up with a subtle prod or even a cheeky little tweak but we seem to have tired of sub/dom and the often tiresome power games that might have been hot but seemed to have dreadful consequences. We eventually discovered that playing with the dark forces of violence and cruelty was dangerous. Who'd have thought it? say the general public, shaking their heads at the idiocy of it all. Well, yes, perhaps we should have caught on to that one a little quicker. So now it's a matter of forging an equal exchange. Match up the yin and yang. Let the water find its own level. Having said that . . . as she's doing some sort of backwards lap-dance right in front of me, taunting me with those gorgeous honey cushions, I might as well plant one upward SMACK on the lower curves and watch her flesh wobble up and then down.

Ride the ripple. Watch the wave. She gasps and sighs. So, while we're here, we might as well have a few more of those liveners. Just to drop some spice into the pot. And maybe her scent is a little stronger now.

She peels her flimsiest knickers down and waggles her bottom cheeks at me with a lascivious smile. Lawdy. Miss. Clawdy. Great Globes of Fire. Big heart. Big butt. Something splendid to grab hold of. And knead and stroke and kiss and . . . Stop slobbering, boy, slow down. Most of it's pheromones and scent, of course. The merest hint of gaminess does help. While it's nice that scene players' asses tend to smell more like Body Shop gift packs these days, there should be a touch of truffle in the mix or there is no reason to get excited about these dark delights. It's time to poke the tip of my tongue through the puckered ring, a moment to hear a long slow grateful moan and breath exhalation.

Back then.

"Oooh! You are spoiling us, Ambassador," she said.

It's the kitschiest ad ever, supposedly upmarket chocolates on a silver salver at the ambassador's reception and the grateful guests greasing up the host. But I know where I would rather be. Between four walls with Madame Petra. Needless to say she would prefer to doing this in a fetish club. To show off. To be validated. I'd rather snuggle up in a burrow somewhere but then why should we agree? We're a *couple*. Sometimes. These times.

One or two gentle slaps towards the base of the buttocks send soft ripples upwards, warms her a little, says hello and remember the zillion times we did that? Breaking through many pain/pleasure barriers, untying a few psychic knots left-over from various traumas. Converting past pain to present pleasure.

"No, let's do it face to face," she said, as I'm starting to manoeuvre her somewhere I could ease in. "Let's stare in each other's eyes."

And be smothered by your desire for a long future together? Can't do it. But you can't say that out loud. Not and keep your teeth. How do I get out of this?

"I don't want a relationship any more," she says, spotting me looking like a frightened rabbit. Being drilled by the headlights of decades more responsibility, not the first thing you are looking for after an acrimonious divorce. "I *told* you that."

So she did. But the cold wind still howls. And she's still Miss Bossyboots. Paid to be bossy during the day and always glad to take her work home with her.

I'm still in thrall, despite it all. Still in harness.

It's time.

Rather than mess everything up like young people would, we

follow our ritual. Moisten the earth before you plant. Follow the anal sex code: glove, lube, fingertip, finger. Although we don't need rubber gloves, being among friends. Flawlessly filed fingernails goes without saying . . .

Maybe I would have got thrown out for some other reason. Marriage is just a business to women. They have to be more hard-hearted than men about it. And when they've extracted the breeding sperm it's time to downsize. Sorry. We don't really need an armchair occupier and remote control operative, thank you very much. The children might find you entertaining. They might *love* you. But I want *money*.

Write out one million times. Don't marry for love. At least mistresses don't want your money, should you have any, or your sperm for breeding. They don't want you to meet their parents. They just want warmth. Heat. A bit of a break from the bleak midwinter of most people's lives.

So let's get back in the warmth. In the flat with the chocolate brown sofa. Back to where membranes sing and deep grunts signal rich, yeasty pleasures. Our heart's desire. Rude health. Ruddy ruttings.

Some may have heard enough of men burying their faces deep into the widening cheeks and licking feverishly while gently rubbing the clit bar with the tips of their fingers and rootling deep inside the vagina with a busy thumb while snuffling in the scent of life and death. But there's plenty of soap operas on the telly. I'd rather do this.

And what's THIS? An actual erection has appeared, a minor miracle in the Chinese year of crystal MDMA and K-addled hog . . . We have lift off. Queue here to enter the tunnel of death.

Feverish fingers fiddle with the condom, unscrew the Prince Albert ring that is really best left out of this delicate nudging, easing, teasing . . . and . . .

"More lube!" she said, yelping a little, also sending out little thought darts intended to lodge deep inside my aura, their sharp steel tips sending out a little starburst of pain which would remind me – forever, hopefully – that the anus has no natural lubrication.

Let there be lube. This be the law. Pour on the oil. Water the earth. Then plant carefully. And slowly.

In.

Again.

"Aaaah!"

This time a soft long sigh of pleasure. It has been said that women can lie about vaginal intercourse. They can fake orgasms, fake every single thing about it. But there is less room for the thespian's art where the ass is concerned. And no more space for words any more as we head for space. Orbiting Saturn. Dark side of the moon.

Stirring the brew brings us close to fruition. After which there will be a final abandoned sprawl waiting for a brief smudge of sleep. Hugged by a golden ring.

Some call it a starfish. Perhaps it's a pink snowflake. Which will one day dissolve in crisp, cleansing air. As we all will. Becoming a different energy. Matter in motion.

Someone, something, somewhere else. Wafted along by the wind and the waves.

For ever.

In the Stacks

Kristina Wright

He came in one evening shortly before the library closed, looking for information on nautical knots. I pushed my glasses up on my nose and searched the data base. Four titles, all about knots. He smiled, this quirky little smile that hinted at some secret I couldn't begin to fathom, thanked me and left with three of the books. The fourth didn't have enough pictures, he said. He liked pictures.

I forgot about him. You tend to forget the ones that only come in occasionally, that ask one question and never come back. But he came back. I don't remember how long it was. A month, maybe two? But he came back and something about that little smile reminded me of the knots.

He wasn't handsome in the classical sense. He was average looks, average height. The kind of guy who could be really cute if you liked him or nondescript if you'd only met him once or twice. But the smile, that made him stand out. It would be awhile before I'd notice that his eyes held the same secretive amusement as his smile.

The next time he came to the reference desk he asked about the Marquis de Sade. Not his fiction, a biography. Not a usual request for a small town library in the heart of Virginia. I checked the database. Just two biographies on the Marquis. He took them both. I felt a little strange leading him back toward the biography section, deep in the shadows of the nonfiction stacks. Maybe it was the smile.

I pulled the books and handed them to him.

"Ever read him?" he asked, tapping the cover of the top book. I could feel myself blush as I shook my head. "Uh, no."

That smile again. Amused, knowing. "But you know who he is."

Not a question, but I nodded. Then I hurried out of the stacks and back to the refuge of my desk with a muttered, "I have patrons waiting." I didn't and he knew it. I think I heard him laugh.

After he left, I looked him up. It's against the rules, but I needed to know. His name was Justin Brant and he was forty-one years old. I knew the neighborhood he lived in, it wasn't far from my own townhouse. I also knew the types of books he liked – historical biographies of questionable characters and action-adventure. Harmless enough. Yet something about him stayed with me long after he left.

I'm embarrassed to say I checked the status on the de Sade biographies for the next couple of weeks. He renewed them both once. I found that interesting. Either he didn't have time to read them or he was being very thorough in his research.

He came in one night just before closing. I didn't see him at first; I was reading over some paperwork when I felt his gaze like a weight on my shoulders. I glanced up to see him staring intently at me.

"May I help you?" I asked, sounding colder than I felt. My palms were already beginning to sweat and he hadn't said anything to me.

He smirked. "No, I found what I was looking for this time." He gestured at the stack of books in his hand. The title of the top one mentioned nude photography.

"Oh."

The smirk deepened. "I was wondering if you'd like to have coffee sometime, maybe one night after work?"

"I don't think so," I said quickly, glancing around to see if anyone had heard him. "I mean – thank you, but I don't think we really have much in common."

The smirk never faltered. "No? What a pity. I thought I turned you on."

He was gone before I could pick my jaw off the floor.

I was curious, I admit it. So when I pulled out of the parking lot half an hour later, I turned left instead of turning right. I drove the five miles to the street where he lived. I turned on the street in a very nice subdivision and I drove along the main road that circled the hundred or so houses. I found his house, tucked in a cul-de-sac. I was so intent on making sure I had the right house number, I didn't realize someone was getting out of the Mercedes in the driveway. It was him!

I sped away, heart hammering in my chest. He couldn't have seen me, he wasn't looking in my direction. Still, I could feel my cheeks flush hotly as I drove the few miles to my house. Whatever his charm, I wouldn't do that again.

I almost dreaded seeing him at the library again. Almost. Here I was, thirty-seven and hopelessly single, mooning over some pervert who used the library as his dirty bookstore.

Still, there was something about him that suggested he'd be able to tell me all the secrets I'd been wanting to know. Questions I wasn't even sure how to ask. Maybe he was a pervert, but if he was, so was I. Because he had my mind going down a road it had never been, and my willing cunt followed.

By the time I saw him again, I was debating calling him. It would have been highly inappropriate and I could have lost my job for it, but desperate times call for desperate measures, to my way of thinking. Who am I kidding? I wasn't thinking, I was only feeling. And it felt good.

Strangely enough, it wasn't the library where I saw him next, but the grocery store. I was standing at the bakery counter, choosing a loaf of bread, when I heard a familiar laugh. I jerked my head around just in time to catch his smile as he turned and walked away. My cheeks flushed hotly, but instead of ignoring him, I followed him, bread forgotten.

"Wait. Hey! Mr Brant, Justin – wait."

He turned and looked at me. We were standing alone in the wine aisle. It was after ten o'clock and there were few people in the store.

"Yes?"

I stopped in front of him, suddenly speechless. "I was just – I mean—"

He arched an eyebrow. "How did you know my name?"

My face felt like it was on fire. I couldn't think of a good lie quick enough. "I looked you up," I blurted.

"I like that."

That made me feel warm for an entirely different reason. "Can we go some place?" I asked, emboldened. "To talk?"

"Talk?"

I felt like he was teasing me. "Yes, talk," I said, suddenly angry. Not at him, at myself for being so foolish. "Never mind, forget I asked."

He grabbed my wrist with a gentle, but insistent pressure that was impossible to ignore. "I don't forget anything," he said. "Ask me again."

Part of me screamed to get out of there and away from him. Part of me never wanted him to let go of my wrist. "Would you like to go somewhere and talk?" My voice was soft, I could barely hear myself, but he didn't seem to have a problem.

"Good. You're learning."

There was a condescension in his voice I wouldn't have tolerated from anyone else. So why was I taking it from him? Something about his confidence, maybe. Or maybe I was just ready for someone like him. In any case, his approval sent a little thrill through me that I hadn't experienced in a long, long time.

We each paid for our groceries, waiting in line silently. Then he told me to follow him. I liked that better than going with him. I was curious, but I wasn't stupid.

He drove to a coffee shop about a mile from the library. I'd passed the place a thousand times, but I'd never been there. I parked next to him and followed him inside.

The waitress nodded to him as if he was a regular. We sat in a booth near the back, the only other patron an elderly man sitting at the counter. Justin sat across from me, studying me with dark, unblinking eyes.

"What?" I said, fidgeting nervously.

"Sit still."

Like an obedient dog, I immediately quieted. Then I frowned.

"What's the matter?" he asked.

I shook my head. "I don't know."

"Yes, you do. Tell me."

I started to say I really didn't know, but I could feel my frown deepening. "I don't like you."

He chuckled and it was a soft, seductive sound that washed over my skin like a touch. "No. What you don't like is how you respond to me."

I opened my mouth to deny it and he held his hand up.

"Don't. Don't lie to me and don't lie to yourself. You respond to me and it confuses you."

I thought about that for a moment. "Yes," I said, though it hadn't been a question.

The waitress came over and took our order – a black coffee for him and a hot chocolate for me. When she was gone, he stared at me once more.

"Why do you think that is?" he asked.

I'd lost track of our conversation for a moment, so caught up in his steady gaze. "What?"

His lips thinned to a straight line. "Pay attention. Why do you think it bothers you to respond to me?"

I didn't like the conversation, but I knew if I continued to argue with him, he would leave. I wasn't sure how I knew it, but I did. I thought hard for a moment, trying to put my feelings into words. "Because I'm used to being in control."

"And I make you feel out of control?"

I played with the salt and pepper shakers. "You make me question myself."

"Interesting."

I felt like a science project. I also felt a need to clarify myself. "It's mostly curiosity," I said, sounding defensive even to my own ears. "It's not like this is going anywhere."

Again, that soft, sexy laugh. "Oh, really? Is that what you think?"

I didn't get a chance to respond because the waitress brought our drinks. I waited until she'd gone off behind the counter once more before saying anything.

"I think I'm going to be very careful around you."

He nodded. "Smart girl."

We talked then, about inconsequential things. My job as a librarian, his as a college professor. I wasn't surprised he taught college. He had the air of a man comfortable in academia, in instruction. I wondered, almost jealousy, if any of his female students had experienced his disciplining side. Somehow, I didn't doubt it.

An hour slipped by and my cocoa grew cold. He pulled a few bills from his wallet and tossed them on the table. I felt an irrational disappointment to know our time together was over.

"Don't frown," he said.

"I didn't know I was."

He reached across the scarred table and circled my wrist with his fingers. I could feel my pulse jump and I knew he could, too.

"You're upset it's time to go."

I swallowed hard, but I nodded.

"So, don't leave me just yet. Come to my house."

I gently tugged my wrist free of his grasp. "I can't go with you. I don't even know you."

He studied me carefully, as if memorizing me. "You know me. And you're afraid of what I know about you."

Almost against my will, I asked, "What do you know about me?"

His fingers took my wrist once more. "I know you're nervous, a little afraid." His grip tightened. "I also know if I asked you to go to the restroom and remove your panties, they would be soaking wet."

I gasped, but I didn't attempt to pull away. Nor did I deny his statement. How could I? I'd been wet since I'd spotted him in the grocery store.

He smiled. "Good. I didn't want another argument." He rubbed his thumb over the pulse in my wrist. "Now, do you want to come with me?"

I didn't miss the double entendre. "I don't know."

"Honest enough. Would it make you feel more comfortable to go to your place?"

I thought for a moment before I shook my head. "I don't think so."

A frown line creased his brow. The pressure on my wrist grew tighter. "Then what?" Then, a smile. "Oh, I think I know."

Again, my pulse began to race. "What?"

"Do you have a key to the library?"

"Oh, God."

More pressure. "Answer me, please."

I nodded.

"And there's a security system, I'm sure. You know the code?"

"Yes," I whispered hoarsely.

My mind racing as quickly as my pulse. Could I get away with it? Yes, probably. The library was tucked away off the main street through town, no one would be likely to notice if we slipped in through the back door and didn't turn on the lights. But just because I could get away with it didn't make it a good idea.

"Don't think about it. Just feel. React. Respond. The only consequences are the ones you make for yourself."

I didn't believe him for a minute, but I knew I was in too deep to say no. Even the threat of losing my job wasn't enough to keep me from sliding out of the booth and walking toward the door. I was going to do it. Not because he told me to, but because I wanted it.

The library was dark and silent, the parking lot empty just as I knew it would be. He'd followed in his car and parked beside me in the employee parking area. I lead the way to the employee entrance, keys jingling in my trembling fingers. At the door, he put his hand over mine as I went to insert the key in the lock.

"This is it. If you don't want to do this, say so now and it's over." He caressed my hand with the most delicate of touches. "But if we go inside, be prepared to give up your control."

I'd already worked it out in my mind, but when he put it that way, I hesitated.

He smiled, and it was a wicked smile. "But if we do go inside, I promise you won't regret it."

I turned the key and entered the security code. My hands were hardly trembling by the time I lead him into my office behind the circulation desk. Now that I'd committed to this, I was feeling calmer.

He sat in the comfy chair in the corner, leaving me standing in the middle of the room between my desk and the door. He looked around, studying the pictures of Paris and Milan hanging over my desk. My office window looked out onto a pretty garden area with reading benches. At this hour, all I could see were the lights from the parking lot.

"Close the blinds," he said.

I didn't argue or question. The last thing I needed was a nosy teenager, or worse, a cop, driving by and peeking in the window. While I wasn't quite sure what was going to happen, I was pretty sure I didn't want anyone watching.

When the blinds were closed, he nodded. "Good. Now turn the desk lamp on."

The lamp he was referring to was more decorative than functional. I quickly obeyed and the parchment lamp shade cast an intimate golden glow across my office.

"Now, strip."

Whatever I'd expected, it hadn't been that.

I fumbled with the buttons on my blouse. There was still some rational part of my brain that couldn't believe I was undressing in front of a stranger. In my office, no less.

The blouse fell away, leaving me in my bra and conservative skirt. I paused, waiting for him to say more, but he didn't. He only stared.

I reached behind me and unzipped my skirt. The motion forced my breasts up and out, and I watched his eyes drift to my chest. My nipples responded to his gaze as if he touched me. I felt them tighten, pushing out the material of my bra.

The skirt pooled at my feet. I reached for the clasp of my bra, afraid that if I hesitated, I wouldn't be able to do it.

Justin watched as I removed the bra. He watched as I slipped out of my shoes. My legs were bare, the summer weather and a good tan making stockings unnecessary. My panties glided down my thighs and then I stood before him naked.

"Very nice," he said. His voice was cool and distant, as if he was admiring a piece of artwork. "How do you feel?"

"Vulnerable," I whispered.

"And?"

"Excited." The confession came at a price. I could feel myself blushing and knew he could see it on my neck and breasts.

"Good. That's how you should feel."

A long moment went by as he stared at my and I resisted the urge to fidget. Finally, when I couldn't take his silence any longer, I said, "Now what?"

"Impatient?"

I nodded, though I wasn't sure what he was asking for.

"Do you like pain?"

The question took me by surprise and I blurted, "No!"

He tsked. "Get dressed."

"What? Why? What did I do?"

Justin stood quickly and I took a step back. "You misled me. I thought you shared my interests."

"I don't know—"

He closed the distance between them in two long strides. My back was up against the wall, the soft brush of his shirt against my bare breasts. My breathing was ragged and harsh. I realized I sounded like a woman in arousal, not someone who was afraid.

"You know exactly what I'm talking about. I'm interested in exploring pain. Namely, yours." He took my nipples between his fingers. "If you want me to stop, simply pull away."

I couldn't have moved if the security alarm had gone off.

"If you want me to continue, ask me to hurt you."

His words were soft and surprisingly arousing. I lowered my head, ashamed and embarrassed by my feelings, my gaze falling to my nipples imprisoned in his fingers. The sight of my pink nipples against his tanned fingers brought a soft moan to my lips.

"Well?"

"Please."

"Please what?" His fingers just barely held my nipples. "Don't play games with me, little one. You won't win."

I raised my head until I met his gaze. "Please hurt me, Justin."

Almost immediately, he began to twist my nipples. If I had thought about it, I might have said the pain began even before I asked for it, as if he knew I would ask. The pain intensified, a warmth flowing from the tips of my breasts across my chest, radiating a steady, constant pressure that became more and more intense.

I wanted to squirm, to cry out, but something in his expression made me stay still and quiet, my back pressed to the hard wall while he tortured my tender breasts. He gave my nipples a particularly vicious twist and I bit my lip until I tasted blood. It hurt, no doubt about it, but there was also a heaviness in my cunt, a corresponding tingle in my clit with every painful twist of my nipples.

"You please me," he whispered. He leaned close and gave me a chaste kiss on the lips that seemed incongruous with the rest of the situation. "Your threshold for pain is going to be a delightful challenge."

I wasn't sure I liked the sound of that, yet I felt myself smiling in spite of the pain. "Thank you."

He tugged my nipples out from my breasts, stretching the already pained skin, then released them. The ache began as the blood flowed back into them and I moaned softly.

"Nice."

Before I could respond, his hand was between my thighs, squeezing my cunt. The sensation was pleasurable at first and I pressed against his palm. Then he exerted the same pressure on my pussy that he had on my nipples and I gasped.

"Pain with pleasure," he murmured. "There's nothing like it."

I wanted to ask him how he knew, if he'd ever felt pain during sexual arousal or if he only liked to inflict it. The words died in my throat as his fingers found my clit. With a quick, steady motion he kneaded my swollen flesh roughly. So rough, in fact, my body couldn't decide whether it felt good or hurt. My hips moved of their own accord, alternately thrusting against his wrist and pulling back as far as the wall would allow.

"Don't think about it," he said. "Let your body decide what it likes."

I closed my eyes and rested my head against the wall. My body was aching for release, that much I knew. Justin seemed to realize that, because each time my body would tense for orgasm, he would pinch my clit that much harder.

"Please," I begged, though I could barely speak loud enough to hear myself. "I can't take any more."

He chuckled softly and rolled my swollen clit. "You'll be surprised how much you can take."

I shook my head, denying him – or denying myself? I couldn't be sure.

"You're going to come on my hand," he said, matter-of-factly. "You're going to come and it's going to be stronger and harder than anything you've ever experienced."

I kept shaking my head.

"Yes, you are. And it's going to hurt, which is going to confuse you more." He pushed a finger in my drenched cunt, then slid another one in for good measure. "But you're going to love it and you won't want it to stop."

He was finger-fucking me now, hard. Hard enough to lift me up on my toes with each thrust of his hand. I whimpered and moaned, clutching at his shoulders with my hands, but not pushing him away.

"That's it," he coaxed. "Feel it, feel everything. Come on my hand. Let your body have what it needs."

I was moaning now, almost screaming with the intensity of the sensations he was causing. I could feel his cock, hard and insistent, pressing against my hip bone as he angled his fingers higher into my cunt. He wanted me. He was giving me pleasure and hurting me at the same time and he wanted to fuck me. The fact that he wasn't as distant as he sounded made me relax.

"Come," he said. And though his voice was as harsh and cold as his fingers in my cunt, I knew he was enjoying me.

With his fingers driving into my cunt and my clit rubbing against his wrist, I came. I clung to him, whimpering and sobbing as I rode a powerful orgasm, his demanding cock bruising my hip, wanting me.

"Yes," he hissed, close to my ear. "It's what you need. Show me what you need."

I sagged against him, no longer caring I was naked and vulnerable in my own office. All that mattered was the orgasm, the release. What he had given me, what he had taken from me. They were one and the same. I came and whimpered and said his name like a prayer.

He lowered me to my knees, his hand cradling my head against his erection. The fabric of his pants was soft against my cheek and I nuzzled him, weak and satisfied and still craving more.

He pressed my head against his cock, hard, then harder still, until I thought he might leave a mark on my skin from the zipper. I let him rub his crotch against my face, wanting only to please him.

He gave my hair a tug, forcing me to look up at him. "What do you say?"

My brain felt fuzzy, my speech slow and thick when it finally came. But I knew what he wanted. I knew it instinctively. "Thank you."

"Your pain arouses me," he said, holding me against his cock as proof. "That's the first lesson."

"Will there be more lessons?" I dared to ask, looking up at him. My heart was throbbing in my chest, afraid he was going to leave me now that he'd proven he could have me.

He smiled. It wasn't a pleasant smile. "We've only just begun."

I Want to Watch you Do It

Mike Kimera

"I want to watch you do it."

We've been kissing; really kissing. My eyes are still closed
and my mouth is wide open when Karen pulls away to make her
bizarre statement.

"Do what?" I say, trying unsuccessfully to pull her back into
my arms.

"I want to watch you masturbate."

"What? No. I mean, why?"

"You need a reason? I thought you did it several times a day."
Karen places her hands on her hips and holds her head to one
side in that way she does when she wants me to know that I'm
being difficult.

"I do not. Well, not several times. Once or twice maybe.
When I'm by myself."

Karen looks unconvinced.

"What do you think about when you do it?" she asks.

"I don't know. Coming, mostly." I'm feeling foolish and
confused now.

"I think about being fucked," she says, "with my hands tied
above my head in the centre of a Moorish harem." She holds
her hands up and sways slightly at the hips. "With the Sultan
taking his pleasure while his other wives stroke themselves from
sheer excitement."

I try to grab her hips but she twists away, falling back on to
the sofa, legs spread wide.

"Or I imagine I'm on stage," she says, "men and women

lining up to lick me to orgasm. It's a charity Lickathon, televised around the world."

Her hips thrust forward and her head rolls from side to side on the cushion. I stand between her legs and she sits up. This girl has very strong stomach muscles. Her face is just in front of my fly and I want desperately to be in her mouth.

"Are you sure you don't want to masturbate? You look as if you need to."

She's laughing at me, the cow. But my cock never gives up and I hear myself asking, "Couldn't we just fuck? You've made me as hot as hell."

She sits back on the sofa and folds her arms. "No. I want to watch you do it."

"But why?"

"I want to know if you look the same."

"What?"

"You know, whether you still get that 'I've-been-consti-pated-for-so-long-but-it-will-soon-be-over' look."

"Bloody hell." If I was a real man, I'd leave right now.

"Don't take offence. I'm just curious." She makes that sound so reasonable. Like it's something every woman has to find out eventually.

"Look, I'll strip if it will help," she says and starts to unbutton her blouse. I'm still thinking about sulking until she reaches the third button. She has beautiful breasts.

She looks up from under her fringe, her hands frozen on the fourth button, and says. "Wouldn't you like to stand over me while you do it? Hmmm?"

"What if I knelt?" She slides to the floor in front of me. "And touched myself like this?" she says rubbing one prominent nipple with her thumb.

"Fuck," I say. I'm so eloquent at these moments.

"No, wank. Come on, you'll enjoy it."

So I pull my cock out. It is very hard, thank God. I push it in Karen's direction but she moves back.

Karen's right: looking down at her is a rush. I pull back the foreskin with my finger and thumb. She's watching with the same close attention as when I showed her how to hold a golf club. I slowly start to stroke up and down. I don't normally do this standing; for some reason it's more difficult than lying down. My legs are starting to tire. I move faster, my whole fist around my cock now.

Karen is fascinated. "Doesn't it hurt, grabbing yourself so tightly?"

"Nnnnggghhhhhhhh," is all I manage in reply. I'm thinking about coming now. Wanting it. Rushing for it.

Karen's face is right in front of my cock. Vixen that she is, she opens her mouth and licks around her lips.

"Fuck, fuck fuck, fuck." I say, in rhythm to my hand. My buttocks are clenched and I'm rising on tiptoe with every upward stroke.

Then there is nothing but me and the need to come right . . . now!

My eyes are closed. My calves are screaming. My hand is a blur. And I'm coming.

I open my eyes just in time to see the slap coming but not in time to turn away.

"You bastard," Karen cries out.

"What the . . ."

"You complete shit."

For a moment I wonder if I've woken up in an episode of "My Life as an Idiot."

Karen is actually crying now. And hitting me. It hurts.

Feeling stupid and vulnerable with my sticky cock hanging out, I grab both her wrists and hold her to me until she stops struggling.

I manage to get her to sit on the sofa.

"What have I done? Did I get some in your eye?" I think I'm doing well: sounding concerned and sensitive and everything.

Karen shrugs out from under my arm and pokes me in the ribs, hard. Even as I wince with the pain I can't help but notice that the last button of her blouse has given way in the struggle and her breasts are now free. God, I want them.

"You enjoyed that," she says, making it obvious that this is a bad thing.

"But you told me to enjoy it."

"I didn't tell you to enjoy it that much."

"What?"

"Rita was right about you."

"What's Rita got to do with this?" Rita is my ex-just-before-Karen-girlfriend. She never forgave me for falling asleep on top of her after sex one night.

"She said you preferred wanking to fucking – and she was right. To think I defended you."

I can see it now. Rita, my female Iago, pouring poison into Karen's ear. Or am I getting Othello and Hamlet mixed? Anyway, I imagine Rita saying nasty things and Karen being defensive and loyal.

"So you decided on an experiment?" I said.

Karen nods her head, little nods that end with her leaning against me. This is a good sign.

"And I enjoy masturbating more than I enjoy fucking you?" Another nod.

I take Karen's shoulders and make her look at me. "There's a flaw in your methodology," I say, pulling her blouse open further and pushing her shoulders back.

"You see," I say, dropping my head and letting the flat of my tongue graze her fat little nipple, "what I like best," my tongue works on the other nipple, "is feeling you come."

I suck half her breast in my mouth and hear her say, "Truly?"

"Let's go back to where we were and I'll demonstrate." I take her by both wrists and pull her to her feet. She doesn't move to cover her breasts but she does glance down at my now-shrunken cock.

"Poor thing," she says, as if she was talking about an over-tired puppy, "I think you may have killed it."

She starts to bend, to curtsy, saying, "Maybe I could save it if I gave it the kiss of life?"

You'd think that was the perfect offer, wouldn't you? She's

literally going to go down on me. So why do I feel like this is
another test?

"Leave it." I say. Shit, I didn't mean to bark at her like that.

Karen looks up from her curtsy, arms outstretched, breasts
jutting, one eyebrow raised, mischief in her eyes.

"Yes, O Masterful One," she says, bowing and making a real
curtsy.

My first instinct is that she's making fun of me again, but
something in her posture makes me wonder if she's also sending
a message. Nothing Karen says ever has only one meaning.
Sometimes I don't find out what a conversation was about until
weeks after we've finished it.

It's lucky I've just come. For once I'm able to concentrate,
even with Karen half-naked in front of me. Maybe she had a
reason for telling me that when she masturbates she imagines
being taken with her hands bound or being licked to ecstasy?
Because she's a faster thinker and a smoother talker than me,
Karen has always been the one in charge, but maybe it's time for
me to take control, to show her that I also have a pretty skilled
tongue?

I have an image of Karen twisting helplessly as my tongue
plays tunes on her clit. My cock salutes the idea with enthusiasm.

"Gosh," Karen says, "whatever that glint in your eye is, it
was shock therapy for our dying patient here."

She hasn't stood up from her curtsy.

"I was thinking . . ." I bring her to her feet, letting her fall
forward onto my chest so that I feel the warmth of her breasts
through my shirt. Before she can say anything to confuse me, I
let go of one wrist and twirl her around by the other in a dance
move I didn't think I was capable of. She comes to rest with her
back against my chest. ". . . about making you come." I fold her
arm down and across her chest and press both of our hands into
the round softness of her breasts. Karen presses her backside up
against my erection. I'm certain I know what she wants.

"And then come again." I slide my free hand up her thigh
and across her mound.

"And again." She spreads her legs so I can slip a finger between her labia. I feel her hand close under mine, kneading her breast. I like this "being in charge" thing. I'm pumped up with excitement as well as lust. Life seems full of possibilities – and all of them end with Karen coming on my tongue.

I let the tip of my finger push her labia apart. But I don't enter her, so she brings her free hand down to guide me.

"No," I say, softly but clearly.

Her hand moves back to her thigh.

I bite her neck before saying: "Relax. Just do what I ask and don't say a word until you come at least twice. Nod your head if you agree."

Karen stiffens. She may be small, but she's strong. I doubt that I could hold her if she didn't want me to. I feel her heart hammering and half expect her to start hitting me and calling me names again. Then she nods. It's a small nod and after it her head is hanging forward, her hair half covering her face. Waiting.

My mouth goes dry. This isn't a game any more. It's something different, something important. God, I hope I don't fuck this up.

I let go and she just stands there, holding her breast with one hand, head tipped forward, other hand on her thigh, like some action figure that's been posed and forgotten.

Time slows down. Normally sex with Karen is an urgent thing. I get so aroused that I want to do everything at once. But this time it's different. I'm just as aroused, maybe more aroused than I've ever been in my life, but it's all focused on Karen, on what she wants and how I can give it to her. It's scary . . . but it's as sexy as hell.

I feel so calm. I only become aware that I've decided to use my belt to tie her when I hear the noise it makes as I pull it out of my jeans. Karen hears it too: her head raises but she doesn't turn around.

I stand behind her pressed into her back, and reach my arms around her. My hands seem to know what to do. I slip the belt around her right wrist and pull it tight through the buckle; then

I tie the other end of the belt in a knot around her left wrist. She shivers and presses back into me.

"Lift your arms. Put your hands behind your head." I sound calm and reasonable.

"Good girl," I say when her hands are in place.

I run my hands over her flanks, letting my spread fingers brush her breasts. She stretches like a cat, arching her back into my chest. Her eyes are closed and she's smiling.

"You are beautiful," I say.

I unzip her skirt and push it down to pool at her feet. She's wearing plain cotton panties that ought not to be sexy but which I find exciting today. My thumbs slip into the panties and I push them down. Normally she'd laugh or tell me to hurry but this time she lets me drive. I even have to lift her feet one at a time to clear her panties and skirt away.

The image of her standing above me, hands tied behind her neck, breasts spilling out her shirt, sex exposed and vulnerable, almost overwhelms me. It is so . . . Damn, I don't know what it is except that I want more of it.

I move in front of her. I lift her head and kiss her lips, gently and with complete attention. Only our lips touch. I concentrate on the full soft wetness of her mouth. I feel strong and needed.

Karen's eyes are open when the kiss ends. I expect to see some question in her eyes. Instead I see only trust and desire. In some strange way, that summons my next move. It's as if she is providing the music and I'm improvising the lyrics.

"Get down on your knees and lower your breasts onto the coffee table."

She raises an eyebrow. Will she refuse? Then I realise how difficult it is to get down on her knees with her hands tied.

"I'll help," I say and she smiles.

It's obvious that her hands can't stay behind her head like that. I push her arms up over her head and then use the belt to pull her hands down the front of her body and between her legs. Now her weight is on her chest, her breasts pushed together by her arms, and her fingers can reach her sex. I push down on her back and pull hard on the belt between her legs to make sure she knows how I want her.

She's expecting me to fuck her now. I always like taking her from behind. But I decide to surprise her.

"Slide a finger of each hand into your cunt. I'm sure it's wet enough. Hold your labia and spread them for me. No, don't lift off the table. Stretch. You can reach. Good girl. Make circles with your thumbs but keep your cunt open; I want to see it drizzle."

Karen groans, maybe with pleasure, maybe from frustration at not being fucked, but she obeys.

I watch before putting my hands on her tight arse cheeks and pulling them apart.

"Keep stroking."

Karen pauses. We haven't had anal sex. She doesn't like the idea and she says she's too small. Looking at her tiny arsehole, I think she may be right.

"Trust me."

I wait until she pulls at her labia again, then I lower my mouth onto her arsehole. She bounces against the coffee table, but there's nowhere for her to go. I make a small wet circle around the brown ridge of her arse. I can taste her sweat and smell a faint whiff of shit. It ought to be gross, but it feels wonderful.

When I push my tongue in she cries: "Fuck, yes." I decide not to reprove her for speaking; I'm too busy pushing into her. My tongue finds its way out of the dell of her arse over the small mound of smooth flesh between arse and cunt and then back up, making a spiral back into her arsehole. On the third of these circuits, I let my nose follow my tongue down towards her cunt.

Karen has both fingers buried in her cunt. I let my tongue flick across them, then pull them out and suck them. When my mouth finally finds her cunt, Karen pushed back so hard I think she's going to break my nose. I force her legs a little wider apart and turn my head sideways so that I can extend my tongue up and down her slit like a finger. She's wet and smells of sex and sweat. I can't resist pushing my nose into her cunt. I'm crazy for her smell.

I lift my mouth and say, "Rub yourself, Karen. Show me how you frig yourself."

To my surprise, Karen doesn't push inside herself, she just presses on her mound. I press my thumb against her arsehole in the same rhythm, not entering her but just keeping the pressure on. After only a few seconds, she comes with a low growl I've never heard her make before.

Before she can relax, I slip two fingers into her and bend towards the roof of her cunt, searching for that little ridged spot the makes her explode.

"Oh, God, you can't . . ." Karen just can't do the silence thing.

Her sentence ends when I find the spot. I'm kneeling to one side, my erection against her thigh, one arm across her hips, holding her down, the other hand pressing her up again and again and again. She twists and bounces but I won't let go.

At first I think she's peed herself, but the gush over my fingers is slick and the smell is sex, not urine. When the gush is over, Karen goes limp under me.

My calm deserts me. What If I've hurt her, ruptured something? What if she's bleeding?

"Are you okay?"

Silence.

I pull her up off the coffee table. Though her eyes are closed I can see tears. Shit, I must have really hurt her. How could I be so stupid?

I turn her to face me. I have both hands on her face when her eyes open.

"That was wonderful," she says.

"But you're crying?"

She just nods, as if crying is the most sensible thing in the world. Then she lifts her arms and laces her belt-bound hands behind my head.

"Look me in the eyes while you fuck me," she says. So much for me being in charge.

We move so that Karen is on her back under me. I take my weight on my arms like a gentleman. She keeps her arms full

extended with her hands behind my neck. I know I won't last
long so I rock slowly, pressing against her mound. It feels like
coming home.

It's hard keeping eye contact. She laughs when she sees how
difficult I find it, then she grabs my ears to help me stay
focused. When she's certain I'm looking straight at her, she
wraps her legs around my waist and squeezes. I come with so
much force I feel like some of it must be gushing out of my ears.
And I closed my eyes, damn it.

Unbelievably I'm suddenly hit by the need to sleep. I roll off
Karen. She snuggles into the side of me, one leg over my thigh.
"You can untie me now," she says.

I fumble with the belt until one of her hands slips free. She
slides it down my belly to rest it on my shrunken cock. Even so,
I can barely keep my eyes open. She lets go of my cock, leans
across my chest so that her breasts are pressing into me, and
makes a show of forcing one of my eyes open.

"Rita said you liked to sleep a lot."

Fuck, I'd forgotten about Rita whispering sweet malice in
Karen's ear.

"But today I found out something that she doesn't know,"
Karen says.

"That I'd rather have sex than masturbate?"

"No."

"You still think I prefer wanking?"

"Shush, don't speak when your brain is impaired, you'll only
embarrass yourself."

I think that's an insult but I'm not sure, so I stay silent.

"What I found out," Karen says, "is that you love me."

She puts a finger to my lips to prevent me from replying.
Then she kisses me on each eye. I slip into sleep, content.

Chinchilla Lace

Cervo

Chinchilla High

Marblehead rolled down the covers to her knees and let the weight of his right hand enjoy the ride back up her thigh to her patch of black wiry fur at the top. He paused and rotated his wrist for a while as he kissed her. She moaned in such a way that he thought the time was right for the next move.

Sliding down the mattress, he lifted his huge frame so that his cock and balls dangled just beyond her reach. His pecs glistened smoothly over her. She could not quite reach them either. Then he smiled and gently lowered his mouth with its large white teeth to her pussy. He moved his tongue in a slow pattern until he settled on a spot that made her shove herself hard into his mouth. That was fine with him.

The sun from the window warmed his large, hard ass as he continued to slurp at an even pace. The sky was slate on the horizon. Snow coming. She screamed a little, beat on the mattress a lot and yelled for help after a while. She got it. After a long while, he let her come, and she collapsed with her legs wide apart in the middle of the sweaty sheets.

"You are so bad," she said. He wrapped her in his arms. In ten minutes, she was asleep.

Marblehead got up and stroked his dick as he looked down at the wet hair around her pussy. The skin was a nice shade of brownish purple beneath the black cloud of hair.

"Mmmhmm," he said to himself as a man will after a job well

done. He headed for the kitchen catching a glimpse of the other rehabbed brownstones on the block. His house in Upper Manhattan had tripled in value in the last three years. He made a large pot of coffee, which was not easy to do with an erection that threatened to get caught in the utensil drawer. The kitchen counters were done in veined black marble.

He poured himself a cup and then leaned his ass against the counter. With his free hand, he slowly massaged his dick even harder. He liked waiting to come. Patience made the whole thing a bigger deal. Then too he enjoyed watching the ripple of his arm as the muscles danced beneath his tight skin when he jerked off.

He really wanted to fuck her in the ass to see how she liked it, but he was so thick that he wondered if she would split. He had not actually raised the subject yet, but he had placed the head of his cock against her asshole a couple of times. Clearly she was torn about the idea as much by the thought that she might be torn in half herself. He did not believe in pressure when it came to fucking.

His hard-on was approaching a volatile state and felt like hot granite when there was a bang at the door. It was one hard bang. It had to be Toodles. Nobody else would take the risk of banging on his door. Not many people knew he lived here. His mailing address was a numbered box in Carnarsie.

He put on a silk robe and took off the police lock.

When Toodles came in, he said, "You been bangin' all night? Smells like the fuck farm in here."

"Yeah, well, that could be," muttered Marbles, the name Toodles called him.

"Look to me like you ain't done yet." He was inspecting the tent in the front of Marblehead's robe.

"Gimme a minute." At which point he went into the bedroom and closed the door. He gently rolled her onto her tummy and then lifted her up so that she was on her knees near the end of the bed. Making sure she was still damp, he eased the thick head of his cock into her pussy from the rear and began to pump. She seemed to be asleep still, but he knew she was playing possum. She wrapped her arms around her pillow, turned her head to one side and pretended to snore. In so doing, she pushed back hard against him with her pussy as open as possible.

A man of skill and control, Marbles fucked her with majestic certainty for another ten minutes. His balls slapped her thighs in a way that made them a little tender but it was not unpleasant. She clearly thought they felt great as she enjoyed the heavy whapping sound of his balls on her skin. His cock felt like a tree limb moving inside her and she was fond of trees. At last she gave a hard wiggle and the scent of her pussy filled his nose. He exploded inside her, pulling her asscrack hard against his hips in a grip that she could not have broken with pliers.

"Hoooo . . . not a bad fuck," he said under his breath. He tended to understatement. She was babbling now and starting to cry. Then he bent over her and kissed her shoulders following the ridge of her spine to her hips with more kisses. By then she was nearly asleep again.

When he came back to the livingroom, Toodles said, "Take a shower, man. You been rolling in pussy. I can't drive the Caddy with no big-ass hard-on, you hear?"

"You can't do nothing with no hard-on, Toodles." Toodles had been chipping white bitch about six days a week since he was fourteen. He was so big across the chest by then that nobody bothered to tell him to stop. He had just turned forty before Christmas.

By the time he was tossed out of pro football at 20, he was also doing steroids and uppers. He balanced the mood swings with a little tab now and then. This pharmacological mix did not do much for his sex life, but he sure made an impression wherever he went. That was enhanced by his black leather porkpie hat, that he wore on the front of his enormous skull, and the wide black cashmere overcoat he sported in winter with a pocket for a shotgun inside. His orangey brown pigskin gloves were a little out of place with the cashmere coat, but nobody noticed his gloves. Few people forgot his large dead eyes.

"We gotta see a guy," said Toodles in a dreamy voice.

"About a horse?" asked Marbles.

"Horse? No fuckin' horse this time. Chinchillas."

Marblehead was used to this sort of lateral focus from Toodles and did not press it.

"Forget about it, let's go. Chinchillas, hunh?"

"Yeah, chinchillas. Dead chinchillas. Big fucking fuss, if you ask me, over some dead rats." By the time they got to the Caddy, it had started to sleet. Last week's snow was still on the ground with a layer of ice underneath that. After they crossed into Brooklyn, even the heavy Caddy waddled a little in the slop.

Toodles plowed the Caddy through a ridge of slush and pulled up to the curb at the corner. A hard wind pushed at the windows. The heater felt good.

The streets were empty. Here in Red Hook they were among the last in the city that were paved with granite cobble stones. They were slippery and good for breaking your ankle if you had to move fast. Marbles hated them. Two blocks down they could see a ratty bodega that might be open. Otherwise the inhabitants had left the neighborhood for work, left for good or were left for dead. Here and there buildings that had survived demolition stuck up in isolation like old, broken teeth. Sleet slapped the windows after the engine shut down.

They got out of the car, went around the corner and headed three blocks north. They both knew appearances were deceptive. No building here sold for less than a million bucks, even though there were no windows in lots of the window frames. Everyone wanted to get in on the boom to come. Some buildings were being rehabbed by the new owners who occupied one of the floors.

"This is one ugly shithole," said Marblehead. He stuck to no-load tax-free bond funds. Real estate was too much work and he needed tax relief in his bracket.

His eyes swept to the top floor of the brick building across the street.

"Marbles, you ugly. You ugly as this place," said Toodles. Toodles had bought two houses in the area in the last six

months. He was having them gutted by his cousin from the
south who owed him for his down payment on a house in Sea
Bright, New Jersey. His cousin was good with a hammer.
Toodles had never used a hammer, but he knew how to pound
things without one.

"Yeah, Toodles, I'm ugly. I am. I admit it, but I ain't fuckin'
crazy like you."

Toodles' vision went out of phase like an old black and white
TV with the horizontal on the fritz. The left side of his head
throbbed. The right side buzzed. His fingernails dug into his
palms even through the cashmere lining of his hand-made
pigskin gloves. He waited a moment for things to clear in his
head. He did not like to be called crazy.

"The guy in there?" he said, changing the subject.

"The guy's in there all right. He walkin' around. See behind
the shade there?"

"Maybe he's an asshole. A nervous asshole."

"Could be. Could be."

They crossed the sidewalk shoulder to shoulder. Together
they were half again as wide as the door. Toodles was tall and
wide in the shoulders. Marblehead was taller with long arms.
His neck seemed to start at the top of his head and flare out to
his shoulders from there. He was slow on his feet, which had
ended his career in the ring. The ring had also left him with a
jaw that creaked when he chewed. It sounded like a rusty
rendering machine chewing a bone. He had a warm smile,
but not many people got to see it.

Toodles was scary. Women never knew whether to be turned
on by him, scared to death of him, or both. He did not think
much about sex. The front door to the building was not locked.
The lobby was stuffy and warm. Marblehead held the door for
Toodles. They walked quietly up to the third floor landing and
paused to listen for a breech closing or a cylinder snapping into
place.

"Why's this guy in Red Hook? He an asshole?" asked
Marbles.

"You gotta gun?"

"Gun? Why I need a gun for an asshole? He an asshole, right? So why's he living here?" Marbles did not like guns. Too many ways to fuck up with a gun. Toodles didn't mind either way. He got where he was going gun or no gun.

"No . . . well, yeah, I guess," said Toodles scratching has forehead. The steroids aggravated his skin. "He an asshole, all right. I mean, where the fuck else should he be? He's a Yuppy. Got alligators knitted on his G-string and what have you like that. They all wanna live in Red Hook. It's cool now."

"Smells like cat piss to me."

"No, that's herbals, Man. Herbal shit."

"Herbal shit?"

"Aromatherapy or some shit. Makes 'em feel better."

"Sheeeit, man, gonna take a lotta herb make you feel better in this fuckin' place."

They got to the top floor. Marbles leaned on the front door of one of the apartments. He let his weight settle on it. The metal skin on the door sagged and buckled. The door popped open. The guy was standing in the living room with a T-shirt that didn't cover his naked dick. The room was large and nicely decorated with a large bank of windows leading to a wide narrow balcony. Doors led to other rooms off the living room.

It was an odd building, having three bedroom apartments and marble stairways. Nearly abandoned in the 70s, it was now a coop. Only the top two floors were occupied as yet.

"Where's the fuckin' chinchilla?" asked Toodles as he marched over the fallen door. He kept his eye glued to the guy's eyeball in case he twitched looking for a sidearm.

The guy was the whitest guy that Marblehead had ever seen. He looked like a dishrag on two icicles. He could see the guy's eyes flick to the right toward a doorway. Marbles started toward it to check.

"You got the five hundred?" asked Toodles.

Marblehead went to the doorway and looked inside. The room had an enormous walnut sleigh bed, satin sheets and a sea of embroidered pillows. All this shit would go for three, three and a half grand from Manhattan. There was indeed a guest face down on the bed. A small pile of cushions supported the hips of a girl who was now out cold with a martini glass in her hand.

She wore the floor length chinchilla which was now pushed up to her waist. Her creamy ass and pink pussy were in full view between her legs. Her feet were in her open-toed sandals with three-inch heels. They were covered with pale gold sequins. The shoes went with the coat and her pale strawberry blonde cloud of hair between her legs.

The guy looked astounded, like they had interrupted his strip croquet game. It was around his eyes.

"Not yet," said the guy, with a hopeful wheedle underneath it.

"Too late," said Toodles.

"That coat's worth 80 thousand . . . Take it."

"That coat worth shit to me. I don't move shit like that. Frodo give you the coat for 8 thousand. You paid Frodo 7,500. The coat worth 80 grand. He needed cash. You got a deal, man. Ten cents on the dollar. You got a deal. Now you stiffing him on the small five. That's fuckin' dumb, you know? He wants his five hundred."

"I don't—"

"– have it." Marblehead finished the thought for him and paused.

"The nays have it, Asshole." Then Toodles and Marblehead walked over to the guy. They ripped off his shirt which left him naked. Then they picked him up and shoved his head through the glass of one of the windows, which also broke out the old wooden frame. Then they paused to let him take in the moment. After that, they threw him through the window, assuming he would land in the street, but he managed to grab the iron balcony rail.

The metal was so cold it was peeling his skin off his bare hands and feet, but the guy did not care. He did not want to fall off the balcony. He was pulling himself back over the railing when Toodles picked up two retro Eames chairs. The guy was almost back over the rail when Toodles stepped through the shattered window frame and then smashed the two backs of the chairs together like a huge pair of cymbals. The guy's head was between them.

"Toodleoo, Motherfucker," said Toodles, using his trademark method of saying goodbye. The guy fell over backward like Wiley Coyote having a bad dream. Toodles chucked the chairs over the rail, where they landed on the guy in the empty street. It was starting to fill with snow. In an hour he would be buried in the gutter.

"Gotta move the Caddy before they plow. Don't want to have to dig the fucker out," said Marblehead, but Toodles knew they had to get the coat if they were not going to get the five hundred. The girl snored evenly, but it was not convincing.

"You could fuck her in the ass, and she wouldn't say nothing," said Marblehead. The girl tried not to flinch about her possible ass-fucking.

"No, man. No time." He had to get to a dentist appointment back in Manhattan. With luck they would beat the traffic and he could meet his connection first.

"You might mess up the coat, fucking her, anyway." Then Marblehead picked up the coat with the girl inside it folded them over his arm. He patted her on the ass to calm her.

"I gotta carry you. You got no shoes."

They went back downstairs.

The walk back to the Caddy was miserable with sleet melting down their necks. He plumped the girl down on her bottom in the plush back seat.

Marblehead said, "You need to wizz?"

She shook her head no. Her bladder was screaming for relief but she didn't want to bother these monsters.

"You pee in that coat, you dead, you hear?"

She started to cry. Toodles looked at her and grunted.

Marbles turned to him, "She gotta pee. I can tell. It's a panic reaction. I'll take her down to the bodega."

As she had no shoes but the sandals, Marblehead picked her out of the back again and carried her along the street to the bodega. This time he carried her like a bride. When he walked in with the girl in his arms, he told the owner she needed the powder room.

The owner would not have allowed this invasion of his dingy toilet, but he realized that the top of his head did not come all the way up to Marblehead's nipple, so he figured the girl could pee on the floor if she liked.

"Careful of the coat," Marbles told her as he set her down on the toilet on her butt, as gently as a butterfly landing. He gathered the skirt of the fur around her and put it in her lap to keep her warm. Then he closed the door and went back into the store. He looked around. He grabbed a tiny bottle of mango nectar from the chill cabinet. He thought of the stuff as gourmet cusine à la Puerto Rico.

"You got any snowballs?"

"Snowballs?" asked the owner, who looked baffled and turned his eyes to the slush in the street.

"No, man. Snowballs with coconuts. Pink, you know."

The owner realized they were discussing snacks and not slush. That was better than talking to this lunatic about possible murders he was planning to execute in the next ten minutes. He tried smiling at Marblehead, who did not smile back.

Instead, Marblehead paid for the fruit juice and the snack cakes with a twenty. He told the owner to keep the change as the stuff was placed carefully into a paper sack with a little napkin. Then Marblehead asked for two coffees which the owner put in a separate bag.

The owner was starting to feel brotherly about Marblehead when the toilet flushed. There was no sink in the little bathroom so she couldn't wash her hands.

The girl came out of the little room at the back of the store. She was blushing now because she figured everyone was thinking about why she had gone in there, and now she couldn't wash her hands. But, she did feel a lot better. The owner gave her a little package of towelettes saying, "That's on the house," with a soft smile. She mopped her tiny hands and then he gave her a couple of paper napkins. She dried her fingers and then blew her nose loudly on the last one. She had been crying and was still sniffling.

Marblehead handed her the two bags and picked her up again since she still had no shoes. He cuddled her against his chest. She could feel a hard length of pipe in his breast pocket, but she felt safe. The coat fell open, revealing that she was naked except of course for the chinchilla. The store owner gently put the coat back over her. She smiled at him as Marblehead took her out the door and through the sleet back to the Caddy.

"Come back and see us," said the owner, and then he threw up with relief on the floor.

Marbles surprised Toodles with the fresh hot coffee and gave the girl the juice and the snack. "You can have some of my coffee if you want something hot after," but she was still trying to figure out why he had given her the snowballs. So was Toodles.

"We gonna have a fucking picnic? How about the Flatlands? I got a shovel in the back." He let his eyes flick toward the girl.

"Hey, we can take her to my place. She can decide what to do from there. She ain't gonna bother us, and if she try, who listen to a naked-assed white girl running around in the snow on Lenox Avenue? They just call Bellevue. One way ticket to Ward's Island."

She pulled her feet up onto the seat and started to nibble the coconut. She had the message.

They got the Caddy out of the snow and slush with a little shoving and rocking. Then they started back to Manhattan.

"One fucking ways, man. Pain in the ass." Not wanting to be stopped, they turned the corner and started to weave their way out of Red Hook. Two minutes later, they passed a large lump in the snow. Toodles looked at it briefly.

"Asshole," said Toodles to himself. He looked at his watch, happy in the knowledge that he could see his connection before he got to the dentist. Marbles found he was thinking about the girl waiting at home in his bedroom, which was giving him an enormous erection.

The girl in the chinchilla fell asleep in the close warmth of the

Caddy's plush back seat. The soft fur of the coat allowed it to fall open again. Coconut shreds had gathered at the corner of her mouth. A few bits of it fell on her little pink nipple. Ten minutes later they crossed the Brooklyn Bridge to Manhattan. It snowed like hell. Red Hook wasn't plowed for three days.

Chinchilla Downs

"Some fuckin' outfit for fuckin' February in Brooklyn," Frodo muttered. She was climbing down the front stoop in her stilettos from the little apartment he had rented for her in the PR section of Sunset Park. His dick started to wave a little at her from inside his pants. She was in gold pedal pushers, a caramel tube top with one vertical purple stripe over her left breast, a white down jacket and pink pumps with high heels. Her hair was piled high on her head and her makeup was perfect. Little ringlets of shining black hair framed her face and emphasized her huge almond eyes.

Frodo found her totally adorable. He crammed his plaid water-proof snap-brim cap onto the remaining strands of his hair. Then he worked his way around the battered Chevy Caprice to help her over the ridge of grey frozen slush. He gave her a kiss and gently patted the firm, round curve of her bottom. Her little white teeth were as shiny as the snowflakes that swirled out of the sky. She looked him in the eye warmly, having no idea what he had grumbled when she came down the stairs since it had been in English. He settled her in the front seat. When he got in the driver's side, she smiled her serious smile, reached across the seat and gently squeezed his joint. She was a very gentle girl when she felt like it.

"Boys," she said and giggled deep in her throat. It made good enough sense to Frodo for him not to care. He thought about her delectable ass in those thin pedal pushers and cranked up the heater as they headed toward the docks.

Once there, Frodo was wrestling with two problems and he could not get either one of them straight. He parked the crud-covered Caprice on 30th Street under the Gowanus Expressway. His girlfriend now had her head in his lap and was slowly sucking him with a circular licking motion. She was doing a very good job, which was making him lightheaded. As an experienced suckee, he could not deny that. But, at 72, he was having trouble keeping his mind on her ass crack, even though it was tantalizingly visible from the top of her gold hip huggers.

As with all Latin women, Frodo thought of her as "PR". She was 27, but looked 18 to most men without them even having to squint. They hoped she was at least 19. She had been shipped to the States in a cargo container from Honduras along with fifteen other girls and two boys. Once in Jersey she was forcefully invited to work off her travel expenses by learning to be fucked in the ass four times an hour by customers.

She had proven less than meek with her Lithuanian owner/ pimp. He had two older women haul her pants down to her ankles in a warehouse near Newark Airport. One of them pointed to an oil drum lying on its side. The other whacked her across the mouth prison-yard style. She pressed her lip with her fingers to stop the blood. They figured she couldn't do much with her pants around her feet, but she could do enough.

The pimp sauntered up to her pleasantly and threatened to ice her if she didn't bend over and take it. He was busy scooping a handful of all-purpose grease out of a plastic tub. She saved them both the trouble by cutting his throat with a razor blade she had hidden in her cheek. As she squatted down to haul up her pants, she shoved the used blade into his mouth, slicing into his tongue. It took skill to stay out of the blood. There was a lot of it. The two older girls who worked for the dead pimp did not seem disappointed when she walked out of the warehouse.

Anytime Frodo watched her walk away, his heart would pound in his ears. He had picked her up outside a truck stop in Bayonne. She was hitching with no idea where she was going. Hers was a classic wonder of an ass, in his estimation, and he was a devoted and respectful follower of Latinas from all angles. It could be a risky habit, given their volatile male relatives and friends, but very exciting. If you could get a Latin girl to grace you with a smile, the sun belonged to you. She was also not a bigot about his being a little older. He liked small boobs with dark puckered nipples. He planned to marry her, if he could figure out how to ask her.

Even with those nips in mind, he figured it would be Yom Kippur before he came again because of his second problem. He had a cash flow emergency that needed solving right away or he would not be seeing 72 and a half. It was a question of hedging his profit and loss. Frodo did not like red ink. He made between a half and two million a year, but he was always invested up to his eyeballs. If interest rates dipped too far, he was cash poor and the nature of his relationship with the IRS did not allow for going to a bank. So he borrowed from a discreet Brooklyn associate named Tony.

He owed Tony ("the Crunch") Cavallo 8 large for a two-week loan. It was nothing, but it kept Frodo from taking bigger losses. Tony had not gotten his name for his skill with opening filberts, but nuts were his specialty. Frodo had two nuts and two grand in his pocket and he needed both pairs. The vig was mounting and he would be tapped if he ponied up the other six. He did not like to be tapped, as it brought back unpleasant memories from his dismal childhood in Utica selling kosher food in his father's store. Tony was from Bay Ridge, a place he had never once left. He had Bell's Palsy on the right side of his face. On top of that he was mean and ugly, but he had money from gambling and a midnight Mercedes-to-order business he ran for select customers. Frodo did not want to excite his displeasure.

In the trunk was a big part of his second problem. It was a 60-thousand-dollar chinchilla coat from the many that hung in his warehouse in Jersey. He dealt in furs and gem stones whenever he could, as they were hard to trace. Besides, they seemed romantic. He had lots of these coats, but it was the off season for coats and the economy was on the skids. Who knew? All of a sudden the broads from Saddlebrook who had bought two fur coats a week were hooking in trailers.

His girlfriend was working his pants down a little, which was not such a good idea in broad daylight under an expressway, but undeniably racy. He had a buyer for the coat. The guy was a citizen who owned a condo in Red Hook. He wanted to buy the coat for ten cents on the dollar. So naturally Frodo had told him the coat was worth 80 thousand instead of 60. If he was going to get robbed, Frodo thought, he would pick up the extra two grand. It was only money, but there was a principle here. This way he could cover the vig and a lot of the loan from Tony C. and still have some cash.

The problem was that he was sure Sylva, the girl now sucking his dick, would want the coat once she saw it. He was mistaken in that, but he had no way of knowing it. She saw a future in Frodo that extended beyond evening wear. She started sucking harder which made his vision blur and then she began to cradle his balls in her hand. She rolled them gently in her dark little fingers. Then she tickled the skin just at the point where his balls met his crotch. Frodo thought that was an idea with a future.

He had the impression she really liked him, even though he had not the slightest idea why, since she spoke no English and he spoke nothing else. He was not even quite sure of her name, which sounded like "Wilma", like the broad in the Flintstones, but then again it sound like "Sylva", too. He liked Sylva better, so he called her that. When he did, she would sit next to him and hold his hand, so he figured he was close enough. It was very comforting to be close to her and quiet together while they listened to the slush melt on his apartment balcony. They shared things like overstuffed pastrami sandwiches. Of course, it was not so bad when she was sucking his brain out of his skull through his dick. He had developed a complex palate for her pussy, which changed flavor with her mood. Now and then they fucked, when he had time to deal with the headache the Viagra gave him.

She sensed that he was distracted in some worrisome way and so slowly began to wiggle her little fingers under his balls. Soon she was tickling the rim of his asshole. Just as she eased in her finger to the second knuckle, the Fur-Coat-Guy squealed his tires in three slots down in his "pre-owned" Lexus. The shining silver car was as inconspicuous as a fart in a confessional. The guy jumped out, wearing assorted rugged gear from L.L. Bean, and yelled, "Hi!" as he waved at Frodo. His hair flopped around like Hugh Grant's and he had carefully not shaved in a day and a half. Frodo wondered if this was the guy's idea of tough.

Frodo sat on her finger in the battered Chevy Caprice and thought, "Great. Now I got two assholes working here." Just then she licked the hole in the head of his dick and gently wiggled her finger in his asshole. That turned the key to his heart and Frodo had an orgasm of supremely voluble pleasure, causing him to groan loudly. The guy dodged around the front of the Lexus and started running to the Chevy. The windows were a little steamed by now.

"You okay?" Asshole shouted. "You know older guys have to be careful of the cold." In Frodo's mind, his customer went from being The Guy in that instant to The Asshole. Frodo wondered where his nephew had found him. He could picture row upon row of assholes trying to look like fur trappers in downtown Manhattan. They had met at some bar in Tribeca where this guy was trying to impress him about how he wanted to buy a nice fur "under the table." His nephew told Asshole he understood and would he like a deal on a fur coat (the nephew knowing that Frodo needed to get some cash moving).

Asshole leaned into the nephew breathing sushi into his face and said, "Yeah, Sport," which sounded kind of faggoty to the nephew but the Asshole said he had cash for the coat. There were two problems with non-criminal citizens, civilians, or, as the pros called them, assholes. They wanted to tell you things you didn't need or want to know, and they wanted to rip you off to make themselves feel smart.

"My name's Aston—" said Asshole at the car window.

"Yeah, yeah," said Frodo, "And my name is Dick Nixon, but I don't want it to get around. I know who the fuck you are. Just a minute."

At this point Sylva sat up and looked at Asshole, who she

immediately dismissed quite rightly as an asshole. Then she turned to look out the windshield and lit a Marlboro while her fingers toyed absently with her left nipple under her coat. Frodo was very good at licking nipples and he would get around to doing that soon enough. Still, she was a little anxious to get started from all that sucking.

Frodo mopped up his wad and zipped while she dabbed a little come from the corner of her mouth. Then Frodo got out of the car. He buttoned his plaid polyester car coat and they walked to a pillar in back of the car. They confirmed the price and Frodo went back to the trunk. He undid a padlock that went through a chain in a hole in the trunk lid and hauled out a black garbage bag with the coat in it.

"Cash first," he grumbled.

"Don't I get a look?" asked Asshole.

"You want me to get a model? Try on a chinchilla coat under the expressway here, Sonny? There's a cop shop about ten blocks that way. You think if they go by on a doughnut run, they might get some idea it's a tax-free transaction? The rats around here are mean enough to steal the fuckin' coat and eat it. Never mind the people."

"Oh, yeah, yeah, what was I thinking?" Asshole smiled at Frodo who looked at his customer like he was an old piece of cheese. Then the news got worse.

It seemed that Asshole only had 7,500 on hand, but was good for the rest in a couple of days. He pointed to his car like it was collateral. Frodo figured the guy leased the car, but he needed the seven and a half.

Once the bag was secured, the Guy drove back to his condo in Red Hook. Along the way he stopped under the Gowanus again and picked up fifty dollars' worth of coke (generously laced with baby laxative) from a local Mexican dealer. The dealer waved at passing cars now and then. The guy figured they were regulars. The cars all looked the same to him as they were covered in salt and street grime, unlike his pristine Lexus. He chuckled about stiffing Frodo out of the cash he still had in his wallet. He hadn't done pre-law and art history at Swarthmore for nothing.

His condo was not yet the swank chick trap it could become, owing to the nearby garbage treatment facility, but time and developers would fix that. He picked up a quart of Tanqueray gin on the way home. Once there, he placed his rubber paddle with fake fur glued to one side on the pillow and washed his orange and blue dildo. Then he put out various jars of lubes and creams.

Checking the clock, he ordered a round-the-world pizza delivered from Tony's on Court Street. He and the guy on the phone chuckled over the name, they being two men of the world. He then put on a Sinatra disk and slipped into his midnight blue ultra-suede jumpsuit with the zippers going front, back and sideways. It drew attention to his dick. It never crossed his mind that most women already knew where it was. He was ready.

Shortly thereafter, Peaches McGuire got out of a cab and banged open the unlocked front door of his building. Every inch of Peaches was pale, creamy pink except her large brown eyes, her strawberry blonde hair and her rosy little cunt. Her nipples were a dark shade of pink. Her tongue was a captivating luminous pink and she liked the way men's eyes fixed on it when she smiled and put the tip of it right between her teeth. She could be a very bad girl at times and she was still smart enough to stay clear of the flying drool.

After doing an MA upstate, Peaches had come to the City to work for a very hip urban planning firm in Chelsea. Two months later, the only planning the city was doing was how to keep from defaulting on its bonds. She was laid off. Rather than return to Poughkipsee and her boyfriend, Boxer Barton (heir to a once prosperous Chrysler dealership), she decided to plow a new furrow in a field where her pink endowments would not go to waste. She answered a classified ad and took employment as a fantasy escort. It was a concept developed by an unemployed epidemiologist from Bangkok. For five hundred bucks she would do whatever the geeks wanted as long as they didn't touch her. She would touch them with anything from whips to oatmeal if they liked, but they had to sit on their hands.

She had assumed this arrangement would be no more lucrative than urban planning, but she was wrong. She soon found that the male population of New York City is so driven, exhausted, nervous, guilt-ridden, nipple-starved, delusional, terrified and perpetually, constantly horny, that they thought this was a hell of a deal. In fact, when she coolly removed all but her panties and bra, it would be hard to argue the point, and hard was the name of the game. She usually took off the rest if she was fairly sure they would pull a muscle.

She went through the Guy's chosen repertoire of tricks, opening a zipper here and shoving in a dildo there. He got the chinchilla out of the garbage bag. She tried it on as requested. He studied her face. He seemed to like her getting the feel of this coat she could never have. Being a girl of insight, she saw that in him and wished she had a bigger dildo.

She did a modest amount of stroking and more spanking than he had expected. In time, he blew his lid while staring at her nipple from an inch and a half away. It was snowing hard by then. Getting a cab would be impossible and, having nothing else to do, she had got a little drunk. She dozed while the guy took a shower to wash the Vaseline out of his ass. When he was under the water, Peaches checked his wallet. She was a forward-thinking young woman. He had asked her for a real date, which meant one of two things. Either he was falling in love with some idea of some other woman he had in his head, or he intended to stiff her. The question was, did he have the cash at all?

She rolled over onto a pillow with the coat pulled up to her waist. This allowed her to inspect the wallet in peace. She reasoned that men never thought about much else if they had a clear view of her ass and pussy. She looked in his wallet and found her five hundred along with another seven bucks left over after the gin, drugs and pizza. She took the five hundred.

At that moment, the front door of the apartment hit the floor as though it had been punched out by a concussion grenade. The biggest, hardest males she had ever seen clomped over the door and started talking to the guy in unhappy tones. He had come out of the john in his T-shirt with his dick hanging out.

The look did not suggest dealing from strength. She deposited her five hundred in a zippered, hidden pocket in the coat and pretended to have passed out.

What the guy had not noticed was the grimy Chevy Caprice chugging along Third Avenue behind him. Frodo had seen him stop to pick up the coke. Frodo had known the dealer for quite some time as they had done some business together in hideous retro furniture from the sixties. Chairs that had cost 20 bucks new then were worth two thousand now, even beat to shit. Then too the dealer did evictions in the Bronx on the side, so he had a line on some choice pieces. Frodo did the brokerage, selling the stuff to art dealers in Manhattan who sold it to assholes.

Having seen the coke deal right on his turf, Frodo got angry. He had been stiffed by an asshole, because understandably enough he wanted to get busy and worship Sylva's ass. He realized that you should not try to think about more than one asshole at a time. Distractions should be avoided, so it was sort of his own fault. Being stiffed, however, was out. So he called his nephew, the real estate broker in Manhattan. He had paid for his nephew to go to Yale, so a little favor would be reasonable in return regarding this guy now known as Asshole.

The latest hot real estate location was Harlem near the Park, and the nephew had tried several times to buy a perfectly restored brownstone from a huge black man who declined to sell. In his research the nephew found out the homeowner was called Marblehead and did all sorts of highly unpleasant things for lots of money. So the nephew called a contact who got a line on Toodles, who got hold of his old colleague Marblehead, and voilà. Within an hour Marblehead had joined Toodles in the walk up to and over Asshole's front door. Then they showed the guy a window of opportunity that left him three stories up without a floor.

Frodo did not care about the coat. It was used goods now anyway. He did not care about the five small. He did care about the guy, who was clearly an asshole with the gall to treat him like an asshole. The guys should know that they were the assholes. Otherwise there would be asshole anarchy. Now and then you had to let them know. So Frodo bit the bullet and sold a couple of T-bills before maturity, lost 5 percent and got liquid again. By five o'clock he had a hundred and seventy five thousand back in the bank. About half of that would go to Marblehead, but in business you got expenses. Frodo was not cheap, just thrifty. The guy had gone to flight school but flunked out, having no airplane.

By seven that night Tony Crunch was off Frodo's ass and Frodo was tenderly exploring Sylva's. She lay on her tummy on her new gold satin sheets with lace ruffles on the pillow shams. She felt like a safe little girl, which she had never felt before in her life. She was reading a Spanish language bridal magazine which he had bought her by way of a proposal. He slowly tugged her thong from between the smooth mocha cheeks of her flawless bottom and left behind little kisses in its wake. The wedding was going to take place as soon as she could figure out a way to show him where Honduras was on a map. She was happy though to stay in Brooklyn. Honduras meant zip to Frodo but whatever made her happy.

Sylva had seen the coat and couldn't care less about it. Chinchillas were nasty little fuckers, whereas Frodo was a very nice, patient, caring, attentive and rich fucker. He was also an old fucker. They both knew the marriage would not last very long, as Frodo was reaching the tape at the end of the race. She would make out like a bandit when he crossed the finish line, a career he fully endorsed. When he died, she would get the ratty old Chevy. The seats were stuffed with cash and bearer bonds. Then there were the warehouses in Jersey.

A month later at the wedding reception at Maria's Gourmet Cuisine in Coney Island, Frodo said, "Fuckin' Lexus, my ass. Dumb fuckin' asshole." Sylva fed him a tiny, delicate piece of sweet, white wedding cake with creamy icing. He smiled the smile of a man who would be forever in love and they very gently kissed.

Turning the Tables

Rachel Kramer Bussel

Slinking amongst the overly bedazzled crowd, I slide my way to
the bar, careful not to trip on my Cinderella slippers and long,
velvet gown. And while they're not glass, they may as well be;
they are clear, tall lucite, more like stripper shoes than orphaned
fairy tale footwear, but they seemed like fun, a modern twist on
everyone's favorite orphan. The fact that I'm at the party at all
is only a testament to my friendship with Marlene, aka Princess
Leia, who keeps swooping in and out carrying trays of food and
admonishing people not to remove their costumes. She had a
strict admittance policy and, fearing that I wouldn't get in, I
adhered to it, even though I wasn't even sure I was in a party
mood. Nothing like the chance of not getting in to make me
want to be part of an inner circle.

I'm making my way through my cocktail, trying to find
someone I know, or might want to know, when I see a gorgeous
nymph of a girl, the kind who my heart speeds up for, the kind
who makes me want to pull them by the hair and never let go.
She is dressed as a classic schoolgirl, not surprising in this
crowd but still charming nonetheless. Her hair spurts out in two
brown pigtails, tied with those rubber bands with big pink
beads on the end that I haven't seen in about 20 years. Her skirt
is short and plaid, on top of strategically ripped fishnets, her
shirt white and sheer, her bra the exact opposite. A studded
collar beams out from around her neck, but I've been watching
her for an hour and know she is alone. This isn't a slave collar,
but an I-want-to-be-a-slave collar, even if that desire only lasts

a night. Her bottom lip is pierced smack in the center of it, a surly circle daring anyone watching to touch it. Daring in that defiant way that really means, stay away. But I can't, or don't want to. She is the kind of girl who challenges me, who makes me want to tie her up with her own fishnets, make her defy all her own practised coolness to beg me to fuck her. It's Halloween and although there are far more original outfits at this party, I only have eyes for her. I approach her slowly, keeping my eyes on her until she is forced to look my way, even though others are vying for her attention. Her bright red lipstick glows against her pale skin, and though she's probably 21 or 22, she could easily pass for 5 years younger, her sullen eyes and daring look just asking anyone who'll try to have their way with her. My hand is practically itching to grab her, to get her across my lap, her ass exposed, but before I race too far ahead of myself and completely scare her away, I pause and regroup, taking a deep breath and trying to pretend that she's just a pretty girl at a party who somehow hasn't set off a rush of heat inside my brand new black lace panties.

As I approach her, my mind is racing with all the delicious games I want to play with her but all I say is "Hi," deadpan, not giving anything away. I lean against the table, trying to play it cool. She looks me up and down and then sticks a finger in her mouth, sucking on it like a lollipop, her eyes twinkling with girlish mischief. I take a step closer; I need to teach this brat a lesson. She finally takes her finger out of her mouth and holds it out to me, approaching my lips as if she is offering a sample of the best dessert ever. She's being deliberately naughty but I don't think even she knows the kind of punishment I want to dole out to her. I grab her outstretched hand but instead of taking the proffered finger, I push it behind her back and press her up against the wall. She's wearing a choker, the kind that kinky girls like to wear to signal that they're not your ordinary schoolgirls, that they're far more cut-class-and-smoke-in-the-bathroom types than ponytailed-cheerleader-in-a-mini-skirt. Only they don't know that those are often the kinkiest girls of all yet, so they dress up much like this, but on her somehow it works, less of an act and more of a display, an offering. I tower over her thanks to my sharp, spiky heels, well worth the pinching and puffiness my feet will later feel to be able to look down at her like this. I stroke her neck with my fingertips as she looks up at me, her eyes wide and mouth slightly slack.

The tables have turned in only a moment, but one that has brought us both exactly where we need to be. My cunt is threatening to go into overdrive if I don't give it some attention, and with each second that passes I'm torn between tormenting her further and putting her lipsticked little mouth to good use. I pause for a few moments longer, looking deep into her eyes, making sure she wants this as much as I do. As we stand there not speaking, my hand wrapped around her wrist, daring her to break away, I can feel the infinitesimal changes in her stance, her breathing, the ever-growing red creeping along her skin, the faintly faster breaths escaping from her mouth even as she tries to maintain her cool. We are both playing a game of chicken, wondering who will break first, who will admit to being so wet she cannot stand one more minute of this tension-filled foreplay, and both of us will win whoever goes first. I inch closer to her, and almost laugh at how highly charged things have become between us, before we've even told each other our names. I'm glad that I got a manicure today, glad my nails are just long enough and red enough and intimidating enough to make her flinch slightly as I rake them lightly along her delicate neck, then bring them towards her mouth, which is open just enough for me to slide two digits inside her. Gone is her teasing lollipop offering she made to me earlier; she knows she has no choice as I push my fingers inside, feel her hot, wet mouth fasten around them. She closes her eyes and I watch the muscles in her neck contract as she sucks on my fingers, ready for anything I have to give her. Just as she's getting really into it, has made my fingers the focal point of her entire body, I remove them and bring my hand up under her skirt. Her fishnets are an optical illusion, only covering her up to her thighs; above that point I meet goose-bump-covered flesh, and quickly make it my own, pinching along her upper thighs, claiming her for the night.

She doesn't dare protest, and I know she secretly likes the way I squeeze the tender skin between my fingers, the way that zap travels right up into her nearby pussy, the way with the slightest movement my hand will brush across her cunt and feel her wetness. Because of course even though her skirt is short enough to be considered scandalous even at this party, she's not wearing any panties, not caring who might get a peek at her, and before I can even think better of it my fingers are stroking her along her very wet opening, making my own cunt suddenly ache in a most torturous way. I'd love to sink to my knees and taste her for myself, lick along this slickness my fingers are exploring, bury my face in her juices and suck on her clit, make her grab my head and claw the wall with desire. But, as risqué as this party is, that would be going too far. I loop a finger through the collar and tug on it, making her look at me, then pulling her around so I can lead her into the private closet that only a select few know about, the one that rivals the size of my room and is perfect for fucking, according to Marlene. Leading her along by the studded choker, my hand at the back of her neck, I prod her gently with the occasional brush of my knee against her ass. We are both silent but our walk speaks volumes. I tug on the collar strategically, and shove her inside once we reach the coveted closet, the walk having almost exceeding my patience. I slam her up against the wall and bring my hand back under her skirt, pressing urgently against her cunt, sliding the edge of my hand through her slick lips, then shoving three fingers inside her, my other hand holding her by the neck. "You're a little brat, aren't you? A tease? With that lollipop and little girl look, and those I-need-you-to-fuck-me eyes? This is what you wanted, isn't it, sweetheart?" I croon at her as my fingers probe her sleek walls. But she surprises me, more agile than I've given her credit for.

"Actually, no, that's not what I'm looking for at all." She pushes me away from her and then manages to get me up against the opposite wall, propelling me across the room with her tiny body. "Put your hands up," she says, the cop language working her too, and I do it, too stunned, surprised and aroused to protest. I hear her fumble and then the awful sound of a knife tearing its way up my long velvet skirt, cutting it away until I feel a breeze against my ass. The bitch just ruined my precious thrift store dress! I know I could take her, despite the knife, could turn around and wrestle her to the floor and show her who's boss, but despite her appalling behavior – or maybe because of it – I am now soaking my panties and even more turned on than before. Her fishnet-covered knee comes slamming into my pussy and hits me just hard enough to send a rocket of desire jolting through me. She leaves it there, kneading it against me, and I reach up and hold onto Marlene's closet rod for support, needing something to keep my balance as she works her knee back and forth and has my pussy clenching and way more than ready.

"You think that just because I'm short, or I look the way I do, that I don't know that you want me to fuck you too? You think I don't know that your pussy is pounding right now, that you need it just as bad as I do?" Every word out of her snotty little mouth is just sending me further into overdrive. She moves her knee and rips the dress even further, then yanks down my thin panties in one swoop. They land around my ankles and I move to lift a leg but she doesn't let me, so I stand there, trapped by the flimsy fabric and my own lust, fully exposed to her.

She slides her fingers along my wetness, teasing me just as I did to her, and tears come to my eyes as she taunts me with the nearness of her fingers, almost sliding them in and then back right out, not going near my clit either but simply over and over my slit until she finally takes pity on me and slides those same fingers easily into me, pressing and pushing and expertly working my cunt, though by now I'm so turned on she could do practically anything to me and I'd respond. And she does, her fingers somehow knowing exactly what I need, making me come in a fierce series of spasms that have me holding onto the rod above me for dear life as I push down against her probing digits, her small but powerful fingers that have tears streaming down my face at the intensity of it all. I haven't come like this with someone else in years, haven't let anyone that close to the real me, haven't indulged in quite so much vulnerability, and with a stranger no less. She keeps her fingers there, waiting, her other arm wrapping around me, hugging me as she presses herself to me, and I let her, any composure I once had gone as quickly as it took her to shove me across the closet.

I finally let go of the rod, wipe my face and turn to look at her in the dim light coming in under the door. We still don't speak, but she gets my message as my eyes probe hers, thankful and needy and just a little bit shy. The dress is ruined, but I don't care. Marlene will surely understand as I ditch the dress and slip into one of hers, a flowery summer sundress that has me feeling like I should be out picking flowers or skipping along a field. The girl still looks the same, but somehow all her outer symbols take on a new meaning, not quite menacing but not quite bratty either. I'm still not sure what to make of her, but I let her take my hand as we make our way out of the closet. The party is still in full swing; nobody seems to have missed us. And then I'm not quite sure what to do – how does one make small talk after someone has rocked you to your very soul, gotten inside you so thoroughly and completely you're not even sure who you are anymore? We smile at each other, sweet, sad smiles, and then I go back to the punch table and she goes back to her corner, each of us more than slightly shaken. I wonder if I'll see her again, but even if I don't, she's taught me never to judge a girl by her costume.

Exceptions

J.D. Smith

I've never been a man for ass. The allure of the gluteal has always eluded me; the female form offers far choicer real estate just around the corner, and just a few blocks to the north. Jennifer Lopez's hip-checked rise to stardom is a bigger mystery to me than the tax code, and when Sir Mix-a-Lot recorded "Baby Got Back," I admired his enthusiasm but couldn't share his bulbous faith.

There have been exceptions. From time to time a particularly taut or ample-and-inviting derrière sheathed in a tight skirt might catch my eye, but those were but merely passing things.

The biggest exception, the one that changed my life, stood in front of me in the cashier's line at the company cafeteria. I nearly dropped my tray.

As she turned I saw a fairly pretty woman. Her eyes were a pleasant blue, but watery and a little too far apart. Her breasts stood like Appalachians rather than Rockies.

Then there was, in all its subequatorial splendor, her ass. Not a "bottom", or a "behind", or some other euphemism. Not a butt or a rump, one of those labels that sounds like a cut on a butcher's chart. No. An *ass*, and one that had to be taken on its own round terms.

Ample? Yes, like the lower reaches of a cello. This ass could claim its own zip code. Taut? I couldn't say – yet; it was too soon to bounce a dime off those lower slopes of Paradise. Soft? Again, I couldn't say, but there was no jiggling or sag, no speed bumps of cellulite. *Firm* seemed to be the safest guess. Not sculpted or overflowing, but molded like an English pudding. Remember the bumper sticker? *Life is uncertain. Eat dessert first.*

I reached in my pocket for cash, and when I looked up she was gone.

My cafeteria receipt was my only souvenir of our not-quite meeting. I tucked it, a scrap of hope, under a refrigerator magnet at home. I resolved to save my money: I'd need every spare dime for flowers and chocolates, for reservations at fondue restaurants, for ties that didn't clip on.

For the next week the time stamps on my receipts ranged from 11:58 to 12:47, but I'd received none of them in her presence.

At a corporate headquarters of more than two thousand people she had many places to be present, and many ways to go absent. She might have been a temp, a consultant on assignment from one of the regional offices, or an interviewee who didn't make the final cut. Or she might have been an embezzler, absconding to the south of France or packed off to prison. I had no way of knowing. The employee directory wasn't searchable even by gender, let alone ass.

Each day at a different time I'd wolf down a mini-pizza – or frozen yogurt, sometimes so quickly that my head hurt while looking over the room. Other times, playing periscope for my manly parts, I'd linger over broccoli-and-cheese soup or a slow-nursed double espresso, scanning every table twice. Or I'd make multiple trips, buying first a bagel, then a sandwich, then a cookie.

In five weeks I gained seven pounds. I began to explore for her in other restaurants, partly to walk off my meal.

To paraphrase the song, I was looking for lunch in all the wrong places: the food court of a boutique-ridden mall, the mysterious buffets with fluorescent macaroni and cheese, the nouveau-deli sandwich shops and malt chains with aspiring folk singers perched on stools. I never looked in the hamburger chains or chicken shacks. I couldn't bear the thought that she might keep her figure – especially its most prominent feature – by frequenting grease pits.

Wandering, and some days walking instead of eating, I lost the seven pounds I'd gained, and then some.

Ass ass ass ass.

During my beret phase in college, I read a short story titled "In Dreams Begin Responsibilities". I never learned what the hell that meant, but dreams did provide a great starting point.

Such as *spanking* that ass. Not hard, and not with anything but my open hand, but just to get the feel of it. Her ass. Name, apostrophe-s, ass.

Ass ass ass ass.

I wondered what Tito Puente could have done with that ass. What had he done with others? To the end of his days, after a hundred albums, Tito never stopped smiling. I know why. Have you ever seen the women on the covers of salsa albums?

Maybe I was falling into a fetish. There was only one thing to do: research.

Two hours in the library stacks among old National Geographics left me unmoved. An Internet search at home, where no one could look over my shoulder, proved no more help. The paintings of Rubens showed too much of a good thing. The animated Betty Boops did nothing for me. Betty Grable packed an ass that was simply unfinished, as if the sculptor had gone out for cigarettes and never come back. I got a little misty-eyed realizing that the generation that saved the world from Tojo and Hitler couldn't have enjoyed a better fantasy. I clicked into a narrower but jam-packed niche, filled by sites like Cheekster, Back 40, Ass-o-rama, GluteGlutton, and ButtSteak. I marveled at the sheer variety: skirted, jeaned, hot-panted, gartered, thonged and bathing-suited, as well as bare-ass naked asses. Their shapes and sizes ranged from fashion-model meager to vast mud flaps. Between these extremes were the majestic bubbles of Rio's Carnival and the spring-loaded buttocks of competitive ballroom dancers.

Alas, none moved my blood from its usual course.

Homework done, I went into the field. At the theater I watched an eye-level parade as the end credits rolled, and at coffee shops I pretended to read while women walked out. On the bus I gave up even the pretence of reading. A week of this gave me only caffeine-spiked insomnia, teeth gummy from Jujubes, and a fragment of popcorn kernel stuck in a filling.

At work e-mail piled up ethereally in my inbox, and the message light on my telephone blinked like an eye splashed with picante sauce.

Anything truly awful gets an acronym. TB. DOA. HR. The white top copy of the form that also named me a marked man lay on my chair like a metaphorical thumbtack when I returned from another lunch hour where I had walked but did not eat. The time appointed, hand-written on it in a round, feminine hand, was 11:45 the next morning.

I divided the afternoon between vending machines and housekeeping. After animal crackers, I moved my personal files from hard drive to disks, in case the next day was my last. The security guys don't give you much time as they escort you from the building, and they don't necessarily care if the door hits you in the ass on the way out. After yogurt-raisin trail mix, I scavenged empty copy-paper boxes and started filling them with the objects that had for three years and seven months made my desk my very own space: bobbleheads from all four major team sports and two political campaigns. The picture of me with the previous CEO at the company picnic, taken only weeks before he won an orange jumpsuit for insider trading. After cheese curls late in the day, I speculated about who might have an opening or offer a letter of recommendation.

I went home to a night of fitful sleep, tossed through dreams about voluptuous sand dunes and swelling loaves of bread, hot from the oven. But overnight, my stomach had shrunk to the size of a pea. I couldn't eat breakfast; I nursed my coffee like warm beer while an idiot DJ talked about how many moon pies he had eaten on a dare.

The first hours at work passed like kidney stones. I watched my e-mails mounting like so many love-starved rabbits and filled a few more boxes until it was time.

At HR, before I could so much as read a New Yorker cartoon, I was whisked out of the reception area and down the hall. The receptionist knocked once on a door and opened it just wide enough for me to pass through, like the entrance to a lobster trap.

The face on the other side of the desk looked vaguely familiar. At first it was a struggle, like a baseball announcer trying to figure out the destiny of a long fly ball on a windy day: it can't be . . . it can't be . . . it may be . . . could be . . . looks like . . . probably is . . . has to be . . . yes, yes, it is – a Home Run!

It was her.

Visible only from the desktop up, truncated like a newscaster, and, just as cruelly, visible only from the front, was the object of my dreams – who would also serve as the agent of my termination.

Good morning. I am Irene Nalgala. Nice to meet you, Mr Brown.

Actually, my name isn't Brown.

Sometimes there is confusion in the files. Mr. Johnson, is it?

Not that, either.

I'm sorry. At least she was getting closer. *Mr. Jones?*

Third time was the charm.

Please have a seat.

I settled for a chair.

Have you been informed of the purpose of our meeting this morning?

Not really. My imagination, though, had done a good job of filling in the blanks. *Am I being dismissed?*

She lowered her voice like a funeral director comforting the bereaved. *Oh, no, Mr. Jones. Nothing of the sort.*

I waited for the other shoe to drop, and it did, on my head. *You are probably aware, Mr. Jones, that your productivity recently has not been consistent with what your supervisor tells us is your usually impressive level. Part of what we'll be discussing in our session is the company's policy of assisting employees who are experiencing personal difficulties that affect their performance.*

The polysyllables rolled along. I nearly looked for a Teleprompter on the wall behind me, but knew my looking would only be looked at in turn and find its way into my ever-expanding file.

She passed a form across the desk. My name and contact information were already filled in; I simply had to mark boxes next to conditions from alcoholism to yeast infection. I stopped for a moment at endometriosis to ask what it meant, then wrote a particularly large X.

I passed the form back across the desk with the gravity of a chess move, then waited. She – I could not think of her as Irene, or even Ms Nalgala – scanned the form with the ease of someone who had seen every possible combination before.

It looks like we have a baseline to work from, she said, *and it's certainly good that you're not facing any of the challenges listed. As I'm sure you know, however, not every potential source of difficulty appears on the form. Are there any other issues that might be drawing your concentration away from work?*

One or two, depending on how she counted. *Such as?*

Bereavement, financial difficulties, the end of a relationship, some other recent loss or disappointment.

I mentally checked other "no" boxes. Over the last five years not even a car had died on me. Relationships had come, fortunately, and gone. What other losses? The credit card that slipped through my still-greasy fingers and down a manhole as I walked out of a rib shack in Memphis had long since been replaced. What disappointment? Basketball? On no day, on no court, would I ever dunk, but I had grieved and moved on.

None of her "other" categories quite fit. What would fit? Someone who had worked retail lingerie might know, but not me. For now, though, I didn't have to volunteer anything. I could ingratiate myself, maybe even declare myself later. All I had to do was sit back and wait for the next question, which was:

Are you having an intimate relationship with another employee?
My inner lawyer emerged. What was "intimate"? What was
"relationship"?

Please, Mr Jones.

At least she knew who I was.

*The sessions will remain confidential unless there is information
connected with a crime.*

"Crime"? Did she have a licence for that ass?

I told what seemed like the most useful truth. *No, I'm not
having an affair with anyone in my department, if that's what you
mean.*

Are you thinking of having an affair with someone here?

Funny she should ask. *It has crossed my mind.*

*I appreciate your candor, Mr Jones. I hope we can continue to
build on this trust.*

Me, too.

*I might be able to reassure you somewhat. You may recall that
company policy restricts only relationships within the same department. Employees are free to socialize with anyone else, as long as
their behavior is not disruptive of the workplace.*

As she sorted through the stack of forms that was becoming
my dossier, the bare ring finger of her left hand emerged from
between the pages, unlined and smooth as her magnificent
lower slopes. My heart, and other organs, leapt. Yet this didn't
seem to be the time to speak.

Her delicate hands sifted through the papers a second time,
more quickly, then came to rest like the wings of a disheartened
bird.

*I hope you'll excuse me for just a moment. I have to find another
form that we need to complete the intake session.*

Ms Nalgala – or was it Dr Nalgala? – stood and walked to a
file cabinet behind her desk. She crouched to open the bottom
drawer and rocked back on her heels like a major league catcher.

Words formed in my brain and turned into action that I could
muffle, like a sneeze in a theater, but had no way to stop. *Hold
that pose!* And then two more syllables slipped out. *Baby.*

She turned. *Excuse me, Mr Jones, did you say something?*

Yes, but not something I wanted to repeat just yet. *I, uh, might need to blow my nose.*

There is a box of tissues on the corner of the desk. I will be with you in a moment.

I pulled a tissue out of the box and brought it to my nose. I blew once, then again. Nothing. My sinuses had become a small Sahara.

She stood up – to my eternal sadness – and returned with a final form that forced me to give my voluntary consent to counseling.

She scooped the papers into a folder with an air of finality. *We have come to the end of our session for today, but we will be in touch* – There was an idea – *to schedule your next appointment.* She said something about needing lunch before her next appointment, and I was wafted out of the room in the way that people behind desks know how to do these days.

But I was not fired. The knot in my stomach unraveled, and at once I was terribly hungry. Hungry like the wolf, as the college kids said who hadn't even been born when the song came out. Unpacking my boxes could wait. A thought seized me. Where would she, Irene Nalgala, go for lunch if she had only a short time between appointments? The burrito cart on the next block fell by a voluptuous wayside. My destiny might be served on the steam tables.

No one seemed to hear me singing snippets of songs as I made for the cafeteria. Almost every song that included the word *love*, I discovered, could be sung instead with the word *lunch*. Who's to say that the O-Jays wouldn't have taken the Lunch Train, or that the Ohio Players might not have taken the Rollercoaster of Lunch? Certainly not me.

A plan came as I waited in line for purportedly "Athenian" chicken. I could see if she needed Tabasco sauce, or some other, more appropriate condiment. Or I could simply take a table that would let me watch her lushly appointed coming and going. I took my laden tray and added a slice of pie and a cookie, perchance to share, to my usual diet cola. If there had been birds in the cafeteria, they would have sung sweetly.

I lined up at the left-hand cashier and watched the right-hand line began to move faster until there stood ahead of me, at about a two o'clock position, her. And her *ass*.

My blood sugar must have plunged, or at least that's the explanation I prefer. My hands shook as I set my tray on the rails. Which was still a foot away. The tray fell, carrying me with it. I hit the floor with a clatter of stainless-steel silverware and the clank of unbreakable foodservice crockery.

I couldn't tell if my bones had proved as unbreakable. Still shaken, with one lavish mashed-potato sideburn, I sat up and checked for damage. Others came to help, but I waved them off and gathered myself. Waiting for heads to turn away from me, daubing foodstuffs from my face, I saw the lunchtime crowd as I had never seen it before: a profusion of shoes and pants, a moving forest of legs.

Just a little above two stiletto heels rested a pair of exquisitely chiseled and delicate ankles, detailed like the ivory sculpture that fills Asian gift shops in every shopping mall.

I could clasp each of those ankles in a hand like a prized gem or a precious egg. I could polish them with my tongue. The ache of my bruises faded. The embarrassment of being spattered from head to foot with lunch vanished.

I have never been a man for ankles.

But there are, of course, exceptions.

Worship

Elspeth Potter

At your monthly doctor visit, the nurse uses a special tool to cut your wedding ring from your grotesquely swollen finger. "Only one snip," she says, as if that makes it better. "A jeweler can fix it again, good as new."

The mutilation will still be there in your mind's eye, a severing of a sacred bond. You will never wear the ring again: you can never get it onto your finger after this, even at night when the swelling is down a little.

Your husband picks you up out front. He's been getting a haircut while you listened to the rheumatologist. You can smell the fresh barbershop smell of the talcum on his collar, see little flecks of dark hair on the back of his neck, muscular and strong. He can lift you in and out of the bathtub when your knees or hips, or sometimes both, are too stiff.

He opens the door of the car for you, and helps you fasten the shoulderbelt and fumble on your sunglasses. "Any new prescriptions?" he asks, as he pulls out into traffic.

"No," you say. His hands on the steering wheel are big and square and strong, the nails neatly trimmed. You had fallen in love with his hands first. You can see the gold band on his left ring finger, and you wonder if he ever takes it off, if he ever looks for a woman besides you, a bedroom gymnast to ease himself. He's a good-looking man, your Jeffrey. His eyes are brown as coffee, and full of good humor. He plays tennis once a week with his friends from the Masonic Hall. You feel like a chunk of slowly petrifying wood. You imagine not being able to move at all, someday. Your doctor has said that knee or hip replacements are a possibility, so long as your overall health remains good. You don't want to think about that just yet. You don't want to think about what will happen when your elbows freeze up.

Old people have their hips replaced. You are only fifty-six. Jeffrey is fifty-eight and has hardly been ill a day in his life. You had fibroids. You had your gall bladder out. You spent six hours on your tail in the yard once because you'd slipped and couldn't get back up again. If you didn't love Jeffrey more than you love yourself, you'd be jealous of his health and vigor.

You can't believe he's still with you. Even though he spends vacation days taking you to the doctor. Even though he is willing to help you get up off the toilet in the middle of the night when your hands can't grasp the rail. If that isn't love, you aren't sure what is.

You never thought it would be like this when you married him. You and Jeffrey were going to be one of those couples that went hiking in Nepal or spent their weekends rattling around the countryside buying folk art and old milk bottles. Instead, you can hardly walk around the mall.

Jeffrey says, "There wasn't any line at the barber shop, so I was done early. I got us something."

"What?" There's a brown paper bag on the seat between you. Jeffrey stops the car for a red light. You let him reach in with one hand and tug something out partway.

"Juh – Jeffrey—"

It's a dirty video. You've never seen such a thing in your life, except in shop windows you'd hurry past. You know Jeffrey doesn't own any, and he gave up girlie magazines in high school, he told you once. So why? You don't know whether to be hurt or simply astonished.

He's grinning at you like a little boy, and you settle on astonishment. The light turns green, and he accelerates and says, "I went next door to the coffee shop, and the magazine on my table had this article about spicing up your love life—"

"Jeffrey—" You have no love life any more. Not one that involves sex, anyway.

"I thought it might be fun." He smiles at you sidelong; he's watching the traffic. Jeffrey's a careful driver.

"Where did you get the tape?" you ask, trying to make this a normal conversation.

"That place behind the dry cleaner's. It's a rental," he says, after he turns down Revello, the street that leads to your subdivision. "Lucille, there were college girls looking at the adult videos. The clerk didn't even look twice at me."

"We're not college kids." You don't mean to sound so abrupt. But you talk to him like that all the time. Sometimes your words just stab out like the piercing pain you can't control. And Jeffrey takes those words in, calm as a feather pillow. Muffling your pain. Never complaining. You can't tell how you hold him, why he stays. Since you can't see his motives, you're not sure he will always be there, even though you try to believe in him. It's been twenty-four years, and you can't quite believe.

"I can take the video back." He turns again, and now you're passing your neighbors' houses. You wonder if any of those couples, in between cutting their grass and buying vinyl siding, rent dirty videos behind the dry cleaning place. You've never been in there; Jeffrey always goes in to get whatever it is: John Wayne, mostly. Sometimes a caper movie, or a historical drama. You've only had a VCR in the last year or so, a gift from Jeffrey. You have a special remote with big buttons that you still have trouble using sometimes, if your hands are especially stiff.

Jeffrey's pulling into the driveway before you realize you never answered him. The truth is, you'd like to do something fun with your husband, especially something different. A dirty movie wouldn't have occurred to you, but why not? The VCR is in the privacy of your bedroom. He's paid for the rental already. You've been married for years; this shouldn't be able to shame you.

You want to do some tiny thing for your husband.

Jeffrey's putting on the parking brake. You clumsily pat his hand and say, "Are you going to make popcorn?"

*   *   *

The movie is dispiriting. Some of the women have visible scars from breast enlargement surgery, and the men aren't nearly as attractive as Jeffrey. You're leaning back against his chest instead of your gray corduroy "husband" pillow. The real husband is warmer and smells like the barbershop and a hint of sports antiperspirant. His arm is wrapped around your waist, firm and comforting. You've both been criticizing the sets, the plot, and the acting ever since the tape started with some ads for films with titles like "Ass-rassic Park," but the criticizing is fun. You'd never realized before that Jeffrey never liked skinny women with big breasts. He comments, "She looks so off-balance she'd keel over in a good wind."

You point out the obviously fake hair of one of the men. "I thought bald was sexy? You know, Kojak?"

"Or Captain Picard," Jeffrey says, referring to the character from *Star Trek* you'd once admitted, reluctantly, you liked. "That guy's no Captain Picard, but he does have a pretty big, uh, phaser."

You try to pretend you're not laughing. Jeffrey's hardly ever raunchy and when he is, it's always very funny to see him blush. "Maybe the hair is a disguise," you comment. "He's really on the City Council but doesn't want the voters to know."

The only time you both fall silent is when one of the women is performing oral sex on two of the men. You and Jeffrey have never done that. Not either way. Where you grew up, people talked about it like it was dirty, like you'd get germs. That was something prostitutes did to men in their cars. Jeffrey never brought it up with you, or you with him. Now all you can think of is that the woman isn't using her hands. At all.

You could do that. You don't need your hands to do oral sex. "Suck his cock," they say in the movie. When you think of doing that for Jeffrey, those words don't seem so disgusting.

"Turn it off," you say.

He does. "Tired, Luce?"

He kisses your temple. It's been a while since you've sat in bed together, touching like this. You touch all the time, but all of it is him helping you get out of bed, get into bed, climb stairs.

Like a nurse and a patient, not a husband and his wife. Jeffrey
kisses your neck, and it feels just as good as it used to feel.
Better, because it has been so long. You love the scratchiness of
his cheek as he nuzzles under your chin. You say, "Tired of that
movie. It was terrible."

"I thought they'd at least look a little more enthusiastic."

"Maybe they were bored. I mean, if all they do all day, every
day is have sex, it would be like . . . like . . ."

Jeffrey says, "Wonder Bread? White rice?"

You say, "Generic dog food?"

You both laugh, then silence falls, because sex hasn't been
like Wonder Bread for either of you for a long time. Jeffrey
kisses your neck again, and you lean into him a little more, and
say, "Unbutton my blouse for me." You'd dressed up for the
doctor visit, which meant something other than your usual
decorative T-shirt and sweats.

Jeffrey says, "I bet I could do that with one hand." His arm
tightens around your waist. You guess he doesn't want to move
from this current comfortable position; neither do you, but if
the two of you don't move, the picture in your head, of his cock
in your mouth, will never happen.

"Can you take all of my clothes off with one hand?" You're
wearing a loose skirt with the blouse, and had awkwardly heeled
off your sandals when you got home. Nylons are one thing
you've never missed.

Jeffrey looks a little surprised, but he doesn't ask that you're
up to, which you'd thought he might. Maybe he knows. He
shifts your body carefully back against the husband pillow and
kneels on the bed beside you. He starts unbuttoning your plaid
blouse, with one hand, just like he said. His other hand, big and
hot, rests on your hip.

Your skirt and underwear take some work; you have to lift up
a little; it would have been much easier if you'd been standing
up, with a wall or Jeffrey there to lean on while you stepped out
of it. But neither of you makes that suggestion. His free hand
moves to your waist. When Jeffrey unclasps your bra, you can
see his hands are trembling, just a little. Then you're nude, and

staring into his beautiful brown eyes. You hold out your arms and he comes to you.

The embrace is pretty uncomfortable, but you're able to stroke his back a little with your forearms. There's some kissing, and you savor the taste of mint toothpaste and the scrape of his afternoon beard on your face. When Jeffrey sits back and starts unbuttoning his shirt, you notice with surprise that your nipples are hard and tender, and not from cold, either.

Jeffrey keeps glancing at you as he's undressing, and you can read his desire and worry like a road map. He's about to say something, but you want to be in charge. You want to have control over something in your life. Before he can speak, you say, "Hurry up and come here."

"You sure you don't want to finish watching that great movie first?"

You pretend to think about it while he's stepping out of his khakis. You look at the clear delineation of his shape underneath his Y-fronts, and you remember how silky-soft his skin is over his penis, and the soft hair on his balls. Finally you say, "We can turn it on again if I run out of ideas."

Jeffrey sits down next to you and puts his hand on your thigh. "I got a few ideas myself," he says.

"You picked the movie. I pick that you—" You consider how you might manage this. You swing your legs over the side of the bed. "Come stand over here."

"You're in charge."

You smile. "Yes, I am. I want to try this," you say, when he's standing between your spread legs. The height's just about right. You can see his cock that you used to love touching so much give a little bob hello. You lean forward and lick once over the slit at the tip, your own kind of greeting.

Jeffrey sucks in a breath. You let your tongue dip in deeper, and find that you've pushed a little too hard; his penis is trying to escape, it's so encouraged. You look up at Jeffrey's face, which is wide-eyed and a little pink, and tell him, "Hold that still for me."

His big hand wraps around the bottom of his shaft, and you

start licking around his little cap. He doesn't taste bad, like you might have thought. He tastes mostly like the rest of his skin. A little sweeter and muskier, maybe. And a hint of pepper without pepper's heat.

Carefully, you open your mouth and suck the head past your lips and it feels so good, so solid and warm and sweet, that you want to bite down and chew and swallow and then do it all again. But you don't do any of that. You suck gently for a moment, then your neck cramps up and you're bent over, whimpering, and being bent over hurts your back between your shoulders and down above your tailbone and Jeffrey is having to lift you onto the bed and gently, gently straighten out your limbs as tears of frustration roll down your nose and all over your face and onto the pillow, and curses spill out of your mouth like the tears.

Jeffrey massages your neck and back until the muscles loosen up. You've done the exercises, everything your physical therapist told you, but it isn't enough. It will never be enough. You'll never be healthy again, not like you were.

Jeffrey gets up and goes and sits on his side of the bed, the right side.

You say, "Why do you stay with me? Jeff? Why?"

He says, "Because I love you." He reaches into your purse, there on the nightstand, and pulls out the twist of paper wrapping your severed wedding ring. "I married you in sickness and in health. And I meant it." He takes your ring and puts it on his pillow. "With my body I thee worship. Remember that?"

He's looking at you like you'd always dreamed someone would look at you when you were a little girl, and for many years after, until the company picnic where you saw him with a pitiful bag of potato chips and he saw you with your silver platter of deviled eggs.

Your body isn't worthy of much worship. It has surgical scars and cellulite and varicose veins, and a few misshapen brown spots from a childhood in the sun. You wonder how Jeffrey can worship your body when you can find nothing in it that is satisfactory. You close your eyes. You've gotten used to doing as Jeffrey says. Usually he's right. If only you could just give in and let him do your thinking for you. You'd have no doubts then, no emotional pain, no regrets or grief. His love for you would be enough, until he was parted from you by death. "I remember," you say, softly.

He smoothes your hair and strokes the side of your face, leaving warmth and taking away mourning. He's smiling. "It's time for some worship, Luce." He settles back against the headboard. "Can you see me?"

You can see mostly his lap. His erection has perked up. You consider reaching for it but a twinge from your sore muscles keeps you still. Maybe it's worth the pain, to have him in your mouth again in that intimate kiss.

You see Jeffrey's hand come down and cover the head of his penis and close up tight. "Like this," he said. "It was like this, only better. I could see you liked it."

"I want to suck you in all the way," you say, the words tumbling out, a blush heating your face. "I want to . . . suck your cock. Rub it like I want to rub it with my tongue."

Jeffrey rubs and you can see his belly go taut and his back arch, just a little, and you see his big, strong hand tensing, so rough and dark over the tender skin of his cock. You remember the first time you saw his hand on your breast, in this very room, in the afternoon sunlight.

His hand tightens, tugs, holds; his fingers relax and he does it again and again. You can see his shoulders tighten each time his hand pulls. You want him to come and you can see he wants it, too.

"I want you to come," you say. The words spill out and his cock twitches in his grip. "Tell me you want to come."

"I want to come," Jeffrey says, his eyes staring into yours and his hand quickening its motions. You're pretty sure you're not breathing. "I want to come for you."

"Faster," you say. "Faster, faster, faster," once for each stroke, and it's like your words are your mouth and his hand and you can almost feel that satin flesh on your tongue and then his cock is jerking and spurting and it's like you did it. You.

"God, Luce," Jeffrey says when he's done. He's made a mess but you don't care. He reaches over and pats your hand and gets sticky semen all over it, then he carefully arranges himself along your body and it's the best feeling in the world. "You are so fine," he says in your ear, and that's better still.

"Next time, no movie," you say. "Just the cock sucking."

Jeffrey laughs. "I love you."

Resignation

N.T. Morley

9 December

Ms. Antoinette Childress
Chief Preceptor
Birchwood Heights College for Young Women
One Birchwood Heights Lane
Merrington, VT

Dear Antoinette:
It is with regret that I, Felicity Hamilton, must tender my
resignation as an employee of Birchwood Heights College for
Young Women, effective at the end of the fall term. Since the
start of the school year, I have been employed as Residential
Preceptor for Hall A of the Carrigan Memorial Dormitory.
Given the rumored proclivities of Miriam Carrigan, I suspect it
will come as no surprise to you that Hall A is an assemblage of
incorrigible miscreants, troublemakers, budding criminals, aspiring whores, accomplished tarts, sluts, exhibitionists and
saucy deviants of a most unpleasant nature.

In the event that you have mislaid my no fewer than fourteen
memoranda pleading for disciplinary assistance in bringing the
residents of Hall A under control, I have detailed below just a
few of the choicest misdeeds committed by the student body.
Please note that I have refrained from listing the almost daily
ritual of birchings, canings, paddlings, and bare-bottomed
spankings that being preceptor of Hall A has required of me,

not to mention the litany of unscheduled panty inspections, strip searches, and review of the shower surveillance cam to prevent (or correct) any improper hygiene practices. Such a list would take far more time for me to pen than the few days remaining in the fall term.

1) On 1 September, the night before the first day of school, freshman Monet Williams was discovered in the laundry room with sophomore Murietta Davis. Ms Williams was quite busy having her head dunked in the laundry room washing machine by Ms Davis. It shames me to say, Antoinette, that both girls were in their bra and panties: When pressed for an explanation, Murietta said she "just wanted to show the little slut how we do the upperclassmen's laundry here at Birchwood."

When it was pointed out to her that she was hardly an upper-classman, Murietta turned quite scarlet and used a flurry of bad language to abuse this residential preceptor. Apparently, Ms Davis had misrepresented herself to Ms Williams as a junior, almost as serious an infraction of our rules as dunking a fresh-man's head in the washing machine. In following with Birch-wood policy, Murietta was instructed to bend over the washing machine while Monet retrieved my preceptory paddle, and the sophomore was subjected to a stern paddling from both wronged parties, as well as a fervent dunking by her erstwhile victim.

Sadly, I must report that the story does not end there. Later in the evening I discovered Murietta and Monet in that very same laundry room. Monet was mounted once more on the washing machine as it went through its spin cycle, and her hand was quite firmly entangled in Murietta's hair, forcing it be-tween her naked thighs for ministrations of a most distressingly Sapphic nature. Monet was heard to utter the following state-ment: "Oh, yeah, bitch, you like that, don't you, bitch, you love eating that freshman pussy, bitch, oh look, here comes that bitch Hamilton, maybe if you beg she'll give you what-for again, slut."

I should point out, Antoinette, that this malapropism on Monet's part is a direct quote, helpfully captured on the audio track of the laundry room's surveillance camera.

Needless to say, Monet soon found herself in quite the same position Murietta had occupied, following on Birchwood's policy of making the punishment fit the crime. It saddens me to say that I discovered the little slut was sodden as a Peruvian summer, and my discovery of that fact propelled Monet well into the throes of a violent sexual release as she orally serviced her classmate. Since, of course, Monet had gone so far as to call me as well as Murietta a bitch, there was little left to do other than to administer my own similar punishment to Monet. Antoinette, I know it will shock you to know that as Monet was being punished, Murietta discovered her to be as vulnerable then as before to sexual stimulation – quite repeatedly, I must add.

2) On 14 September, during our weekly inspection immediately after shaving period, I discovered that sophomore Katrina Miller's otherwise impeccable mound had been sullied by hints of lipstick of a shade senior Jeannette Johnson informed me is popularly called "cocksucker red". As you know, Birchwood policy strictly prohibits the wearing of cosmetics except for weekly Bridal Trainings.

Since Jeannette appeared to be little miss know-it-all, she was employed to administer a stern birching to Katrina in an attempt to elicit the source of the forbidden cosmetic enhancement. (Jeannette, it must be noted, administered said birching "to this little whore's behind with pleasure" – her words.) Upon punishment, Katrina admitted that the lipstick had come directly from the mouth of sophomore Emily Wilson who had apparently assisted in Katrina's shaving and been so overcome with Sapphic temptation that she had applied shocking oral attentions to the freshly-trimmed orifice. Emily, of course, denied the incident, and it took extensive investigation by the helpful Jeannette to discover that the sophomore tart had secreted the lipstick in a most unsavory place. Antoinette, my intention is not to shock you, but Emily clearly achieved her release during Jeannette's extensive rummaging in her sodden netherpassage.

Since, obviously, Emily had displayed a proclivity toward both lipstick and tonguejobs, she was punished by being instructed to administer both to the turgid furrows of the entire hall. It took most of Sunday and into Monday to accomplish this task, but the residents of Hall A were most obliging in their participation, and Emily clearly learned her lesson.

3) The previous incident led me to believe that Jeannette Johnson was quite a proper young lady, having learned quite well the principles of behavior at Birchwood. Unfortunately, I must report that this is not the case. On 15 October I discovered (upon routine weekly inspection of the residents' panty drawers) that Jeannette was harboring quite a monstrous secret among her prim cotton underthings. Wrapped in a pair of heart-adorned boxer shorts, I found a Sapphic tool of a most unimaginable nature. When I confronted Jeannette with this item, she brazenly admitted that it was hers, informing me that she had planned to "strap it on for your mother, bitch". Confronted with this reprehensible attitude, I summoned the residents of Hall A into Jeannette's room and "strapped it on" for her, demonstrating beyond the shadow of a doubt to all present that Jeannette's eyes were considerably bigger than either of her passages.

Though it got quite cramped in there with more than twenty girls witnessing the punishment, I must say that it was made somewhat easier given the fact that weekly panty inspection requires all residents to be naked (to ensure that no contraband underthings can be hidden in untoward spots). The close quarters did require no fewer than four girls to crowd onto Jeannette's single bed as I punished her, but as they were all reclined lengthwise, it was possible to accommodate them. I selected the four most poorly behaved girls (Marica, Serena, Twill, and Penny) to get the most advantageous view of Jeannette's savaging, which presented its own problems when I discovered all four of them locked in Sapphic couplings right beside me! Needless to say, these four girls were administered punishments identical to Jeannette's, the hated phallic tool still glistening with the plentiful gushings of Jeannette's passage.

I have enclosed the specified member here, confiscated for your inspection, unlaundered, for the purpose of documenting the copious humitude of Hall A's resident snatches. My intention is not to shock you, Antoinette, but as you know, residential preceptorage is rarely pretty.

4) Finally, and most egregiously, one week ago Friday, virtually all the residents of Hall A were discovered well after lights-out in freshman Erica Nottage's room, making quite a ruckus. Upon entering I discovered Erica splayed on the bed, attired most shockingly and bound wrist and ankle to the head and footboard! Junior Cecile Morrow and sophomore Pandora Drew had stripped themselves bare and were applied with some fervency to young Erica's body, Pandora administering body-slams to the poor girl's face with her legs spread quite wide while Cecile caned her lace-pantied sex. All this occurred while the other residents of Hall A cheered the girls on.

Extensive interrogation brought out the fact that Erica's roommate, freshman Veronica Wallop, had discovered Erica so appareled in anticipation of sneaking out for a date with a boy (an infraction that carries a penalty of immediate expulsion). She had summoned the other girls, who had wrestled the transgressing freshman to the bed and begun to administer their own brand of punishment. Antoinette, I don't mean to shock you, but Erica was clad in just the barest of dresses that would have been considered exceedingly inappropriate had it adorned a worn-out whore in a Thailand brothel, and was so far beyond Birchwood's dress code as to suggest that our young Erica had been replaced by some sort of doppelganger. Furthermore, the insufficiency of the girl's undergarments in covering her underlips – not to mention her posterior, which was hidden (or shall I say "revealed") by nothing more substantial than a fragrant scrap of dental floss – was so shocking as to elicit a gasp from my lips when I saw them up close – as did the fact that they were badly in need of a determined wringing-out.

Erica refused to admit that she'd dressed up for a date, regaling me instead with a fairy tale of how the other girls had forced her to dress up like this so they could "whore her out down by the waterfront."

Unmoved by Erica's improbable account I informed the

freshman that if she wanted to make a slut of herself she could quite effectively do it without leaving Birchwood. Though Erica protested at first, she soon learned her lesson, discovering that a date with boys, in addition to being strictly against the rules, was wholly inadvisable. The other residents of Hall A were commended both for their apprehension of their wicked schoolmate and for their enthusiastic participation in her punishment (which took the remainder of the weekend, and then some).

How I wish I could end the story there, Antoinette! It was soon confessed to me at weekly panty inspection that the "official" account of things was not in any way accurate. This confession was elicited from Veronica upon discovery of a black lace garter belt – a garter belt! – in her panty drawer along with black fishnet stockings. Apparently Veronica had conspired with the other girls on the hall to overpower and dress up young Erica, whom they considered to be "too stuffy for her own good – or ours." Though several girls had helped her smuggle in an array of lace garments for the forced transformation, Veronica had been unable to part with the garter belt and stockings, which she considered quite fetchingly sexy.

Since Erica's account of things now appeared to be accurate, I had no choice but to reverse the previous state of affairs, requiring each of the participants in the scheme to return Erica's lingual attentions to the wronged girl's nether regions. Erica was quite eager to participate in this punishment in order to set right the state of affairs. In fact, as she was serviced she could be heard uttering language that was quite inappropriate for use during a disciplinary session at Birchwood. Needless to say, this indiscretion was corrected as soon as Erica's recompense was completed – each girl at whom she had hurled an encouraging or demeaning expletive was invited to hurl the same back at her tenfold, and thereafter to administer a few swats to the potty-mouthed trollop's well-used bottom.

As you can see, Ms Childress, there is little I can do to maintain discipline on Hall A. I am at quite a loss, finding myself as incapable of maintaining order as I was of behaving when I was a student here just a few short years ago. As you know, I was disciplined quite severely for indiscretions and oversights, and I think this account should establish that I've not learned my lesson yet. That is why I've submitted my application for Birchwood's graduate program in Home Economics, with the humble aspiration that you'll accept me as a candidate for student residence at Birchwood – preferably on Hall A. Clearly, Antoinette, I deserve it. My hope is that, given my catalog of the indefatigable sins of Hall A's residents, you will take over the residential preceptorage of this incorrigible hall yourself. I'm quite hopeful that your firm hand, so much more experienced than mine (as I discovered many times when I was a resident on Hall A during my undergraduate studies) will render the otherwise inveterate tarts as obedient as possible, and produce the kind of young ladies of which Birchwood can be proud.

Miss Childress, I implore you to consider my application for residence on Hall A. In my mind, nothing else will correct my failings as a preceptor.

Sincerely,

Felicity Hamilton
Residential Preceptor
Carrigan Memorial Dormitory, Hall A
Birchwood Heights College for Young Women

Handwritten note at bottom:

I believe we should discuss this letter in person Felicity. Please meet me in the laundry room at 6:00 pm on the last day of class.

On second thought, assemble the hall's other residents there as well. See you at six.

Miss Childress

Guided Tours

Jolan Sulinski

Lewis cautiously peered into the cup of thin, dark sauce and sniffed it. He shrugged, and in a single, smooth motion, he poured it over the pile of slender brown noodles set before him. The sauce flooded through the noodles and out from under the red lacquer box that was their home. Lewis twitched slightly as the cold sauce soaked through his trousers. His fellow travelers froze. Half of them tensed, ready to be chased out of the restaurant by a katana-wielding chef. The other half choked on suppressed laughter.

The Japanese said nothing, only blinked at the silly gaijin, and continued their meals. A waitress rushed over with a washcloth. May, the ever-nonplussed tour guide, offered Lewis her napkin. A flurry of apologies and reassurances in Japanese and English thickened the air.

"Mr Hoffman," said May, "Dip the soba in the sauce next time. One mouthful at a time."

"Yes. Well. Maybe next time we should just tie my hands behind my back and let me bury my face into whatever is put before me. It will be only slightly less embarrassing."

May smiled and touched his arm. This small touch managed to wipe his brain of the incident entirely. He would've joyfully rammed edamame up his nose if only she would consent to keep her fingers there.

Lewis had not traveled much, even though he was a carto-grapher by trade. He made maps; he didn't use them to go places. Leave the data collection to the graduate students. Why should he get his hands dirty? He did the same thing day in and day out, each week a replica of the one before it. Get up, go to work, eat a microwave burrito and fall asleep in front of the TV. His life was smooth and precise, as unwavering as the lines of latitude.

The inspiration for this trip had come in December. One day, Lewis went to the bank and found that all the doors were locked. This was strange for a Wednesday. He stared hard at his reflection in the glass, and saw himself surrounded by piles of white. He turned around and noticed, for the first time, that everything was covered in snow. He checked the calendar function on his watch and saw that it was the 25th. Lewis couldn't recall autumn. He felt ill.

Lewis had some vacation time to use. He decided to go someplace exotic, to shock himself out of his stagnation, but knew he wouldn't get very far on his own. Still, he had mixed feelings about taking a tour. He didn't want to get stuck following a stiff itinerary with whiney retirees wearing their pants hiked up to their tits.

After a brief search, he got a good deal on a package to Japan with a small local company called Chawan Tours. It offered modest-sized groups, a relaxed pace, and plenty of time to wander on one's own, just what he was looking for. Japan! The other side of the world! Everything would be different there: the food, the language, the architecture, and with any luck, himself.

Lewis's expectations of the tour company were surpassed. The guide, May, was an inspiration. It was as if she had just stepped out of a pulp fiction paperback, the brilliant and daring heroine in a crisp white shirt that never stained and khakis that never wrinkled. One got the impression that she could go anywhere and do anything. As a guide, she had a gentle touch. She was happy to let her charges make their own discoveries and their own mistakes. She stood calmly aside and assisted only if asked, or if, presumably, the situation was life threatening. One could easily imagine her inside of a ramen shop calmly sipping beer while Godzilla gobbled up busloads of salarymen a block away.

Lewis took a liking to her immediately. She was cool and self-possessed. She was quiet, too, which lent an air of mystery to her. Lewis developed an astounding crush on her over the course of the tour. Every night he dreamt of her. He shut his eyes and she wrestled crocodiles, scaled mountains, drank whiskey straight from the bottle, took him to bed.

Lewis awoke every morning with an erection that taunted him, for these were dreams and would remain so. He was shy. He was smart and happy-go-lucky, too, but these qualities tended to fail him just when needed most. He became clumsy both linguistically and kinetically before the object of his desire. Awkwardness is generally not something women look for in a man, he found.

But this day, in the restaurant, the gods were in a good mood, and they smiled upon Lewis as he stood there with wet pants. Sometimes, making an ass of oneself does not destroy one's chances for romance. Rather, it is one's opportunity to prove how charming and gracious one can be under such circumstances. And so Lewis did not lose love but encourage it by the Soba Incident.

The next day the group had some free time in the afternoon and split up. Lewis stood on the street as usual wrestling with an armful of tourist brochures, all half unfolded, as if he was inventing a new and particularly ugly school of origami.

"Mr Hoffman."

Lewis started. May was beside him. She had taken a special interest in him, or so Lewis imagined. Maybe it was just that obvious he needed more guidance than the others, lest he walk grinning into an open manhole.

"I could show you a garden of such intoxicating beauty that you will never want to leave it. Unless, of course, you have other plans?"

He followed her. At first, they didn't talk much. May apparently had no need to speak, and Lewis was so busy trying to think of something clever to say that he was rendered completely dumb. This did not escape May's notice, and she began to ask him a series of questions. "Where are you from? Where do you work? What do you think of the beer here?" The gentle small talk put Lewis at ease. How else can a friendship begin? But Lewis could not wait to get past these preliminaries. He wanted to know why she was so quiet and so cool. He wanted to know what she dreamt about. He wanted to know what she looked like when she was asleep. He wanted to know what she looked like in the shower. He wanted to make her laugh. He wanted to trade secrets with her. The world seemed different when May was near. It engaged him, he saw that he was a part of it, not some disembodied imp amusing himself by reducing it to two dimensions, and for once, he wanted to see more of it.

They left the crowded sidewalks behind and followed a path through a quiet wood. Fallen needles and moss absorbed all sound. They reached a tiny gatehouse, and May gave the monk inside some coins. He handed her a brochure, which she passed over to Lewis.

The temple grounds were built on a narrow strip of land ascending the side of a mountain. Switchbacks cut through a meticulous garden with forest on either side. It was quiet and peaceful. How could such a place exist in this world? It was heartachingly beautiful.

They reached the uppermost boundary of the grounds and sat on a worn stone bench. The view overlooked the city and the mountains on the other side of it.

"I hope," said May, "that there is a place like this inside each one of us. And I hope we each find it." She turned her eyes from the distant peaks and looked at Lewis, who met her gaze. He had been transfixed by her, not the view.

Those eyes. So much to explore in those lovely dark eyes. "I hope so, too," he said softly. She smiled.

They descended. Along the way, May told him the names of the plants and pointed out the techniques that brought out certain effects in the garden. "I learn something new every time I come here," she said.

For the rest of the tour, whenever the group had free time, Lewis went with May. She took care to instruct him, and she intervened whenever he was about to do something that would give the Japanese a hilarious story to tell their friends over tea. This was fairly often.

"You're a good man, Mr Hoffman," May said. "You just need a little guidance."

On the last day, May escorted everyone to the airport. She was not returning with them to the US, but was off to see what sort of trouble she could get into in Southeast Asia before making her way back to the States.

The group had a farewell drink together. When the boarding call for their flight came over the intercom, Lewis tried to say something to May and failed. I had a wonderful time, thanks to you, he thought. "Um, er, I'll be going now," is what he said. He followed this with a series of unintelligible gurgling noises, the music of his nervous self-loathing. He had gone on this trip in the first place to wake himself up with an unapologetic slap, and here he was at the end of it, the same clumsy idiot who began it.

He fumbled with his bag as a language he had never heard before poured out of his mouth. He wondered if perhaps aliens had abducted him when he was a child, and the long-dormant brain-implant of an extra-terrestrial tongue was only now becoming active. He looked into May's dark eyes, and his heart crumbled.

May grabbed him by the collar and kissed him. Lewis' command of English was restored, and they agreed to meet each other in their native land. Lewis could have ripped up his plane ticket and soared home on love.

Back in the States, a romance swiftly blossomed between Lewis and May. They took great pleasure in unraveling one another's mysteries, and they found that they complemented one another. Lewis borrowed May's sense of adventure, and she borrowed his calm. She was fascinated by his lack of restlessness, something she had never known.

Lewis still dreamt about May, but his morning erections no longer taunted him, because he got to go to bed with her in real life, too. She was a passionate and generous lover. Lewis felt very lucky. And very awkward. Shyness, it would seem, had invited itself along for a ménage à trois.

"Is there anything you'd like to try?" she asked him. "What can I do for you? I'll do anything."

This was hard for Lewis. There he was in bed with an amazing woman who had put herself at his command. He imagined all the jerks who had picked on him through school, and the women who wouldn't even give him the time of day. If only they could see him now. He was so happy. And so in love. And so paralyzed.

He couldn't think of a single thing to say. A thousand dreams and fantasies lingered in his brain and pestered him at all hours when he was apart from May. His penis felt harder than it had ever been before. Lewis was certain that when he finally came to orgasm, his entire flushed body would come out of his cock, and there would be nothing left of him. He craved this annihilation, and his body screamed at him to say something, anything!

May was silent. She caressed his face. Lewis could barely make out her mouth in the darkness. Was she frowning? He had to speak up.

"I don't know," he creaked. Oh, charming, Lewis. You'll be shown the way out now.

"Let's make it multiple choice, then. I could: a, suck your dick; b, fuck you; or c, give you a hand job."

Lewis mustered up the courage for a weakly whispered "b", and she happily rolled a condom down his cock, climbed on top of him and fucked away.

He loved to have her on top. He didn't have to worry about his performance, his inexperience, or his shyness. She fucked and he responded. He could open his eyes and see how pretty she was, reach up and touch her soft breasts, watch them swinging and bouncing as she went to work on him. It felt good. Really, really good.

This sort of positive conditioning worked wonders over time. Eventually, she could ask him what he wanted and he'd answer. At first, it was always the same thing, but later he branched out a bit. He became more comfortable using dirty words. Being able to say, "I want to come between your tits," was reliably rewarded, and while the words slowly lost their shame, they never lost their erotic power.

One night, May confessed to him that she had never really enjoyed being on top before she met him. She used to feel too vulnerable, ungraceful. She trusted him and felt so safe with him, she explained. He seemed to like it so much, and she was eager to please him. Lewis was incredulous. How could May ever lack confidence in anything? It was a sweet confession. Things were going well, and Lewis was very happy.

It was true: things were going well – for Lewis. But having lunch in a restaurant one day, when May told him that she was thinking of breaking up with him, it occurred to him that he hadn't really considered if she was happy.

"You don't know my favorite position, do you? You never ask me how I want to be pleased. You never give me multiple choice. Why is it always up to me to initiate sex and make all the decisions in bed? I don't know if we'd ever fuck if I didn't shanghai you into bed. We probably wouldn't be sitting here at all if I hadn't lost my patience and kissed you in the airport bar. Don't you find me attractive?"

Lewis sat there stupefied and ashamed, gazing into his soup. The icy grip of panic tightened around his throat. She thinks I'm a terrible lover and she's going to leave me! He thought of all the times he had been mysteriously, coldly dumped, without explanation and without ceremony. Well, truthfully, he had only dated a handful of women, and he hadn't made it into the sack with most of them. No, he could quite successfully repel women without going to bed with them, thank you very much.

Lewis wasn't demonstrative enough, and he knew it. They were lovers and he treated her with all the emotional tenderness of a distant cousin. He felt worlds of joy when she was at his side, and he hadn't shown her even one of them. He'd never given her flowers. He'd never given her much of anything. He'd never said, "I love you." Let's face it, Lewis. Dating you is like dating a slab of cement, only with less feeling.

Even now, Lewis said nothing. "You're losing me! Don't you care?" May shouted. He had never heard her raise her voice

before. He kept staring at his soup, too sad to even move. May
left the table. She did not return.

The next two weeks felt like years.

Sometimes there was simply sadness. The strength of Lewis'
love for May became the strength of his grief. When he could
bring himself to eat, the food tasted like he was chewing on a
mouse pad. He had trouble sleeping. He moved slowly. His
muscles ached. Lewis thought of what he had lost, and he
became angry with himself. That he should be so careless, so
cowardly! He was a worm. He hurled an endless stream of
insults at the mirror. "May deserves so much better than you,"
he snarled.

Then there was frustration. He sent her e-mail and left
messages on her answering machine. His words were, alas, as
lame as ever. "So, just wondering how you're doing," he'd say.
He cringed even as the words came out of his mouth.

The frustration was replaced by a quiet despair, and Lewis
took refuge in his work. There was always his work, where
things made sense, where he knew what he was doing.

One day, a letter arrived. Well, it really wasn't much of a
letter. May was a woman of few words, and they were always
straight and to the point. A small card read: "The guided tour.
My place, Tuesday, 6 p.m. Come well-rested, well-read, and
hungry for pussy. Love, May." The room swam a bit, then lay
on the beach panting. Lewis skimmed through the rest of the
contents of the envelope: photocopies from books on sex and
downloads from the Internet all about cunts and how to be
friendly with them. Page after page of diagrams, techniques,
and suggestions.

Lewis' mind drifted to May. She wasn't like the others. She
knew he could be a bonehead, but instead of dropping him, she
was willing to help. She was there for him. At his side. On top of
him. Under him. A shiver ran down his spine. He held in his
hands, he realized, the first draft of a map to pleasing May. The
area would have to be visited, explored; details would have to be
worked out. This could take some time.

He sat down and read the papers closely. He imagined

undressing May and spreading her legs. His pants began to feel too small, and he undid them. He touched himself as he imagined touching her. It wasn't the same; he was desperate to have her there, to see how she would react to this touch and to that. He stroked himself softly, slowly, then quickly and firmly. He closed his eyes and tried to see her face as he adjusted his caresses. She furrowed her brow and arched her back, or her hips moved with his fingers and she scarcely breathed. Her taste flooded into his mouth. They both moaned and cried out. His hand felt wet, and he opened his eyes and saw his semen on his fingers. He caressed himself as softly.

"I love you, May," he whispered.

Lewis studied every night, but he was still nervous when he knocked on May's door. I may have been an idiot in the past, and I may be an idiot in the future, but please, just this one night, let me be good to her! Let me be everything she wants – He was dizzy with love and already half-hard.

May opened the door. She wasn't wearing anything special, just the usual white dress-shirt and khakis. She stood for a moment without moving, as if wondering whether to let him in or not. Lewis realized with horror that he hadn't brought anything.

She reached out and enfolded him in her arms. He hugged her back. May shut the door. "You're a good man, Mr Hoffman," May said. "You just need a little guidance."

She took Lewis by the hand to her bedroom. He had been there many times before, and yet he still would be unable to describe it had he been called upon to do so. One night at a bar, she suddenly asked him what color her bedroom was, and he honestly did not know. It had become a running joke between them. But the simple reason was that he could only see her when they were there.

A candle on the nightstand cast them in a kind, warm light. May released his hand to prop up some pillows against the headboard. He didn't want to stop touching her, not for a second, and as soon as she let go of his hand he ran his hands down her back and settled them on her hips. She invited him to sit on the bed against the pillows. She kissed him, took off her pants, crawled onto the bed and sat between his legs facing away from him. Lewis grasped her breasts and nuzzled her neck. How he had missed the smell of her! His penis strained inside his pants against her ass. She spread her legs and leaned back against him.

May took Lewis's hand in hers and moved it down to her pussy. At first he tried to move it himself, but she held it firmly until he surrendered control. "Mons pubis," she whispered as his hand moved through a mound of dark hair. The rest of her cunt was shaved, making it feel all the more slick. She guided his fingers over it gently, getting them nice and wet. "Labia majora." She ran them over the thick outer lips of her vagina. "Right, and left," she said, taking his fingers from one side to the other. She took them down low to a firm piece of tissue. "Perineum." A little higher, "This is what's left of my hymen." Lewis rested his head on her shoulder. He had been with her intimately, but still he knew so little. The topography, the history of her was awesome.

May spread her lips open with her other hand. "Labia minora." These were a much different shape and far more delicate than her outer lips. "Right, left. Vagina." She touched his fingertips to the wet gate and massaged herself. She arched her head back onto his shoulder and groaned lightly. They moved on. "This is the clitoris. Its only purpose is to give me pleasure."

"So is mine," Lewis whispered. May squeezed his hand and grinned, caught off guard, and sighed happily.

"This is the shaft, this is the hood, and this is the head. It's very, very sensitive." She moved his hand up and down her cunt until his fingers were dripping wet. "When I masturbate, I usually use two fingers, like this, on the hood." May moved her fingers rhythmically up and down, sliding the hood over the shaft. She became wordless, lost in sensual concentration. Her breathing became quick and shallow. Lewis kissed her neck. His fingers left hers to their pleasure while he played over her juicy opening, ever so slowly probing and pressing, moving first just to the tip of one finger into her, then two, deeper and deeper. May rubbed herself at a fever pitch and Lewis could feel her tighten around his fingers. Then she relaxed and moved slowly.

Lewis pressed his cheek into her shoulder, squeezed her breast and thrust his fingers deep inside her. Cervix, he thought to himself. She was in his arms totally, a divine geography of endless delights.

May returned to her quick pace. She began to rock her hips and Lewis moved the full length of his fingers in and out of her pussy to match her. Her hot tender space grew tighter and tighter until May convulsed. Lewis felt the pulsations deep inside of her as she made small cries.

She rested. Her cunt felt even warmer and wetter than before. Lewis slowly withdrew his fingers. She turned around and lay over him like a blanket.

After some time, May sat up next to Lewis. He was taut with desire, eager for her to release him. But she made no move to touch him.

"I can give you guidance, Lewis, but in the end, you have to find your own way."

"What if I get lost?"

"Maybe you're already lost."

She was right. He didn't know where he was, and he had no map, no compass. He suddenly felt panicked.

"Don't leave me," he blurted out. "No one has ever shown me the patience that you have. I'm sorry I haven't appreciated you as I should—" His throat tightened, and he couldn't force one more word out.

May brushed her fingers against Lewis' cheek. She left the bed and dressed. "Let's go for a walk," she said, holding her hand out to him.

They silently traced their usual route to the nearest park. May's gaze was forever distant, and even when they at last came to rest on a bench, she looked not at Lewis but at the wooded horizon. "I think it's time for me to move on," she said.

"Take me with you." Lewis was as surprised as May at his

words. He wondered if the impulse was truly his, or if he was only borrowing it.

May shook her head. "Not this time. Maybe, someday, we'll find each other again." She looked about her, as if she was leaving a place she may or may not ever see again, and she got up and walked away, without looking back.

Lewis felt exhausted, as if he had just returned from a long journey. What could he have done differently this night? Why had he been abandoned? He had taken the tour and been left behind. No one had bothered to see him safely home.

But he no longer wished to be home. He watched May's receding figure and felt pain and love and an electric anticipation for an unknown tomorrow. Lewis had reached his goal: he had been shocked out of his stagnation. No exotic locale could have done this. Only a woman.

Cracked Butterfly

Teresa Lamai

I'm glad the industrial district is always this deserted after six. I can't stand human beings after a day in criminal court. The desolate November wind smells of burning garbage; I nearly fall every time it gusts out from between the buildings. I'm halfway home when a sideways, freezing rain lashes into me.

My breathing echoes in the dark hall of my apartment building. I want to push through my door, fall on the carpet in the dark, turn up music so loud it would vibrate my ribcage, rocking me into exhaustion.

Instead I see a streak of warm light under my door.

A moment later I'm in Tal's arms. My apartment is filled with the smell of tortillas, with music, with Tal's broad shoulders and lush, ringing voice. He squeezes my waist through the dank coat and I hold his temples between my palms. I refresh my eyelids in his glossy curls, press my cheek against his and inhale. He has just shaved.

"I thought you were still on tour. Oh my God, don't move." My voice squeaks. He laughs and kisses my forehead. His skin smells like cinnamon bread.

"I wanted to surprise you. You were going to eat caramel ice cream for dinner, weren't you, Rosa? And you're soaked." His warm mouth finds mine and we stand motionless, kissing softly and drinking each other's breath. One by one, my cells come back to life.

I'm still holding his face when he breaks the kiss and looks down at me. Tal's eyes are almond-shaped, tilting towards his temples in gorgeous arabesques. Their darkness is almost inhumanly beautiful, absorbing rather than reflecting light. I do everything I can to make them glitter like jewels. His lashes flutter and I know he has a question for me, unspoken.

His hands, slender as a pianist's, move over my hips. I squirm.

He unbuttons my coat and slides it off, letting it slump wetly on the floor. My suit jacket lands on the couch.

He lets me kiss his wide cheekbones and smiling lips as he busies himself with my blouse. I rip out the last three buttons and sigh when he pulls it off. The air is cool, but my bones feel warm for the first time in weeks.

"No bra? I thought you were in court today. Good lord, woman." I'm tugging at his curls, trying to pull him to the darkening nipples.

He runs his tongue along my belly, leaving a damp line just under my navel. Kneeling, he smoothes his hands up under my wool skirt. I kick my shoes behind me. My knees buckle when he hooks his fingers into the waistband of the pantyhose and pulls. My skirt follows quickly.

He pauses and I look down. "When did you get a red thong?"

"It's laundry day."

"Damn. Let's see. Goddamn."

I close my eyes when he moves behind me. He fits one hand over my pubic bone and pushes my ass into his face, sinking his teeth into the cool mounds. His other hand is flat against my belly. My pussy swells; I sway side-to-side, letting the thick lips kiss. His hair tickles the small of my back. I shift my hips, tilting my silk-covered cunt towards his snaking tongue, panting "ah, ah," to the dark ceiling.

He stands. I turn, winding my arms around him, lifting a leg to circle his waist. I run my tongue from his collar to just behind his ear, warming his neck. His hands grip my ass and he pulls the cheeks slowly apart, listening to the wet labia separate.

"There's plenty of time, Rosa." He covers my mouth again in a long, clinging kiss. "Mmm, that's just how your cunt kisses me back."

I don't see his hand moving – I squeal when he pinches my nipples. He grabs my shoulders before I can step back. I laugh, but his eyes are distracted; he takes several short breaths before he speaks. "Rosa, I want you to let me use you like I did before. I haven't been able to think of anything else while I've been away."

So that's the question. My breath catches.

Neither of us meant to go that far, the night before he left, but the need exploded in us the instant his hand closed over my wrist. I've melted each time I remembered being bound and bent over his desk, his right hand forcing my neck into the polished wood while his left hand held my vibrator. I came the way I'd always needed to, filling the house with long, braying screams like a woman giving birth.

I look down. "Okay, yes. Yes." This compulsion is absurdly strong.

"Take off your panties. Come into the bathroom."

I follow slowly. He has a pair of handcuffs dangling over the shower rod. I let out a snort. He turns and tells me a safeword. I toss my panties at his chest.

"Face the tub. Put your wrists in the handcuffs."

I pause. He leans against the opposite wall. "In the bathroom?" I shove a nervous, simian smile toward him and he lets it fall, unacknowledged. I turn quickly, reaching for the cold metal. They click benignly around my wrists. I don't quite believe they'll hold. Tal is silent behind me.

"Um, okay—" I say after a few moments. I start to twist my head, looking for him.

The first slap, more on my hip than my ass, knocks me to the side. The cuffs cut into my wrists as I hang, feet splayed. The second slap burns, the third stings.

"Don't speak. Don't turn around." Tal's mouth is at my right ear, but his voice seems to come from every corner of the room. My nipples are tight, straining at empty air.

I struggle to my feet. "Ow," I say pointedly.

He fits his left arm around the front of my pelvis and lifts me backwards, off my feet, spreading his legs to take the weight. He hits my ass with his right hand, swinging the weight of his back into five blows. Shock keeps me from yelling at first. Setting me down, he massages the shaking flesh gently, using both hands. It's unbearably hot and I feel bruises forming.

He has never spoken to me so gently: "I have a large, uncomfortable gag, Rosa. It'll stretch your mouth, press on your whole tongue. Most likely it'll make you salivate all over your chin. The ties will get tangled in your hair. I'd rather see you control yourself. Can you?"

I lick my lips when I can catch my breath. I watch the goosebumps rise along my arms.

"Good." He kisses the back of my neck.

I hear the scarf before I feel it. It's one of mine, wide red silk. Tal fits it snug over my eyes.

I hear him move in front of me. A scraping in the tub, then his breath coming from down below. He's moved my stool into the tub. Panic rises in me, stopping just at the top of my throat.

"I have the gag ready, sweetheart, and other things to hurt you with," Tal whispers. Something cold and hard probes rudely at my anus, then leaves. He grips my pelvis in both hands, tilting it forward.

Water's running. A warm cloth is on my belly.

I moan as softly as I can when his delicate hands reach my cunt. He lathers briefly and I feel one of my small razors working the hair off the mound. He tells me to put my right foot up on the side of the tub.

He spreads the outer labia and lets one of his fingers stray just close enough to be sucked in. I gasp and rock towards him, my body ready to break into a rhythm. My cunt coats his finger and he stops as the scent fills the space between us.

"Don't move, Rosa. I'm serious."

I feel a cold length of metal, flat against me. I freeze and bear down hard on my terrified stomach.

"A straight razor is the only way to get a close shave up in here." He tickles me and I clench my teeth.

"You know the safeword. But then we'd only be half-finished."

Moments later he tells me to switch legs. My thighs are trembling. I press my left foot hard against the cold porcelain. He finishes with a few efficient swipes, then sponges away the soap.

A long silence follows. The air tickles strangely.

I feel him whisper something just over my clit. His mouth closes slowly over the naked, slick labia. His kiss is thorough. I move in circles, impatient, trying to press my clit against him. My inner lips swell towards him, as if begging for his tongue. He stops. I hear him swallow.

"Tal, fuck me." He must be ready to finish this game.

In answer, he stands. His hand slides under my hair and presses, soft and firm, against my cheekbone and under my skull. It holds my head still as his other hand lands loudly on my left cheek, just enough to make my eyes sting.

I hear him leave.

When he returns, he takes the blindfold off, sliding the knot tenderly from my hair. He is holding a key, and he unfastens the right cuff just long enough to turn me around. My wrist clicks back into place. His face is satiny with sweat. He is still dressed. His eyes are dazed and grateful.

He kisses my cheek. "I'm going to take you out, Rosa."

My blue silk dress is hanging on the back of the bathroom door. His rucksack is on the floor, the contents spilling. I see the gags and he laughs softly.

"Oh, she's mad? She thought I was kidding?" He kisses my mouth and runs his tongue over my neck where the veins are throbbing. He whispers into my hair, "I love you. Are you all right, really?"

"Tal, it's time to fuck me. We're not really going out."

He kneels and pulls something from the rucksack. A tiny, plastic, powder-blue butterfly, maybe an inch in diameter. Black straps dangle from it.

He lifts my feet out from under me and slips the straps round them. I hiss when the cuffs bite into me. When I can stand again, I realize he's fitting the straps over my hips like a harness. I twist to look; the butterfly rests lightly over my raging clit.

The labia are ready to swallow it. It looks ludicrously innocent.
I can feel that I'm blushing, hard.

"You know the best part?" Tal's narrow eyes are on mine.

"It matches my dress?"

His hand moves to his pocket and the butterfly jumps to life.
It hovers, buzzing greedily as if I were a deep, thick-petaled
flower. The vibrations spread through my labia to my ass. My
cunt is furious and I pull at the shower rod. Plaster shakes loose
at the bolts and settles to the floor. Tal looks ready to eat me.

"Tal, Tal." My voice sounds small and tight. "It's not
enough. Tal."

"Pace yourself."

"You motherfucking . . . motherfucker." I'm moving my
legs, grinding my hips until I see him crouch down to watch
more closely.

"That sounds like a hurt word. I'm afraid it's quiet time
again. But if you really want a gag, keep talking. I have this red
one. It holds your jaws apart."

He opens my cabinet and finds some make-up. He grabs a
fistful of hair at the base of my skull while he wipes the sweat off
my forehead and upper lip.

"You look delicious as you are. You don't need any blush. I
want to add lipstick, though." He leans into my swinging
breasts, still gripping my hair.

He murmurs like someone drunk with love as he licks the top
of each breast. He can only manage two or three words between
kisses. "If you try – to sneak away – and rub this off – you'll
wear bells – all night." With the lipstick he smoothes my black
nipples into long, sticky, crimson peaks. I want to cry but even
that release won't come.

When he turns the butterfly to low I can breathe again, but it
still takes all my concentration to keep my hips still. I watch the
long, smooth curve of his cheekbones as he reaches over my
head. His throat is a little swollen.

"We've been meaning to go dancing for so long," Tal purrs.
He unlocks my wrists and massages my arms. He slips the dress
over my head and helps me into my shoes.

He holds my head gently now, questions fluttering over his lashes again. I lean forward and bite his pink lower lip. When I pull back his eyes are pure limpid bliss.

Señor Frog's is crowded on Friday nights, a tiny neon box, tucked under the freeway overpass. Salsa beats through its thin walls. Crowds huddle against the wind, hurrying over the black ice that gleams multicolored over the parking lot. Inside, chairs and tables have been pushed to the corners. The dance floor, the lobby, the dark hallway to the kitchen, every inch is thick with dancers. The crowds clear reverently for the best couples. A haze of smoke and perfumed steam hangs under the low ceiling.

I'm brought straight back to my cunt when the butterfly jumps again. My cry isn't heard over the music, but I turn to Tal's eyes, hard as ebony. I try to move away, but we're pushed hip to hip. We've eased into a slow merengue, his hand resting on the small of my back. Our bellies cleave, his shirt buttons flick over my nipples. In my mind, I undress him quickly, suck him hard, and impale myself on him several times, here on the uneven floor. I doubt many would notice.

He tugs at my hair and kisses my ear. "Dance with anyone who asks."

He's gone. The butterfly is on low. I clasp my hands together tight, looking down.

Soon I'm asked to dance. A tall, quiet man tries to lead me in country dances I never learned. I do my best to follow, watching his feet, almost forgetting the relentless little sting of pleasure. I look up to find his eyes transfixed on my vivid nipples. I can't keep them from pushing out farther. Just before the music finishes, the butterfly surges to high and I have to stop moving, clutching my hands over my mouth. Two desperate moans escape. My partner stops, alarmed, asking if he's stepped on me. I do what I can to reassure him. I thank him, panting, and stumble away into the crowd.

I can't find Tal.

But he must see me because the torment ebbs as soon as another man asks me to dance.

A hazel-eyed professor rests his tense fingers on my back, shaking as if I were a silk-covered bomb. He ignores the music and moves me in a slow orbit across the floor. He cries out at the end of the song when my fingernails sink into his wrist. I leave without looking at him.

A Haitian man, dreadlocks flying, twirls me on every fourth beat. The room spins in front of my eyes as his dark hands nudge my shoulder or tug my wrist. Our stomachs meet as a new phrase starts; his teeth flash as he laughs. He is irrepressible, radiant as a bride. I press my forehead to his at the end of the song, watching his full, soft lips as he speaks. Tal turns me up, and I pull away.

A very young student asks me. I wait for him to look up at my face before I say yes. His drenched silk shirt is nearly sliding off his smooth chest. He carefully strokes my neck as we settle into our rhythm and I smile, imagining that's step five in some article he's memorized: Ten Moves Chicks Dig.

He turns me and I see Tal, watching. Girls surround him like fireflies.

I make it to Tal before he can reach his pocket. He grabs at my wrist – but it's I who leads him to the women's bathroom.

Two elegant grandmas are sashaying out just as we arrive. One winks at me. I slam Tal against the far wall, harder than I meant to, then turn towards the door.

The ladies are still there.

"We're not well," I tell them. I lock the door.

I turn back to a heap of clothes. Tal, naked, is sitting on the counter, gleaming under the vanity lights. His skin is flushed and velvety as rose petals. His cock swings up, vein-covered. Stretched to its capacity, hard as a gold ingot, shimmering like fresh honey. His knuckles are white as he braces himself on the grimy ledge. His eyes are wide and starving.

My hair falls over his belly and clings to his wet skin. The sweet head of his cock nearly chokes me. I stretch my lips over him, tickling his balls, running my tongue over the crinkled, pulsing flesh. My jaws ache but I would do anything to coax that choked falsetto cry from him.

He's begging now. I jump on the counter, one foot on either side of his waist. I lower into a squat, letting him nuzzle into my slick folds.

There's a knock at the door. I slap Tal's face when he looks over.

He grips the counter hard and pushes his pelvis up as best he can. I reach under him to feel his clenching ass. Sweat drips between my fingers. I lift my cunt away from him and bend down to lap at his stomach.

I start to come as soon as his nails sink into my shoulders. I am bent over so swiftly that the breath is knocked out of me. He fits his hand over my skull and presses my cheek into the countertop. He throws my dress over my back.

I try to reach back towards him, hands curling.

"Jesus, Tal. You have to do it."

He slides in as soon as I begin to speak, so the last word stretches into an unhinged wail. He only has time for one slow rotation of his hips, caressing my wet, aching inner walls. The butterfly cracks as I grind it into the formica.

As he starts to thrust, I push my hands into the mirror so that I can writhe against him, pleasure flashing from the base of my spine, spreading through my body. For a long moment I'm half-dead, stretched still as my cunt opens and closes on him like a sea anemone.

He releases my head and collapses on me when he comes, sobbing, "Fuck, fuck," with his last thrusts. Stars circle in front of my eyes, white and gold and violet.

Five minutes later, the icy wind sucks the air out of our lungs. We cling to each other, shaking, disheveled, laughing madly. The steady pulse of music fades behind us as we run to the car.

Secretly Wishing for Rain

Claude Lalumière

My palm pressed between Tamara's small breasts, I feel her heartbeat. The raindrops pounding on the skylight reflect the city lights, provide our only illumination. Tamara's fingers are entwined in my chest hair; my perception of the rhythm of my heart is intensified by the warm, steady pressure of her hand.

This mutual pressing of hands against chests is our nightly ritual. Our faces almost touching, we silently stare at each other in the gloom. This is how it is for me (and how I believe it must also be for her): I abandon myself to the dim reflection of light in her eyes, the rhythms of our hearts, the softness of her skin, the pressure of her hand; I let go of all conscious thought or intent. We whisper meaningless absurdities to each other. One of us says: "There are fishes so beautiful that cinnamon nectar spouts from their eyeballs"; the other replies: "Your mouth is infinite space and contains all the marvels of gravity." Most nights we explore each other's flesh, reveling in each other's smells and touches. Deliriously abandoned in each other's embrace, we reach orgasm, remembering the loss that binds us. Some nights, as tonight, we simply fall asleep, snugly interwined.

The cliché would be that I was jealous of Andrei's mischievous charm, his tall-dark-and-handsome good looks, his quick wit, his svelte elegance, his easy way with women . . . but no. His omnipotent charm defused the pissing-contest resentment that heterosexual pretty boys usually provoke in the rest of the straight male population. Everyone – men, women, straights, gays – was helpless before his androgynous beauty, his complicit grin, and his playful brashness. Perhaps I was even more helpless than most.

Andrei avoided being in the company of more than one person at a time. Whoever he was with enjoyed the full intensity of his meticulous attention. I never felt so alive as when I basked in his gaze.

Andrei may have been desired by many, but few had their lust satisfied. Men weren't even a blip on his sexual radar. Most women also fell short of his unvoiced standards – the existence of which he would always deny. The women who could boast of the privilege of walking down the street arm in arm with Andrei were tall and slim with graceful long legs, hair down to at least their shoulder blades, subtle makeup, and cover-girl faces. And, most importantly, they had to be sharp dressers. Age was not an issue. I'd first met him when we were both nineteen, and during the seven years of our friendship, I'd seen him hook up with girls as young as sixteen and women as old as fifty-five. All that mattered was that they have the look. Actually, that wasn't all. Andrei possessed a probing intelligence. He read voraciously, and he expected his assembly-line lovers to be able to discuss at length the minutiae of his favourite books. Invariably, he grew bored with his women, or contemptuous if they read one of the books in his pantheon and proceeded to display the depth of their incomprehension. Rarely would he declare to the injured party that their short-lived romance was over. Instead, at the end of an affair, he'd simply vanish for several weeks without a word. Even I – his closest friend – never found out where he vanished to.

Ten years ago, Tamara had been one of those women. The last of those women.

At nineteen, I moved to Montreal from Deep River, Ontario. I wanted to learn French, to live in a cosmopolitan environment. See foreign films on the big screen. Go to operas. Museums. Concerts. Art galleries. Listen to street musicians. Hear people converse in languages I couldn't understand.

I never did learn French. I'm often embarrassed about that. Montreal isn't nearly as French as most outsiders think, and it's all too easy to live exclusively in its English-language demi-monde.

I'd taken a year off after high school, intending to travel, but I never did. I never had enough money, and I languished resentfully in Deep River. I applied to McGill University for the following year, was accepted, chose philosophy as my major.

In early September, less than a week after classes started, I attended a midnight screening of Haynes's *Bestial Acts* at the Rialto. I'd heard so much about that film, but, of course, it had never come to Deep River, even on video. There were only two of us in the theatre. The other cinephile was a stunningly handsome guy I guessed was about my age. He was already there when I walked in, his face buried in a book, despite the dim lighting. I sat two rows ahead of him.

After the credits stopped rolling, the lights went on, and I felt a tap on my shoulder. When I turned, the handsome guy – Andrei, I would soon learn – said, "I feel like walking. Let's go." I had no choice but to obey; I didn't want to have a choice. So I followed him, already ensorcelled.

We walked all over the city, and he brought me to secret places where its night-time beauty was startlingly delicate. The water fountain in the concrete park next to the Ville-Marie Expressway. The roof of a Plateau apartment building – its access always left unlocked in violation of safety regulations. We snuck into a lush private courtyard covered in ancient-looking leafy vines; the windows reflected and rereflected the moonlight to create a subtly complex tapestry of light. All the while, we talked about *Bestial Acts*, trying to understand it all, to pierce the veil of its mysteries.

As dawn neared, he said, "You've never read the original story, have you?" There was disappointment in his voice.

I felt like this was a test. I looked him straight in the eye. "No. Before seeing the 'adapted from' credit on the screen tonight, I didn't even know about it."

His face changed, and he laughed. He'd decided to forgive my ignorance. He dug out a paperback from the inside of his jacket. "Here. Read this. Let's have lunch on Sunday, and we can talk some more."

The book's spine was creased from countless rereadings, the corners furled and frayed. It was a collection of stories called *Ethical Treatment,* and the back-cover blurb said that the author lived here in Montreal. Andrei saw my eyes grow wide; he told me, "No. I didn't write that book. That's not a pseudonym. I don't even know the guy."

So we had lunch that Sunday, and then became nearly inseparable.

As for all those women of his – well, yes, I admired their beauty; but they were unattainable, too glamorous and self-confident for me to even fantasize about. Was I jealous of them? Of the love he spent on them? No; it was abundantly clear that I was permanent, that spending time with me took precedence over his dalliances. And they were only ephemeral mirrors into which he'd gaze to see his own beauty reflected.

As I do every morning, I wake up at six. The rain is still splattering on the skylight window. Although it's summer and sunlight should be flooding the bedroom by now, under this thick blanket of dark clouds, it's still as dark as midnight.

I turn around and spoon Tamara. My nose rests lightly her shoulder; I breathe in her unwashed aromas. She is intoxicating. Her soft back is luxuriant against my chest. My semi-erect cock jerks lightly, probing the smoothness of her buttocks.

She moans, but she's still hours from waking up. She rarely wakes before noon. Then, eventually, she heads out; without a word, without a goodbye kiss. Brunch with friends? Museums? The gym? Does she even have friends? I can only speculate. She always returns past eleven in the evening, and we go to bed together around midnight.

I get up. Normally, I would go jogging, but I'm too fed up with the rain.

*   *   *

Andrei never worked. But money never seemed to be a problem. I was curious, but I knew better than to inquire. Whatever he wanted to share, he would tell me.

Actually, it's not fair to say that he never worked.

He wrote. He wrote for hours every day, the words pouring out of him with the relentless flow of a waterfall. He never tried to publish. He disdained the very idea of publication; nevertheless, he was supportive of my futile efforts at getting my own work into print.

He wrote poetry, fiction, philosophical ramblings, and other prose that segued from genre to genre. All of it was brilliant. Yes, I envied his way with women, but what inspired my jealousy was his prodigious literary talent. It often took me months to finish a short story, while he would write several of them a week, in addition to countless other pieces. And he worked on a number of long Proustian novels simultaneously, each of them accumulating wordage but never seeming to reach any kind of conclusion.

We'd spend sleepless nights poring over each other's work with a harsh and unforgiving love. We questioned every word, every comma, every idea. We revised and reread and rearranged. He was unfailingly generous with his talent and editorial acumen. His input imbued my feeble scribblings with a depth of allusion and empathy I could never have achieved on my own.

If he was aware of my jealousy, he never showed any sign of it. He considered me his only friend and let no-one but me read his work. And so my jealousy was tempered by exclusivity. Although I urged him time and again to seek publication, I secretly thrilled like a teenage girl who, magically, knew that she – and no-one else – had the privilege of sucking the cock of her favourite rock star.

Tamara and I rarely talk, rarely spend any time together, save for the nighttime in bed. Our lives are separate, save for that nightly communion. We are strangers.

Occasionally, she walks in on me, whether I'm in my study or in the living room or taking a nap, and asks, "Read to me."

What she means is, "Read me something of Andrei's." And I always do. Sometimes I grab a book, sometimes an unpublished manuscript. Andrei left so much behind. She nestles into my lap and chest, and I enfold her as best I can, breathing in the heady blend of sweat, perfume, shampoo, and lotions, wishing for the weight of her body to leave permanent impressions in my flesh.

When I stop reading, we neck like teenagers, fondle each other tenderly, hungrily, with unfeigned clumsiness.

Before, she used to read voraciously. Now, all she desires of the world of literature is to hear me read Andrei's words.

During most of my years-long friendship with Andrei, I never had a lover, never seriously pursued anyone. Andrei had awakened the writer in me, and that was all that mattered. I'd quit school. I supported myself with a string of meaningless jobs, and devoted all my spare energies to, inseparably, my writing and my friendship with Andrei.

I met Tamara one late afternoon coming home from work. I had noticed her further down the line at the bus stop: dark wavy hair to below her shoulders; complex features that managed to be both softly round and strongly aquiline; a large mouth; full lips; a brownish-olive tint to her skin; tall and svelte, yet with a pronounced curve at the waist. I thought: she's Andrei's type. Gorgeous. Glamorous.

The bus was crowded. She sat down next to me. My throat dried up. I was suddenly overwhelmed with desire for this woman. I knew that Andrei would have no problem initiating contact with this beautiful stranger, but I lacked his grace and confidence.

As the bus took off, each of us dug a book out of our bags. We were reading the same book, *Bestial Acts*. Probably buoyed by the film's cult celebrity, the author had expanded the story into a novel – much to its detriment.

We looked up at each other, and we both laughed. I don't remember who started talking to whom, but we fell into an easy, friendly conversation and ended up eating veggie burgers and gourmet fries on St-Laurent, and then walked down to a cocktail bar in the Gay Village that played postmodern lounge music in a colourful high-kitsch decor.

We laughed easily with each other, and she frequently touched me, letting her hands linger just long enough for me to know she meant it.

It was nearly two in the morning when I walked her home. She gave me a firm hug; I felt her breasts press against my chest, and she surely felt my erection. She grinned as she disengaged, and, while holding both my hands, she kissed my cheek – the contact with her lips made me shiver.

I watched her climb the stairs to her second-storey apartment. I stood there for a couple of minutes after she closed the door behind her.

I don't remember walking home, so lost was I in my reveries of seeing her again.

Next thing I knew, I was lying naked in bed, prudishly fighting the impulse to masturbate while replaying moments of my evening with Tamara.

And then I remembered that I had promised to meet Andrei that evening.

Ten years after Andrei's death, I still have no other friends. I have no lovers but Tamara.

My days are always the same.

I wake up at six. I work until noon. Often that consists of editing Andrei's large inventory of unpublished manuscripts. Sometimes, I work on my own writing.

I go out for lunch. There's a wonderful pressed-sandwich shop on St-Denis. If it's too crowded, I go for noodles. These days, there's a noodle shop on almost every corner.

In the afternoon, I catch a matinée movie, then I go shopping – books, CDs, DVDs, clothes, food – hoping that something, anything, will bring me pleasure or elicit any kind of reaction. Nothing ever does.

I drop my purchases at home. I check for messages. Then I go out for dinner. Usually Indian. Sometimes Thai. Or something new I read about in the newspaper.

I come back home around eight in the evening, put on some music, make some tea. I read until I hear Tamara come home. Then I get ready for bed.

If the weather's bad, I just stay in all day.

It's the middle of the afternoon, and it's still raining. It's as dark as dusk. It's been like this for five days straight, and it's been having a languorous effect on me. I've noticed that Tamara, usually less sensitive than I to the weather and light, has been somewhat morose of late. I do not pry. We never pry into each other's affairs or emotions.

But today I'm feeling a bit better. I'm just off the phone with my agent. She had good news for me. Dardick Press has made a six-figure offer for my new novel. Not that I really need the money, but they want the book. My book.

To the outside world, I'm the author of a wildly successful thematic trilogy of Proustian ambitions; of an allegorical fantasy novel the *Washington Post* welcomed by trumpeting: "Finally, an English-language writer whose depths of empathy and imagination surpass Márquez"; of an immense thousand-page short-story collection praised for its cross-genre audacity, the precision and beauty of its language, and its parade of heart-breaking characters; of a poetry collection that stayed for more than a year on the bestseller lists; and of a blockbuster philo-sophical novel – adapted once as a film and once as a television mini-series.

Although all of these appeared under my byline, none of them are mine (well, I snuck two of my own short stories into the collection; I still feel guilty about that). I did edit the manu-scripts into their final format – I was certainly familiar enough with much of the material from my years with Andrei – but they were his works, not mine.

Despite Andrei's immense posthumous success under my byline, my own work has been consistently rejected by publish-ers: "Let's not oversaturate the market," "We're not sure how to categorize this one," a litany of insulting excuses . . . Until today, that is.

I feel like celebrating, but I can't think of anything appropriate. Take Tamara out for lunch? I fantasize further: maybe we could even go on vacation. Spend a few weeks in Venice. I've always wanted to see Venice. We can certainly afford it.

But we never travel. We never do anything together. We stay here, slaves to our habits and our grief.

Besides, I would never dare upset the fragile equilibrium of our tacit agreement with even anything as mundane as a lunch invitation.

Just then, Tamara walks into my study. She's dishevelled, clearly having just woken. She's wearing black panties and a white camisole that contrasts vividly with her skin. I'm still visited by images of our fantasy holiday; seeing her – so beautiful, so subtly out of my reach, the constant pain that haunts her imbuing her with an aura of delicate fragility that I find, despite myself, overwhelmingly arousing – I catch my breath in admiration.

She doesn't notice, or she ignores me. Does it really matter which?

Nevertheless, for a second, I even half-convince myself – both fearing it and desiring it – that she'll propose an outing or even converse with me. But no. The inevitable words, full of mournful loss and despairing love, come out of her mouth: "Read to me." Not even waiting for a response, she heads towards the living room.

I rise from my desk, my hand resting for a moment on the third volume of Andrei's Proustian trilogy, but then, emboldened by my agent's good news, I mischievously and pridefully grab a copy of my novel manuscript instead. Tamara won't know the difference.

I join Tamara on the couch, and she snuggles up to me. She smells delicious. I nibble on her bare shoulder, and she moans, grabbing my hand and rubbing it against her breasts. She nuzzles my neck and whispers, "Read."

Momentarily, I feel guilty for deceiving her. But I start to read my novel, and I quickly get seduced by the allure of my own words, my own characters.

I'm only a few pages into the manuscript when Tamara suddenly gets up.

She mumbles, "I'm tired . . ." – heading back to the bedroom, not even glancing at me, shutting the door.

For the next five days – after I stood him up for Tamara – Andrei didn't answer my calls. Was my friendship ultimately as meaningless to him as his dalliances with his glamorous girlfriends? Had I finally suffered his inevitable rejection?

Tamara called me, and we saw each other once. We went for a walk on Mount Royal. She held my hand. She sensed my dark mood and did not push.

Her goodbye hug conveyed less promise than her first; she asked me to call her soon. Translation: if you want me, show it.

I mumbled that I would, knowing that I'd made a mess of what should have been a great evening. I had been much too distracted by my anxiety about Andrei.

Finally, I showed up at his apartment without calling. He hated it when people did that.

When I got there, there was a girl with him. She was stunning: the kind of face that stared back at you from magazine covers; long, shapely legs; delicate toes; toenails painted bright orange peeking out from elegant high-heeled sandals. She was crying.

I ignored her. I didn't say anything. I stood firm and did my best to stare Andrei down. I needed to prove to him that I aspired to be his equal.

He surprised me. He smiled at me, turned towards the girl, and said, "Get out. Can't you see that my friend is here now?"

She opened her mouth to say something, but then closed it sharply, visibly trying to hold on to some degree of dignity.

She didn't even glance at Andrei, but she shot me a disdainful sneer as she hurried past.

The rain never lets up. I stay in all day. Tamara never leaves the bedroom. I hear her use the adjoining bathroom a few times.

Finally, at midnight, I open the bedroom door. I get undressed and slip into bed.

Tamara is feigning sleep. I know her body language and the rhythms of her breathing too intimately to be fooled.

We do not press hands against each other's chests tonight. We do not whisper absurdities to each other. We do not touch. We do not have sex.

We've never skipped our ritual before; in sickness and in health.

A despairing loneliness chews on my innards, chasing sleep away.

Tamara gets up in the middle of the night. I hear her bustle in the kitchen. When she's done eating, she climbs back into bed, carefully not touching me, and falls asleep immediately.

I stay awake until dawn.

I realize that the rain has finally stopped, the clouds finally gone. Sunlight hits Tamara's bare shoulder. I yearn to kiss it, to taste her. But I dare not.

I didn't know whether or not to believe Andrei, but I didn't question him, didn't push my luck. I was too relieved, thrilled, exhilarated that our friendship was still intact. He claimed not to care that I had stood him up. He hadn't been in touch because he'd spent the last few days with the woman he'd just thrown out of his apartment. He had known it would only last a few days.

Suddenly, it seemed so egocentric to think that Andrei would have been affected by my absence the other night. I chastised myself for my arrogance and self-importance.

Nevertheless, I told him all about Tamara. Was it he or I who suggested that we all three get together for a meal? I suggested it, I think – but was it only because he wanted me to?

I called her from his apartment; we would meet there on the weekend, and he would cook for both of us. Already, my mouth watered. Andrei was a fabulous cook.

We spent the rest of the night as usual: we pored over his latest writings until sun-up.

*   *   *

I am running. The morning sun spurs me on. I am exhausted from my sleepless night. My muscles are complaining because of the days of inactivity I imposed on them during the recent rains.

But I run, nevertheless. I don't even notice where. I just run and sweat.

I come back home. I look at the clock. It's nine fifteen. I've been out running for three hours. I walk through the bedroom to get to the shower although I don't have to. I could use one of the other bathrooms. But I want to gaze at Tamara.

She's not in bed.

I call out her name, look through every room.

She's not here. She's never awake this early.

I go out again.

I run.

I run until the pain and exhaustion is all that I can feel. I just run; and sweat – so much that it's impossible to distinguish the tears from the sweat.

I knew, of course, that whatever spark I ignited in Tamara's imagination would be dimmed by the greater conflagration that Andrei would provoke. I was not wrong.

They were beautiful together, but I also knew that Andrei would soon tire of her.

Pathetically, I fantasized about consoling her after Andrei inevitably broke her heart. Fearfully, I never spoke to Tamara – about my feelings, about Andrei who discarded lovers like flakes of dead skin. Boldly, I imagined telling Andrei he had no right to use Tamara like a disposable mirror, when I could love her more truly than he ever would. Stupidly, I confronted Andrei in such a way.

It would be inaccurate to say that we had a fight. I said my piece, and he just laughed at me. I got angrier, and he just laughed harder.

"You're my friend," he said, between guffaws. "But go home now. When you get over your anger, come back, and we'll work on one of your stories." He was still laughing.

I left his apartment, melodramatically slamming the door, feeling self-conscious for doing so, but unable to express myself any other way in the face of Andrei's dismissal.

There are messages from my agent. Details to work out. Contracts to sign.

So what? It's not like I need the money.

Am I betraying Andrei's legacy by publishing my own work under my name? Should I use a pseudonym? Or maybe scrap the whole idea. I'll never be the writer he was.

I lie on the couch all day. The phone rings. Again. And again. I let it ring. Tamara wouldn't call, and there's no-one else I want to talk to, even if, as I fear might now happen because of my transgression, we never see each other again.

When Tamara wakes me by caressing my cheek, I realize that I had fallen asleep.

Andrei's relationship with Tamara lasted a full year, months longer than any of his previous affairs. I had barely seen either of them since I'd stormed out of Andrei's apartment like a bad actor. After a few weeks, I visited Andrei twice, but my resentment was too overpowering, and the encounters were forced and awkward. I was physically unable to be around Tamara without feeling nauseous. So I stopped calling them, and I never heard from either of them. Occasionally, I'd spot them downtown, but I always managed to creep away unseen.

Then one day I found a handwritten invitation in my mailbox. I recognized Andrei's precise, feminine script. There were no details, save for a time and the name and address of a restaurant. I dreaded some sort of wedding announcement. Or that he'd finally shooed Tamara out of his life like all the others before her. I didn't know which of the two I feared more.

Of course, I went. I was lonely, bored, and miserable, and I missed my friend.

I'd never heard of the restaurant, so I was unprepared. I'd dressed casually, and this turned out to be an intimidatingly swanky establishment. I was sure they weren't going to let me

in. True to my expectations, the maitre d' sneered at me when I
stepped through the door, but when I said Andrei's name, he
repeated it almost reverentially and instructed a waiter to escort
me to Andrei's table.

Andrei's table turned out to be a private room, lushly decorated with museum-quality reproductions and fresh flowers. I
recognized Debussy's String Quartet – a favourite of Andrei's –
playing at just the right volume. The table was set for two; there
was an empty chair waiting for me. Tamara sat in the other
chair.

Tamara asked, "What are you doing here? I mean – Where's
Andrei?"

I shrugged. "Andrei sent me an invitation. I didn't know
you'd be here."

"But it's our anniversary. Where—?"

I knew, then, that Andrei had left her. And indeed he had,
but that wasn't the whole truth. That came later.

Before either of us could say anything more, the waiter
brought in the hors d'oeuvres.

Tamara said, "But we haven't ordered anything."

We learned that Andrei had arranged our evening's menu in
advance. We ate in silence, but not even that tense awkwardness
could mask the heavenly taste of the food.

We finally spoke to each other when it came time to argue
over who would get the cheque, but we were informed that
Andrei had already paid for everything, and that not even a
gratuity would be accepted from either of us.

Befuddled, we walked out together. We glanced at each other,
and we both laughed at ourselves. Still chuckling, Tamara took
my arm, and we walked together through downtown, all the
while talking like dear old friends. We didn't utter a word about
Andrei.

When we parted, she gave me a chaste kiss on the cheek, but
there was genuine warmth in her smile. Silently, I cursed
Andrei for what I believed he was doing to her.

The next day, I received a couriered letter, requesting my
presence at the law office of Laurent Tavernier the following

Monday at nine in the morning. Not a little alarmed, I called to know what this was all about. The attorney's secretary told me: "We can say nothing of this matter until the appointed time."

Tamara called me every day. She was worried about Andrei's disappearance. More than once, she cried over the phone. As much as I wanted to, I couldn't bring myself to tell her that I thought Andrei had deserted her. I grunted noncommittal responses and sidestepped any suggestion that we should meet. I refused to follow Andrei's transparent script, no matter how much it matched my own desires.

The following Monday, I was startled to see Tamara sitting in the attorney's waiting room. A few minutes later, we were both ushered into Tavernier's office, wondering to each other what Andrei had planned for us this time.

This is what we learned: Andrei was dead, had poisoned himself on the day he'd set us up to meet at the restaurant; Andrei was wealthy, worth millions of dollars, all of which was now ours . . . in a joint account, no strings attached. Tavernier needed our signatures to make this official.

In addition, Andrei bequeathed all of his writings to me, with instructions that I seek to publish them under my own name only and that, with his blessing, I should edit his works as I saw fit.

There was a letter addressed to both of us; the attorney read it. It was terse.

I had nothing more to write, it said.

But that wasn't true. In death, Andrei was writing the script of my and Tamara's lives, and we followed every stage direction like fawning understudies.

I almost speak, but Tamara shushes me. I can't decipher her expression.

She's sitting on the floor, next to the couch. She looks away from me and into her lap. I hear the rustle of paper.

I look down and see that she's holding my manuscript. My novel.

She starts to read. I cry.

I cry because I see her mouth form the words that I've written, because I hear the tenderness in her voice when she speaks my words.

She reads a few chapters. She takes her time. She forms the words carefully, imbues their articulation with a slow sensuality.

Finally, she pauses. She looks at me, and she's crying too. She says, "I like it."

When I come back from my morning run, Tamara is still asleep. Her feet are sticking out from under the sheets. This is one of my favourite sights: tenderly domestic and deliciously sensual. I fantasize about straying from our scripted lives, about indulging in spontaneous intimacies outside the confines of our rituals, and . . .

Fuck Andrei.

I look at Tamara's sleeping body and let the sight of her overwhelm me.

I stoop down and kiss her toes. I slip my tongue between them, slide it around each one. I nibble on them.

She moans, still asleep, and throws off the sheets.

The sun hits her skin, from her nipples to just below her luxuriant pubes. The prospect of transgression makes my blood rush, but I rein in my impatience and move with slow but focused intensity.

Cupping her heels, I raise her legs in the air. Below, I catch a glimpse of her moist vulva, framed by her butt cheeks and by the backs of her thighs. I bend down and breathe on her wetness. She gasps, still asleep.

I smell her and close my eyes. Her pubes tickle my nose, and I can't help laughing.

That wakes her up.

I fear her reaction to this unscheduled intimacy, but she opens her arms in invitation.

I let go of her legs and fold myself into her sleepy embrace.

"You're sweaty," she mumbles. I'm still wearing my jogging clothes. "I love your smell." Have we broken free? Can we write our own lives? Together. Finally, truly, together.

She disentangles herself and sits up. She hugs me, drowsily rubbing her face against my chest.

She pulls off my T-shirt, and she runs her tongue from my belly button to my armpit.

She squeezes my stiff cock through my shorts, and we both laugh.

She smiles coyly, letting go of me, then runs her hand in circles around my crotch, never quite touching it. She gently bites my nipples.

She moves as if to squeeze me again, but then she pulls away and slips behind me.

She hugs me from behind, bites my shoulders hard enough to hurt, sinuously licks my nape. I feel her breasts squish against my back, and I get even harder. Her hands start to slip into my shorts, brushing against my pubes, but, again, she pulls away, laughing.

I grab for her. I lock her wrists in my hands and push her down on the bed. I bite her nipples – alternating from one to the other – and she gasps and squirms. I pull her up and place her fingers on the elastic waist of my shorts. She pulls down my shorts, takes my dripping cock into her mouth.

She delicately scratches my chest while her mouth goes up and down the length of my penis. I could come right now.

But I pull out of her mouth. I stick my thigh between her legs and rub her moistness against my skin while I play with her breasts.

After a while, I turn her around and push her down on the bed. I run my wet, hard cock on her skin, from her butt crack, along her spine, to the side of her neck. Her tongue slips out and licks me.

Leaving my cock next to her mouth, I reach down and grab her ass. I fondle it, kiss it, bite into it. I dip a finger into her moist cleft, and I tease her anus. She squirms and coos. I plunge deep into her asshole with my wet finger, and she screams in pleasure. I wriggle my finger inside her, slide in and out tenderly. I look at her writhe with delight, and my heart swells up.

Eventually, she pulls her butt away and flips over.

She again takes my cock into her mouth. She pushes her crotch up against my mouth, and I slip my tongue inside her vagina. I pull back slightly and gently kiss her labia. I tease her by running my tongue on either side of her clit, never quite touching it.

Meanwhile, her mouth slides up and down my cock; her fingers play with my balls.

Then, she lets my cock slip out of her mouth, and works on me with her hands.

I can barely keep from bursting. I struggle to hold on just a little longer.

I cover her vagina with my mouth and work on her clit with my tongue. Her breathing changes, and I can tell she's going to come soon.

In a sudden, almost violent, move, I pull away. She whimpers.

I grab her feet and run my teeth against her soles. Her whimpers turn to moans. I spread her legs, my tongue licking her inner thighs. Her moans become sharp cries. I kiss her belly. My hands find her breasts, my fingers squeeze her nipples. My lips find her mouth. My cock finds the wet opening between her legs.

I plunge deep into her; and she screams, comes, and then whispers the syllables I desperately want to hear, the inevitable name: "Andrei . . ."

And then I come inside of her, and the jism spurts out of me in neverending waves. In my mind's eye, I see the beautiful face of my dead friend.

The Gift

Dahlia Schweitzer

The martinis were strong and lunch took too long, but it was my birthday, so I didn't really care. I've always been pretty good at not showing how drunk I felt, and today was no different. Making my way back to my desk, a neat grin on my face, my feet methodically moving left, right, left, right in my pointy black patent leather heels, I slid into my seat and exhaled slowly.

All I had to do was stare at my monitor and type a few words, and no one would know I was wasted off my ass. I just had to keep my mouth shut, my face focused, and then I could leave.

"Rachel?"

I turned around.

"Um, someone left this at the front desk for you."

Michael reached forward and placed an artfully wrapped package on top of "To be Filed." I stared. I knew this package would have impressed me even if I wasn't seeing double – the bow was red luscious silk, the paper was smooth as satin and as brilliantly red as my fingernails, and the box covered half my desk.

"Do you know who dropped this off?" I asked, turning around, but Michael had already gone back to the mailing room, leaving me alone with my unexpected gift.

I glanced around – no one seemed to have any interest in me or my enormous red box. I debated whether to open it now or save it for later, but I couldn't resist; and so, with a sigh and a tingle of anticipation, I delicately slipped the bow off and ran my nails under the tape. Letting the wrapping fall down the sides, it made a satisfying hiss and exposed a white cardboard box.

I looked once more at the wrapping paper – no note, no explanation. Having no idea who would give me such a large present, much less deliver it to my desk, I opened the box and peered inside, hoping the contents would provide some answers.

At first, all I saw was a neatly folded stack of black lace, underwire, and red ribbon. I looked around the room – no one was watching. Was this some kind of joke? I reached in and lifted up the material, groping with my left hand to see if there was anything underneath. My fingers found a slim metal chain – and nothing else.

What the fuck? I looked around the room again; still no one was watching, no one was snickering, no one was paying me any attention. Time to figure this out, I thought. Quickly, I slid the fabric out of the box and into my briefcase. As I stood, I reached into the box one last time, grabbed the chain, and dropped it into my suit pocket before striding confidently to the restroom, all traces of inebriation eradicated by curiosity and adrenaline.

The bathroom door locked; I placed my briefcase on the shut toilet seat and opened it. The pile of lace and ribbon eyed me suggestively. I shook my head, grinning – this was the most intriguing birthday present I'd ever received. Lifting up the fabric, it took form and I laughed. Barely enough material to cover anything worth covering; anyone lucky enough to view it would be desperate to see what was underneath – and it was the perfect size.

Within moments, my suit hung neatly on the hook behind the door, and I was wearing a decadent mass of material – all crisscrossed and tied and finessed around my breasts – the underwire fitting perfectly under my cleavage, the ribbon wrapped around my waist and lacing up the back of the corset, the red silk creating a pattern of Xs against the sheer black lace of the rest of the garment. The box had also thoughtfully contained a pair of black thigh-highs topped off with an inch of red lace.

I didn't dare leave the stall to look at myself in the mirror.

Slipping on my heels, I leaned back and closed my eyes. Running my finger against the ribbon's smooth satin, I tried to remember when someone had last stroked me this way. It had been too long.

My last boyfriend and I had split up almost a year earlier, and between my work schedule and my distaste for bars and one night stands, I'd slept alone every night since, which made this gift all the more mysterious. No one had shown interest in me lately, and the only appointments I made these days were with co-workers and clients.

As I ran my fingers back and forth over the trail of red ribbon, eyes closed, breath quickening, I let my mind wander. By the time my fingers reached between my legs I was all wet. With a rush of need and desire, I shoved first one, then two, inside; pressing along the curve of my body, breathing deeply, every inch of me focused on the hot wetness of my pussy. I slowly started to push them in and out, my left hand making its way along the fine bone of the corset's underwire, cupping my breast and pinching my swollen nipple between my fingers.

The pain from my nipple, combined with the swelling of my clit and the pressure of my fingers, following a martini lunch, almost made me pass out. I slid back against the wall of the stall, falling into the corner, sweat glistening on my face, hair in my eyes, as I pressed in and out, harder and faster, feeling every inch tighten, every inch beg for more, my clit craving the pressure of my fingers, my pussy craving the pressure of a cock. I alternated as quickly as I could – a few seconds outside, a few seconds inside, my fingers darting across the edge of my clit, back and forth, round and round, and then inside – quick, as deep and as hard as I could shove. In and out, round and round, back and forth, every motion of my right hand echoed by my left across my breasts.

Both breasts had long since been liberated from their lacey confines, and they swung over the underwire, quivering as my hips thrust forward and my entire body began to shake. I could feel myself starting to come – the hint of delicious pleasure teasing me on the edge of my horizons, a promise of what would come if I kept at it, if I didn't let up, if I shoved harder and deeper, if I pinched stronger and tighter, if my fingers moved faster and my hips pushed further.

Leaning against that damn bathroom wall, hair around my shoulders, breath heavy, face flushed, my wetness leaking down my thighs, I kept moving – my fingers, my hands, my hips, until I could feel the sensation building and building and building and then – with one big rush, I exhaled as millions of tingling sensations rushed through me.

A huge grin on my face, I shoved my briefcase off the toilet and sat down. My chest was heaving, my head was spinning – and I felt magnificent. I couldn't remember the last time I'd masturbated, and certainly not the last time I'd done it in a public restroom. It had been way too long. What a birthday present.

When David left, I'd gone onto autopilot. Getting close to someone else seemed like too much work and way too much risk. It was easier to focus on my friends and my job and my apartment. Without anyone to run their hand between my legs, without being woken in the morning by someone pressing up against me, it was easy to forget that my body served anything but clinical purposes.

The last ten minutes had been a delicious reminder.

With my clit still throbbing and my nipples still swollen, I unhooked the corset and stepped back into my suit. I looked at my watch – only an hour or so until I could leave without guilt. I bent down to pick up my briefcase when a loud tinkle startled me out of my reverie. I glanced over to see a pile of silver chain against the edge of the toilet.

I smiled to myself. I'd totally forgotten. What the hell was that? Reaching over, I picked up the large circle at one end and lifted – it was a very delicate, very finely linked leash, the clasp attached to a matching very exquisite, finely linked collar. I smiled to myself. Whoever put this gift together certainly spent a lot of money. I'd never seen a chain so expensively made; they definitely knew how to pick things out. That outfit had fit me perfectly, and my flesh tingled at the feeling of cold metal against it.

Suddenly remembering a small makeup mirror in my bag, I fastened the collar around my neck, letting the leash hang down over my shirt. I couldn't resist. I opened up my mirror and looked at myself. I looked naughty. I couldn't remember the last time I felt naughty, much less looked naughty – and it felt hot. I loved the way the chain looked against the collar of my white shirt, the metallic glitter of the leash against the sober gray of my suit. I ran my fingers down the metal and felt chills down my spine. Delicious.

I unclasped the leash from the collar and slid it into my bag. I kept the collar on. I wanted its cold reminder to stay with me the rest of the afternoon. Doing my best to keep a straight face, I made my way back to my desk. I felt like everyone must have heard my moans or at least noticed the excessive time I had spent in the bathroom, but no one paid any attention, no one commented on my pinkish cheeks or unruly hair. I patted my hair anxiously as I sat back down at my computer, realizing I had forgotten to check my appearance in the bathroom mirror.

"Um, excuse me?"

The meek voice came from behind, and I spun around guiltily. The girl had long curly brown hair and huge brown eyes behind small tortoiseshell frames. I noticed her lips, which were large and seemed just slightly dry and cracked. For an instant, I wondered what it would taste like to lick them wet.

"I really hate to bother you, but—"

"It's no problem," I said reassuringly. "What can I do for you?" She looked vaguely familiar, but I couldn't think from where. I tried to remember if I owed her any paperwork.

"This is terribly awkward," she flashed a nervous grin, her hands anxiously twisting together, "but, you see," and then it all came out in one sudden rush. "I went out at lunch and I bought myself a present and I left it on my desk while I ran to answer the phone and the lunch receptionist thought it was for you because my name is also Rachael and the regular receptionist told her it was Rachel's box, and I don't know exactly how it happened but she told Michael and somehow he thought it was yours and then I asked him if he'd seen it and he said oh no, he had thought it was for you, and he gave it to you, and I don't know if this makes any sense, but I wondered if you knew where my box was?"

I smiled. Of course. Of course it wasn't for me. Of course not. How ludicrous. Only in my life. I smiled at her, at this darling girl with the dry lips and the nervous hands.

"Nice to meet you, Rachael."

She laughed shyly, her hands resting for an instant against the edge of my desk.

"Why don't you have a seat?" I asked, motioning to my extra chair. She sat down and stared at me, wondering.

"The box is here," I gestured under my desk, showing her where I had tucked the package before my trip to the bathroom, "but the contents are in my bag. I'm sorry."

She looked at me, confused.

"I couldn't resist. I had to try it on."

She laughed again, a bit longer this time and a bit less shy.

I reached into my bag and pulled out Rachael's outfit and slipped it back into the box. The leash I placed carefully on top, before handing it all to her.

"I'm really sorry about this. You must think I'm terribly strange." Her eyes stared straight into mine.

I smiled back at her. "Not at all. I think you're wonderful. It's the best birthday present I've ever gotten."

"It's your birthday today?" she exclaimed in wonder.

"Yes, yes, it is." I couldn't help smiling at this delightful girl.

"Oh, God, I had no idea. Why, then you must keep this. It should be yours." She pushed the box back at me.

"No, no, no. It's yours. I tried it on. That was amazing enough for me. It's your outfit. It belongs to you."

There was a pause while we both thought about what to say next.

"Please. I'd like you to have it."

I couldn't stop staring at her lips. "No, no, thank you, it's not really me, anyway. I like my underwear to be brighter than the clothes I wear on top . . ."

She laughed again, this time the shyness almost gone, the

brown eyes bigger and browner than before, and I began to notice little hints of gold inside them.

"You know," she leaned over to me and said, in a soft whisper, "they have corsets in red and pink and blue . . ."

My first thought was that her lips were only inches from mine. My second thought was that I'd never kissed a girl. My third thought was that a pink corset might be the best thing I could ever buy.

"Will you take me to the shop? I want to go."

"Of course!" she exclaimed. "If you won't let me give you mine as a birthday present, perhaps you can let me buy you another?"

"Only if you let me buy you a drink after?"

I couldn't believe it. I was flirting with a girl. I was flirting with a girl named Rachael. I was sitting at my desk, flirting with a girl with my name, and all I could think about was how her lips would feel between my teeth.

"I would love it," she said as she stood up. "Shall I stop by your desk at six?"

"That sounds great." I couldn't stop smiling at this creature.

She leaned over again, her lips inches from my face, and my breath stopped. What was she doing? Was she going to press her lips against mine, her tongue in my mouth, running against my teeth, her breath mixing with mine? Was she going to kiss me at my desk?

"You can keep the collar," she purred, and then turned to walk away.

I closed my eyes, waiting for my heart to return to normal. Two more hours until six.

Bells on Her Toes

M. Christian

Jasmine died two years ago. She showed up three weeks ago. Should have expected it, knowing Jasmine as well as I did.

I didn't know she was back, not really, for almost a week. Stomping around my little Long Beach bungalow, the one she had called my shell, I caught glimpses of faint reds, gold, of the hazy glow of sunlight through baggy tie-dyes, and of God's Eyes turning in the windows. They were just there enough so you knew you saw something, but was always a part, always a fragment of something. Same with smells: incense, patchouli oil, pot, cheap wine, and that simple lemon perfume. Same with sounds, walking from the little kitchenette into the living room you would catch the slap of leather sandals on the hardwood floors, the opening clap of *Stairway*, and that tiny sound, that special sound that would always mean bells on toes. Jasmine.

She had outlasted the ghost of the sixties by a few years, Jasmine had. Even though she'd been born in '71, she was a spirit of the Merry Pranksters, of Airplane, of the Summer of Love, acid, pot, Fat Freddy's Cat, the Stones, and tie-dyes.

It wasn't easy being a flower child in the age of the World Wide Web, ecstasy, coke, NIN, Courtney Love, Belly, and body piercings, but Jasmine pulled it off. She drifted with a smile on her face, and those fucking bells on her toes, through life – hitching rides with only good people, taking only the best drugs, being friends with only good people. She was a ghost of the sixties, a spirit of the Haight and the Diggers.

Now she was just a spirit.

I never could figure out how she could exist. She was
fascinating in the same way a Mary Keene painting (admit
it, you've seen them – big eyed children) can be: innocence
distilled to the point of being surreal. Jasmine could hitchhike
with Jeffrey Dahmer and get out alive, and with some money to
help her on her way.

If there was a sin in Jasmine, in her perfect fortune, this
unblinking good luck, it was that it didn't leave much room for
depth or brains. Jasmine was a spirit who walked slowly
through life, letting it bump her this way and that. Never
ask her to meet you anywhere, never make plans around her.
Jasmine was pot and incense and a soft, warm body that fit so
comfortably in your arms, but she wasn't someone you could
count on. No one who knew her said it, but we all knew it was
true – and having her turn up two years after we all put her to
rest in the Long Beach Municipal Cemetery proved it. She was
late for her own funeral.

I can't really remember the first time I met Jasmine. Maybe it
was that party to celebrate Rosie getting her first gig at the Red
Room. Maybe it was that picnic that Robert and Steve threw
down at the remains of the old Pike. Maybe she had just shown
up on my doorstep like she always seemed to, jingling her tiny
silver bells and lazily sweeping her tie-dye skirt back and forth.
No place to sleep that night and Roger Corn was always up,
awake, and willing to take her in.

God knew what we had in common, save we . . . fit somehow.
We didn't talk music (Airplane! NIN! Joplin! Love!) or books
(Kesey! Coupland!) or anything else for that matter (You're
always so damned happy! What do you have to feel sad about?),
we just fucked and played and took our respective drugs (Coffee
& weed! H and Pot!). The spirit of the 60s and one hack writer,
making his bread and butter writing porn, *True Detective
Stories*, and articles on how to get your cat to use the toilet.
We just seemed to go together somehow. We tolerated each
other because we liked to fuck and kiss each other. Relationships can be based on worse things.

When I got that call, Rosie so calm and collected, I was sort of ready for it. Jasmine wasn't someone who collected a lot of uniqueness. She did kind of what you expected her to, so when the phone rang and Rosie said that Jasmine had "passed on" I knew almost exactly how, where and why.

The funeral was sparse and sad for such a little spirit. The four of us in the cemetery. We had all pitched in to get the coffin. It was a colorful affair, you had to give it that: Rosie in a gaudy color-blast of a red sequined gown and boa, Robert in his own retro seventies platforms and polyester, Steve in his sixties with his beads and (where the fuck did he score that?) Nehru jacket. I wore something aside from black. It was hard to find, but I managed to score a brilliant red shirt from a friend of mine. In many cultures – my shitty education not enough to tell me exactly where and who – red is the color for the dead.

Two years later she was paying me a visit.

The first time I realized that something was going on I was scared shitless. I was washing my coffee cup out (my only lucky one), high just a wee bit from this shitty Mexican that Rosie had scored for me, and I felt someone behind me. Thinking it was Montezuma's revenge acting through the weed I shrugged it off. Then the someone put their arms around my waist and hugged my little pot belly. I screamed, dropped my cup (*Java is the Spirit of Creativity*) into shards of ceramic, jumped into my Docs and ran over to Steve and Robert's.

You'd think that ODing on H in Rosie's apartment would be enough to keep a girlfriend down.

After a day or so Rosie had convinced me that it had just been lack of sleep, too many sips from my favorite mug, and a sudden flash of missing Jasmine. Rose said she felt her own late ex touch her sometimes – when she was in just the right mood. Of course there are differences between a dyke who'd gone off a bridge on her Harley and Jasmine the flower child overdoing the nostalgia just a bit.

Back in my place I kept seeing those flashes of Jasmine's colors, smelling her smell, and hearing her bells. And some-times, just before drifting off at three A.M. I'd feel her body warmth – just the heat of her at first, you understand, slip into bed with me.

Then, about two weeks after that first touch in the kitchen, I was coming from the living room into the kitchen, new mug in hand (*Coffee is the Last Refuge of the Sleepy*), straight for my Saint Coffee machine and there she was: sandals, tie-dyed drawstring pants, simple white cotton shirt, scarf tied over her head. She was just there – as I'd seen her a million times: joint burning in one hand, twirling a few strands of her blond hair in the other, chewing her lips at some newspaper headline or another and – while she'd never actually said it – you could still hear her thoughts clear and distinct: *Why don't people get along*? Like she had on many mornings, as she had countless times.

And there she was again, after two years cold in the ground.

Then she wasn't. She was there for about as much time as it takes to blink and think, for a panicked second, *is that really her*?

That was the first time. There were quickly others.

Jasmine liked to get in the bath tub with me when I was practicing my Death Trance Meditations. I like to sit in warm water with the lights off and think about myself in terms of flesh, blood, bone, hair and where all those pieces could end up, say, in a million years. You can get into some profound thoughts, lying in the dark, in the water, like that. And it can really mess with your head when the door would crash open and this demented hippie chick, all bounce and giggle, would come storming in jingling her tiny silver bells to pull off her balloon pants and squat herself down on the john to take a piss. We used to fight about it, especially when she and I didn't even know she was in the house. You can imagine the shock she made after she was dead.

Mornings were Jasmine's favorite time of day. If I'd let her she would go on and on about the opening of the day, with the accompaniment of birds singing and the soft applause of butterflies. She would wax cliché about the possibilities "dawning" (and giggling at the pun) with the new day and wonder how many adventures she'd have by sunset.

I am a Creature of the Night. I run from the burning rays of the sun and seek solstice in the cool darkness of my shell. But, still, I would always get up on a cheery blast furnace of a morning and be happy as a clam – especially when Jasmine treated me to one of her early bird special blowjobs. She liked that word, "Blowjob" – said it sounded so cute. And, boy, was Jasmine skilled in its performance. Just the right amount of tongue, suction, lips, wet, dry, hands. She used to wake me up with soft kisses along my leg to let me know she was there and what she was up to. Then the kisses would run up to my stomach. A hand carefully placed over my cock and balls would warm them and add some sensation. When her mouth did finally touch my cock, it was after those soft, soft hands had stoked, teased, tickled and coaxed me into a painfully intense hard-on. Then the mouth. Then the real ride.

Mornings haven't been the same since she died. The sun must be a little brighter, stronger now. But then that one morning came. I was sleeping off my usual late-night writing stint (with a celebration of a new one finished: *I was a Teenage Trailer Park Slut*) when I got this amazing hard-on. I was so zonked that I really can't tell you if it was because of Jasmine or just because I was remembering my past with her, but there it was: long (no brag, but seven inches), strong and mighty. It was a mechanic's cock, a soldier's cock, a fuckin' basketball player's cock (okay, one of the white ones). I was proud of my cock, pleased with it that morning. With a hard-on like that, even hack writers can go out and become president (if you know the right people).

Then Jasmine started to work on it. Dear dead Jasmine. Maybe because of my half-zonked condition, maybe because I just missed those lips, that throat, but I didn't do what I should have done: run screaming into that intense morning. But I didn't and dear dead Jasmine started to really get down and suck at my cock.

Death did not diminish her knowledge of blow-jobs, it seemed. She was all of Jasmine rolled into that one cock-sucking. I could, in fact, just squint enough and see her as I

M. Christian

had seen her on all those mornings: her firm, slightly heavy body folded over, her face concentrating at my cock, with her right hand between her legs as she humped herself along with her sucking.

God, I could feel every inch of Jasmine – even if I couldn't see her. I could feel her tongue playing with the ridges and corona of my head, I could feel her lips play over my skin and veins, I could feel her throat – hot and firm – as I grazed it during her sucking. When I came, it was so good it hurt real bad, and my come shot into an invisible mouth and vanished into ectoplasmic nothingness just as real, live Jasmine had liked to swallow it.

Other people would have run – to their pastors, to the cops (why?), to some science guy with a gizmo to exorcise the latent spectral energies, to their priest (who would rattle their beads and speak some Latin). But most folks don't consider themselves a Child of the Night, groove on gloom, or hate any color save pitch black. Besides, Jasmine had been a sweet girl (tinkle, tinkle) and one motherfuckin' hot lay.

The fact that she was dead and haunting me didn't really seem to bother me at the time.

Jasmine was great for surprises. She liked to catch you unawares and get caught unawares herself. I can't remember how many times I'd "caught" Jasmine in the living room, or on the toilet, in my bed, rubbing one of her little, soft fingers up and down on her little moist slit. She was like a little kid in that, her body and other people's used to give her so much pleasure. Death didn't even slow her down.

Listening to the newest Lycia, all moan, cemeteries, statues, clouds, rain, and mourners, I would get the strong impression of flowers, macramé, pot and the distinct sound of the tiny silver bells on toes jingling merrily away and look next to me to see Jasmine, half there and half not, not quite developed, not quite visible, legs spread wide, fingers gently rubbing up and down on her gumdrop-sized clit.

She became, over those weeks, to be more and more in my life. More so than she had when she was alive. Flesh and blood, Jasmine used to come over maybe, tops, three times a week.

Then I wouldn't see her for months. Once a year passed before I walked in to see her dancing, naked, with headphones on in my living room, the air thick with Mexican greenbud. But now that she had passed on, time seemed different to her. I would expect to feel or feel this spirit of Morrison, of Cream, of Sergeant Pepper at least once a day. Dancing in the living room, reading the Sunday paper in the kitchen, masturbating on the toilet, spooning with me in bed.

Bad? No, not at all. I felt special that of all the people she lived with, had fucked, had fought with, this one grungy hack writer living in a cheap-ass bungalow in Long Beach was the one she wanted to spend eternity with.

But there were other times, too. I would walk from the kitchen into the living room, coffee cup in hand, straight for my Mac with visions of *Truck Stop Bimbos* running through my head like a pneumatic chorus line, and I would see her, standing by the window looking at something only the ghostly Jasmine could see. What bothered me more than anything was that Jasmine, alive, never really had an interest in the traffic on Oleander Street. Jasmine wasn't just an echo drilled into me and my cheap-ass stucco walls. Something of the real Jasmine was here with the spectral one. Something that was missing something.

It became pretty obvious when she started to get . . . distracted by things. Right in the middle of one hot and nasty morning blowjob, her ghost would stop right in the middle (*coitus spectoralus*) and I would get the definite impression that she was either looking out that window again or maybe trying to remember something that she had forgotten.

Rosie, my only expert on dead relations coming back to cop a feel, got real quiet as she poured me Darjeeling tea, then said: "When Bolo left this world—" Rosie's ex who tried to jump her Harley from the Queen Mary to Catalina "– she came back to visit me a couple of times. It was like she just wanted to say good-bye in a way she couldn't when she was living. When she had done that, she just faded away."

"Yeah, but I don't get the vibe that Jas is here for a reason. It's like she just sort of moved back in."

Rosie stirred her tea with a chiming that reminded me way too much of Jasmine's tiny silver bells. "I got the impression from Bolo that she knew where she was going and that she was just stopping by. Remember, we are dealing with Jasmine, here. She could have gotten lost."

Great, a girl who could get lost in a Safeway had taken the wrong turn between death and the afterlife and was now trapped in my house.

It got worse soon after. The sex was still there, but now it was . . . sad. The one thing the flesh and blood Jasmine wasn't was sad. The best way to get rid of her, in fact, was to get depressed: she'd vanish like pot smoke to find someone more cheerful. I have always had a hard time putting on a happy face, the one reason why Jasmine and I never stayed together for too long a time. Now, though, it looked like she was stuck in my dark little bungalow.

And it was making her sad. It wasn't something she was used to, getting sad, and it was hitting her hard.

I heard her cry one day. I was hard at work on something for a porno mag specializing in dirty buttholes "– and the guys who love to lick them" when I heard this weird sound. A sort of choking, wet sound. I hadn't ever heard it before.

I found her next to the bed, curled into a partially invisible fetal position. Jasmine was crying. It was that heaving, nauseous kind of crying, the kind you do when your cat gets run over, when you know you've taken way too much of the wrong kind of shit, when you're lost and know you can never find your way back.

I'm not a very altruistic kinda guy. I don't really know where it comes from, or doesn't: I just really don't give a flying fuck for a lot of folks. Yeah, I'll take Steve to the hospital when his T cells are low, or hold Rosie when she thinks too much of Bolo, but I don't really see those things as being good. Good is, like, helping fucking orphans or something, or giving change to the smelly crackhead who hangs out, or passes out, at the Laundromat. I don't have that kind of temperament.

I really didn't care that much about Jasmine. Yeah I'd bail

her out when she got busted for forgetting her purse and eating up a storm at some diner. Yeah, I'd give her whatever I had in my checking account when she really needed it. Yeah, I'd always let her in, no matter what was going on in my life. But she was just a pal, and a really good lay. I honestly didn't think of her in any other terms.

But then she was dead, and crying in my bedroom.

I could guess the cause. Bolo was a dyke who always knew where she was going and how exactly to get there. She was an iron-plated mean mother who knew what the score was – despite her profound depressions and mood swings. Jasmine was flowers and pot and the Beatles. She could get lost walking from the bathroom into the bedroom.

It wasn't all that hard, once I made the decision to do it. One phone call, to Rosie. Then into the bathroom.

I hadn't done my Death Trance since she had manifested herself those two weeks ago. It was just too much of a temptation for her and the shock of her walking in had been way too much when she was flesh and blood. Since she was a ghost – well, I don't really want to see if I'm cardiac prone.

Had trouble sleeping a few years back. I was lucky enough to have health insurance at the time, and so was able to see a doc who could actually give me pills. I had only taken one – the fuckers were so strong that I stopped taking them and simply started staying up late.

I took five and lay down in the warm water.

We are nothing but matter. We are nothing but the flesh than hangs on your bones, the blood that gushes through our meat. Bach took shits, Aristotle got piss hard-ons, Mother Teresa the runs, Ghandi really liked enemas, Lincoln got wind. We are animals that have learned to walk upright, that have trained themselves to use the next best thing to fishing with termites with a stick: the nuclear bomb.

I didn't have to think long. About the time I was drawling analogies between Sartre and seals that know how to play *Lady of Spain* on car horns, I was interrupted by a tiny sound, the sound of cheap Mexican toe rings chiming their tinny, cheap tones: the tinkling of tiny silver bells. Then the sound of Jasmine pissing into the toilet.

But this time it didn't sound mischievous: It sounded sad.

The pills had started to take effect, I braced my feet against the tub so I wouldn't drown and whispered, as loud as I could (which was just loud enough for the dead to hear), "Follow me."

I don't know what she saw, but I started to hallucinate pretty badly. Either the pills, or I had really started to fade, myself – I don't know. I was in the kitchen, full and real and solid, looking out my window. The sun was bright, so bright that I had to close my eyes against the brightness – but for some reason it reached right through my eyelids and right into my brain. I realized then that it couldn't be the sun – for at least the obvious reason that sun never came in that window, anyway.

No tunnel, no saints (or sinners, either), just that bright light. I felt myself start to come apart, like the flesh I had always talked about, thought about in my trances, was starting to unravel and decompose around me, leaving just the lightweight fragment of Roger Corn left. It wasn't a pull or an enticement, it was just a direction that I was walking myself to.

Jasmine. Somewhere I thought that, and reached back into my apartment for her, but I couldn't seem to find her. I looked in the bedroom, the bathroom (I looked so silly lying there in the tub, mouth hanging open), the living room, all the closets, the kitchen . . . everywhere. No Jasmine. Not even her ghost.

Then that sound. Her sound. Cheap bells on her toes and a smile on her face. I found her masturbating in the bedroom, chubby legs wide and open, finger dancing on her clit. Typical. I smiled and took her hand and pulled her towards me, into me –
– and then pushed her away, into the brightness.

The cops and firemen busted down my bathroom door about that time. I don't remember much after save the sound of their tools smashing my interior door to cheap splinters. I probably don't want to remember being naked in front of all those macho public servants, having a tube run down my throat and having all that guck and pills poured out. Rosie had come through, with perfect timing.

No repercussions, no real ones at any rate: what's another botched suicide, after all. At least I had accomplished something with this one: a spectral repercussion.

She's gone. You'd expect that. Gone wherever magical little Deadheads go when they OD. She's with Janis now, with Morrison and Lennon – in a place where the seventies never happened and where everyone gets along.

And, yeah, I hear those damned happy bells now and again.

Two of Cups

Elizabeth Margery

The first time I saw Esmee she was reading Tarot in the square in front of a soaring brick and stone church. What I would come to know as French, African, and Spanish blood was blended in her dark luminous eyes, high cheekbones, and queenly posture. Dressed like a younger, hipper incarnation of Marie Laveau in a long ruffled skirt and tignon, she laughed and chatted with the tourists.

She shuffled and dealt like a pro, slim golden fingers bridging the oversize pasteboards with ease. I watched from the shade of a flowering tree as she told the future for a few bucks a pop, her patter in Creole-spiced tones as sweet and slow as honey. She noticed me, too. Her inquisitive glance felt real as a touch on my skin, even as she assured a stout, perspiring woman of opportunities on the horizon. When the woman hauled herself to her feet, Esmee beckoned to me, smiling.

I hesitated. Not because of the cards, though some of Papa's congregation would consider them a risk to my immortal soul. Papa would disapprove mightily as well, though from distaste for the mystical rather than belief in its dangers. I hesitated because of the danger to my heart, the danger of making a fool of myself. What could it hurt? I asked myself as I stepped out into the sun.

"What'choo name, cher?" she asked.

"Kristina." I sat on the rim of the fountain.

"From up north? Me, I'm Esmee." She'd set what looked like a large TV tray covered with a black velvet cloth next to the curb of the fountain. Only room for a three card spread – past, present, future – because, she explained shrugging, "les flics" sometimes looked the other way, and sometimes not.

"Gypsy laws," she said darkly.

And sure enough, as soon as she laid out my cards a cop strolled into the square. Her eyebrows rose, but I'd barely gotten a glimpse at the bright colors and archaic forms before he headed towards us. Esmee bundled the cards into the cloth and folded the table. We scurried into a nearby café; half in real urgency, half in smothered giggles.

From the shelter of the area defined by awnings, ropes, and potted plants, she gave an impudent smile to the cop. He cocked thumb and finger at her like a gun, smiled sourly and walked on.

"Private property," she explained with satisfaction.

We sat at a small wrought-iron table, her paraphernalia stowed beside us. The waiter brought café filtres without being asked. We sipped and smiled a little self-consciously, my sundress and sandals making a strange contrast to her voluminous garments.

"Would he really have arrested you?" I asked.

"Maybe. Maybe not." She flashed a gamine grin at me, square white teeth gleaming. "For sure, he'd hassle me, run me off. Me, I don't feel like running today."

"I thought that was all part of the local charm. Jazz, ghosts, voodoo?"

"In theory" – she pronounced it "tee-o-ry" – "but not in practice. If you don't have a license or work for a shop, they treat you like a panhandler. If you do, you don't make any money."

"What about my fortune?" I wondered if she remembered the cards, if she'd read it here.

"Pfft, that's easy," she said, winking. "Same as mine, when I read my cards first thing this morning: 'You have been lonely, but you will meet a beautiful stranger. Your life will change.'"

I caught my breath, unsure whether she meant what I thought or not. Unsure what I wanted her to mean. I was afraid it was wishful thinking on my part, though her slow smile and dark gaze seemed to indicate otherwise. For years, I'd been taking my holidays in exotic cities, hoping for excitement. Perhaps, just perhaps, that excitement had finally arrived.

"So, how much do I owe you?" I asked, reaching for my handbag to cover my confusion.

"For you, nothing." She shrugged; a delicious gesture that caused her off-the-shoulder blouse to shift distractingly. "We'll share it, yes?"

"Are you sure? Don't I have to cross your palm with silver to make it come true?"

"Not much silver in American money these days. Cross Etienne's palm instead. Get the tip? Come, walk with me, cher." Esmee dropped a couple of tattered dollars on the table and I hastily scattered a handful of change. The maitre d', a very dark man with dreadlocks, kissed his fingers to her and smiled.

Outside, she slipped her hand through my arm as though it was the most natural thing in the world. Our strides matched nicely, shoulders brushing as we strolled out of the sun-struck square and down a tree-lined avenue. At home, I would have felt self-conscious. At home, I would have had good reason – Pastor Nilsen's librarian daughter. Here I enjoyed the glances we garnered: a lovely darker woman in the garb of the last century and a tall, blonde woman in aggressively modern tourist attire.

We talked. She was actually a student at the local college, slowly putting herself through evening classes. Not an actual refugee from another time, she told fortunes, did other things. Like gumbo, she said, a little bit of this, a little bit of that.

"Can you make a living?" I asked, though truthfully her gypsy existence sounded like heaven. I'd had enough stability to last a lifetime.

"Not bad during the season," she said cheerfully. "More fun than waiting tables, washing dishes, yes?"

More fun than shelving books and collecting quarters, too. I asked, "Do you believe in the Tarot?"

"But, of course! We make our own futures, you know, but we make them of the past and the present. It's all there."

"What if you see a bad future for someone?"

"Mmm, bad fortunes are bad for business. Like a sundial, I only count bright hours. I might warn, you know? Don't travel next week? Like that, but the other, no. People come here for pleasure, to leave sorrow at home."

I suppose I thought Esmee was looking for a new place to set up. I didn't realize I was walking her home until we arrived at the door.

"Come up?"

My footsteps and breath stuttered to a stop, color scalded my cheeks. "Don't you need to . . . work?"

"Too hot for the tourists now. They'll be back in the evening," Esmee said, stopping one step up. "I'm not wrong about you, cher, am I?"

I almost asked, wrong about what? I didn't, couldn't. "No," I whispered, "not wrong."

"Then come up."

Up, indeed. Three floors up, but at least it gave an excuse for my flushed face and pounding heart. Her apartment was small, a bed-sitting room decorated in nouveau-hippie: India-print fabrics and squashy pillows. The room smelled of curry and incense. The single window had no real curtain. It probably didn't need one with its view of rooftops and tree crowns, but she'd hung a beaded curtain of rainbow-colored plastic. The slanting afternoon light threw drops of jeweled brightness on the dusty floor. She kicked off her slippers with a sigh of pleasure.

"Sit down. I'll get some wine."

I chose a cushion and slipped my sandals off. My sundress wasn't long enough to make sitting on the floor easy. I finally settled for curling my legs to one side. Esmee, returning with two lovely but mismatched stemmed glasses, sank gracefully to sit cross-legged, her skirts billowing around her. She lifted her glass and held it until I copied her. "Bon chance!"

"Good luck?" I sipped. It tasted like chablis, but I'm not sure I could have told the difference between champagne and turpentine at that moment.

"To good fortune," she corrected. "The good fortune that brings us together."

The atmosphere in her room was suddenly so thick that I could have written my name in the air with my finger. No, not my name – "I Want You," in large letters. I'd dreamed, if not of this, then of a hundred variations of it for years. But in those fantasies I hadn't been paralyzed, staring like a fool, afraid to trust my luck.

Esmee took the glass from my fingers, placing it and her own on the floor beside her. She caught my wrist and turned my palm up.

"Do you read palms, too?" I asked, then felt like an idiot when she dropped a kiss into my palm.

I had never been so conscious of the size and shape and structure of another's hand. Her fingers were shorter, her palm broader, but size for size, very like my own. Callused and strong, but so different from a man's. When she leaned towards me, I met her halfway, drawn like iron to a magnet.

That first kiss was like a sixty-second faint with my eyes open. Her full lips were warm and lush, tasting faintly of wine. Our lips clung, as though my flesh was loathe to part from hers. The second kiss was even better, deeper. Her tongue was small and quick and pointed like my own, a *pas de deux* instead of a duel. She touched the planes of my face, tracing eyelids, cheekbones, and the curve of my jaw delicately, reading me in Braille.

"I've never done this before," I whispered against her cheek. "Been with a woman, I mean."

"But you wanted to, didn't you?" Her tongue traced the inner curve of my ear and I shivered when I felt her breath against the moisture.

"Oh, yes."

"Don' worry. Like fallin' off a log, cher. It's easy."

God, yes, it was easy. Like falling off a log, like falling off a cliff, like falling in love. Easy and total and irretrievable. Whatever I'd suspected in the past, I knew for certain now. I reached out and caught her shoulders, warm and solid beneath the ruffled blouse. A simple push bared her breasts, the garment catching at her elbows for moment before she slipped her arms free.

She reached for me on another kiss, canting her head to fit more perfectly as she groped for the zipper on my sundress. The slur of my zipper underscored the inhale and exhale of our breathing. Her laughter against my mouth as she fumbled for the fastening of my bra went to my head more than supermarket wine could ever do.

"Stand up," Esmee said urgently and I did, dizzy and unsure of my footing amongst the pillows. She shimmied out of her blouse and long skirt in one gesture, nothing beneath them. I undressed quickly and didn't worry about whether she thought my hips too wide, my breasts too small. All my attention was on her.

She was perfect – smooth café au lait skin over a solid, close-coupled frame, curly dark hair cropped close to her elegantly shaped skull. Her nipples were generous and dark.

"Like Hershey's Kisses," I said, touching one with reverent fingers. The tip hardened.

"And yours like raspberries, all pebbled up. A pretty good combination, cher, raspberries and chocolate." Esmee bent and drew my nipple into her lips. We were of a height so when she straightened, our breasts nuzzled together, firm and soft. "Come here, sugar."

She drew me towards the bed: several mattresses stacked together, her coverlet a patchwork of velvets and satins all in shades of maroon. Her tawny skin was marvelous against it, and I wondered if she'd chosen it for that reason. I wondered other things, too. I wondered what she'd feel like under me, on top of me. What she'd taste like.

"Don't look so worried, bébé. I'll teach you." She laughed then, and patted the bed. "I almost said, 'I won't eat you,' but of course, that's not true! At least I hope not."

I sat on the edge of the bed. "I want to go first. Eat you, I mean."

"Soixante-neuf is nice," she said. "You know, sixty-nine?"

Too distracting for the first time, I thought and besides, if I couldn't do this or couldn't do it right, I didn't want to owe her. Failure seemed highly unlikely. I'd never felt this sure about a first time with any boy. But still. I shook my head. "Please?" "Sure." Esmee lay back, spreading herself before me like a landscape of gently rolling hills and wooded valleys. Her generosity made me catch my breath. I kissed her mouth, her throat, and feasted on her breasts. It wasn't imagination; she smelled and tasted of cocoa-butter.

She had a racing stripe, a line of darker pigment that ran from below her navel to her sex, like an arrow showing the way. Goosebumps rose on her belly as I ran my tongue down that stripe. Heart thumping, I settled between her legs. I lost my concentration for a moment, distracted by the contrast between Esmee's honey-colored thighs and my pale freckled hands; the contrast between my fantasies and the reality in my arms, inches from my lips. Uncertainty stilled me. "I want this to be good for you."

"It will be. You got an advantage, girl. Just think 'bout what you like and do it. It'll be fine." She touched my hair. "You'll be fine."

I kissed the hollow of her hip on each side and rubbed my lips and nose across the crinkly black nest of pubic hair. She smelled like me but also different, salt and musk but warm, like a tropical sea and also flowers. What sort of flowers bloomed on tropic isles?

I parted her outer lips and marveled at her. In theory, I knew how a woman is made – how I was made – but this was different. I'd always thought of women as being all neatly tucked up inside, not bobbing absurdly out in front like men. Caring for and even pleasuring myself had never challenged that notion, but her sex was a structure more subtle and complex than I expected.

Her inner lips were a baroque fantasy, ruffled like an orchid and richly pink. Ah, yes, orchids! Her vagina was a mysterious well of deeper hue, her clitoris prominent. She caught her breath as I gently slipped the hood back to expose the tiny inner knot, then released a long sigh as I touched it with the very tip of my tongue.

The first taste led to a deeper kiss and it was like having oral sex for the first time ever, not just the first time with a woman. The act for its own sake, not as a way station on the road to something else, but an end in itself, and a thing of mutual pleasure. Her every shift and sigh fed back to me.

Her musk grew stronger, her thighs dewed with perspiration as they tensed and relaxed, and her sighs became murmurs of pleasure and then moans. Time spun away from me. I came back to myself to find her clitoris fluttering like a tiny live creature between my lips. When her cries told me "too much" I set it free and dropped my forehead to rest against the arch of her pubic bone, breathing hard into the hollow formed by her outspread legs, filling my lungs with her scent. Though aroused, I felt no desire to move. I could have lived in the canyon of her thighs forever.

Esmee plucked at my shoulder. I crawled up the length of her body slowly and collapsed against her. The planes of our bodies meshed like drowsy serpents – my shoulder under her arm, my cheek against her bosom, the swell of her hip into the narrow of my waist. "Cher, if you never done that before, you got natural talent you been pure-dee wasting."

She scooted down till she could kiss me. The taste of her lips through the taste of her sex made me reel. Sweet tangle of lips and tongues, sweet mingling of perfumes, sweet mixture of desire.

"First time ever," I whispered, still feeling solemn, "but not the last."

"Dieu, I hope not. So what you think 'bout eating pussy?" she asked and kissed my temple.

"It's wonderful, and – I don't know – it's so easy. I thought it would be harder, the first time."

She laughed, a rich caramel laugh, that I felt as much as heard. "Well, why would it be hard?" she asked with perfect logic. "Hard's for men, not for us. Your turn now, bébé."

She sat up, leaned over, and kissed me, lips as soft as rose petals. She slipped one finger into me, gathering my fluids so her touch slid silkily over my clitoris with just the right pressure. When my hips rose to her hand, she flung one leg over my thigh and rubbed her sex against it, rough hair and hot, wet labia riding me. We rocked together, drinking each other's sighs and whispers, until I shuddered to climax.

We lay twined together, her soft, damp weight a precious burden until she shifted and propped herself on an elbow. She touched a finger to the end of my nose and frowned in mock sternness.

"There's just one thing about eating pussy I gotta warn you about," she said.

"Oh, really?"

"Yeah. It's wonderful, but it ain't filling. Course, it ain't fattening either! There's a Thai restaurant down the way. Coconut soup and garlic shrimp? We can bring it back here." She pushed herself up and sat cross-legged, smiling.

"Is it good?"

"You never had Thai? Second best thing you'll ever eat! Trust me, cher. I told you your life was gonna change. The cards, they never lie."

Screen Play

A.F. Waddell

In a dimly lit room I stood at the bottom of a winding staircase; the sound of wind chimes played from an upstairs porch on a hot night. I wore a white blouse, tight red skirt, and spiked high heels. I watched the man walk toward my front pane-glass double doors. His brown hair was slicked back; his cheekbones were prominent; his long thin nose slightly flared over his mustache. He jiggled my door handle; the door was locked. As I watched him he searched the ground for something. Picking up a large stone, he used it to break my glass door pane; he reached inside and turned the lock. He threw open the door and approached me, holding and kissing me and unbuttoning my blouse. His hand rubbed my cunt through my silk skirt and panties.

"Maybe . . ." I whispered.

He lowered me to the floor. He pushed up my skirt and pulled down my white panties, slipping them over my thighs, knees and calves, and over my strapped, spiked heels. I breathlessly shook.

I awoke moaning in bed from another orgasmic dream; I'd mentally recreated a scene from the film *Body Heat*. I was Mattie Walker, my perfect, fit-in-a-champagne-glass breasts throbbing in my perfect white blouse, my hungry cunt throbbing in my perfect red skirt. I recalled the first time I'd seen the film in the early nineteen-eighties. In a cold, empty house I'd sat huddled under a blanket. I was emotionally and physically transported to the lush, warm, wet environs of South Florida –

was it my imagination or did steam visibly rise from grass and earth, from Mattie and Ned, as they fucked in the boathouse?

I thought of my vibrator nestled in the night stand drawer. I deferred. It was getting late. I got up, dressed in a robe, and went to the kitchen for coffee. I took a cup of Colombian into my office and checked my schedule for the day. I'd get off easy today: only one appointment, later in the day. Driving southwest through the hills in my Jeep was relaxing, a perk before hitting the freeway. To the sound of Santana's *Samba Pa Ti* I floated through green-hilled space. Highway 120 was winding. With my tendency to speed I had to be careful, lest I totally lose it on a curve. The hitchhiker stood on the west side of the highway. He wore a blue flannel shirt and jeans. His long dark hair was tied in a ponytail. What would he be like? I wondered. A snake-hipped stud with knowledge of the *Kama Sutra* and Tantric sex? A masseur and sex magician? A lover who'd spend hours discovering and lingering on a woman's sensitive spots? Did he smell of recently showered male and exotic fragrance, his hair of coconut shampoo? I imagined the male bouquet drifting from his skin and through my nostrils, into the limbic system of my brain. *Get a grip, girl. He's probably a serial killer.*

Dr Wellman's office was located on Citrus Avenue between Back, Neck and Shoulder Pain, and Anti-Ageing Clinic. I walked the maze between offices and entered the lobby at 3:50 p.m. The receptionist, Melanie, was pretty, perky and tan.

"Hi! Have a seat, Ms Waites. He'll be right with you."

I sat on a cream-colored leather sofa. The decor reminded me of a Woody Allen film set, with its calming vibes of neutral shades white, off-white, eggshell, oatmeal, beige, mushroom and sand. At 3:59 I walked into the office and took a seat opposite Barry. We sat in comfortable overstuffed chairs.

"How've you been, Anna?"

"Busy."

"Anna, are you taking care of yourself? Exercising? Eating right? Socially interacting?"

"Yes, yes. Who are you, my mother?"

Barry smiled. "How's work going?"

"I'm adapting my novel into a screenplay, remember?"

"That's right. Wonderful. Your novel about the female independent film maker?"

"Yes, that's right! But I wonder if people will pay to see yet another inside-the-industry satire. No action figures or computer games will result. Industry accountants will likely be unenthusiastic."

"Do the work, Anna. You must complete the work in order to get to the next work."

"Yes."

"Sleeping well? Dreaming?"

"I dreamt of Mattie again. That I was Mattie."

"Why do you suppose you dream of being a *femme fatale*?"

"I suppose I'm attracted to the power. The sexuality."

"Yes? . . ." Barry rested his chin on his intertwined hands and leaned slightly forward; the furrow between his brows deepened.

"Dr Wellman, do you realize that Mattie's character is bad, and isn't punished for it? Quite unusual for a story, for a film. Oh. And don't forget Bridget in *The Last Seduction*. Another exception to the rule."

"Anna . . . we don't use the b word in this office."

I smiled. "Sorry! And . . . this morning I fantasized about picking up a hitchhiker."

"Yes . . .?"

"Spontaneous sex with a complete stranger would be hot."

"Well, yes, but a distinction must be made between fantasy and reality. Many fantasies are meant to remain unrealized. Violating prohibition is however a strong basis for eroticism."

I had images of forbidden fruit. Dates. Smooth and rich on the tongue. High-carb. Sugary. Dangerous. I took Citrus Ave to I-5. As I drove north through green foothills, the air quality improved; dusk gave fantastical quality to the hills and lights. Pockets of housing development imposed, their squares and rectangles backing out, pushing between the natural curves of the foothills, boxes juxtaposing green jutting breasts. Driving East towards Shadow Valley, I looked forward to getting home,

putting on a robe and puttering around the house. I wondered
when my muse might visit and send me scurrying to my note-
book or word processor. At home I reclined on the sofa and thumbed a magazine.
Goddess targeted a female professional demographic. I skimmed
the food section and made a mental note on the Salmon and
Spinach Diet. I skimmed the health section and noted the latest
miracle supplement. I skipped ahead to Indulgences. Blurbed
were spas, vacation getaways, and specialty services. *Retreat
caters to your special needs. Nestled in the natural environment of
the Golden Haze foothills, our facility offers the utmost in comfort,
privacy, and natural beauty. Our select, discreet staff is here to
indulge you. For more, visit our web presence at retreat.com.*

I went into my office, signed online and accessed the site. The
design was simple, understated, clean. Shades of light blue,
cream and black were accented by soft focus photos of foothills,
cabins, interior design, and bodies under the hands of masseur
and masseuse. I accessed the reservations page. A link provided
a request form. *Let us assist you in designing your experience.*

Interesting, I thought. I bookmarked the website, got ready
for bed, climbed between the sheets, and randomly took a book
from the night stand. *The Mind of Eros* by Frederick Borman
Ph.D. could be a deeply psychological read, but also included
sexual fantasies and experiences. I liked to skip around. I first
hungrily, then sleepily read. The dark-haired woman sat in the
center of the small movie theater; she seemed to be the only
woman there. Men watched the screen with a focused yet wild
energy. In giant close-up, a pink quivering cunt and cock
devoured and attacked the other. Reminiscent of some nine-
teen-fifties' American sci-fi/horror film, sans the cheesy costumes with visible zippers in the back, slimy odd-shaped
creatures wrought havoc and spewed mysterious, dangerous
fluids. A large prick pumped a perfect, hairless, tanned, pink-
edged wet cunt. The Maw-Creature appeared impossibly small
to accommodate the Prick-Monster which inched inside it,
stretching and spreading its edges.

A pink belled tip and shaft vigorously slid through slick

fingers and thumb, fingers and thumb, fingers and thumb. From its slitted tip spurted whiteness into brunette hair. It ran onto a soft tan face over heavily blushed cheeks, over cotton-candy-pink lip gloss, over a delicately dimpled chin. The dark-haired female viewer looked at the screen. Recognizing her own face, her jaw slackened as the cinematic action reflected in her eyes.

I awoke and touched my face. Lying on my back in bed, I stared at the ceiling and replayed my unusual dream.

Under a skylight I crawled on the hardwood floor and arranged three-by-five-cards. Breaking down a novel into key film scenes could be torture. How to effectively condense, yet retain meaning? I agonized. Many screen treatments in any case eventually suffered drastic re-writes; the further into the process one got, the less original meaning likely remained, until a work could appear unrecognizable. Casting-wise, Cate Blanchett and Jeremy Irons might devolve into . . . who knew?

I thought the first scene would be of protagonist Claire giving direction on a film set. Scene two would begin a series of flashbacks: Claire in the early years, as continuity person and script supervisor on various low-budget location films, including the comic relief of behind-the-scenes on horror films. Relationships would be broken into love scenes, interspersed with her industry climb and disappointments, climaxing in her Cannes win for *Sighs And Whispers*.

I gathered my three-by-five cards, mixed them up, and threw them into the air. I spun and chanted as the cards fluttered to the floor. Not bad! I thought of their re-ordering.

I drove West on Mountain View. It had been a while since I'd seen him – since he'd closely stood, caressed my shoulders and neck, and run his fingers through my hair. Rick was a good listener, sensitive, and had a sense of humor. I'd date him, I thought, but then we'd have sex and break up, and I'd lose a damned good hairstylist.

"What are we doing today, Anna?"

"A trim and a blow-dry, please, Rick."

Draped in plastic at the shampoo sink, I leaned back, closed my eyes and relaxed into the experience. Wet. Lather. Rick's hands vigorously massaged my scalp, moving in circles, moving skin over bone, massaging nerves and limbs. Rinse. Condition. Rinse.

Back at his work station, I sat as he precisely combed and trimmed my hair. He continuously re-positioned my head, as if I was a fidgety child. At the next station a female stylist did a man's hair. It was funny, I thought most men came into a hair salon with a maximum of two or three inches of hair, yet the stylist could take forever to trim a quarter-inch. She did a Hair Styling Dance of sorts, delicately fluttering around the man, smiling and chatting and flirting.

"Let's blow this dry, Anna, I want to double check the line."

"I want volume and tousle. Every hair needn't be in place."

"Sure! Lean forward and flip your hair, please."

Through the fringe of my hair I noticed the intersection of his thighs and groin; his well-tailored navy cotton slacks; the tucked black cotton shirt; the thin black leather belt with the silver buckle. Stylist and patron seemed often body parts to one another, varying with the point-of-view.

"How is it? You like?"

I looked at my hair. It was full and wavy and not too short.

"It's good. Thanks, Rick." We smiled.

I drove East on Eucalyptus. Town & Country Centre boasted an upscale grocery market. I aimed my Jeep towards the parking lot and put it in a space between a Mercedes and a BMW. Dear God, I thought, Christmas decorations were up. Red, green and gold frou frou contrasted the clean lines of the beige stucco building. The upscale neighborhood seemed sometimes surreal, perhaps too quiet, too clean, too calm, with lurking noise and dirt and chaos threatening sudden explosion.

Inside, market patrons had a weird social energy, sugary perkiness covering vitriol. Perfect suburban dolls shopped in tennis dresses, smiles drawn back over teeth that would love to bite. Suntanned champagne blondes filled their carts. Clothing fashion changed little throughout the year in Southern California; the temperature changed little, and might allow halter tops, cut-offs, and platform sandals in December.

The produce department boasted obscene abundance; it seemed the vegetables had been inflated with a bicycle pump, or were futuristic monsters. The produce area smelled wonderful, I thought, as I touched Japanese eggplant, English cucumber and Italian squash. To my right a man shopped and watched me. Was it my imagination, or was he slightly smiling and smirking as I handled the green and purple vegetable shafts?

An instrumental version of *Let It Snow* played as I wandered the store aisles. At the bakery, red and green packaging contained myriad sweets. The world shimmered with candy. The Muzak was seeping into my brain. I had to get out! I focused on filling my small basket. Mixed baby greens. Zucchini. Chicken breasts. Merlot. Chocolate ice cream.

At the express lane, Aileen rang up my stuff.

"Paper or plastic?" asked Kyle.

"Paper, please."

In the kitchen I unpacked groceries and poured a glass of merlot. It tasted fruity, plummy, spicy, low-herbal. I stood and looked out my kitchen window, sipped, gulped and poured another glass. On the counter I preheated my grill. I heavily spiced a boneless chicken breast, put it on the grill, and put down the lid. I mixed baby greens with extra virgin olive oil. Wine chewed at my empty gut; I drank more. My brain clicked, warmed and sweetened. I stood at the counter and wolfed down my chicken breast and salad.

I went into the living room and put a DVD into the player. I sat on the sofa. Energetic acoustic guitar began the film soundtrack.

"Garbage!" began the dialogue.

The beautiful young Southern woman discussed imagery with her therapist. Garbage. What if garbage cans were actually producing more garbage? she wondered. The doctor smiled. They'd soon be discussing masturbation, the woman blushing and stammering, denying her need. Fast Forward. The woman sat on a plaid sofa in a hot, sparsely furnished room. She wore a gold blazer, black tee shirt, black mini-skirt, and black leather cowboy boots. A man in tee shirt and jeans sat on the hardwood floor in front of her, looking up at her. His camera rolled. "Do you remember the first time that you saw a penis?" he began. She narrowed her eyes, parted her lips, cocked her head to the side and began to talk. As she shed her blazer and rearranged herself on the sofa, her leather boots rubbed together, making soft squeaking sounds. Fast Forward. In a bedroom, a man and woman shouted at one another. "Did you have to masturbate in front of him?" he demanded of her. "No. I wanted to. So there!"

Sex, Lies, And A Video Cam was another favorite film of mine, transporting me to yet another humid Southern clime. I'd felt voyeuristic viewing its seeming raw intimacy and dialogue; I'd thought its editing amazing; it had inspired my purchase of black leather cowboy boots. I soon slept on the sofa, in blue screen light.

I opened my eyes to filtered sun. I got up, made coffee and went to my desk. I checked my schedule: no appointments for the day. I sipped my coffee and tiredly made notes on my writing projects. A drive to the coast might be inspirational, I thought. I took a shower, dressed in a pullover scoop-neck sweater, skirt, and leather sandals.

Highway 120 wound through velvet hills and grassy flats on its way to the sea. The two-lane road could be lonely, with little traffic. The dark-skinned hitchhiker stood on the north side of the road. He wore a Henley shirt and jeans. His dark hair was tied into a ponytail. I passed him, checked the rear-view, braked, and pulled onto the shoulder. He smiled as he loped towards the Jeep. I unlocked the passenger door. He hoisted himself into the leather bucket seat, threw his bag to the floorboard, closed the door, and fastened his seatbelt.

"Hello. Thank you much for stopping. *Gracias.*" He warmly smiled, his dark brown eyes making direct contact with mine.

"Hi. Call me Anna."
"I'm Manuel. Manny."
"Where are you headed?"
"Caida Del Cielo. Heaven's Fall. The beach."
"Where's that?"
"Near Fuego Que Sopla. Blowing Fire."
"It's on my way."

Darkness was beautiful, I thought. The deep reds of roses and blood and wine; the tan to brown of bread and chocolate and exotic skins; the dark liquid of brown, drowning-pool eyes pulling one in. Contrast could be interesting, I thought; sophistication and innocence; vanilla-cream swirling with caramel-tan.

"Where are you coming from, Manny?"
"Palmville."
"Do you hitch much?"
"Do you pick up much?"
We smiled.
"Would you like a beer? There's a cooler in the back seat."
"Thank you."

Over a hill, the road turned and opened to the Pacific Coast. Heaven's Fall seemed deserted. I saw no parking area. I wondered where to park.

"Don't park too close to water. The sand is wet and deep," Manny cautioned.

"Thank you, Manny. Do you have time for another beer? Or do you need to meet someone?" I glanced the pier and the vast, empty shoreline.

"I'm meeting no one."

I parked a distance from the shore, near a small dune. I scavenged a blanket from the back and spread it on the sand.

We wordlessly sat on the blanket next to the Jeep, drinking amber lager, getting stoned on nature and negative ionization and brew. I wasn't sure whether minutes or hours had passed.

"Let me touch you . . .?" he asked.

"Where?" I smiled.

"Here . . . here . . . ." His hands brushed my cheeks; he lightly ran his hands down my neck to my breasts.

"Soft *pechos* . . . sweet *pechos* . . ." He gently pulled a bare breast from my sweater. His thickly sensual lips took my nipple; his mouth pulled. He stood and pulled me up and kissed me. "Wait," he said, opening the rear passenger-side Jeep door.

He lifted me onto the edge of the high bucket seat. He pulled down my scoop-neck sweater; my breasts lightly hung over the purple velvety material. He pushed my stretch skirt up around my waist. I sat, legs askew on the leather seat, grains of sand sticking to my skin, the sea wind blowing against me. He knelt and placed his hands on my lower inner thighs, slowly moving up. I leaned back and more widely spread my legs. His head moved towards my center; I held it and felt the texture of his hair, removing the tie that held it. It softly fell and draped my thighs. His finger centered the outer lips of my cunt, moving into the inner.

"Ahhh . . . *ostra rosada* . . . pink oyster . . ." he murmured.

Licking and entering me with his tongue then fingers, he moaned and intermittently gave soft voice. "*Mar salado* . . . salty sea . . ."

The Spanish language would never be the same, I thought. It now seemed even more beautiful, if that was possible. I clenched and came around his fingers.

"Wait." He pulled away, his erection straining against his jeans. He unzipped his fly and lowered his jeans, releasing his prick. He fumbled in his small travel sack, pulling a small square brightly-coloured packet from it. *Gallo* read the lettering; the art was of a red rooster. He removed the white condom, held the tip, and rolled it onto his brown erection, vanilla-white engulfing caramel-tan. The wind grabbed and whipped the empty condom wrapper down the beach. I dripped onto the leather seat. He held my hips and slowly slid his cock into me. He moved deeply into and out of me, gliding clitoris and G spot, clitoris and G spot, clitoris and G spot. Orgasm rolled from my wet center, sensation becoming sound, escaping through my O-shaped mouth. I envisioned my orgasm having come from the sea and returning to it; my cries metamorphosing into ocean roar.

"*Caliente, caliente* . . . hot . . . *mojado!* Anna!"

In front of my television, I drank shiraz and ate take-out crab and shrimp enchiladas and squash with red peppers. I clicked my DVD play button. *Sexo En El Camino* was subtitled. Miguel entered his girlfriend's bedroom, and her, in rapid succession, with no foreplay. The girl had long dark hair, perky breasts, a thin build. In a fascinating, non-American quality she had lots of thick, dark pubic hair.

The film's logic seemed to imply that women were in a perpetually pre-moistened state. It worked. The sex was quick and intense and hot, with penises and vaginas artistically filmed in shadow.

Fast Forward.

In a dilapidated motel room in Oaxaco, the young naked Sergio stood with an erection.

"Drop the towel," commanded Gabriella, from the edge of the bed.

He stood in front of her and kneeled.

"I'm wet for you. Eat me . . ." she said. He lowered his mouth to her and began to lick. "Wait! Let me take off my panties!" She laughed. He very soon fucked her, in another quick, intense scene. Miguel watched his friend from a doorway, a hurt look in his eyes.

Fast Forward.

The two young male friends and the older woman drove through mountainous jungles and small villages towards an allegedly mythical beach, laughing and telling stories, stopping in rundown cantinas for beer and food. At the beach the three fucked. The men fought and drove away together. She stayed at Heaven's Mouth for the rest of her short life. Fade to black.

I sighed and thought of a spontaneous, passionate man who made love in soft whispers, intense cries and beautiful words; who could have been manifesting Tourette's or channeling spirits as he thrust and came.

I drove 120, and I-5 to the Citrus exit. The generica of strip malls seemed somehow obscene. I pulled into the medical plaza and parked. I walked the maze between offices and entered the lobby at 3:50 p.m. I took a seat on the sofa in Dr Wellman's lobby. "Hi, Anna! He'll be right with you."

Third Person Singular

Richard V. Raiment

Cassandra loves my bottom. "Your lovely little girly ass," she calls it. But it's never me she makes love to, never me she goes down on. It's always Tatiana, Mei Lei, Rosa, or whatever other girl she has staying with her.

They're all illegals, of course, which I am not. All struggling to find a way to stay in my homeland and usually finding it with someone's cock or cunt in mouth or other moistened orifice, and usually in front of a rolling camera, at the game, or both.

Tatiana, her latest, is typical of them – a tiny wisp of a thing but beautifully proportioned, tits and ass cheeks like two pairs of apples, small and plump and ripe and rosy. Lots of head-hair for Cassandra to play with, almost no hair anywhere else.

My bottom, at least, is fuller and rounder, and my hair – as Cass requires of us – is long and falling to my shoulders. Just like Tatiana I am otherwise shaven, the mound of my pubis smooth and bald as a baby's bottom.

I am what I am because of Cassandra, and I love her. It seems to me I have loved her forever, even in lives we've lived and no longer remember. I have loved her the most since that day at school long ago. The day I told her I loved her, when she told me I could and I first learned the price, bent over the changing room bench, my gym shorts round my ankles. Cassandra's hand was down the front of her own shorts, playing with her little jewel, while Miriam – an early acolyte – whipped my ass red with my gym shoe, and spanked me until I wept and came.

I love her still, and have been hers for several years, now. I do not mind that she finds pleasure in my pain, in my routine humiliation. It is as it ought to be. The feelings that stir in my loins and flood my parts I know I should not feel. I do not deserve her, could never deserve her, and the chance to gaze almost constantly upon that perfect, wonderful form, is worth any price. I am glad to serve her.

Cassandra brokers influence. That is her life and way.

It is gloomy beneath the table in the dining room, the illumination of a hundred silver mounted candles lost behind the thick white damask table cloth which hangs almost to the floor. Plush carpet cushions my knees. I am naked and warm, but I do not really like it here, do not really like what I must do.

Cassandra and Tatiana are greeting our guests in the hallway – I can hear the buzz of voices muted by distance, tablecloth and nervous discretion. I can picture them in my mind. Six people, almost always; three men of power and influence and three women who are the real owners of it, all of them gleaming and well-dressed. All excited by the luxury and taste which surrounds them, by the promise of unknown wickedness, and by the sight of their hostesses.

My love and her other lover are wearing nothing, unless you count the body paint. I watched them apply it to each other and wished they would do so to me. But they didn't – they never do.

Black, white and amber rippling stripes, white abdomen and groin, make each a tigress. There are subtle hints of matching color about their brows, their eyes and cheeks. But it is the white diamond on each black-painted pubis which most excites the guests and it excites me, too.

Cassandra, I know, is introducing Tatiana, encouraging them to ogle her, remarking on her beauty. She shocks them deliciously by telling them, right in front of the gently smiling, inscrutable naked girl, that Tatiana gives the most wonderful head. She tells them there is no greater joy than to have Tatiana's tongue dance a piquant ballet on her own sweet, glistening, clit. And I know they stir, small pink cobras of cock uncurl from sleep in soft warm undershorts, pink orchids bloom to a touch of dew, and they all want her, eagerly or apprehensively according to their gender and experience.

Tatiana takes their coats and leaves on Cassandra's implication-laden promise that they will "see more of Tatiana later."

I hear a feminine gasp of delight as they walk into the room, see a shadowed ghost of hall light falling through the doorway before it closes, hear Cassandra's voice explaining, telling them the rules, telling me the rules for the night.

She calls this one "Russian Roulette", although sometimes it's Chinese Roulette, Cuban, Thai or whatever, depending on the girl. It's a game of pairs and pairings that they have all agreed to. I hear her soft, dark voice invite them to sit down, introduce Raoul to fill their glasses. I have never met Raoul.

It is no longer dark, seven pairs of hands carefully – according to the rules – lifting the cloth into their laps as they sit down, but forbidden to peep beneath the cloth. At the top of the table is one pair of naked legs, white diamond gleaming on black-painted shaven pubis, the lovely slit of my lovely Cassandra brightly pink in the sun-bronzed darkness of her, tempting but yet untouchable.

My first course comes with theirs. They are seated in pairs, man and partner, on the three broad sides of the table around me, and in front of me, now, an elegantly tailored pair of dinner-suit trousers, side stripe gleaming. I rest my hands on his blind knees, feel the body tense, sense the tension around the table as some suddenly arrested motion of his or rapid change of expression tells them he's been chosen.

Beneath the cover I unbutton and unzip him, draw the thickening impostor through its tailored exit, firm the cotton gently beneath the weight of his balls, and grip him in my lip-protected teeth.

I'm not displeased to meet the little stranger. I quite like cocks, their blind ebullience, their babe-like hunger. This one grows less little by the instant. It fills my mouth, stretching my lips as I slide upon him, feel the silky wetness of skin, corded veins registering soft, fleeting pressures on my lips and tongue.

He is all rigid now, and no doubt flushed where they can see it, his five companions watching, wondering, anticipating. The men are hungry for their turn, the women perhaps for theirs. Or maybe they are apprehensive, not knowing what it is like to feel a woman's tongue there. Maybe they are wondering who will be first, which cunt Tatiana's unseen mouth will choose to join with this cock later, the second part of this game.

I am hot myself, and ache with wanting, ache with knowing how long I must wait before she'll thank me, meet my needs.

In the gloom above, a mouth unseen mutters obscenities, the body convulses. Delicious spasms shoot down the length of his hot phallus, spurting unseen white and wet into the warm waiting of me. I swallow, as I must, for she knows I don't much like that and she'll punish me for the slightest yellowing stain upon her snow-white carpet.

I can feel the tension all around me as I turn upon my knees, deciding which cunt it will be. I move towards it, raise the skirt and find no panties. This one is eager. So I let the skirt fall and I can almost feel her disappointment, all of their surprise at her change of posture or expression. I turn to another and find lovely chocolate skin, a livid pink flower under vivid pink knickers, and I press my tongue against here.

Muted laughter. Hers perhaps, or maybe that of the girl who knows I've bypassed her, who thought that my tongue would first be within her, and knows, now, from the tensing body at the foot of the table, the expressions I cannot see, that someone else has it.

I imagine, of course, that it's Cassandra's clit, and tease it and play with it as long as I dare, darting and wetting and licking and pricking. I feel it moisten with my wetness and hers, feel her soften around me, and then she shudders and softly moans. I wish it was Cass who was coming so wetly, filling my mouth with her potion.

A warm word above and behind me, a man expressing pleasure and probably him of the fresh-emptied balls who will be her post-prandial lover.

I choose to take her partner's cock next, hoping it is chocolate as hers and full-creaming. Then I open his flies, and there's a disappointment, of sorts. But I don't really mind. This one is gorgeous, fully engorging, and fully engaging, a monster in skin. It pries me wide until it quite hurts and then explodes like a hydrant, white liquid to the flame that burns only higher inside me. It hurts now. I want her.

And now I take pity on she that I spurned and moistly I pair her with the dark girl's big partner, pretending her Cass again, tonguing Cass's clit again, finding the gush again and hearing her whimper. Cass never whimpers.

The last man sounds angry in his civilized way. He knows from Cass's earlier instruction that the rules mean the two pairs chosen leaves a third which is wanting but is left unrequited. A woman's voice protests, sweetly, sincerely, that she really doesn't mind. Everyone knows fully her secret relief – and I can feel Cass's soft smile, see it clearly behind my eyelids.

My choice is her choice, and I know her choice always, when a woman is reluctant. In an instant I'm at those soft panties, so girly, naïve, and I'm at the pink flower that's full, hot and frightened in its nest of roan curls, and I'm tonguing my Cassandra with all of my being, sending all my love searing in wet, white-hot lapping. I hear her mewing, her body soft-shaking as if she is weeping, and then she is weeping a flood in my face and pooling full wet in the chair.

His cock, last now and wanting, is ripe for playing. I play him till long past dessert, leaving him trembling, leaving him shuddering, as I finish my own final course.

It's an age until they leave; I'm wet with their juices, sticky and full, thirsty and hungry and hurting. There is a slow burning ache of a heat deep within me, the pain of my wanting intense.

When they're gone to the rec room, with its beds and benches, its plush and velvet, I can creep to the peep-hole and watch them. Tatiana has rejoined them and I watch the couples I've created coupling. I match their faces to trousers and skirts, whilst Cass and her lover hover, watching and smiling, two tigers in happy embrace, fleetingly breaking to caress breast or ass, bestow fleet finger-blessings on cock or pink clit and smile their encouragement.

Our guests are sure it was Tatiana, of course, who pleasured and ate them through their own gourmet courses, and do not know of my existence. In consequence she has their gratitude, shares close secrets. If that's not enough she's always got the videotape, although she rarely has to threaten it.

And I have . . . what?

I have served Cassandra, I have loved her. I have done as she requires me, given in entirely to her will, so that later I may watch them, as I sit cuffed to my chair: Cass and Tatiana mutually astride, each with her face between the other's thighs, each supping at the precious fount until they're full.

And then they will untie me. They will lie side by side in silence, softly kissing, and allow me to lick their pink lips clean, to seek to please them.

I do try, really. For if I please them I'm rewarded. The strap in Cass's hand beating heat into my ass-cheeks, the close metal cage unfastened from my cock which strains against it, checkered patterns of red pressure lines upon my hot and thrusting flesh.

Then Cass, the strap in hand, will ride Tatiana's tongue again as I slide my aching want into the pink Russian wet-walled vault of Cassandra's gentle lover, seeking to pleasure Tatiana's pussy. I close my eyes, and pretend once more that I am fucking *her*.

Richard's Secret

Saskia Walker

"A gimp?" Richard was a sex slave? Could it be possible? I swallowed, breathed deep and tried to make sense of what Tom had just told me. "But what does it mean . . .?" I looked up at him, spluttering the words out. "I mean, I know what it means . . . I just don't know what he means by it, by approaching us."

Tom rested his hand reassuringly on my shoulder. There was a look of deep concern in his eyes and he was watching me carefully for my reactions. Oh, how I loved this man; when he had said he had something "a bit heavy" to talk to me about, I thought the worst was about to happen, that he was going to say there was another woman, that he was leaving me. The last thing I expected was for him to reveal this, Richard's secret. Richard's darkest secret.

I had actually known Richard longer than I had Tom. He had been working in the international trade department when I was transferred to the London branch, about six years earlier. Admittedly he was the dark horse in the department, and the office gossips plagued him with questions about his private life, all of which he managed to avoid and dismiss without being in the least bit offensive.

To me Richard was just a shy, reclusive guy; a small man, and very attractive in an understated way – nicely packaged, dark hair and vivid blue eyes. I just assumed he was comfortable around me because I was the only one who didn't quiz him about his private life. That was also how I had learned more about him than the tenacious office gossips. He lived alone in an apartment overlooking the Thames and enjoyed a number of extreme sports, like acute and prolonged bouts of mountain biking, martial arts and kick boxing. I supposed that was what gave him his good packaging – the guy worked out, you know – but none of that seemed to go with his shy, understated image. Neither did this fetishistic sexuality that I had just learned about, but then . . . maybe it did kind of make sense?

I had kept the personal information he gave me to myself, which is why he liked me, I assumed; he appreciated that kind of respect. Now that I reflected on it, I guessed he had been even friendlier to me since Tom had arrived on the work scene and moved in with me two years ago; but shy single men often feel more comfortable around women who are attached. Little did I know he was observing Tom and me with this kind of proposal in mind. He wanted to be our sex slave, our gimp. My heart rate went up several notches and my body was hot, almost uncomfortably hot. I fanned myself with a magazine while trying to come to terms with the conundrum, and the rather extreme effect it was having on me – I had to admit it the idea made me horny as hell.

"Suzie, I can see you are interested, my love." Tom folded his arms. He was standing in front of me and nodded down at my breasts, where my nipples were swollen and crushed beneath the surface of my silk blouse. There was no hiding it. My sex was clenching, my body was on fire.

"Yes, I can't deny it . . . the idea of it makes me hot, but you know . . . I want *us* to be okay." I eyed his long, lean body, the fall of his dark blond hair on his neck. I couldn't bear to lose this man . . . hell, I could hardly get through a day without wanting us to meld our bodies together and fuck each other senseless.

"It won't affect anything between us, it's just an adventure." He began to stroke my face, pushing back my hair where it was sticking to the damp heat of my neck. "He said he will be transferring soon, so there wouldn't be any awkwardness at work, it would just be a one-off." My, he had thought of everything, and he'd obviously been planning the whole thing for quite a while, too. Tom lifted my chin with one finger, his thumb stroking gently over my lower lip. "He said it would be up to us, he said we could do what we wanted with him." There was a dark, suggestive look in Tom's eyes.

"I see . . ." I mumbled, not sure if I did.

"One thing I'd like to see . . ." His voice was hoarse. He ran a finger down the collar of my blouse and into my cleavage. He slipped one finger inside, pulling the blouse open, looking at the shadow between my breasts. His other hand lifted mine and led it to his groin, where his cock was already hard inside his jeans.

"What . . .?" I wanted to know. The blood was rushing in my ears; the magazine in my hand fell to the floor.

"I'd like to watch him going down on you." His eyes were filled with lust. I groaned, my hips beginning to shift as I rocked back and forth on the hard kitchen stool, my sex hungry for action. He leaned forward and kissed me, his tongue plunging into my mouth. My fingers fumbled with his fly buttons, and then I was bringing his heavy cock out and stroking it with my whole hand. He pushed me back, over the breakfast bar. He was going to fuck me, right there and then, and I was ready; sweet Jesus was I ready. I hoisted my skirt up around my hips. He dragged my knickers off and pushed my thighs apart with rough, demanding movements. He stroked my inflamed clit, growling when he saw the juices dribbling from my blushing slit. Then he fucked me while I perched on the kitchen stool, pivoting on its hard surface with everything on display.

"Get your tits out," he whispered as he thrust his cock deep inside me, his body crouched over me. I pulled my blouse open, my hands shaking as they shoved my breasts together, kneading them and tweaking the nipples, sending vibrant shivers through my core. I was whimpering, jamming myself down on his thrusting cock as hard as I could. Tom watched with hungry eyes as my hands crushed my breasts. I suddenly remembered Richard blushing when I had caught him looking at me over his monitor, just the other day. Was he aroused then? Had his cock gotten hard as he thought about me and Tom? He had glanced away, furtively, his color high. Dear God, the man had been thinking about us doing this; maybe even thinking about doing this *with* us. He had told Tom his dark secret, and Tom was now rutting in me like a wild man. I was on fire. I whimpered, my hands suddenly clutching at Tom's shoulders. I was about to come. I had never come so bloody fast in my entire life.

"You look very beautiful, Suzie," Richard said. My fingers fidgeted with my neckline, nervously. "I always thought you looked like Audrey Hepburn with your hair up like that." He smiled; he seemed quite calm now, and he was leading the situation even though he was going to be the slave. We were nervous, but then we were the novices; presumably he had done this many times before. I glanced at Tom. He had chatted happily about work while we made our way through several glasses of wine, until now – until Richard had moved the conversation on to a personal note. Now Tom had grown silent and watchful.

"Thank you," I replied, swigging another mouthful of wine. Both men were staring at me; the sexual tension had risen dramatically. "It's the little black dress," I added, with a smile. That morning I had told myself that I wasn't dressed any differently; I always wore stockings, garters and high heels to the office. The little black dress underneath my jacket was the new addition. It was very soft and clingy, and now that I had abandoned the jacket I felt good in it. Besides, what does one wear when one is about to take on a sex slave?

"You want to know what I've got in the briefcase, don't you?" He'd seen me looking at his black leather briefcase when we left the office that evening, the three of us headed to Tom's and my place for drinks. Yes, I had been curious. I nodded. "I like to wear a mask," he said. "I've brought it with me and I'd like you to put it on for me."

My sex twitched. The combination of power and deviance he had suggested in that simple comment hit my libido like a narcotic entering the bloodstream.

"Okay, I'll do it," I replied, as nonchalantly as I could manage.

Richard stood up, taking off his immaculate suit jacket as he did so, and placing it over the arm of the sofa. He picked up the briefcase and carried it over to the breakfast bar, where he set it down, flicked the combination lock and opened it. Tom and I both watched with bated breath. Richard undid his tie, rolling it slowly and tucking it into a section in the top of the briefcase. Then he lifted something out of the case and turned back to us, leaving the briefcase sitting open on the breakfast bar. As he walked back to me, I stood up.

"It's perfectly safe," he said, allaying any concerns we might have in advance. "It was handmade, for me." He passed the soft, black leather mask into my hand. I turned it, feeling it with my fingers. It was cool to the touch and incredibly soft, molded, with laces down the back and breathing holes for the nose, a closed zip over the mouth. A powerful jolt went through me when I realized that there were no eye holes; Richard would not be able to see what we were doing once he had the mask on. My eyes flitted quickly to Tom and I saw that he had noticed that too. Richard undid his shirt, revealing well-muscled shoulders and torso. He dropped it on the sofa and stood in his black pants, looking from one to the other of us, for our consent.

"Turn around, and I'll put it on." Even as I heard my own voice another wave of empowerment roared over me. Richard smiled slightly and inclined his head.

Tom suddenly stood up. "I think you should take that dress off, first," he instructed. The mask dangled from my hand. Richard's eyelids fell as he looked at the floor, hanging his head, but I could see that he was smiling to himself. The atmosphere positively hummed with sexual tension. Tom's instruction had completed the dynamics of the triangle. This was it; the scene was set for action.

I put the mask down on the coffee table and pulled the soft jersey dress up and over my head.

"You can take one look at her, before she puts your mask on." Tom's eyes glittered. Richard's head moved as he looked back over to my stiletto-heeled shoes, up to my stockings and the scrap of fine French lace barely covering my crotch, then up and on to the matching balconette bra that confined my breasts. I

Saskia Walker

knew I looked statuesque and glamorous in this, my most
expensive underwear, and I could see that he approved.

"Thank you," he said, his gaze sinking to the floor again.
Before he turned his back he passed something else into Tom's
hands. It was a set of intricately carved manacles. As Tom
looked down at the object, Richard turned his back, bent his
head and put his wrists behind his back – awaiting both the
mask and the manacles. Not only would he not be able to see, he
wouldn't be able to touch. Tom looked at me, his eyebrows
lifting, a wicked smile teasing the corners of his mouth.

Tom came forward and enclosed Richard's strong wrists in
the manacles. Then it was my turn to take action and I moved
over, heart pounding, and began to ease the mask over his head.
It pulled easily into place and I gently tightened the laces,
gauging my way until the mask was molded tight and secure
over his face. When the knot was done Richard slowly descended to the floor and squatted down on his knees, eyes
unseeing, his head cocked, as if awaiting instructions.

We circled him, taking in the look of this creature, as he had
now become, kneeling between us in the center of our personal
space. I had prepared the room well, with the furniture pushed
back and subdued lighting. He knelt between us with his
masked head lifted up and back, his strong arms manacled
behind him, his cock a discernible hard outline in his pants.
With Tom towering over him, Richard presented an image I
would never forget.

Tom nodded at me, pushed an armchair forward and in-
dicated that I sit down.

"Do you remember what I said?" He kissed me, then pulled
my knickers down the length of my legs and up, over my heels,
stroking my ankles as he did so. I nodded. "Good." He smiled –
it was devastating, wicked – and then he grabbed our slave
around the back of the neck and urged him forward. "Your
mistress is one horny bitch. I want you to go down on her, and
make sure you do the job properly. I'll be watching." With that,
he unzipped the mouth on the mask and slowly lowered Richard's head into the heat between my thighs.

I couldn't believe this was happening – Tom was so dominant, so strong and commanding. I was getting wetter by the
second. I couldn't look down at the man between my thighs; I
felt a sudden rush of embarrassment and strangeness as he
crouched there, unseeing and yet so sexual. My eyes followed
Tom as he moved away. He was looking into the briefcase that
had been left open on the breakfast bar. What was in the
briefcase? I wondered, again. Then I felt the surface of the
mask, cold against my thighs as Richard moved his head along
them, feeling his way toward the hot niche at their juncture.
The tip of his tongue stuck out and I felt its blissful touch in the
sticky, cloying heat of my slit. He used his tongue like a digit,
exploring the territory of my sex, before he began mouthing me,
his tongue lapping against my swollen lips and over the jutting
flesh of my clit. It felt so good; my embarrassment was quickly
replaced by something else: sheer rampant lust. I tried to stay
calm and take my time; I had to resist the urge to gyrate on the
edge of the seat and push myself into his obedient face.

After a moment I became aware of Tom's presence again and
looked up, gasping for breath. He had stripped off his shirt, his
leanly muscled chest bared for my eager eyes. I purred; he blew
me a kiss, and then grinned.

"Stop now." At the sound of the order Richard's head lifted,
cocking to one side again. "I've found some of your other toys
and I intend to use them. Do you understand?" Richard
nodded. My fingers clutched at my clit, replacing the tongue,
keeping myself on the edge while I tried to see what Tom was
holding in his hands.

He pocketed a shiny blue condom packet, and gestured at
Richard with a stiff leather cock harness. Tom looked dangerous now. He always had a certain edginess about him during
sex, but I'd never seen him quite this intense before.

"You really are a deviant one, aren't you?" He gave a deep
chuckle. Richard hung his head in shame. "Oh, but there's no
need to be so embarrassed, we can both see you've got a stiffy,
Richard." With that he crouched down on the floor and
grabbed at Richard's belt. He opened the buckle, the button

and zipper in the blink of eye and, yes, Richard did have a stiffy – a major stiffy.

"You are a bad boy, and did you get hard when you had a taste of Suzie?" Richard nodded. "Right, I'm going to have to take care of this. No one said you were allowed to get a hard-on did they?" He pulled Richard forward so he was kneeling straight up, his pants falling down around his knees. He wasn't wearing underwear and my eyes roved over him in appreciation. Tom pushed Richard's head to one side and bent down, his hand measuring the other man's cock in a hard vigorous fist. God, what a sight! I shot two fingers inside my slit, probing myself while I watched Tom handle Richard's cock.

With some effort, he pushed the cock harness over Richard's erection and secured it with the stud fastener around his balls. He was almost entirely covered. I could just see his balls squeezed up inside the circles of leather, and the very head of his cock pushing out of its containment. The harness was extremely tight and I could see the effect it was having on Richard, his whole body growing more rigid by the second, as if he was being gripped in a hard heavy hand, his blood-filled cock bursting for release.

"Get back to work on Suzie, right now." Tom pushed him back between my thighs. By then I was on the very edge of the chair, my legs spread wide to get more of him. Tom walked behind him and pulled the condom out of his pocket, turning it over in his hands. He looked at me; his green eyes glittered like gemstones. His eyebrows lifted imperceptibly and his mouth was fixed in a devilish smile. He wanted my approval. I whimpered, my head barely nodding, but I really wanted to see him doing it. Tom opened his fly and got out his rock-hard cock. He pumped it in his hands for a moment, his eyes on mine. This was one of my favorite sights; I couldn't get enough of seeing him with his hands on his cock, and he knew it. He looked down at my chest, growling. I followed his gaze and saw that my nut-hard nipples were jutting up from the edges of my bra, my breasts oozing out of the restraining fabric.

Tom eased the condom on and then knelt down behind

Richard. When Richard felt his legs being pushed apart his mouth stopped moving and clamped over my sex. His body was rigid between us, his buttocks on display to Tom, his face pushing in against my sex, his muscled arms bound tightly behind his back. If I rolled my head to one side I could see his harnessed cock.

He remained quite still, his tongue in my hole, when Tom began to probe him from behind. Tom's face contorted and I felt Richard's head thrust in against me as he was entered from behind. My hips were moving fast on the chair, moving my desperate sex flesh up and down against the leather mask, his mouth and the rough edges of the zipper. I couldn't help it, I was gone on this.

Richard's cock looked fit to burst. Tom pulled out and ploughed in deeper, his teeth bared with effort and restraint. He must have hit the spot, because Richard's body tensed and arched, his tongue going soft and limp against my clit. I glanced down and saw his cock riding high and tight in its harness, then it spurted up under his arched body, which was convulsing.

"You made him come," I cried accusingly, but with delight, and a dark laugh choked in my throat. Tom grinned at me and then jammed into him hard again.

"Suck her good, Richard; I want Suzie to come next."

Our obedient slave began to tongue me again. I gasped my pleasure aloud for Tom – Tom, my gorgeous lover, watching me. It was just like our sessions of mutual masturbation, but with Richard's darkest secret filling the void between us; to-night he was the gap across which we watched each other's deepest pleasures rising up and taking us over.

Tom's lean body was taut, his hands gripping on to Richard's hips, the sinuous muscles in his arms turning to rope. His eyes were locked on mine, urging me on as he sent Richard's tongue lashing my clit again and again with each deep thrust. I began to buck, wildly out of control, shock waves going right through the core of my body and under the skin of my scalp as wave after wave of relief flooded over me, and then Tom threw back his head, roaring his release as his hips jerked repeatedly and he shot his load.

Tom sat across the breakfast bar from me. He sipped the rich black Colombian coffee I had made us, his fingertips running against mine as he eyed me over his cup. He smiled as he put the cup down and lifted my fingers to his lips.

"You looked incredible," he whispered, kissing my finger-tips. It was an extremely intimate moment; he was looking at me with possessiveness and something akin to awe.

"So did you," I replied and I meant it; I was overwhelmed by my lover. Richard had long since left us, but the images he had given us of each other would be with us for a very long time.

"Do you think we'll ever see him again?"

"Maybe," he replied. "Maybe not. Would it bother you if we did?"

I gave it some thought. I pictured us casually speaking to him in the office, the way we used to, but this time the three of us would be looking at each other and knowing what had gone on. The idea of it made my pulse quicken again.

"No, not in the least." I liked the idea. I smiled at Tom. Not only had we seen each other anew, but Tom and I had become part of Richard's secret, part of Richard's darkest secret.

Mileage

Tom Piccirilli

I. Me And Pepito

My agent Monty Stobbs wanted me to make a pitch to one of
the new twenty-something mega-producers in Hollywood. I'd
moved out to LA expressly for the purpose of meeting the
mover and shaker industry kids, even if they did have razor-
wire moussed hair, wore steel toed boots, and rode Harleys to
lunch meetings. It seemed unduly aggressive to me but I made
the effort to get over it.

The only trouble now was that this particular kid was back in
Manhattan, staying at a five-star hotel about thirty-four blocks
from my old apartment.

"He's there setting up an urban drama for next season,"
Monty told me. "One of them witty Mafia shows, with the
goofy hitman who cracks wise while he's digging graves behind
Kennedy Airport. The teenage son of the mayor falls in love
with a goombah's daughter. The mayor's trying to put her
father in jail, the big boss puts a contract out on hizzoner.
There's even dancing. The teens do this big number outside
Lincoln Center."

"Are their names Tony and Maria?" I asked.

Monty didn't get it. He frowned at me without catching the
drift and said, "I thought you didn't read the trades."

"Christ."

"Anyway, in a week he flies off to Sicily to set up some of the
Italian location shoots. You've got to catch him before then. But

I can't afford a plane ticket right now. I don't see any turn-around until the Zypho units hit the video store next month. I'm tapped but I can front you bus fare. Otherwise, it comes out of your pocket."

"Monty, it was about this time last year that you were promising me a penthouse apartment on Sunset and my own private masseuse by Christmas."

"I can rub some Passionate Midnight grape-flavored lotion into your shoulders if you want. I think I have a quarter bottle left on my night stand from when that dancer Betty the Ta-Ta Queen was here last month."

Just thinking about Betty brought a deranged expression to his face.

He saw the look in my eyes and decided not to pursue that course of the conversation.

"Consider it a tour of America," Monty said. "You'll be like Steinbeck. James Agee. Kerouac. All them road guys. You relax and look at the countryside. It'll inspire you. You'll have half the great American novel by the time you pull into Port Authority."

I didn't have quite have the energy to tell Monty that we were in the age of eight-lane interstates and telescopic, high-powered road rage. I didn't really have the energy to tell Monty anything lately.

"Okay, get me the ticket."

He already had it and pulled it out of his jacket pocket. "I'll drop you off at the station. Your bus leaves at midnight."

"Jesus!"

So. Now I was on a bus with sixty other people and slowly losing my sense of reality. It was like a party where everybody hung back against the wall, didn't make a sound, and generally feared one another.

This was a four-day ride and my laptop had committed hara-kiri rather than face another minute of *Zypho II: Zyphomania – The Return of the Critter from Beyond the Edge of Space*. I got the feeling that Monty wanted a long title on the video box to cover up the picture of Zypho's less than stellar f/x. Hopefully it would edge my name off the credits as well.

I had started out writing in longhand on yellow legal pads hoping to put the time to good use, but reading my own scratchy handwriting gave me motion sickness. By the twentieth hour on the road I was trying to keep myself amused by taunting folks in the next lane to sideswipe us into a guard rail.

It was about two in the morning and I still couldn't get comfortable enough in my seat to sleep yet. I had no co-passenger beside me, but the extra space still wasn't enough for me to completely lie down. I had visions of arriving in New York after four days of insomnia and passing out in the middle of Times Square, waking up with no money, no shoes, and only one kidney.

The moonlight lent a blue haze to the darkness, and the bus' running lights were just enough to allow me to spot her one seat up on the opposite side of the aisle.

She appeared to be a part of the night, swirling, alive, as she turned to look back at me. It wasn't until I fully concentrated, focusing all my attention on her, that I saw she was a Latina woman about my age, smiling in my direction but not exactly to me.

Everyone else was asleep. She gave me the slow once-over, the kind of prying gaze that was frosty and lifeless but held a promise of distant heat. I tried to give it back to her but she ignored me. I'd never been good at this sort of game.

She got up and silently slid into the seat beside me. I generally didn't like these kinds of wordless situations. I enjoyed words, and I hardly ever shut up. When she pressed herself to me and rubbed the meaty palm of her hand against my crotch, I began to suspect I should just shut the fuck up.

It was usually a good call.

Sometimes you had to go with the undertow. You fought your need to rationalize and argue and worry about what the real meaning was behind every act. Especially if you were going insane from boredom.

Her ragged breath blew hot against my ear. I moaned and reached for her and felt that slick electrical itch tingling in my fingers.

"No," she said, "don't touch me."

"Uhm . . . but . . ."

"I don't like to be touched." She began to purr again, leaning into me, pressing herself into my arms while I held them out to my sides, struggling not to embrace her.

She kneeled and I crouched lower, trying to hide behind the high backs of our seats. It wasn't really working, I had nowhere to go. She tugged open my jeans and felt me through my briefs, sort of pawing, her nails lightly grazing me. I scanned the blue gloom trying to see if there might be anyone watching us, anybody else alive in the world, but the shadows became deep and edgeless as she worked me free and stroked my cock. The darkness grew heavier, inside and outside of me.

"Oh, look how cute he is . . . your pee-pee . . ." she whispered.

I checked. He didn't look cute to me at all.

"I'm going to name him Pepe . . . no, Pepito . . .!"

"Pepito? Hey—"

Taking my cock roughly in her hand, she brought her mouth to me and swirled her tongue around the head, slowly working down, her hands on my thighs gently patting like she was trying to urge me to her rhythm.

In the dark, I saw the glint of her eyes looking up as she pushed me farther into her mouth, now shaking her head, no no no, and drawing me out, nodding yes yes, so that her top teeth grazed and tugged at my skin.

Sometimes you want to touch somebody so badly that a fire ignites in your nerve endings and burns away your civilized self. I wanted to snarl and leave bite marks.

I heard the passengers stirring, the muffled sound of cloth on cloth as someone in front of us turned over. My hackles rose. Continuing to pump me, she pulled me forward in the seat and pressed me back again, in control but not taking control, as she rubbed me over her face, swung my prick aside, and tongue lashed my nuts. I was so tired that I watched the scene from outside myself.

Just as I started humping against her cheek, she sucked the

length of my cock down her throat. She took me in completely, clenched her lips, stared up at me, and smiled. We all had to find our pride wherever we could.

She slowly pulled herself off until only the head of my cock remained in her mouth. There was too much of a game going on here and not enough actual fun.

I reached for her hair and she growled, "Don't do that. I don't want you to do that."

I made fists and crossed my arms. I leaned back as her head bobbed over Pepito. I was trying to roll with it, to let her take me away from my utter boredom, but somehow even this was only another part of it. I was frowning in the middle of a blow job. No one would ever believe me.

She licked her palm and pumped harder at the base of my cock before taking me back in. I humped her face and lunged at her mouth erratically, and she rested Pepito near her lips and sort of crooned at him. I groaned and pressed the side of my forehead against the cool metal frame of the window. With a bitter whine, I prodded her some more, feeling my orgasm rising.

"That's it," she said. "Come on."

I jerked away and hit the frame again. There was more rustling of passengers. I bit back another moan as she sucked me wildly, her hair alive in my lap. I wanted to take handfuls of her hair and knot my grip in it and hold her in place while I cut loose. The darkness thrummed with the presence of others. I came and nearly howled in relief as she hungrily swallowed, gurgling softly, gulping as drops leaked over her parted lips.

I wondered if she considered my come on her face as me touching her. I did, or thought I did, as I wafted into sleep.

It passed without dreams. I'd only snoozed for three hours but when I awoke we'd made another stop and most of the passengers seemed to have changed again. I couldn't be sure of anything much except that she was gone and I was being willfully ignored by everybody else.

It took me a minute to realize that Pepito was still pretty

much out there and waving to folks. I'd dozed off before zipping myself back up. I didn't know if anybody had seen or cared, but since I wasn't already in handcuffs I figured nobody had spotted me or had minded if they did.

Actually, he was sort of cute, I noticed, as I slipped him back home. And he remained my one and true friend in a world of quandary, and was always along for the ride no matter how many miles we covered or where the bizarre journey took us.

II. Gnaw The Glass

I'd been on the bus for nearly three days and we'd pulled into more dustchoked towns and cities of smoke and steel than I'd imagined existed between the coasts. I was so tired, constipated, and restless most of the time that I just sat there in an opened-eye coma, fantasizing that I was trapped in hell. For my sins, St Peter had stuck me on a bus for all eternity. Whenever we stopped I gave a wide berth to the driver and tried hard not to call him "Pete". I imagined him with the Book of Judgment in his hands.

If there was anyone from LA still on the bus with me, I didn't know who it might be. Their faces shifted and altered from city to city. Their sighs and snores were the same, the tinny songs in their headsets and the covers of their paperbacks interchangeable. I considered setting my hair on fire just to see if anybody would notice. I was so bored that it was the only time in my life when I thought I might actually be able to stomach watching a mime. I might even join in. Walk against the wind. Pull the rope. Any damn thing.

I kept looking around, hoping to make eye contact with somebody, start up a conversation, but everyone was content in their seats, letting the miles flow over them, one after the other. I began feeling as if my skeleton was trying to make a beeline out of my body – every muscle commenced to ache, and my temples pounded with blood. I really didn't want my obituary to read that I'd died of monotony aboard a New

York-bound bus. Monty would use my death as a springboard to fame and sell my scripts for millions. He'd retire to Beverly Hills and I'd only be remembered for the softcore alien brain juice-sucking scene from *Zypho II: Zyphomania.*

The twilight slowly withered to black and the smell of pine erupted. I had absolutely no idea where I was. I wondered if Steinbeck, Agee, or Kerouac had ever felt such an overwhelming loathing for cars, towns, and people in denim. The only road I wanted to write about was West 4th Street in the Village. I had the sense that once I hit Manhattan I'd never leave again.

I didn't think I was lucky enough to have another woman peel herself from a section of night and come give me head. I wasn't horny but the only survival instinct I had left was the will to procreate. I felt very much the way I imagined a fruit fly might feel during it's twenty-four hour life span. Do the deed and call it a day.

I scanned the sleeping passengers and spotted a blur of movement a few seats ahead.

All I could see of her in the dark was the nimbus of her blonde hair, softly glowing, and the indistinct smear of motion circling before her. I stared and studied her for five minutes before I picked up on the fact that she was masturbating in the shadows.

It got to me, but damn near anything would've.

I stood and glided up the aisle to stand over her.

You could get in trouble for doing a thing like this, but the tedium had given me an ounce of assertion. I lightly fondled her hair, then the side of her face, and stroked her neck for a moment. I held my hand out and when she took it, with her wet fingers, I draw her from her seat and ushered her back to my own.

Okay, so now we were getting someplace. At least she let me touch her.

She slid past me and actually said, "Excuse me" as she passed, loosening her skirt as she took the inside spot. She slipped out of her panties and leaned against the window, reached back and clutched at my shirt, pulling me to her.

I wanted to know her name but didn't want to ask. Maybe St
Pete had stuck me in an eternal rolling orgy without intimate
conversation.

She kneeled on the seat, opened her legs slightly and wriggled
her ass in the dim light. Moonlight swam down and banked
across her face, showing me the silver-lit silhouette.

I ground against her thigh, pressing myself tightly to her. I
leaned forward and she turned and whispered into my ear, "My
ass."

"Yeah?"

"Butt-fuck me."

All right, so maybe that could be considered intimate conversation. Maybe not. Sweat bloomed across my forehead and
that fetid three-day old stink of my body assailed me.

I eased my index finger into her ass and crouched so that I
could lick her from behind. She was wet and streaming, and I
used my tongue to scoop her own juices up to her anus.

You could get funky when you had to. I slipped my finger in
and worked her ass, listening to her quietly sigh, breathing soft
as the sleeping passengers, the silver leaking down her back, her
legs, the lovely blunt curve of her buttock. I rose and angled
myself behind her, placed the head of my cock against her anus
and pushed.

The air surged out of her and she made no other sound. I slid
into her tightness and looked past her out the window at all the
strange miles that lay behind and still lay ahead. The bus hit a
bump in the road and jostled us together even more firmly,
painfully, binding, as we grunted in unison.

I prodded forward into her completely, then slowly pulled
out, reveling in the sense that I was making, then breaking, then
remaking the circuit between us. I became transparent and kind
of floated out of my shoes. I thought that this is how schizo-
phrenics must feel all the time, unanchored from the world, lost
in their own misfiring neurons and too tired to care. She bucked
roughly against me, spiking herself on my cock as she picked up
the pace.

"That's it," she said. "Harder! Harder!"

"Jesus, be quiet. . . .!" I hissed.

I pressed her into the window even more roughly and she climaxed and let out a titter. It took a second to realize she wasn't really getting off on what I was doing – it was the glass window.

She was kissing it, licking, even biting at it. Staring into it with love and wanting. She did not care much for me or Pepito at all.

It stopped me, watching her like that. I'd gotten the vapid look in the middle of sex before – the disappointed frown, the girl calling out somebody else's name – but I'd never been thrown over for a pane of glass before.

This was the kind of thing that could shoot your self-worth to hell.

I tried to bull my way through, but I was hard pressed, slamming my cock into her from behind while the faint ghostly image of her reflection stared back at me. It was new to me, fucking a glass-licker. I suppose there'd been precedent, there always was precedent, but I'd never heard about it before.

She jammed herself backwards and I shoved into her. She moaned and ground her ass against me, thumping, even as she spread herself wider over the glass. It's amazing what can happen to you, how your guts can be plucked and knotted, but there I was butt-fucking her and growing jealous of the goddamn window.

As I thrust she reached down and fingered herself, her juice dripping between her thighs and splashing me each time I dug in. I tried to help, but she kept tilting the wrong way, angling as if she might dive headlong out of the bus. I think she climaxed but I couldn't be certain. We lived in a puzzling age. My nuts tightened and I felt no need to slow myself down and let the act linger. I'd lost her before we'd even begun, and the glass was covered with dried smears of her spit, the outline of her lips.

She murmured to the window and told it how much she loved it, shoved herself back onto me and held herself there, letting me hammer away until I came. I didn't even need to bite down on her shoulder to stifle my grunts. I had no sound to make.

She told the window, "That was wonderful. Oh God, I needed that. You were terrific."

I tried not to sigh. She dropped her skirt and passed me again saying, "Excuse me," and returned to her seat. I was a mess and didn't much care. I zipped up, sat back down, looked out on the American night and made an attempt to curb my paranoia. The glass looked on.

As soon as I caught my breath I'd head to the lavatory and get some wet tissues and wipe clean the signs of an affair I had only a minor part in. I wondered what the Book of Judgment would have penciled in about this particular incident. Pete would not be happy. My reflection stared at me until the face of the moon grew obscured with clouds and I was thankfully left in darkness.

But the glass kept looking down at me – arrogant, vain, and somehow sated.

III. Authority

We pulled into the Port Authority bus terminal on West 42nd Street in Manhattan, about nine a.m., and while I was scrounging up my belongings the driver came back and grabbed me by the collar.

"That's unsanitary, what you been doin' right there, buddy!"

I realized then that, of course, he'd known all along what had happened, or thought had happened. "Look, Pete, nothing like this has—"

"My name ain't Pete!"

"I'm sorry, really, but—"

"Why don't you and that damn Pepito of yours get the hell off my bus before I call the cops!"

"But Pete!"

"I told you, my name ain't Pete!"

I took my satchel, my wavering self-esteem, and my damn Pepito and dragged myself into the terminal feeling like I had detached from humanity and might not ever get back into it.

I was so heavy with fatigue I could barely move as I lumbered among the crowd. I threw myself down in a seat and listened to the roaring bus engines outside, the thrum of the people, and tried to breathe in all the open space. Normally I'd be tracking folks all over the place, my head buzzing with dialogue and camera directions. But now I could barely remember my own name. I got up and pulled my luggage along after me like an angry child, and headed to the men's room.

It had been a hell of a trip so far, but that doomed feeling you get when serious grief is waiting around the corner hadn't left me yet. I'd had it since I was about fifteen but that didn't change matters much.

I used the urinal and spent ten minutes at the sink washing up, staring in the mirror, trying to remember what I was doing on this side of the country again. Hollywood had somehow faded off my back after five days. I felt stripped of most of the things that had kept me going day to day: ambition, desperation, fear. I was aching and exhausted but felt somehow cleansed. I was having a Zen moment of tranquility.

I saw her in the mirror and thought, okay, so this is the capper. I'd been waiting, and afterwards, I could get back on the right rail.

She came up out of the stall like the ghost of all my sins given form, and she swept behind me in one fluid motion as if she'd been meant for this and only for this. I didn't turn but stared at her reflection, trying to make eye contact. She barely acknowledged me although now she was brushing against my back. I'd described women like her in my scripts before as innocent, virginal, snow white, and the girl next door. Her bobbed blonde hair smelled of daisies. I'd never smelled a daisy before, but there it was. She was a homespun beauty that made you think of every Norman Rockwell painting, fireside family moment, Christmas morning, and endearing image that didn't actually exist in the world and probably never had.

"Spank me," she said.

I blinked a few times. I tried not to go, "uyh," but I did it anyway. I kept wondering if I was ever going to visit the good ole missionary position again with somebody I cared about.

I turned around and reached out to touch her hair. I suddenly had an overwhelming need to draw my fingers through a lovely woman's hair, to make a little contact. She dodged me without hardly even moving, as if she'd been trained for it.

"Look, lady, I'm not really feeling frisky at the moment."

Her face fell in on itself and her mouth opened and her eyes spun with pain and rejection. It took some effort for me to quell my curiosity and not suddenly rip into asking her a hundred questions on why a gold-laced girl would spend her time hiding in the Port Authority Men's Room for someone to redden her ass.

"I want you to spank me!"

"No," I told her and started to walk out.

She slid in front of me, blocked my way, tore open her shirt and pressed her tits into my face. "Bite them."

"They're very nice."

"Come on. Bite them! Chew my nipples!"

"No."

"Do it! I need to feel you."

And yet she'd eluded my touch. I'd forgotten how pushy New Yorkers could be, though I had to admit nobody'd ever quite bossed me around like this. It was a situation that locker room chest-beatings were made of. The kind of porn letters I'd send in to the low-end men's magazines for twenty-five bucks a pop.

But I'd never had to live through it before. The reality of ludicrous circumstances, plus my fatigue, was starting to make me feel drunk and dangerous. The trouble with Zen moments is they vanish the moment you remember who you are.

"I'm going to kiss you," I told her.

"What?" She drew back, her frown etched in fear.

"You heard me. I'm going to make out with you. We're going to neck."

"No, that's not what I want."

"Yes, I'm taking you on a date. To the movies. And we're going to sit in the back row and feed each other popcorn!"

"No!"

There was a sudden mad rush of energy and anger that knotted between my shoulders. "I'm going to kiss you and tell you how much I love you!"

"Oh God! No!"

"Bow down before Pepito, baby!"

"You're fuckin' nuts!"

"Tremble before my damn Pepito!"

"Help!"

Of course I was out of my head, but I didn't feel bad about it anymore. Sometimes your confusion made more sense than all the logic you'd build up for yourself. I leaned in to kiss her with visions of a house in the suburbs and three flaxen-haired children writhing through my heated mind. My lips brushed hers and she hauled back her fist and clobbered me.

"Get away, you freak!"

She ran out of the men's john and I stood there with my back against the stall, tasting blood against my teeth. It was just the way of things. I didn't feel relaxed or inspired. I didn't have half the great American novel written. I checked my watch. I had just enough time to get where I was going. I made it out onto 42nd street and headed for the five-star hotel.

It took me twenty minutes. The desk gave me the room and I walked in on the new twenty-something mega-producer in Hollywood, with his razor-wire moussed hair, the steel-toed boots, and a handsome sneer that was supposed to make men respect him and women flush with giddiness.

We stared at each other for a minute. He started telling me all about the Mafia show and somewhere after the fourth time he said "goombah" I stopped listening.

I said, "Can I borrow your phone?"

Maybe he was struck by my audacity. He gave a self-serving grin and said, "Sure."

I called Monty and said, "Monty, I'm not coming back. I'm out of this game."

"But . . . but – wait! What about the movie?"

"Zypho and his love tentacles are going into retirement. See you around."

"You can't! Wait, let's talk . . .!"

I clicked off, handed the kid his phone back, and decided to sit in Central Park for the rest of the afternoon. I had nowhere to go, but I didn't mind. I was back in control.

Prix Fixe

Riain Grey

Appetizer

Homemade hummus served with julienned red peppers, imported olives, and creamy feta-tahini dip.

Cocktail

Our house special – the Frozatini – made with Absolut Citron, triple sec, cranberry juice, and fresh lime juice frozen and blended to perfection. Served in a tall glass with a twist.

Entrée

Today's special: freshly prepared chicken soup with penne, vegetables, and Provençal spices.

Dessert

Banana ice cream with a swirl of dark chocolate fudge, served with chocolate sauce and fresh whipped cream.

Appetizer

Slicing a red pepper has always been erotic for me. When I make the first cut, exposing the pepper's flesh to the air and revealing the bulky bundle of seeds inside, I tingle a little.

Then, pulling its progeny from itself and slicing away the white meaty under-flesh. Seeing the clean edges where the knife has driven, leaving behind only sweet crispness.

I arrange the sliced peppers and olives carefully on the plate. With each incision, each cut, I think of your face, the concentration in your eyes as you bend over me, the sharp curve of your mouth when you smile.

I am already hungry.

Cocktail

With my fluttering 50s apron and slutty pink heels, I feel like Wally Cleaver's wet dream. As you directed me to, I tie my hair up high with pink ribbons and attach my fetter chains to my ankles. Beneath the apron I am bare, my nipples hard against the chiffon and against my hand as I brush my fingers over them, making them fat and juicy for my Master.

In the kitchen, everything is prepared so that I can serve you perfectly. I slice the limes and put the ingredients in the blender. As I mix our drinks, I feel the butterflies winging through me, knowing that soon I will be caught with my ass exposed and filled, my nipples hard, my cunt wet and hot. A drop of come escapes from me and I kneel hurriedly to clean it up, my face flushed with shame. I have twenty minutes before you'll be home. My chains tinkle and sway as I make my way to the bathroom to complete my final task.

The black dildo is already waiting for me. I kneel on the tiles, my pussy wet, my body willing despite the fear churning through me. Bent over, I stroke my asshole, readying it. With a nervous thrill, I remember the sound of your voice this morning as you whispered your instructions, your fingers prying my cunt open, your eyes flashing and dark.

I whimper as I work the dildo slowly into my ass, the cool tiles soothing my hot face. I have never felt like such a slut, my legs spread and my ass high in the air. There is no one to see, but I know that you are watching me in your mind's eye, seeing me bite my lip as I struggle, pushing the thick cock deeper inside. The heat of shame brings longing between my legs, my cunt swollen and hungry, and I almost touch myself before I remember that I am not allowed; that I feel pleasure only at the will of my Master. I want it so much that I am almost in tears as I force the huge cock in, my body stretching to take this piece of you that you have left for me.

Swaying as I stand, I feel a breeze whisper across my cunt and almost come right there. I clutch the sink to steady myself, willing my knees not to buckle. When I move, I feel the thick cock inside, and I imagine you shoving it deeper, pushing me down into my slave cushion.

When you open the door I am kneeling with your drink between my chained hands. My fingers and toes are tingling, my ass full and hot. Without even glancing at me you take the drink and unzip your pants. Put your cock in my mouth. I suckle, greedy to taste your velvet on my tongue. You sigh a little and I suck harder, licking and nipping, already so excited that my face contorts and my body arches up towards yours.

You pull away and I can feel you watching me, regarding me with the cool detachment that covers you when you Master me. Your voice is gentle steel. "You have a giant, black dildo stuffed in your ass," you say slowly, with precision. "Why is that, little cunt?"

Hot pain splashes across my face. I can feel the finger marks where you've slapped me for not responding soon enough.

"I asked you a question, cunt. Why do you have a black dildo in your ass?"

My cunt floods, my face reddens, but this time I respond tentatively.

"Because it pleases Master?"

"Wrong," you say calmly. "Slave has a dildo up her ass because slave likes to be degraded and humiliated. Because slave needs to be used this way."

We both know that you're right, and I moan with the trueness of it, trembling beneath your gaze. You kneel over me and hold the base of the dildo, waiting for my answer.

With the sound of your voice, still steady, I feel myself fall, reaching towards the hot ocean that threatens to drown us both. "Yes, Master," I gasp, and you start pumping the cock into my ass. I twitch and whimper. My tongue lolls out of my mouth as I pant beneath your touch.

"Such a good girl," you purr, "my sweet slave, come for me, little slave, with your Master's cock in you," and that's all it takes. I'm grunting and pushing my ass against your hand, my come spraying onto the cushion and dripping down my legs, and I'm begging – "Take me apart, Master, fuck me" – the words twisting out of me as I come. It's another kind of coming, the filth that I speak, as cathartic and healing as the pain that you so carefully inflict.

When I finally rest beneath you, you reinsert the dildo. You stroke my hair and face. "Now drink your cocktail, little one, while I get you your dinner." Your smile is so bright and true that I find myself brushing away tears as I settle onto my pillow to wait.

Entrée

My slave is so beautiful, kneeling in front of me, but I try not to let her know it. I just take the drink and give her my cock to suck, her face wild, her hands fluttering to stroke my thighs and balls. I let her suck for awhile, knowing the pleasure it brings her, before moving my attention to the fat dildo she has in her ass, the base peeking out shyly.

She jumps a little when I address her, lost as she is in the moment. I can tell how uncomfortable she is, and yet how excited, how proud she is to be owned this way and to do as I bid her. I pitch my voice as softly as I can while I torment her with hard truths about herself, watching her wriggle and writhe in dismay. Funny that this foreign thing, this plastic device, could have such power, and yet we are both swept away by it.

I grab the dildo, forcing it into her again and again as she cries out beneath me. Her ass is hungry and offers no resistance; as I fuck her I listen to her mews of delight and feel almost dizzy with my own lust. I want to put my cock there, instead, and spurt my come into my slave, my darling girl, my most precious possession.

When she starts to come, when her whispers become grunts, I am ready. She doesn't see the bowl I slip under her, so that her boy-come squirts into it hot and slick. She bucks and squirms, her face glorious and her mouth making words she hardly knows she speaks, begging to be fucked and filled, taken and torn. The words twist in her mouth, fierce and enraged with her need. She gives a final gasp and I whisk the bowl out of her sight.

Once she is still and calm, I fill her back up with the black cock, so that she will remember what she is, and I touch her cheek, so that she will remember whom she belongs to. Before I go to get her dinner, I rub her own come into her hair, delighting at the feel of it in her curls.

When I bring the dog bowl out, her eyes widen, but she knows not to speak. She casts her eyes down at the floor. I move slowly, aware that she is dying to know what is in the bowl, what she will eat at my command. I sense her relief when she smells it.

"Now, slave, I know that my bitch in heat likes meat, so I went out and got the best, yummiest dinner that I could for my beloved puppy."

As soon as she relaxes, I bring the other bowl out from behind my back.

"But if you don't eat it all, you'll have this instead."

I know she remembers the taste of her own come and doesn't like the overwhelming tang of it.

"Maybe I should mix it in for you," I mock, "let you taste your own filth."

She shakes her head violently, eyes closed tight, but obediently opens her mouth for me.

I set the bowl in front of her and wait for her to notice that there is no spoon. She looks up at me for instruction. The trust in her electric eyes feeds me.

"Yes," I say, "that's a good girl. Go ahead and eat, sweetest bitch," and she bends over the dish, her small pink tongue darting out to lap at the soup.

"Do you like your dinner, pet?" She nods so sweetly that I almost lose control and take her into my arms.

She slurps at her food the way I like her to, puppy-dog noises deep in her throat, and I can see the freedom shining on her face as she transforms into my favorite animal. With her tongue out and eyes closed she looks like she does when she comes, messy and wild. I move around to finger her and her sopping cunt betrays her need.

As I fuck her with my hand I feel her concentration waver, so I shove her face back into her bowl – "Keep eating, little bitch, and maybe Master will let puppy come." A shudder works its way through her body as she crouches over her bowl. She is wet and smooth, warm on my fingers, and she begins to thrust backwards as she laps, moans escaping her mouth as she eats. It doesn't take long for my little puppy to writhe and twist under me, making a mess on the floor, her juices spilling out hot and salty.

"I think puppy's all done," I tell her. Even as she quivers I can feel her acceptance, her innate awareness of what will come next. "Come over here and clean up this mess you made."

She clatters around quickly, her chains swinging against the floor.

"Go ahead, little bitch," I say, "lick it all up."

My puppy does a good job, gets every drop, and my cock throbs, the ache to be fucking her and holding her and kissing her, deep in my chest. The dildo is still in her ass and I give it a little shove to keep her balanced on the edge of arousal. I feel her sharp intake of breath – she already needs to come again.

It is this that I so cherish, these dark places where we are united in our trust and fear. I always guide our steps so that neither of us will go too far or fear that we will fall. She knows that I will always be there to catch her gently and bring her safely home.

Crouching on her pillow she is so calm and radiant that I almost forget to breathe.

"I was going to feed you the rest, my darling slave, but we need to do something else, instead. Are you ready?"

With her nod, I reach for her gratefully, pulling her towards me so that I can kiss her, and it's only moments before I am inside her, my cock pressing against her warm flesh. She shrieks and moans. As I fuck her harder I can feel the other cock buried deep inside. I find it with one hand and pump it lightly into her, drawing my cocks in and out of her, feeling the energy that sparks and flickers between us.

"Come for me, little angel, come for me, slave, come for me, come for me." I repeat it like the mantra we share as I move with her, her body warm and sweet. "Come for me, my bitch, my slut, my little girl, my cunt," – and we growl and gasp, breathing together, wild animals howling in the twilight.

When her come erupts out of her, gushing around my balls, I feel myself let go. I am not her Master any more, just her lover making my own sounds into her mouth as I thrust and moan, tumbling into the ocean that only she brings me.

Dessert

After we have tangled together on the floor, our come spilled and shared, I sit in my chair and my slave kneels happily, chained at my feet. I stroke her hair and she rests her head on my knee with a sigh.

I think about how she will look, snuggled next to me on the floor, her eyes closed tight as she tastes the ice cream, licking the sweet coldness from the spoon. Tilting her head up to me, waiting for the next bite. I know how much she will delight obeying me, how much I will delight in watching her face. I know that alone we will always be hungry, and that together we will always be full.

Zoe Clark

Tara Alton

These are my screwed up thoughts about my sex life and other exaggerations. In college, I watched this guy squeezing his zit on his neck in my computer class. It was repulsive and yet fascinating at the same time. I could not look away. He wasn't a bad looking guy either, almost fuckable, except for the craters. The eruption was like a grand finale to his finger ballet, and I almost applauded. As I watched him wipe off the discharge on his jeans, I realized I hadn't even heard what the teacher had said for the last ten minutes, which was a bad thing because she had just given us our instructions for our final exam.

Two years later, I came across this same guy in a redneck bar, which overlooked the lake. It was a rough sort of place, and I was there by myself, nursing a long neck beer. I was thankful I wasn't at home with my mom and adolescent brother, eating Hamburger Helper and listening to her wax poetic about how wonderful the intern girls were in her office. When she did this, she reminded me of a husband who didn't have a clue that his poor wife might not want to hear about the strippers and waitresses he recently flirted with. It made you wonder if they were so great what were you? Chopped liver?

I'm not sure if this guy remembered me from college or not, but we danced together all night. It felt good to have his arms draped around my neck. After last call, I blew him in the parking lot, mostly because I was lonely and horny, and I liked the way he had been grinding his hard on against me during the slow songs. Just as he started to come, I thought about that white discharge squirting from his zit in class two years ago. Amazingly, I didn't get sick.

The next morning, with my jaw a little sore because he took so long, I went to work. Much like my mother, I was a business drone, but at least I didn't work at the Secretary of State like her. I worked at a huge corporation in a high-rise building. The field of business wouldn't have been my first choice either, but I wasn't sure what I wanted to do with my life. My mom said if I got an associates degree in Business Administration and if I got a job in an office, I could still live at home, even though I'm twenty-two. So keeping this in mind, I chose a position as an office underling, guiding sheets of paper through the corridors of what I like to think is purgatory.

After getting my morning cup of java, I visited the ladies' rest room. For days now, there has been a red button scotch taped to one of the stalls. Someone must have found it on the floor and thought this was a good way to return it to its owner. The button has been fascinating me to no end. The owner must have seen it by now. There are only two stalls in the ladies' room for Pete's sake, and I've never seen a man wear a red sweater to work, not even at Christmas.

Unable to take it any longer, I finally pushed the button to see if something would happen, sort of like in a panic button type of way. Nothing happened. How anticlimactic, I thought. Disappointed, I flushed the toilet and washed my hands, thinking the episode was over, but I still couldn't get the button out of my mind! It had to be there for a reason. That was when I decided it was a sign from above that I should do something important, and it had to do with something the color red.

The only thing that had stood out recently in the red department was the socks on whom I like to call ABM, Alan Brandon Michaels and/or Aloof Business Man. He was an executive in upper management. I spotted his red wool ankles under a table in a conference room when I was breezing by the doorway. It's not that red socks were a big deal, but for someone who was so impeccably dressed in expensive suits everyday, his shirts superbly ironed, it was.

When I first met him, I thought he was charming and attractive like everyone else. He was in his thirties, and he was tall and broad shouldered with raven hair and a sly smile. Then I realized his moods could be like night or day. You never had a clue what you were going to get. I'd watched him many a time reduce a female coworker to tears in a manner of seconds.

I always wondered what his deal was. I mean, where did he get off? To me, he had everything: a high power job, a Lexus, an apartment in Birmingham, a different beautiful woman clinging to his arm at every after-work function. He had nothing to be an asshole about.

After Easter, I must have caught him on one of his good days because we actually had an interaction. I had been carefully ageing three yellow marshmallow Peeps on my desk for the last two weeks. I'd even named them. I was coming back from the copy room and I saw him steal one.

Furious, I confronted him in his office.

"You stole one of my Peeps," I said.

Like a little kid, he quickly swallowed and looked innocently at me. "I did?"

"Yes. You did. I saw you."

"Do you have any proof?" he asked.

If I'd known him better, I would have walked over to him, pinched open his mouth and looked for tell tale signs of marshmallow between his teeth, but I didn't.

"I would just like to say that Frank didn't appreciate being Peep napped," I said. "He was looking forward to his timely demise in my mouth."

"Who is Frank?" he asked, looking confused.

"The Peep you just murdered."

Mortified by his lack of concern, I turned away and went back to my desk.

The next morning, I found my remaining peeps, Penelope and Oscar, having sex on my desk and a pieces of a cut up pink one behind them. ABM came strolling over to my desk the moment he saw me. Mischief twinkled in his eyes.

"What is this?" I asked.

"They had babies," he said.

From behind him, he pulled out an opened package of pink Peeps with one missing. He gave me his sly smile and handed it to me. How could I stay mad at him? I handed him Oscar. I took Penelope and we ate them. We split the babies between us.

"That was the best sex I've had in months," he said, brushing off his hands.

That was when I realized what his problem was.

Therefore, because of the red button and his comment, I passed him a note that read "YNBPF", which stood for "You've never been properly fucked."

Later when I went to the bathroom, I found the red button was gone. I realized that I should have kept it. I could have started a "signs that changed my life" box or a "new romance with ABM" box. I've always been one for collecting things in boxes, even when I was little. I liked imposing organization on my part of the universe. When I was ten, I used to collect rocks. Mostly they were from the playground at school, but I also used to look for them in yards, gardens and parking lots. I loved stuffing pink quartzite and light gray limestone in my pockets and feeling the weight of them. At home, I stored them under my bed in a shoebox.

At twelve years old, I collected bees in cola bottles. This was more of a semi permanent collection. I'd run around the back yard, trapping the poor bees on dandelions and I'd wait to see if they could fly out of the bottles.

At twenty-two years old, I was collecting interesting autumn leaves from our acre-long back yard that bordered on a woods flaring with red and yellow colors. I thought the leaves were pretty, and they should be preserved like little skeletons of times gone by.

Once again, I was using a shoebox, the only difference being this wasn't a Buster Brown shoebox. This was a shoebox from my "come and fuck me" 4-inch black patent leather pumps.

Today, I thought I was looking quite the rustic girl in my faded blue jeans and red plaid flannel shirt with my shoulder-length auburn hair tied back as I worked on my collection when

I came across Justin, my neighbor, who was having a smoke behind an oak tree.

Justin was my age, but he had dropped out of college and he went to live with his Dad in California for a while. Now he was back home living with his mom. When we were seven years old, we once had a session of doctor in an abandoned car in a field. During high school, I fooled around with him in my bedroom a couple times in an "I'm bored and you're in the vicinity" type of thing.

For the first time, I noticed the contrast between Justin and ABM. It was striking. Justin was perpetually unkempt. He always wore ancient jeans and an army jacket. His T-shirt logos were always ten years behind the times, mostly pot leaves and heavy metal bands. You could just see the bong collection and black light posters in his room. The only jobs he'd ever kept for more than a week were pizza delivery boy and video rental store clerk.

A few weeks ago, we had a brief grope session at a garage sale. It's not something I was proud of. It happened during a moment of weakness. My motives for being at the garage sale were not pure either. I wasn't there because I was looking for a funky seventies burnt orange colored sofa or the last piece of bone china for my mother's plate collection. I was being nosy because I had never liked these neighbors and I wanted to see what crap they were selling.

Justin showed up almost the same time I did. I hoped he wasn't following me. He appeared to be fascinated by the tools while I checked out the board games. Eventually, he came over by me.

"So why are you back here?" I asked. "Did you fall out with your Dad?"

"Nothing like that," he said. "I was missing shit."

"They don't have shit in California."

He shrugged.

"There is shit anywhere you go," I said.

Justin sighed.

"My dad said I could come back anytime," he said.

I moved away, looking at a table of partially undressed and rejected Barbie dolls. I rather liked the way their limbs were all clacked together.

Justin held up a pair of granny panties.

"Is this your style?" he asked me.

"No."

"So what is?" he asked.

"None of your business," I said.

To get away from him, I ducked behind a clothes rack, but he followed me. Without permission, he grabbed my ass and slid his hands down my jeans, apparently to find out what kind of underwear I was wearing. The only thing I was wearing was a tiny thong. His fingers hit bare skin. The protest I was about to launch died in my throat. His fingers inched along my skin, his breath in my ear.

Part of me wanted to yell at him, "get your freakin hands out of my pants." The other part of me wanted to tell him to move on down to my crack. Suddenly, an old lady yanked open the clothes to get a better look at a blue floral print house-dress.

We scurried out of there like mice.

I hadn't seen him since. Glancing at him now, I wondered how he could look even scruffier.

"You wouldn't be wearing that thong again?" he asked.

"What about it?"

"It was interesting."

"Interesting how?" I asked.

He shrugged.

"Are you wearing it?" he asked.

I nodded.

He stepped in closer. I felt a weird flip flop in my stomach. Like he was unveiling an important painting, he lifted up the corner of my flannel shirt, unzipped my jeans an inch and brushed his fingers along the skin of my hip.

Gooseflesh tickled my skin. Suddenly, this stomach churning desire tormented me. I yanked down my pants the rest of the way and, turning my butt so it faced him, grabbed the tree for support.

Gone was the clumsy teenager who I had to show which hole was which. It felt as if he knew my body as if he had the owner's manual. It astounded me. Whom had he been fucking? That blowjob with zit boy in the parking lot seemed like nothing compared to this.

A few molar-rattling minutes later, it was over. I turned around, zipping up my pants, dizzy with my lingering orgasm, when I caught his expression. He looked all detached, like Joe Cool, as if he'd done me a big favor. Then he lit up and flicked his match.

It fell in my leaf box. Whoosh! It went up in a ball of flame. It never had a chance. I stared in horror at my newly incinerated collection.

"You can fuck me from behind," I cried out, storming back to my house. "But you better not burn my leaves."

Since my leaf collection was gone and the garage sales gave me an idea, I've now decided to collect naked fashion dolls, not exclusively Barbie either. And, as an added bonus, I'm rubber banding them together in sexual positions. As I child, I never did like playing with their hair or constructing elaborate dramas, but now I sort of liked the idea of their naked limbs entwined together in sexual parodies.

When I'm finished, maybe I'll submit my collection to an art gallery, or I'll take photos of them for a coffee table book or I might just give them to my little brother.

After dinner, on my way outside to take out the trash, I found an envelope on my car. I opened it. Justin had made me an artistic rendering of a leaf in charcoal. Basically, he traced a leaf as if a five-year-old might in kindergarten. Then he burnt the edges of the paper with his lighter. How original. At the bottom, he wrote, "I want to fuck you again." I added mommy to the end of the sentence, put it back inside the envelope, addressed it to his mother and left it in their mailbox.

Just in case this came back to bite me in the ass, I found my mother in the den watching TV. I told her I was having problems with Justin.

"Why are you hanging out with that loser?" she asked. "Find

a nice boy. One of my interns met a lovely guy. They had a lovely wedding reception in the basement of the church. They served lemonade and cookies."

"If I want lemonade and cookies, I'll go back to grade school," I said and left the room.

The doll collection wasn't coming along as well as I thought it should, so I decided I needed more fashion dolls. I went garage sailing far away from home and Justin, where I found what I needed. After I paid for them, I started stripping them in the driveway. I didn't need the clothes. Onto the pavement dropped a green spandex disco outfit, a pink tutu and a mermaid skirt. A little girl came up to me and asked me why I was taking off their clothes.

"I don't need them," I said.

"Why?" she asked, her eyes big.

"Because they are naked performance artists," I said.

I gave her the clothes and got out of there before she asked her mother what naked performance artists were.

When I got home, I arranged my dolls in order of what I would to do to ABM if he ever decoded the note. Mostly the dolls were blonds and brunettes. I'd been unsuccessful in finding a red head like me. At first, I thought about combing their tangled, disheveled hair, but then I decided to leave them in their natural state.

The girl dolls far outnumbered the boy dolls, so the boys were just going to have to work that much harder. After I arranged them, it looked very impressive. Very horny stuff indeed.

Once I had my collection arranged, I turned my attention to a cardboard box in the corner of my room. My mother, unbeknownst to me, had been cleaning out the attic. She had brought down a box of my childhood stuffed animals. Extracting them, I realized I must have had sex with them all. So many of them had bald spots. Was I that horny of a kid? No wonder little girls liked unicorns so much. Several of mine were my early dildo collection.

I pulled out a particularly sad looking stuffed tiger. He had lost his tail in a tragic accident, or so I had told my friends. Actually, I had been sticking it up inside me to see how far it would go. Its tail was reinforced with a wire so it was quite stiff. Surprisingly enough, with my youthful zeal, I lost my virginity with it. Then I couldn't get the blood off the tail, so I gave my tiger an operation and buried the tail in the backyard.

Now, I felt so bad about what I'd done to my tiger. Was that how you treated your best friend who listened to all your secrets at night? If only I could put things right, but I didn't know how.

Having had enough nostalgia for the day, I put the stuffed animals back in the box, and I went downstairs to do a load of laundry where I made a life altering decision in front of the washing machine.

I've decided to move out. This was the last time my little pervert of a brother will steal my clothes, whack off on them and leave them in the washing machine. In an effort to curb his activities until I can get my own place, I left him a handful of my old granny panties with a note that said if he touched anything else, I'd break his fingers.

Before I moved out though, I realized I needed to find my tiger tail and restore it to my childhood best friend. Taking a shovel from the back yard, I tried to retrace my devirginized steps from all those years ago, but, finding myself unsuccessful, I just started digging holes in frustration.

Justin showed up. If he didn't watch out, he was going to get a smack in the face with my shovel because of his self-satisfied smirk.

"What on earth are you doing now?" he asked.

"I'm going to cut up the people who annoy me and bury the pieces in the backyard," I said.

"You know, if you weren't pretending to be a bad ass all the time, you might be tolerable to hang around with," he said.

"Screw you."

He paused.

"I have," he said. "Screwed you. And that little note trick did not work with my mom. I already told her you were a psycho."

"I'm not a psycho. You are."

"Who is digging holes in her backyard?" he said.

"I'm looking for something."

"Well, let me know when you find it."

He flicked his cigarette butt at me and left.

"Arson," I called out after him.

Once he was gone, I put down my shovel. I felt like crying. This was intolerable. I did have to move out, but the only way I can afford it is to get a raise. To do that, I must move up in the corporate world. I must transform myself from a slacker to a polished, productive and professional employee.

During the next week at work, to improve my standing with the corporation, I volunteered to be a part of the Diversity Committee, offered to type up the last team meeting notes, and let my supervisor know I was up for any special projects. I even changed the type of clothes I wore. Instead of wearing Polo shirts, Dockers and loafers, I chose A-line skirts, twin sets and mules.

Sitting at my desk, feeling very uncomfortable in my panty hose, I got a phone call. I thought it might be my supervisor congratulating me on my new attitude, but it was a man's voice I didn't recognize.

"Who is this?" I asked.

"This note," he said. "What does it mean?"

My heart fluttered. ABM. I glanced around the room. No one was within earshot.

"Figure it out," I said. "You're the one with the private office and huge salary. You should be able to figure out a simple note."

"This doesn't have to do with the Peeps," he said. "Because I made restitutions."

"This is an entirely different issue," I said.

"Give me a clue."

"It's one of your biggest problems," I said.

He paused. I could hear him drumming his fingers on his desk.

"Why did you give it to me?" he asked.

"A red button told me to," I said and hung up.

Tara Alton

The next day, I was trying to decide on what was the most corporate looking snack in the vending machine, pretzels or chips, when ABM came into in the lunchroom. He was looking very good, I might add.

"I figured out your note," he said. "And you're mistaken."

"What did it say?"

He raised an eyebrow.

"You've never been properly fucked," he said. "But you're wrong."

I looked him up and down.

"Why are you still so aloof and uptight, then?" I asked.

"To keep the underlings in their place," he said.

"Do you consider me an underling?"

He bought a package of miniature jawbreakers.

"Of course," he said. "But a very cute one who likes the same snack foods as me."

Opening the package, he offered me some. I let him pour the hard little balls in my hand.

"Why the note?" he asked.

"I thought it might help you," I said.

At home that night, I began my photo shoot of my naked fashion doll collection with an instant camera. Looking at the pictures, I told myself I really had something here, but if only I had a second opinion. Whom could I ask? Not the trinity of horror: Justin, my brother, my mom.

Taking the photos to work with me, I put them in an interoffice envelope with "private" written on the front and left them in ABM's inbox. The last photograph was a self-portrait of me holding a naked doll. Three cups of coffee, two packages of pretzels and four hours later, I got a phone call at my desk from ABM, summoning me into his office.

"Close the door," he said.

I closed the door behind me. With a great air of disbelief, he held up the photos.

"What is this?" he asked.

"I'm creating a coffee table book and I wanted your opinion," I said.

He sighed and looked relieved.

"What makes you think I'm qualified?" he asked.

I shrugged.

"I needed a male perspective," I said.

"Ah," he said, raising an eyebrow.

"Do you do think they are interesting?" I asked.

There was a pause. He cleared his throat. "What is?" he asked.

The way he was looking at me was telling me he was thinking something else. Suddenly, I felt warm.

"The photographs," I said.

"Well, I'm not interested in the dolls themselves," he said.

"In the positions?" I asked.

He looked through the photos again as if he was considering a business proposition. I stepped in closer. I noticed my note on his desk. Alongside it was a note pad with a million scribbles on it. He must have worked for hours trying to decipher it. I tried not to smile.

He held up a photo. The girl doll was straddling the boy doll in his lap.

"I like this one," he said.

"My personal favorite," I said.

He looked long and hard at me.

"I probably shouldn't be entertaining this idea, but I'm not getting any younger," he said.

Leaning over his desk, he kissed me. The way he mashed his mouth against mine was pretty exciting, and I was so taken aback by the suddenness that I stood like there a dummy letting him shove his tongue down my throat. I hadn't realized his hands were so massive but alongside my head, they seemed to engulf me.

The next thing he did really blew my mind. He hauled me over this desk to him, my body contacting his papers and his half-eaten club sandwich. It was sort of like in the movies where two characters knock everything off a desk to get it on, only we didn't flop on the desk in a mad passionate embrace. He pulled me onto his lap, much like his favorite fashion doll photo.

As his hands roamed for access to my bare skin, I bit his ear lobe.

"Oh, God," he moaned, which was a nice response, although a little bit too loud for this point in the getting it on with your boss stage.

Wanting to up the stakes, I pinched his nipples through his nicely pressed shirt.

"Holy shit," he cried.

I smiled. He was such the liar. He had so not been fucked properly before.

Hopping off his lap for a second, I yanked up my skirt to give him better access. I expected him to pull down my thong, but he ripped it off. My favorite thong. Justin had touched it at the garage sale and by the tree. I felt a pang as I stood there, looking at it on the floor. I decided if he got his dick out in the next three seconds, I would forgive him.

"Come on," I ordered, motioning at his crotch.

He got the clue and, with some major fumbling, got it out. Not bad. I'd seen better, but it would do.

I climbed on board, commandeering this love ship. The pace was mine. As I thumped my pelvis against him, he seemed so overcome by the power of my pussy; he could barely hold his hands on my hips.

The guy was going to come before I even broke a sweat so I grabbed one of my breasts with one hand. The other hand found my crotch, my fingers manipulating my clit like the expert it was. He went right over the edge like a twelve year old finding his first porn magazine.

It was a race against the clock.

"Don't come," I cried.

Suddenly, the office door opened. I found myself propelled through the air and hitting the floor with a resounding thud. Stunned, I looked up to see his dick squirting come all over his desk drawer as he stood to face whoever it was. I barely dodged out of the way.

I heard his secretary say he had a meeting in five minutes and she left. I stared up at him in shock, watching him stuff his business back in his pants. He didn't even glance down at me on the floor.

"That was close," he said.

Picking myself up off the floor, I tugged down my skirt. Never in my life had I been treated like this. A gentleman would have protected me to the bitter end. Not cast me aside like a piece of garbage.

Too angry for words, I gave him a look that said go to hell, picked up my poor ripped thong, my photos and my note. That was when I noticed the huge smear of mustard right across the front of my cream-colored skirt.

In a huff, I left his office. Everyone stared at me, including the cleaning lady. Everybody knew. No one was fooled. Of course, I looked like I had just been fucked, with my disheveled hair and my flushed face, because I had. Now for the rest of my professional career I would be known as the girl who had fucked Alan Brandon Michaels.

I hated them all. I hated this place. What was I even doing here? Then it hit me. I was here because I wanted my mother to approve. I didn't want to work here. I didn't want to live at my mother's. Suddenly, the muddled cloud of childhood confusion broke away, and why, because I'd had my boss's dick in me.

At my desk, I plunked down my stuff on my desk and stopped cold. There in front of my keyboard was the red button. Who had put it there? I flipped it over, and with a groan recognized the florid gold design on the front. It was my button. My mother had given me this horribly, ugly red sweater for Christmas, and I'd worn it once to work to make her happy. Meanwhile her coops had gotten fifty-dollar gift certificates to their favorite stores.

Suddenly, to my amazement, I saw ABM striding purpose-fully over to my desk. I reached for my purse, convinced I was going to be fired right this minute, not that I really cared. I would sue his ass for harassment. I just wasn't in the mood for any more drama right this minute, but he merely stopped behind me and whispered something in my ear.

"I may have to work on being an asshole, but I do care about you, sweetheart."

I met his gaze. He was serious. Nervously, I flipped my button back over on my desk. Suddenly, it felt so warm in my hands.

"Is that the button that told you to give me the note?" he asked.

I nodded.

"Good button," he said.

Beverly's Pastime

Sage Vivant

Everybody needs a hobby. Mine is destroying marriages.

Like any lifelong pursuit, some practice is required to achieve any kind of commendable performance level. I did my practicing as a teenager, using babysitting as my vehicle into couples' lives. I couldn't help but notice at the tender age of 16 that my redheaded milky white skin and burgeoning breasts were a powerful lure – I got babysitting gigs much more often than my plainer-looking friends did. I didn't realize the extent of my power, though, until I was eighteen, when Mr Rosenblum shot a sack full of come onto his wife's face at my bidding. Since then, I've known no greater power than that of eroding the very foundations of people's precious little holy matrimonies.

Fact: men want to bury their faces in my ass so badly that they'll forget years of marital commitments to get there. Exploiting this state of affairs, reader, is just plain fun. Millions of women do it every day. I am no different from them; merely more honest and certainly more memorable.

My distinction comes into play on a much deeper psychological level. Women, you see, have an instinctive urge to lay claim to men. Most of them believe marriage is the ultimate capture.

Women are fools. My goal is to drive this point home to them at every opportunity. Rarely, however, do they take my message well.

I own my own advertising agency in midtown Manhattan. Consequently, I meet hundreds of married couples every year.

At 46, I've met all kinds, but few have cried out for abuse and ultimate destruction more loudly than Melissa and Christopher.

These two walked into the corporate cocktail party like they were at Disneyland. Certainly, Melissa could have worn that forgettably shapeless frock at any amusement park and been quite comfortable. Her husband, on the other hand, cut a more dashing figure. Well-groomed, handsome, dark hair graying gradually at the temples – his posture and grace told me he devoted time to his body.

Both of them seemed a bit shy, but she was downright clueless while he was simply reserved. I decided they were perfect.

I paused at the full-length mirror to smooth my navy blue Armani suit. I'd bought it just yesterday, specially for the party. Elegant yet blatantly sexy, the jacket sported lapels that parted at my chest to reveal enough cleavage to distract anyone, male or female. It was sometimes difficult to find *prêt à porter* to accommodate my 36DDs, but this little number clung to me everywhere as if I'd been the model for its design. The short skirt hugged my round backside with such fetching aplomb, I wished I could kiss my own ass.

Heat permeated my space between my legs as moisture collected in my crotchless pantyhose. I smelled my own arousal at the thought of my impending conquest. As I sauntered over to the hapless couple, the lips of my labia were slick with anticipation.

I don't know if the shimmering waves of my flowing red hair or the jiggle of my corseted breasts caught his eye first, but I knew he was mine from halfway across the room. The frumpy wife turned her head to follow his enraptured gaze. Oh, the fear that galvanized that pudgy face.

"Hi," I said decisively, extending my hand to him. "I'm Beverly Channing." I put my other hand over his when he clasped mine. "I'm certain I've met you before but I'm at a loss to remember where," I continued. I fixed my green-eyed gaze on him while I parted my lips in a hungry smile. I held his hand too long for wifey's liking – in my peripheral vision, I saw her stiffen.

"Christopher Van Dyke," he smiled. His hands were warm. He even smelled nice. *Bulgari pour homme*, I believe. "I'm afraid I've never met you before," he added, stealing a darting glance at his wife to gauge her reaction.

We were off to a smashing start.

"No, I'm sure you're wrong. I never forget a good-looking man," I teased and pressed my right breast into his arm. His color deepened.

He was taller than I but not by much. His wife, at a paltry five feet four inches or so, had the dimensions of a shopping bag. I still hadn't acknowledged her existence.

"Wasn't it Barry Goldman's party last spring?" I persisted. Everybody who was anybody attended Barry's parties. Odds were good that Dudley Dooright here had been on the guest list.

"Well, yes, I was there, but I don't remember meeting you," he replied. His deep voice slid over my skin like a thousand little tongues.

"I was there, too. We never met you," the little woman piped up.

I turned my head slowly and but never quite made eye contact from beneath haughty eyelids. "I have no recollection of meeting you. I was speaking to your husband." I turned back to Christopher, who predictably then felt compelled to introduce his prickly little spouse.

"I'm sorry. This is my wife, Melissa."

I nodded in her general direction, ignoring her chubby hand tentatively extended toward me. She retracted it quickly and immediately reached for a passing canapé.

"Why don't you get us some drinks, Melissa?" I commanded as I continued staring into her husband's face. Christopher, confounded by my impertinence, met his wife's gaze imploringly: *Please do as this woman says. I'm sure this will be over soon.*

"Well, what would you like?" Melissa asked me, appropriately irritated to be serving me.

"Anything. Use your imagination. Surprise me," I purred, still holding Christopher's hand. I had yet to look at her.

She stormed off, waddling toward the bar, unaware that drinks circulated through the party just like hors-d'oeuvres.

He tugged his hand away from mine very gently. I found this clear yet lame attempt to assert his manhood rather charming. He was visibly disquieted by my presence but once Melissa had disappeared, his eyes traveled down the length of my over-heated body and back up again. He took this inventory surreptitiously, mind you, but he took it nonetheless.

"I didn't want to say so in front of your wife," I lied, "but I tried desperately to get your attention at Barry's party. I find you devastatingly attractive."

Again, he blushed but recovered admirably. "I wish I'd known."

"Why?"

He cleared his throat and shifted his weight from one foot to the other. "Maybe I could have given you a ride home."

"Oh, that's not all I would have expected of you, Christopher."

Have you ever had the satisfaction of watching a face work through an internal dilemma? The man parted his lips in involuntary protest and seemed to surprise himself when no words found their way past them.

"In fact," I continued, "why not let *me* take *you* home?"

He grinned and tilted his head to hide his sheepishness. "But we just got here."

"I know of a better party. The three of us could go together."

"Three of us?"

"I assume you've got some kind of code against ditching your wife?"

He chuckled. "Of course. I'm just not sure that she'd, you know, feel comfortable at another party."

"Sweetheart, she doesn't look terribly at ease at this one," I assured him, curious whether he actually was ready to leave his plodding dumpling at the party. Regardless of his desires, I wanted her along with us. Otherwise, what was the point?

I watched said dumpling make her way through the chic and chatty crowd as she tried to squeeze between bodies while balancing two champagne flutes. Horribly unsure of herself and eager not to offend, she disgusted me.

"Here she comes now," I commented in my best monotone.

Christopher turned and satisfaction welled up inside me as I saw his face fall at the bumbling sight of her. He forced a smile to welcome her back.

"Champagne! Thank you, sweetheart." He spoke to her in a fatherly way as he took a glass from her. He leaned forward to give her an appreciative peck on her doughy cheek. As he did so, elbows jostled and the champagne in what was soon to be my glass poured onto my Walter Steiger pumps.

The bitch was starting to incense me.

"Oh! Honey! I think you spilled some champagne on your friend!" she exclaimed, mastering the obvious.

"He didn't spill it. You did." I remarked coolly, surveying my soiled shoe as if it belonged to some street person.

She blushed furiously and looked from her husband to me and back to her husband, undoubtedly waiting for him to come to her defense.

"I saw it all quite clearly. You spilled champagne on my shoe. What I really can't fathom is why you're just standing there when you should be cleaning it up."

Christopher froze, mute with disbelief. Tears welled up in Mrs Van Dyke during the pregnant pause before she crouched at my feet with a napkin. While she dabbed, I attempted to resume my conversation with her husband by taking yet another step closer to him. This movement caused me to squash Melissa's pinky. I heard her yelp and responded by discreetly placing my hand on the top of her head, to keep her crouching.

"Don't even think about getting up until that shoe is spotless," I spat at her. At this moment, I also spread my legs so that if she were to look up, she would be treated to my glistening wet pooch.

"Now, then, Christopher. Where were we? I was telling you about this other party I'd like to take you to. Who do you work for, by the way?"

"I'm with Bozell. I handle Bank of America."

I flicked on my suitably impressed face, to which he responded like the egotist that most account executives are. He no longer seemed to care that his wife was on all fours at a posh cocktail party just to clean up a spill that he himself had made. He still didn't even know who I was or appeared to be interested in finding out.

"Well, then. You need to go to this party more than you need to be here. All you'll find here are people moving up. I'll take you where the people have already made it and are enjoying the spoils."

His face shone with excitement. When I cupped his basket in the hand I'd just removed from his wife's head, his eyes nearly bugged out of their sockets.

"Does that sound good to you?" I squeezed his ballsack ever so slightly.

He nodded, furtively trying to determine whether Melissa could see what I was doing. On her unbalanced way up, she did indeed catch the action and gasped in horror.

"Christopher!"

"Are my shoes clean?" I asked her, boldly staring her down.

She blurted something that has no English equivalent and I ignored it. Christopher's cock inflated in my hand. He blinked and blurted something equally unintelligible.

"Oh, the hell with the shoes. Are we ready to get to that party?" My face was close enough to his ear for him to feel my hot breath. My breast pressed into his arm and the memory of my hand at his crotch robbed him of the power of speech.

"Sure," he finally uttered.

"What? Christopher! What's going on here?" She was a teapot ready to boil, a smokestack about to blow. Her phony suburban manners disintegrated and all of a sudden I noticed where I'd flattened her mousy, outdated coiffure with my hand.

"Nothing's going on, honey. What's the matter?" he cooed to his wife. Unctuous bastard – how solicitous men could be when new pussy was at stake.

"Nothing's the matter," I interrupted. "Maybe you should just keep quiet while I'm trying to seduce your husband."

Her whole face turned the color of her acne splotches. Christopher laughed nervously in an attempt to make light of my comment. "Don't be silly, Beverly," he said with no discernable conviction. "You're doing no such thing."

"This discussion is getting tedious," I announced. "Let's get going." I led the way to the door and out to my waiting limo. It didn't surprise me in the least when they both followed me.

"This is yours?" Melissa observed. Her naïve incredulity bored me so I decided to ignore her. She was probably used to people paying no attention to her.

I made her sit across from me in the limo so that I could be closer to Christopher. When I sat down, I made sure my skirt rode up indecently. I wore pantyhose constructed like stockings and garter belt – generous arcs of bare skin, including an unfettered crotch, characterize them. I nearly squealed with delight as Melissa's jaw dropped at the sight of my neatly trimmed but gaping crotch.

"Your wife seems to be disturbed by my lack of panties," I purred into Christopher's ear. He was as close to me as I'd hoped and upon hearing my disclosure, he looked down at my lap. Reluctantly, he checked his wife's expression. Even Melissa's ample body could not contain her shock.

I led Christopher's hand to my slippery lips as Melissa watched. Once his fingers delved into my wetness, I grabbed a handful of his hair and brought his mouth to mine. Christopher's hand did not leave my gushing pussy. In fact, he was now spreading my juice over my growing clit. She leaned forward and slapped his knee.

"Stop that, now!" she reprimanded.

At the sound of her slap, we stopped kissing and turned to face her ridiculous presence.

"What the hell was that?" I snapped at her.

"I want you to stop."

I sat back in the rich leather seat and stared at her until she averted her eyes. "*You* want me to stop."

"I want you both to stop," the plump lady mumbled.

"Don't you like watching your husband play with my pussy?" I asked, slumping a bit so that Christopher could finger-fuck me. "Tell you what, Melissa. You can play, too."

"I don't want to play," she pouted as Christopher buried his face in my neck. Under the erratic flashes of streetlight through the limo's moonroof, the shadows in her puffy face gave her a ghoulish quality. The poor cow didn't know who to be angry with, me or her amorous husband.

"Of course you do," I insisted. "Slide forward on your seat, there, and get on your knees."

"Why?"

"If you're going to ask questions, I'll have the driver let you out right here. We're only a few blocks from Harlem. Would you like that?"

"No."

"Then do what I tell you. On your knees."

Melissa heaved her unwieldy body forward and landed with a thud onto her knees. The position put her much closer to my excitable crotch.

"Stick your face between my legs and tell your husband what I smell like."

Horror crossed her face for a second time that evening. Or was it a third? In any event, she looked at her husband, who had long since put her out of his mind. His tongue played with my earlobe as his middle finger made squishing noises where I'd led it.

"Christopher!" she wailed, on the verge of tears. Her frustration made me wetter.

"Sniff my pussy, you pathetic whiner."

Her face contorted into hideous expressions before the tears began to flow. I laughed, which disturbed Christopher from his ministrations at my neck.

"What's going on?" It was as if we'd awakened him from a pleasant dream.

"Your wife won't smell my pussy."

"Come on, honey. Just play along. Everything's gonna be all

right," he said distractedly, now moving to kiss my mouth as two fingers pumped my hole. I subtly moved his face into my thick mass of wavy hair so that I could watch Melissa sniff down below. This was a show too good to miss.

She leaned forward as if my muff were rotten meat. With her eyes closed, she ventured closer. I didn't know whether she just didn't want to see pussy up close and personal or she didn't want to see her beloved's hands buried in happy juice. Either way, her extreme unease tickled me and I could only imagine that I was marring her psyche for life.

I loved disturbing her world, upsetting everything she thought was real. Seeing her pudgy form at my mercy while her husband indulged himself on me quickened my pulse. Who needed drugs or alcohol when a high like this was available?

She inhaled dramatically but briefly about six inches from my creamy center, then backed up quickly.

"Are you afraid it'll bite or are you just expecting mine to be as rancid as yours?" I asked.

She stared at me, blustering yet wordless in her rage. Arms trembling, she struggled to hoist herself back into her seat. The violet atrocity she called a dress bunched up over her thick knees, making me crave something from Pillsbury.

"What do I smell like?"

"I don't know."

"Christopher has to know what I smell like before he eats me, don't you, baby?" I purred as I ran my fingers through his hair.

"Mmmm," he replied, still breathing into my red locks. Suddenly, he sat upright, and I giggled, realizing he was finally aware of what had been going on around him.

"Tell him what he can expect to taste, Melissa, or the driver lets you off here." Shouts from a passing car full of foul-mouthed youths reminded her where she was.

"She smells like perfume."

"Is there anything about you that's even been *near* an imagination?" I wondered aloud.

"Let me eat you now, Beverly," he pleaded. I liked his style – urgent yet refined. What was a class act like this doing with such a *hausfrau*? I couldn't wait for his tongue to lap up my juice. But first, some appreciation of the merchandise.

"Not so fast, loverboy. It's a little warm in here, don't you think? Help me with my jacket."

Barely able to restrain a grin, his suave hands dedicated themselves to working the buttons of my Armani jacket. He slid his palms over my ribcage to my sides, pushing the jacket open to reveal my blue corseted torso. The moonlight hit the upper hemisphere of my alabaster globes perfectly, highlighting their smooth, ripe roundness.

I helped him slide the sleeves down my arms until I sat there with the top half of me laced up in a corset, the bottom half with a skirt barely covering my carefully trimmed pubic triangle.

"Melissa, do you think it's right that I'm sitting here half naked with your husband?"

"No, I don't!" The woman sat upright, ready to concur with me, her adversary. What a stupendous fool.

"Then I insist that you match me, garment for garment."

"What do you mean?" The fear returned to her face. Very gratifying.

"Strip, you idiot. Show me what passes for lingerie in the suburbs."

"I most certainly will not, will I, Christopher?" She shot her spouse the most imploring look she'd probably ever mustered. And still it was a pitiful display of feminine wiles.

As for Christopher, he now sat erect, watching our banter like it was a tennis match. He'd never been in so ludicrous a situation but was far more adaptable than his provincial wife.

"I don't see where it can hurt, honey. After all, she's half naked already. I'll even take my clothes off if it'll make you feel better."

"I'll tell you when your clothes come off, sweetheart," I informed him with gentle authority. "For now, I want you to help Melissa slip out of that sweet little frock she's wearing."

He moved toward his frightened wife. She squirmed to get away from him, as if there were someplace she could go. He grabbed her by the shoulders to immobilize her and stared into her eyes.

"It's easier if you just cooperate, Mel."

Mel. It sounded like a pudding flavor. Chill and serve. Watch it jiggle.

He unzipped her polyester sack and guided it over her head. She sat there, weeping, arms crossed over her beige Playtex bra. Even her seemingly inflatable arms weren't large enough to obscure the fullness of her bosom. I estimated that we were roughly the same age, yet this woman's flesh had deteriorated into a slack, overgrown wasteland some time ago.

I sat serenely, observing Christopher's face as he compared our bodies. Such a delicious moment, this silent epiphany in a man's mind when he considers running, screaming, from his sexless wife and into the arms of a beautiful, supple, willing woman.

During this moment of silence, I lowered the window. The purr of its motor went unnoticed but the rush of cool air did not. The Van Dykes turned to me, brows furrowed in confusion.

"Time to put out the trash," I said, grabbing Melissa's dress and tossing it out into the mysterious metropolitan night.

"My dress! Christopher! She threw it out the window!" Just when I thought this woman could panic no further, she lapsed into new fits of fussing. I sent the window back up.

"Now then," I sighed, stretching myself along the length of the limo's long backseat. Melissa sat whimpering as Christopher patted her knee in an attempt to comfort her.

"Come back to your seat, Christopher, and whip out that manhood I was fondling at the party."

Melissa cried audibly now but her husband resumed his seat and immediately unzipped his fly. What he pulled out was a gloriously hard and thick cock. My mouth watered.

I paused, though, to consider what would humiliate this stupid woman more – my giving her husband head or her having to suck him off in front of me. I don't like second-guessing myself and I probably never would have hesitated if I didn't want that cock so badly myself. I would have taken that

fine piece of meat up any orifice, to be honest. Then I came up
with the perfect solution.

"Melissa, I have another job for you."

"No! No more! You're a sick woman."

"Compliments will get you nowhere. I'm about to give your
husband a fabulous blowjob and I'd like to include you somehow in the festivities. Slip your hand into your pantyhose and
play with yourself. Rub your clit slowly if you don't like what
I'm doing and frig yourself like crazy if you do like it. Understand?"

More boo-hooing. I ignored her and extended my stockinged
legs across Christopher's lap. He stroked me from my thighs to
my toes, reverently and slowly. I lifted my toes to his mouth,
where he sprinkled each toe with feather kisses. I alternated feet
and with my free one, I caressed the smooth, purple head of his
surprisingly enormous rod. He moaned as the soles of my feet
skimmed across it.

A sniffle reminded me of Melissa's presence and I turned to
check that she was following orders. She was not.

"Melissa! What's wrong? Can't find your clit in all those
folds?"

"Leave me alone!" she said with all the drama of a made-for-
TV movie.

"Play with yourself or you're out on the street. I think you
know better than to test me."

The bawling chubette struggled valiantly to jam her pudgy
hand into the unforgiving spandex that encased her belly. When
she finally found what she was looking for, I swung my legs
around and sat on them, heading for that delectable cock beside
me.

"Now remember, fast if you're turned on, slow if you're not."
I stifled a laugh – the very idea of this woman having a sexual
response was an outrageous fiction.

Once my mouth engulfed the pure, hard heat of Christopher's pulsating cock, my interest in Melissa's degradation
waned. I diddled myself as I sucked him, primarily for my
own pleasure but also to embarrass her further. I knew she was

watching. I could feel her simpering gaze. How I wanted her to implode into her own depleted womanhood.

My tongue circled his meat as my mouth traveled up his shaft. Up and down I happily went until the driver stopped at the door of my apartment building. I was careful to prevent Mr Van Dyke from spewing his gratitude. There was so much more to do yet.

Ben, my doorman, has seen me arrive home in various stages of undress and in a wide range of consciousness levels. He had never, however, seen me arrive with an overweight, half-naked housewife and her libidinous husband.

"Good evening, Ms Channing," he said, nodding in that remarkably impassive style they must teach them at doorman school. As each passenger emerged, no sign of bemusement or disgust crossed Ben's face. He knew, as I did, that Sutton Place had its share of kink – it was simply more discreet about enjoying it than other neighborhoods might have been. Ben had seen me corseted only once before, on a similar occasion, and let one side of his mouth turn up in a fleeting but appreciative grin.

Melissa wouldn't budge from the car. Christopher had to yank her out by her stout little arms. She landed on the sidewalk like a bag of cement, her rolls of fat reverberating on impact. Her weeping had elevated into a whining drone, her face a smear of tears and unchecked rosacea.

She stood on the sidewalk in all her girdled glory, looking from her husband to me to Ben for signs that we, too, thought the situation untenable. She received no such confirmation. I was as poker-faced as Ben, and Christopher was so focused on his erection that he held it in his hand, watching me expectantly.

Ben let us into the building, where, to my great disappointment, we encountered no one in the lobby or in the elevator. Melissa clung desperately to her husband throughout, despite his fixation on other matters nearer, uh, at hand.

The moment we entered my twelve-room condominium, I spun on my heel and faced the crying wench. I pulled a breast out of my corset and pointed it at her as if to shoot her with it.

"See this boobie, little Miss Crybaby? You're going to suck it if you don't *shut up*. Now follow me to the bedroom," I walked backwards down the hall to keep an eye on her. Terror consumed her as adrenaline raced through my body. Christopher followed behind her, agog and short of breath.

Once in my bedroom, I positioned myself in front of the expanse of mirrored wall, standing like Wonder Woman.

"Christopher, sit on the floor between my legs. Eat me out."

He moved quickly for a man in his fifties.

"Melissa, I'm going to feed you a breast as God intended it to be," I told her, aiming a hard nipple at her. "Come here and suck it while Christopher licks me."

"No!" she sputtered.

"*Now!*"

As Christopher lapped away at what was now a completely drenched pussy, Melissa stepped forward, apparently sapped of any further impulse to protest. She put her lips to my waiting nipple. I snatched it away instantly.

"You *are* a lesbian! I knew it! How dare you try to suck *my* beautiful breasts? Go sit in the corner and suck your own!"

She bawled louder and recoiled, speaking her husband's name to no avail. His face was smothered in juice and he showed no signs of coming up for air. I pointed to the upholstered Biedermeier chair across the room and she scurried over to it. I stared at her until she extracted one sagging breast from the Playtex brassiere and tried to figure out how to get it to her mouth. For a moment, I feared the challenge might get the better of her, but eventually, she stuffed a dark, useless nipple into her mouth.

"Don't let it sit there. Suck it."

She obeyed. A more distasteful sight had never graced my bedroom.

"Remove my stockings, Christopher."

He did so without a single pause from his tongue. Carefully, he rolled the waistband of my silk pantyhose down to my belly and over my hips, then down the length of my long, smooth legs. I watched as he savored the contours of my thighs and the slope of my calves. When they were off, I led him to the bed. I now wore only my corset.

"Unlace my corset now," I instructed as he knelt on the bed and I stood before him. I stared at Melissa menacingly to keep her suckling at her own teat. Christopher's back was to her. He unlaced me with that same wonderful reverence and attention to detail he'd demonstrated earlier. Some men were frightened by my dominance but this one knew that he was born to take orders. His wife had no idea that his strength lay in his submission and I hated her for her stupidity.

He removed my corset tenderly, as if both it and I were fragile. I altered the mood by pushing him onto his back and straddling his face while I dove into his manly goods. As we sixty-nined, Melissa whimpered softly. I would have reminded her to keep sucking but I didn't want to take Christopher's rock hardness out of my mouth. I slapped my face with his cock, licked it wildly, and sucked one ball and then the other into my hot mouth. When my mouth tired, I surrounded his prick with breast meat, smothering it, fucking it, and watching its raw head pop up intermittently between my soft flesh.

Between my legs, he tongue-fucked me with a skill I couldn't imagine him using on his sexless wife. He speared me expertly and rimmed my asshole like he'd been doing it for years. I dripped with delight.

I felt a surge in the base of his cock, signaling impending eruption. I put the action on pause to save him for the main event. Climbing off him, I looked at his pussy-smeared face and caressed it. The man possessed a certain undeniable charm. That charm, however, was not enough to deter me from my goal.

Melissa's breast hung forlornly over her distended belly. She sat there, numb, used up.

"Look at your wife, Christopher. She's the epitome of a sex goddess, isn't she?"

He turned to the corner where she sat but offered no comment.

I got to my feet, watching my heavy breasts in the mirrored

wall as they swayed and bounced with my movement. I enjoyed Christopher watching them, too. Melissa's eyes registered renewed fear as I approached her.

"Get up."

She scrambled to her feet.

"I'm going to do something nice for you. You look like a woman who needs many things, not the least of which is a good diet, but for now, I'm willing to offer you a nice, hot bath. Follow me."

I led her to the master bathroom, tiled in alternating squares of black and white marble. The large round bathtub, which could hold up to five people – and often had – sat atop a three-stair climb. She teetered her uncertain way upward.

"Use whatever you want. Just get in the tub and stay out of our way." I turned on the water for her, bounced one of her unsightly teats in my hand, and walked out.

Christopher waited patiently for me on the bed where I'd left him. He was still fully dressed except for his exposed genitalia. A fetching sight, to be sure, but I wanted to see him fully naked so I demanded that he strip for me.

As he undressed, his cock continued to point northward, an angle that one didn't often see in men his age. I was impressed but didn't tell him so. My pussy ached for his meat but I didn't tell him that, either.

We stood on opposite sides of the bed. As he disrobed, removing each article of clothing as I told him, I turned my back to him and bent over so that his view was of my big round ass with slippery pussy lips virtually speaking his name. I slipped my hand between my legs and stroked myself.

"Christopher, what would you like to do to me?"

"I'd like to have sex with you," he rasped.

"Of course you would, but what would that sex entail?"

He paused. Obviously, he'd never been encouraged to articulate his coital plans before.

I slipped a finger into my steamy hole, doing so slowly enough to let him hear the wetness.

"I'd like to fuck you, Beverly. I'd really like to fuck you."

"How?" I increased the speed of my finger in my hungry vagina.

"Can't we just do it?" He put a tentative hand on my hip. He was on the bed now.

I stood upright. "Did I say you could touch me?" I shot fire at him through my eyes. He blinked but did not waver.

"No. I'm sorry."

"When you see my fingers up my twat, what does it make you want to do?" I resumed the position.

"It makes me want to ram my cock up inside you and pump you until you scream."

I smiled because he couldn't see my face. Ah, the sweet thrill of victory.

"Then do it."

Ram me he did. His thick manhood impaled my backside in one smooth movement, plunging so deeply I thought he might come up my throat. He pounded my ass hard as he held on to my hips to keep both of us grounded. I knew my ass cheeks shook provocatively with each thrust. I adored thinking about my ass.

He fucked for several minutes before I felt him stiffen and prepare for orgasm. I turned to look at his face in the mirror and saw his sweet grimace just before he let loose into my now clenching cunt. He shouted as he spewed, which surprised and titillated me. As his shout subsided, I launched my own, quite without warning. The old man had screwed me into my own release and it took my body by storm. I nearly lost my balance in my delirium.

He collapsed on the bed when he was certain I was satisfied. I joined him seconds later. We said nothing as we caught our collective breath and spiraled to earth. When I gauged he had fully recovered, I took his hand and sat up.

"Let's go see how Melissa is doing." Together, we headed for the bathroom.

There she sat, mired in suds. Our unannounced entrance jolted her and her eyes sprung open. Her Rotundness had taken advantage, it seemed, of my expensive bubble bath to pleasure herself. Such circumstances were enough to bring bile to my throat and yet my curiosity was piqued, for what could have prompted this overfed munchkin to reach that level of arousal? Was it my constant belittlement of her? Her husband's interest in me? My unadulterated beauty?

Whatever it was, I was more than willing to explore some new territory. Christopher glanced at me to gauge my mood. He was undoubtedly trying to anticipate what I might do next but, as we all know, that's not an undertaking for the faint of heart. I shot him a stern glance to ensure his silence.

"I see you've found your pussy, Melissa. I hope its rust doesn't leave a ring around my bathtub."

She squinted at me as if she were wishing some unspoken curse on me. Her face pinched with revulsion and that just made me wetter. I knew I'd already done irreparable damage to their marriage but there's always room for more humiliation, especially for confused and insufferably bland females like this one. I climbed the steps to the bathtub, with no intention of sharing the same bathwater but with every intention of making her think I would.

I walked around the edge of the tub, still wearing my bustier but nothing else. Once I found a spot I liked, directly in front of her of course, I unsnapped the garment and stood before her with nothing between us but suds. The trepidation in her eyes was positively invigorating.

"What are you going to do?" she asked me, voice quavering.

"If you're going to make me watch you jack off, you're going to have to watch me."

I filled one hand with the enviably firm flesh of my left breast.

"Now grab yours," I demanded.

She looked to her husband but I did not. My eyes stayed on her. I heard him say "Grab your tit, Mel."

Somewhere under my dense and fragrant bubble bath, her pudgy hand took hold of a pancake with a nipple. I moved my right hand to my sex, where I spread my labia wide.

"Can you get a good look at this, Melissa? This is the sweet pussy your husband could have been screwing all these years instead of the musty hole that's now stinking up my bathtub. Look at me, you stupid bitch."

She looked. Of course, she looked. Who could look away? Nevertheless, I kept my eyes glued on her and ignored whatever sounds I heard coming from Christopher. I'd already conquered him and knew his allegiance was to me, not her – he wouldn't be stepping in to save her now.

I stroked the slippery folds of my pussy, creaming with every passing second that her gaze stayed on my hand.

"Play with yourself. Follow my lead. Maybe you can learn the timeless art of seduction," I cackled. Her hands seemed busy. I certainly had no plans to check on her progress.

Something made me turn to look at Christopher, whose mood had palpably changed. He stood there smiling wryly, with his jacket open to reveal some tiny digital device. When he took it out of his pocket and held it to his eye as he grinned, I understood that the man I'd just treated to the sex of his life was photographing me with a high-tech camera. Too stunned to move or even hurl well-deserved invectives, I tried to discern just what kind of foul play was afoot.

"You could get dressed, Beverly, but it wouldn't do much good. We've got what we need now. These cameras only hold a hundred images or so."

"What the fuck are you talking about?" I finally spat.

He tossed me the terrycloth robe I bought in Istanbul but most of it landed in the bath water. Mel grinned.

"It was funny that you mentioned Barry Goldman's party earlier tonight," Christopher began. Fiddling with the device, he snapped another photo of me leaning against the Italian marble, breast in one hand, fire in my eyes.

"I was there the night you ruined Barry's marriage. And it was a damn good marriage, you evil slut. What you did destroyed Barry."

"He didn't seem too distraught the night it happened. We screwed like rabbits."

"I warned him about you," he continued, completely ignoring my commentary. "I knew the havoc you'd wreaked with others. He thought he was immune. Did I mention that Barry is my brother?"

"No, I believe you overlooked that. But please – give him my regards."

"I'm going to give him more than that. These pictures are a start. They're likely to make him quite a bit of money, especially when he posts them on the Internet. The footage from the limousine should do well, too. Lots of different angles. Those Web cams are really an innovation."

"Bastard."

"Oh, now I don't think you're in any position to be name-calling, Beverly. You outdid yourself with poor Melissa here tonight. By the way, she isn't my wife."

"I find that reassuring," I said, meaning it, though I didn't believe him for a second. Who would tote a frump like Mel around unless they were under some legal obligation to do so?

"Bitch," Melissa said, throwing my words back at me but sounding so effete, I didn't feel more than a sneer was due her.

"Melissa is my special partner. We play humiliation games often. She enjoys it. In fact, this night was as much for her as it was for me. I'm amazed that a champion player such as yourself didn't know you were being set up. But then, I knew you wouldn't be able to resist the easy target Mel presented. And I knew you and your delusional brain would try to break us up if you thought we were married. You're so predictable, Beverly. You put yourself right where we wanted you."

I said nothing because I was trying to figure out how to drown Mel and have one more go at Christopher. I wanted to fuck him so thoroughly that he'd give me those damn pictures. But what about the Web cam?

"Revenge is really quite sweet," he continued. "There's no telling what these pictures will do to your client base, Beverly. I wouldn't want to be you tomorrow."

"Don't be silly. You wouldn't know *how* to be me."

Mel climbed out of my tub with newfound grace. Though her body was still a repulsive sack of shapelessness, there was no mistaking the confidence that practically beamed from her.

Damned submissives – they had wills of iron under their compliant flesh. It was a mindset I'd never understand or respect. Why submit when you could rule?

"I left you a little surprise in your tub," Mel purred just before she yanked me from the ledge. The element of surprise worked in her favor and I found myself flailing about in her bathwater. It didn't take me long to find my Armani suit, balled up and permanently ruined. And I thought the blue in the water had come from the Himalayan herbs in my exclusive blend of eastern aromatherapy oils.

She'd stained my bathtub, after all. But the stain to my reputation was the more indelible of the two. If I started packing now, I could make it to Canada in just a few hours. Advertising opportunities – and happy marriages – were in plentiful supply there, I'd heard. In fact, one of my former, and attractive, colleagues had just moved there with his wife . . .

The Space Between

Helena Settimana

I make coffee in my kitchen while the wan light of early morning on the lake filters through the louvers of the Venetian blinds in the cottage. It's the last of my Blue Mountain, a gift from the griot, Kayode "Kayo" Mackenzie of Hilton Head Island. I want it for myself and I fear I'll wake Charmaine, who is still asleep in the loft, and I'll have to share my last drop of him. I roll its liquor on my tongue. Strange that I'd feel that way about something as mundane as coffee, but that's the way it is. It's bitter and sweet; something like the man. Something like all that followed our brief acquaintance. The screen door is squeaky and I try not to let it bang as I step out onto the flagstone patio into the dim morning. The air is fresh, and frosted with the resinous smell of pine, like the interior of a cathedral after mass is said. It is still as a church too, hemmed in by trees some seventy feet tall. It's almost light. Soon the morning chorus will begin. Soon the lake will buzz with boat motors and cries of water-skiers. Soon Charmaine will be getting up, stretching, looking for me.

Last night she lay in the space between my thighs and stabbed at my emptiness with her tongue until it was filled loosely, like water outflowing a cracked vessel. I am empty because she is using me. I know that. I'm using her too. We are like mutually supporting parasites. It's his fault. She is using me because I once had the almost-famous Mackenzie, whom she desires. She has not had the pleasure despite tracking him like a camp follower. Of this I am certain.

"I've been in love with that man for a decade," she confessed over *Cuba Libre's* at the old Bam Boo Club in downtown Toronto. Some people idolize singers. Charmaine was like that with poets and artists. So am I, I confess. She responded to Kayo the way women my mother's age swooned over Leonard Cohen. Striped by shade from one of the club's namesake grasses, she swung one sandaled foot under the patio table, her purple-painted toenails coming perilously close to my bare shin. "It's more than lust. It's lo-ove." She flapped her fingers like an excited teenager. I tried not to stare at her cleavage. "I've seen him every time he comes up here. I've even seen him perform *here*," she enthused, waving to take in the whole of the club. "Then I go home and single-handedly console myself that the streets are not paved with talented and handsome men like him, sensitive guys just ripe for the plucking. Any girl should get one. But no," she sucked her teeth, "those ones are rare and worth the wait, not that a girl should go without some while she is waiting."

We laughed, but I was a bit put out. I wished she wasn't so transparently smitten, even if I agreed wholeheartedly with her assessment of Kayo's worth. A girl shouldn't go without a bit of something. I could be that something for her. Like Charmaine, I'm in love with words and most recently with her words. My guru says I shouldn't trust what people say, only what they do, but I'm susceptible to art and sweet talk. I'd been working at bedding Charmaine for six months now, ever since the writers' conference where we met. She's brilliant – a poet as well. I'm a sucker for that sort of shine; that sort of smart-hot. She had always been willing to come out to talk, to shop or share, but I'd wanted more for a long time. I searched her face and the shifting plains and hills of her body for clues, but had found no evidence of my desire returned. That she was so indifferent to me hurt. She thrummed with passion. I quivered back. She was edible. I was hungry. I stared across the table. She looked away. She had broad, high cheekbones, a diamond-shaped face that spoke of her jambalaya roots: Trini, French, Indian, African. Creole. Red. Her eyes were large, and the corners curled down slightly.

This was beautiful. But it was her body; the queenly heft of it, and the way she moved her high chest and broad behind with grace upon slender legs like stalks of grass that I found so compelling. Her ass jutted one way, her tits, belly and chin the other, like those African carvings of dancing girls with long shins and a hand on one hip. That and the words. The words.

We were talking American poets. Slammers. The import Dub set. Spoken-word traditionalists. That's her thing. She brought up Kayo's name and I sat for a long time contemplating my drink and the plate of over-sour escoveitched snapper steaming in front of me. In this moment I sensed a shift about to occur, some rending of the fabric of my universe. "I know him," I said, finally, "personally . . ."

She looked at me with surprise.

"How come you never said so? No. Don't shit me."

"I guess it never occurred to me. We had an affair a year ago."

She weighed this statement against what she believed. "No. No way . . . he'd never. He's a separatist. He's all for *la raza*, Leni."

I shrugged, burning inwardly. Truth was often stranger than art. We invent some of our truths. I couldn't keep my trap shut. Fuck her if she thought I couldn't be telling the truth because he was out there saying he wouldn't touch whitey. There I was, shoving one sacred cow in her face. I wished to fuck she wanted me. There, take that. I attempted the fish. The vinegar rankled in my nostrils and burned my tongue. I pushed it away, called the waiter and asked to see the menu again. . . .

"Well, he did. We did. The only thing he was separating then were my legs. Not long, not deep . . . not love, I'm afraid . . ." She stared at me, disbelieving. "I met him in Charleston. I was doing that article for *Saturday Night*. I have some pictures. Maybe I'll show you. You can come over."

I did have pictures; there was not much to divine from them. They didn't show us, or anyone else fucking. But there is always a story behind an image. In my favorite, he is standing on a narrow, cobbled lane in Charleston, under a huge hanging fern, his bald head turned to one side, his cheek laid across one shoulder. The flash glints off of one earring, dangling along his cheek. The fern stands on the side of his head, looking like a great green jester's cap; a woodland king's crown, sliding off. A church spire rises in the distance at the end of the alley. He is smiling, gap-toothed, goofily at the camera. That was the day after we met. We'd shared breakfast without touching.

I'd been pulled by a bill posted on a telephone pole to attend a slam of Island poets in a backstreet club. I thought, *great*, I could do an extra article on contemporary Gullah culture alive and well in South Carolina. It's why I was there, after all – dredging stories. I went into that place, shining like the North Star. It was fantastic: hot, angry, exuberant. There was much shouting and later, pressing of flesh, the knocking of knuckles in acknowledgment of the groove. I was talking to the performers and he, sliding past my table after his set, did a double take and asked if I had got lost. I laughed and said no. He was very tall, and dark like espresso, with a split in his smile that made him look like an overgrown boy. I was not lost. I was there for the show. Spur of the moment, I asked if I could interview him. He sat down and talked, and that was the beginning. He said to come for breakfast at his hotel. What the hell . . . I did. We drove in his old truck to the Island, after.

Some men are so facile with their charm they astound me. I love that much moxie. He asked. I went. Simple. His sunglasses made him look professorial. He smiled a tiny, tiny inscrutable smile the whole way. We didn't talk on the drive. Not much. I mouthed some appreciation of the raw power of his words. He waxed philosophical and stressed how important his work is to the culture of the Island. The ego – but I got that he wasn't making it up. I suggested we save it for the interview proper. Pausing in speech, he had the distracting habit of touching his tongue to his upper lip. It made my insides twitchy. I looked out the window. I watched his hands, slid my eyes to the side and examined his belly; the tented folds of his loose trousers. If I wasn't conscious of it before, I acknowledged it now: I'd sleep with him, should that occasion arise.

We stopped for groceries. The clerk eyed me with some interest and looked pointedly at Mackenzie, but he offered no explanation of my presence. When we left, I felt the cashier's eyes on my back and didn't turn around.

He stayed on the Island in a beach house, where the ocean raced up to meet the land, and the wind battered the thin grass flat. Sandpipers raced ahead of the surf and chased it back as it sucked in upon itself, sighing. They peeped as they ran. Palmettoes spiked the grainy ground around the house. I thought it was a miracle the place still stood, a survivor of countless storms. The pale yellow paint peeled on the clapboard. I walked up the tall steps, the house high on its pilings, its hedge against the cruelty of the sea. A pelican stood on the roof. I stood outside for several minutes before stepping in.

"Y'all like hush puppies?" he called from the bright kitchen. It was a blaze of sunflower gold.

"Sure. I'll eat anything."

"Greens?"

"Anything, honestly."

"Fried clams?"

"Sure."

"Well if you want 'em y'all'll have to get 'em. There's a pail and a digger out on the porch. Go get us some, then. Know how to find 'em, right?" I nodded. "Make sure you bring 'em in some clean water. Tide's out so it's perfect. They'll be frisky, though. Work fast. See if you can find some crabs, too."

I was back in half an hour, the bucket filled. He puttered in the kitchen, pots clattering, conversing as he worked, and emerged shortly with two steaming plates, topped with sliced tomatoes, dusted with pepper and parsley.

Over lunch and for part of the afternoon, I asked the questions, got my answers, sipped on the Bud he'd pulled out of the fridge.

"Ya'll are welcome to stay and I can drive you back in the morning or whenever y'all have to get back. Nothin' ever happens out here, anyway. They be talking about you back at the store. That's how dull it is in this part. I c'n hear 'em talk about how y'all got lost from the other side. Should be with the country-club folk." He laughed. "Should keep them going for a while. Might as well give 'em something more to talk about. Besides, it looks like the day is turning rough. Check it out." He pointed out to the darkening sea.

A squall had blown up offshore and the surf rose with the tide until water licked close to the verandah's stilted legs.

"Shouldn't we be getting away?"

"Nah. Seen worse 'an 'at. Not likely going to go higher than 'at, and there's a spot down the road a ways where there's more chance of a washout than here. Might not get past that point, anyway. Might as well stay and enjoy the show. It's best if you get out on the porch an' stick ya head into the wind. Always makes me feel like a sea captain. A reg'lar pirate." His twin earrings shook.

So we stood on the porch while the waves sucked at the ground and the rain sliced and swung like a curtain parted and swaying upon itself. It turned and drove itself into us like needles. A huge explosion of lightning made me jump, crashing into him, sodden. We scurried back inside.

"Damn." He was laughing, a big boom, boom, boom of a laugh like thunder.

"I feel like a drowned rat . . ."

"Y'all look like one, too, sorry to tell ya. I'll fetch you a towel and if you like I can throw your stuff over the drying rack. I'll getcha something dry to wear."

He came back with a huge towel and a sweatshirt, then passed me some flannel pajama bottoms with a drawstring waist. "You can change in the bathroom or the bedroom, wherever you like."

"Thanks." I chose the bath, took some time drying my hair. When I came back out, I found him standing in the same place, but dressed in a floor-length plain linen caftan. Barefoot. He looked like a prince. Like Fishburne in *Othello* . . . He was smoking a joint.

"Y'okay?"

"Yeah," I said. "Thanks." I handed him my wet things. He put them on the table and turned back to me.

"You want some?"

"Sure," I said, holding out my hand. "Sure. Love to."

"You need more research for your article?"

"I'm always open for new information."

"What do you need?"

"I don't know what else to ask. So I'll just remain open."

Lightning blued the light in the room.

"You want an exclusive?" That funny smile I'd seen in the truck reappeared.

"Like what? I thought I already had one." He touched his tongue to his lip, again. I passed the joint back, sputtered a little. He put it down. And he kissed me. "Oh," said I. A peck behind the ear, a suggestion laid upon the nape of my neck, an invitation pressed to my lips, an invocation upon my tongue. We stood like that for a long time, tasting. I mouthed his neck, at this darker hollow in a dark hollow near the collar bone. In that spot the smell of salt and wind was strong. I licked it. Salty, too – sweat and sea spray.

"Shoulda jus' given you the towel," he said.

I stroked him through his robe, testing weight, length, breadth and started to feel giddy at the thought of slowly jerking this man off through what looked like an exotic house-dress. Was that all I'd do? Maybe he would just want to be sucked. My legs wobbled. Where would this end? The kitchen table? The paneled wall of the den? Domestically in bed, missionary style?

"Leni, are you in there?" She kicked me on the shin. Charmaine was looking at me. I snapped back to the present. The Bam Boo's purple-haired waitress hovered.

"Yeah . . . just thinking about what you said. You're gonna have to take my word for it. I did. We did. He's not entirely who you think he is. Who he says he is."

After our lunch, Charmaine came over to my house for the first time. I showed her the pictures.

Proof. Sort of.

"Damn, I could just kill you. I'm so jealous I could spit."

"Well, get over it – it's not like I married the guy. He was very cool. He was fulla himself, though. A regular cock of the walk . . . but he was . . ." I sighed, ". . . for two days he was the finest man I ever was with. Sometimes I get mad, thinking about it. You know, you have the fling and it gets under your skin. You want more and it's not there."

"Please put me out of my misery and tell me about it . . ."

"About what?"

"About it all . . . his cock. What he said . . . Sometimes I read his poetry and I start thinking stuff . . . and I want to put it there . . ."

"Oh girl, you have it bad," I said. I felt that shift again, the rip in the universe. If I let something go, I might get what I craved. But should I? I wasn't the kiss-and-tell sort. Still, this could be my ticket. She wouldn't touch me. Fuck it.

So I told her. I told her everything. She *so* wanted to know. I tormented her. I told her about lifting the linen robe very slowly, until it bunched over the high curve of his ass, held there by my fist; how his cock drizzled wet across my rib cage. Her mouth fell open, her lips wet, wet, wet, too. Looking into her mouth I remembered taking him in mine, the smell of salt marsh and wet earth, the clay tang of him as his wrinkled sheath rolled back and my tongue snaked around him, his hands in my hair. This, I told her. With her next exhalation, I was back sprawled on his sofa, exulting in his tongue parting my lips, and his words, "You taste like the sea," eddying over me as he dragged my clit between his gapped teeth and tortured it slowly with the very same clever, pink source of all that jive that had sprung from his mouth. "I'm floating on your sea . . ." And at this her mouth dropped open again, and in it I saw desire, and I leaned forward and put my mouth on hers, and said, "This is how it all went down . . ." On her, I redrew the map – rewrote the history of that travel. The key to this had been so simple, and so unfair to use.

She writhed on the couch beside me, ripe, like a mashy Mission fig – soft. I stroked the narrow silk gusset of her panties, slick already. She was unfashionably and beautifully unshorn, a dense mat of hair peeping all around, spreading to her upper thighs, up the inner cheeks of her ass, the indigo ribbon of her lips glistening then parting slightly: pink, like conch, inside, a recollection of the sea.

I whispered how, for all the gushing wet pouring out of me, he still hurt me with his thing. How it took working slowly, until he said, "Pull the skin fo'ward," and then pushed into me in one slick motion. Farting and sucking from my stretched insides, gales of air caught and released. I bunched my fingers, two, three at a time, into her. She mewled. I pushed, felt resistance, pushed again and again until my hand was clenched around its breadth by her gaping mouth and she broke like surf on it. "Like that," I said. "Big, just like that, Charm. I was bent over the windowsill, with my face in the glass, facing the storm, the rain pelting the window, running down the glass. He made me shoot. That never happened before. It hasn't happened since."

Charmaine grasped my hand, shuddered, jerked like a spastic or a Voudoun in trance, babbled in a strange tongue like that of love; then cried, hiccoughing into my chest.

Later I made her some of the coffee he'd given me; a gift in parting. One of his friends fronted him the expensive Jamaican grind. The stuff cost a fortune. I kept it, sealed in my fridge. Rationed it.

We smoked one too, and I petted her hair, twisted the ends and rewrapped the scarf around it so it stood up in spikes like dragons' tongues. She looked like a queen. She checked my work in the mirror, and was surprised. "You did a good job."

"I have hidden talents." We laughed.

I haven't seen Kayo since that time. A year. We keep missing each other. I'm always where he's not. I don't feel like I'm entirely done. Like the poor SOB jonesing twenty minutes after his first stem of rock, I'm not done. It keeps me on edge. Moist and restless.

I can hear her stirring upstairs. The place is already beginning to heat up. It will be a clear, calm day, perfect for summer idling. I know that part of the past is why she continues to see me, sometimes calling in the night for a fix. We keep apart unless it's to fuck, or in this case to flee into the country. Anais and June . . . Much as I'd like to, I can't call it making love. We'd have to be in love with each other. Seems we're both in lust with him. It's not a fair trade. We don't talk about him, either. That would be too much an acknowledgment of this two-sided triangle. Kayo's the lacuna, the space between, the spirit in the bed. That's my dry, hollow place. If I shut my eyes I'll allow her to be my diviner and I'm her channeler, her shaman. The water flows from the cracked pot, out of the space within its walls. I talk to her. I know the words. Blunt. My fist is his cock – my tongue is his too. It fills her gap. I know what it felt like. I can take her there – almost. I wish it were enough. One day I might have to deal with her finding him herself, except not by accident. She'll go looking. Then, I don't know what will happen. Sometimes I wish I hadn't told her, but in this game the end justifies the means. It's what I dealt for.

In the meantime we revolve about each other in an uneasy orbit, listening to the loons laugh like unhinged spirits on the lake. Pretending. I make her herb tea. I must make a trip into town to get some coffee. I'm out.

The Human Dress

O'Neil De Noux

Cruelty has a Human Heart,
And Jealousy a Human Face;
Terror the Human Form Divine,
And Secrecy the Human Dress.
from "A Divine Image"
by William Blake

Walking along the Bay St Louis levee, my new Nikon dangling from my neck, I found exactly what I was searching for. A black man sat fishing next to an old dock. It was a typically warm Mississippi day, bright and windless. The man, who looked to be in his early to mid-twenties, was handling the heat well. He had stripped down to his shorts. I wasn't as lucky with the heat. Wearing a white blouse and a black wraparound skirt, my long dark brown hair tied in a pony tail, I was so hot I felt perspiration dripping down my back.

As I descended the grassy levee, the man looked up and smiled at me.

I raised my camera and said, "Y'all mind if I take your picture?"

He seemed surprised, but was eager to oblige. He wasn't having much luck fishing. He told me his name was Freddie. Tall and slim, Freddie had a wide smile.

Kneeling on one knee next to him, I focused on his dark face and felt my skirt opening around my legs. When I sat down, I could see that my skirt had opened a great deal and Freddie had noticed also. I closed my skirt and took another couple pictures. But my mind wasn't on the pictures anymore, it was on the rush I felt when I'd noticed him looking up my skirt.

In the past, I had caught men looking up my dress and it always gave me a thrill, especially if they were black. Once, at a shoe store, while I was trying on sandals and wearing a skirt that was much too short, I discovered the black man helping me in and out of my sandals was staring right between my legs. I became so turned on, I tried six pairs before leaving.

Sitting only a few feet from Freddie, I decided to go for the rush again. I pulled my knees up to my chest and rested my camera atop my knees. I looked through the camera lens at him and snapped away. My skirt slowly opened around my thighs. Through the lens, I could see him peeking at me. I felt a flush cross my face because I knew the white panties I wore were very sheer.

After an exciting minute, I put my camera next to me and leaned back on my hands. I closed my eyes and lifted my face toward the sun. The heat on my face matched the heat building within me. I could *feel* him staring at me. When I looked back, he was looking at my ass. With my knees as high as they were, the entire bottom of my panties was open to view.

"So what kind of fish do you catch here?"

"Drum. Redfish. Trout." Freddie finally looked at my face. "Sometimes even flounder." He lifted his line out of the water, checked his bait and put the line back in.

Freddie continued stealing peeks at my panties as he fished. I looked around and made sure we were alone before slowly removing my shoes, one at a time, crossing my legs like a man as I did. With my shoes off, I raised my knees high again and made sure my skirt opened all the way. I like wearing wraparound skirts because they are cool and breezy. I've had plenty experience sitting and keeping them closed. Except for this day, when I worked at my best to open it.

I didn't want to be too obvious, so I grabbed my camera and changed the film. Folding my legs, I sat cross-legged, like an Indian, placing the camera in my lap. Sitting like that caused my skirt to open to the waist. I could see, as I changed the film that my panties were totally exposed. My full mat of dark pubic hair was easily distinguishable beneath my sheer panties. And, since I'm Italian and somewhat hairy, a great deal of my pubic hair was sticking out the side of my panties. I could feel Freddie's eyes right on my crotch, especially when I finished with the camera and put it aside and leaned back on my hands.

My heart raced as I sat with the entire front of my panties exposed to Freddie's peering gaze. After a full minute, I decided it was time to increase the heat. I reached over and pretended to scratch my inner thigh. Then I pulled my panties aside a little and toyed with them. Freddie quit pretending he wasn't looking.

I grinned. "I'm sure y'all have seen a woman's panties before."

I moved my fingers to the top of my bikini panties and pulled them up as if to straighten them. That only succeeded in exposing more of my dark pubic hair. I felt very naughty.

"It's so hot," I complained.

Freddie suggested I take a dip in the bay.

"That's OK," I said.

He decided a demonstration was in order and jumped into the dark brown water. I turned my legs to him and wiggled to the edge of the bank, letting my feet soak in the warm water, all the way to my knees.

Freddie swam back to me. I lifted my butt and pulled my skirt completely out from under me. Then I moved my knees apart to allow him a better view of my crotch as he swam up and stared. Freddie startled me when he touched my foot.

I yanked it back and then laughed.

"Thought it was a crab."

I put my foot back in the water. Freddie tickled it and I pulled it away again. He reached for my other foot; it didn't take long to realize he was pulling my feet apart to open up my legs. I leaned back and let him, asking him not to tickle me, but telling him he could rub my tired, hot feet. He did just that, massaging my toes as he spread my legs.

I had him where I wanted him, at my feet. Then again, he had my legs where they wanted them, open.

Freddie moved between my legs and splashed a light spray of water on the front of my panties.

"That feels good," I purred.

The warm water cooled my super-heated crotch. He lifted a handful of bay water and poured it there.

Massaging my foot, Freddie's face crept closer, just inches from my crotch as he stared at my panties. He lifted another handful of water to drop on my crotch. I leaned back on my elbows and turned my face to the sun again. Freddie poured more water on my panties, and when I looked back I could see his head between my open legs, ogling my wet panties. I'd seen wet T-shirt contests on TV, but I never expected to be the feature attraction of a wet panty show.

Even from my angle I could see my soaked panties hid little.

Freddie began to drop water on my thighs, all the way down to my knees and then rubbed the water against my skin, his fingers rolling up my thighs until he reached my panties. Another handful of water on my crotch was followed by a soft touch.

"That feels nice," I said breathlessly.

Freddie gently rubbed the front of my panties. I felt his fingers working against my pubic hair. I bit my lower lip and looked at him. He smiled back; and I started pumping my hips.

I was so turned on, I felt my heart thundering. I reached around and removed the band from my pony tail and shook my hair out. My heavy breathing increased and I closed my eyes again.

Freddie's fingers moved slightly and slipped into my panties. I shuddered as he fingered my pussy lips.

"Yes," I heard myself say. "Yes!"

Freddie's free hand began working my panties down as his magic fingers manipulated my clit. I panted as my hips gyrated against his fingering.

He pulled off my panties.

Freddie kissed my left knee, then my right knee and kissed his way up my thighs as I lay back and opened my legs completely for him. His mouth joined his fingers and he kissed my pussy.

I came immediately and he sank his tongue into me. I bounced and reached for the pleasure that engulfed me in waves as I lay there with a strange black man tonguing my pussy. For a moment, I realized how incredible it was – us next to this Mississippi bay.

I began to unbutton my blouse, but my fingers stumbled. Freddie climbed out and helped me. Dripping on me as I lay there, he deftly unbuttoned my blouse, unsnapped my bra and had me topless in seconds.

He untied my wrap skirt and I was naked.

He stepped out of his shorts and stood there, his swollen cock sticking straight up.

I went up on my elbows and watched him stroke it. Turning around I looked up at the deserted levee that separated the bay from the roads beyond, then back at the wide expanse of the bay. Miles away, small white houses dotted the other side of the bay.

Freddie took my hand and pulled me up. I walked with rubbery legs to the base of the levee.

I was going to do it!

Trembling as I sat on the grass, I told myself I was *really* going to do it, let a black man fuck me – in broad daylight. How deliciously wicked!

I lay back and opened my legs. Freddie stood between them, with his up-like-a-flag-pole cock. He went down on his knees and let his eyes trace their way from my pussy to my stomach to my breasts. He moved over me until his face was directly over mine. Then he leaned down and kissed me, very gently at first and then harder and hotter, slipping his wide tongue in me.

I kissed him back. I closed my eyes, and felt the weight of his chest against my aching breasts. Then I felt the tip of his cock pressing against my wet pussy. He worked his hips and impaled me slowly, sending waves of pleasure through me, sending me over the top again.

He was gentle, easing the full length of his cock all the way into me. I was so completely filled, I couldn't believe it. I tried my best not to cry out. Freddie rocked me, screwed me, worked my ass into the grass. I worked the muscles in my vagina against his cock and we fucked hard. I came again, this time deep inside.

My God, he was not only big, but hot, super-hot. His body felt like a burning coal atop me as he screwed me good, right there in the sunshine, next to the bay. I closed my eyes and rode with him, letting myself go as he put it to me. His unrelenting cock continued pounding me.

When he started talking dirty, it sent me through another quivering climax.

"Come on, white girl. I want you to come. You like getting fucked by a black man. You like black dick, don't you?"

I clawed at his back.

"Oh, yeah, baby," he moaned. "You like my black dick in you."

"*Yes!*" I cried.

"Tell me how much you like it."

He was pounding me big time.

"Oh, *yes!* Fuck me! *Fuck me!*"

I don't know how long it lasted. I came again and again before he exploded in me like a pile driver. I felt his warm come spurting in me, his balls slapping against my ass. It was fantastic!

I was grateful when he climbed off. I was so hot, I needed the air. After I finally caught my breath, I leaned up on my elbows.

He looked into my eyes and asked, of all things, if I was married.

"Yes," I gasped.

"Good." He smiled. "I love fucking another man's wife."

He leaned over and kissed me and told me how beautiful I was. I lay back and closed my eyes. Freddie kissed my nipples, my belly and my legs and back up again to my neck. Then he lay next to me to finally catch his breath.

I drifted for a while, but a sound above made me sit up suddenly.

Freddie was halfway up the levee. Reaching the top, he peeked over and looked back and shook his head.

"Nothing," he said as he came back down and moved past me to our clothes and my camera. He brought them back.

"I'd like to keep these." Freddie held out my panties.

I nodded. He slipped on his shorts and helped me dress. I stood on shaky legs and he steadied me.

"Can I see you again?" he asked. "You are one beautiful, fine woman." Then he kissed my lips ever so gently.

"Yes," I said. "I want to see you again too."

We planned to meet at the same place again. Next week. Same time. Same day. I hurried back to my Lexus, which I had parked beneath a wide magnolia tree at the end of a dirt road.

My heart raced as I drove away. I could still feel his lips kissing me, his fingers exploring my body. I could almost feel his long shaft sinking into me.

When I got home, my husband was in his usual position in front of the TV.

"Did you find anything? he asked, smiling.

I held up a shopping bag.

"Good," he said and waved me over to his wheelchair. He pursed his lips and I pecked them and as usual, they were cold.

"I'm hungry," my husband said as he looked back at his TV.

I went into the kitchen to fix supper, my heart stammering, my legs still a little wobbly. I tried not to think how long it had been since I'd been good and fucked. Years.

And never like I'd been that afternoon. Never.

I'd found exactly what I was searching for, I reminded myself.

What next?

As I opened the refrigerator door, I couldn't stop my mind from moving forward one week. Same place. Same time.

It rained that day, one week later. Before dawn, a storm blew in from the gulf, sending rain in sheets across our lawn, bending the heavy branches of our oaks, slapping against our picture window.

Sitting on the sofa, I watched the rain as my husband dozed in his wheelchair. Some inane game show droned in the background from his TV.

A half-hour before I was to meet Freddie, I sneaked into the garage and backed my car out and drove away through the downpour. I had to bypass two flooded roads and could not park on the same dirt road, which looked more like a lake.

Driving along the street that paralleled the levee, I slowed as I approached the area where we were to meet. Maybe Freddie was waiting in his own car, or maybe he was across the levee, waiting in the warm rain.

Slowing to a stop, I looked up at the levee and a dark figure stood there in the hard rain. I felt myself smile, felt my heartbeat rising as I backed my Lexus to a side street and parked.

"What better cover," I said aloud as I climbed out into the driving rain storm to meet a soaking man waiting to screw me. I could barely see him standing there, atop the levee. I started up the levee, but slipped on the wet grass.

Freddie rushed down, sliding on the grass and grabbed me. He helped me to my feet and then up and over the levee to the bay side. For a moment, I saw angry Bay St Louis. White caps slammed against the dock.

Freddie leaned close to my ear and said, "I was so worried you wouldn't come."

I pulled his face around and kissed him, my tongue reaching for his. His body responded automatically as he pulled me close. A wave of windswept rain seemed to engulf us momentarily and we pulled apart, gasping for air.

A gust of wind pushed us both back against the levee and swept the rain out of my face. Sitting on the grass, I pulled Freddie close. Incredibly, the rain lessened and the storm's fury seemed to flow away, down the bay, leaving us with a steady drizzle.

Freddie wiped the water from my face and said, "I thought I'd never see you again."

And I knew – I had him. I didn't have to fuck him there in the rain, I had him. But his warm hands moved to my breasts and slowly unbuttoned my blouse. I leaned back on the drenched grass and let him undress me.

Freddie's body was super-hot, even slick with rain, and he sent me to a throbbing climax before gushing in me with long, deep grunts.

The rain stopped as soon as we dressed and stood up.

"Will you come next week? Same time?" Freddie's deep voice was filled with emotion. My hook was well set in him.

I gave it a little tug by not answering immediately.

"You will, won't you?" He looked around. "No one will know."

I sank the hook deeper. "No one can ever know."

He nodded.

"You didn't go brag to your friends how you fucked a white woman, did you?"

"No. I'm not a stupid man."

I reached up and touched his lips with my fingers. "Next week. Same time."

When he started to follow me across the levee, I told him to stay until he heard my car pull away.

"Next week," he said anxiously.

"Next week." I smiled slightly and he smiled widely and I walked away, leaving the hook in him.

That evening I asked my husband if he wanted to watch me shower.

He said there was a game on TV.

He used to sit in the bathroom doorway in his wheelchair and watch me lather up, rinse off, climb out naked to reach for a towel. His skinny eyes would leer at my body parts as I dried off.

He'd back up and sit near the corner of our king sized bed as I sat and blow dried my hair. Finishing, I'd put the dryer away and lay back on the bedspread. My husband positioned himself to see better as I would spread my legs and slowly stroke myself.

It always took a while for me to come and most of the time I faked it.

After, while up on my elbows I'd watch my husband's ashen

face. His breathing was shallow and quick and his face quivered as he stared glassy-eyed at my body.

I'd wait, but he always managed to catch his breath and sink back in his wheelchair.

That was how I thought of the way to take his shortened breath away – permanently.

I didn't show the following week. I let Freddie simmer.

Exactly one week after I didn't show, I dolled up in a pink mini-dress, white thigh-high stockings, a white French lace bra with matching panties and white spiked heels. I curled my hair and made-up my face like the girl at Sak's in New Orleans taught me.

My husband didn't even see me leave.

Freddie sat waiting atop the levee. As soon as he spotted my car, he stood and brushed off his pants. I stopped and opened the passenger door for him. He ran down.

Leaning in the open door, he gasped, "I didn't think you were coming."

"Will you do something for me?"

Freddie looked at my legs. His gaze rose up my outfit back to my face and pouty lips.

"Sure," He said.

"Climb in."

Freddie jumped in and quickly fastened his seat belt. Today he wore a nice polo shirt and dressy tan jeans.

I pulled away and it took Freddie several minutes before asking where we were going.

"To my house. I want to make love to you on my bed."

Freddie looked around again, as if making sure we weren't seen.

"You sure you won't get caught?"

I didn't answer. My heart raced as I turned the Lexus around to head home. My husband was there, sleeping in his wheelchair in front of the TV. Whatever happened next, I told myself, I was in a no lose situation.

He could divorce me, kick me out.

So?

We had no pre-nuptial agreement. I'd get half, eventually.

Maybe, just maybe, it'll shock him to death. He'll hear us, wheel in and see this big black man banging his virginal white wife. The walls of his sick heart will cave in and I'll be free. It was a no-lose situation.

Secretly, more than anything, I wanted him to die.

I parked in the garage.

Freddie hesitated getting out.

"You sure we won't get caught?"

"My husband's in a wheelchair. He's a gentle as a kitten."

Freddie climbed out. "A wheelchair?"

I nodded.

"He some kinda war veteran?"

I walked around and right up to Freddie's face. "Car wreck."

I brushed Freddie's lips with mine.

"He have a gun?"

I laughed. "He's afraid of guns. Always has been."

Freddie's nostrils flared as he took in my perfume. I turned and led the way into the house, through the kitchen and down the hall to the master bedroom. Along the way, I glanced over and saw my husband parked in front of his TV, in front of another inane talk show.

I left the bedroom door open.

Facing Freddie, I started to unbutton my dress.

He stepped up and took over.

With trembling fingers, he removed my dress. Running his hands over my breasts, he kissed my neck. His fingers moved around and unsnapped my bra. Freeing my breasts, he sucked them, nibbling on each nipple, sending shivers through me.

He kissed his way down to my belly. On his knees, he tucked his fingers into my panties and worked them down. He French-kissed my bush, his tongue probing me as he pulled off my heels.

He left my thigh-high stockings on as he sat me on the bed and started taking off his clothes. I lay back and peeked around him, but we hadn't awakened my husband. For a moment I wondered – what if we didn't?

Standing between my open knees, Freddie rubbed the tip of his stiff cock against my pussy lips. I was wet enough for him to slowly, ever so slowly, impale me. I curled my back and took every thick, delicious inch.

Holding my hips, Freddie began fucking me in long smooth strokes.

I cried out and he paused and I pulled him down on me, my lips searching for his. Freddie rode me, dug his dick into me, banged me good. I cried out again.

"Come on," I gasped. "Fuck me!"

"Jesus! You are so beautiful."

Freddie got down to business, sending me through a deep climax as he worked his cock in me. God, he fucked the hell out of me, banging me good and I gasped and cried out again and again as we bounced around my bed.

I held on to his ass as he pounded me, letting out a cry with each stroke.

I almost came again, when I suddenly caught a glimpse of my husband sitting in the doorway. I blinked and looked again and he was there. His skinny eyes were ovaled and his mouth open.

I bucked back with Freddie and felt him about to explode. I reached for the pleasure, my muscles grabbing his dick. Freddie cried out and came and his first hot spurt sent me over the top. We came together in one steamy, gushing, wet fuck.

Freddie collapsed on me and it took a while for us to catch our breaths.

"Man," Freddie finally said. "You were wild." He kissed my lips and I kissed him back.

When he rolled off, I looked at my husband, who hadn't moved. He sat stone-faced in the doorway, his hands gripping the handles of his wheelchair.

Freddie gasped when he saw my husband.

"Damn," he said as he climbed out of bed. "Look man . . . I . . . uh."

It took a minute for him to realize my husband wasn't moving.

"What's the matter with him?"

I shrugged and lay there, spread eagle, Freddie's cum oozing out of my pussy.

Freddie scooped up his clothes and started dressing. Shaking his head, he muttered, "Man scared the shit outta me, staring like that."

My husband's eyes were fixed widely at us.

Half-dressed, Freddie asked if there was any other way out.

"Through the bathroom," I said.

He bolted.

I called out. "Same time, next week?"

Freddie didn't answer.

A few seconds later, I heard the front door slam.

I lay there and watched.

When my husband blinked, I knew he wasn't dead. Not yet. I could see his breathing was extra shallow.

I sat up, my legs still open. Reaching down, I wiped my pussy lips and came up with Freddie's gummy semen.

"Nice African come," I told my husband. "He really put it to me."

My husband made a gurgling sound.

I licked my fingers.

My husband started shaking.

I crawled over and told him what it felt like, being fucked by a real man.

"His cock was so hard and hot and he fucked me good. He fucked my lily white pussy. And it wasn't the first time."

My husband tried to say something, but nothing came out.

I climbed off the bed and checked his pulse. His arm was cold and his pulse shallow, but steady.

I let go of his arm and sat on the edge of the bed.

"He's bringing a couple friends next time. I feel like being gangbanged."

A sound came out of my husband's mouth.

"What is it? Come on, you can talk."

"Mmm . . . Mmm."

I folded my arms.

He tried again. "Mmm . . . Mmm."

"Mmm . . . Mmm," I mimicked him. "What's that? You turned idiot on me?"

"More!" he said clearly.

"What?"

"I want . . . to see . . . more."

He raised his right hand and pointed to the bed. His eyes alight, my husband said it again, "I want to see more!"

Coins For The Ferryman

Robert Buckley

I hate islands.

I cannot understand their allure, the way people marry the words *Island* and *paradise*. Paradise, my ass. An island is a trap, a prison, a fucking Alcatraz, a place that reminds you every day you wake up on it, there's no place else to go.

Pirates understood that. When they really wanted to fuck with someone, they didn't kill him, or even torture him. They marooned him on a goddamned island. And that's what I was — marooned, courtesy of Wang Fu Chu.

That crazy Chinaman – he was affectionately called Fuck You by his nearest and dearest, of which I was one. Nobody understood how he made his money, but that didn't stop the greedy hordes from rushing to jump in behind his flashy parade. Always grinning, he could charm the pig right out of the python's belly.

A few weeks ago, he had more cash on hand than half the world's countries. He sent me to Chaukunamaug Island on a buying mission. He already owned a piece of the island, with a modest ramshackle house, but he wanted more – as much as he could get. I was supposed to charm the locals into giving up their piece.

The problem was, Old Money had set roots down deep in the bedrock there centuries ago and wasn't moving. It had become an exclusive rock, a place from where trust fund brats could sail their boats to the Vineyard, party in Edgartown, then bid "ta" to their envious peers. Social climbers went to the Vineyard to be seen, but pined for an invitation to picnic on Chaukuna-maug.

The only other way on and off the island was a little rust bucket of a ferry that made irregular runs from Woods Hole, but never in choppy seas. It could carry a single car in a pinch, but mostly it ferried supplies and a guy from one of the Cape banks to stuff the ATM at the dock every so often.

I spent my first two weeks being wined and dined by the swells, who enjoyed my company the way they would an exotic animal. It was all very casual, of course: khaki pants and skirts, polo shirts and shorts. A sweater, sleeves tied around the neck when out of doors, was standard uniform. For the most part they were a boring but amiable bunch who had no intention of selling a single clod to Wang. They just liked being asked – it amused them.

Then everything changed. The cell phone stopped working, and so did my ATM card. It didn't take long to find out what happened; it was all over CNN. Wang had split for parts unknown. The SEC and a dozen other alphabet soup federal agencies were two steps behind him but hot on his trail.

It seems Wang had been running one of the biggest, multi-national ponzi schemes in history. He'd taken all the big names for millions, maybe billions. And those big names were pissed for being made to look like chumps.

I had to admire the crazy bastard. Yeah, crazy like a fox. But he left me stranded in suddenly hostile territory. Invitations to dinner ceased, just when I needed to look out for my next meal. Walks through that collection of fish shanties that passed for a village drew cold stares.

I had to go there to use the public phone, even though I had run out of the kind of goodwill that accepts a collect call. I ran in to Walker there. The little prick sneered contemptuously, but didn't say a word. This was the same guy who just days before asked me to fuck his cute little air-headed wife while he recorded us with a camcorder.

Dodie was a screamer who liked to be called dirty names while she was fucked. I was doing her doggie style and brought her right to the edge when I called her "cocksucker." Damn, she came so hard I thought she was having a seizure. She squirted too, even left a puddle on the floor.

Dodie walked a couple of steps behind Walker. Our eyes met and she smiled a little before ducking into Bones Tavern with him.

I made my calls and came up empty. I was shut off. I couldn't expect any money, and had no way to get off the island. None of these sons of bitches would sail me off, even though I must have offended their sensibilities by sticking around, like a big smelly turd under their stuck-up noses.

All the cash I had was in my wallet, a couple of hundred bucks. I figured it would last until the ferry pulled in, or until the feds bothered to come out there to get me. Meanwhile, I had a roof over my head, and the power was still on.

I decided to have a drink.

Bones' place was all raw, unfinished wood, even the bar. Bones was too – raw, that is. He looked even more out-of-place on that hunk of rock than I did. The swells used to whisper about him, about how he'd once been an enforcer for some racketeer – one of the "big ones."

He was compactly built, and gave the appearance of a bullet, amplified by his hairless pate. His eyes were cold, liquid blue. He looked like a man who kept secrets well, especially his own. But he was one more friendly face on the rock.

He smiled and nodded when I sat at the bar.

"Jack D, straight," I said.

He poured a shot and followed it with a glass of water. He leaned toward me as if he were about to communicate some secret intelligence, but glanced to my left and retreated.

Dodie sat on the stool next to mine. I scanned the room but didn't see Walker. I figured he was in the head – that's what they called the john around there.

"Hi, Rick."

"Mrs Walker," I nodded. She frowned.

"I – I'm sorry about – well, I mean, it's not your fault that."

"What?"

"I know people are being horrid to you. I just wanted you to know that – I still like you." She placed her hand on my thigh – my dick twitched.

She was pretty, not exactly a raving beauty, but petite and curvy. Her short brown hair and brown doe eyes gave the appearance of a shy, sheltered girl that contradicted the writhing harlot I'd fucked on Laurence Endicott Walker's high-polished living room floor.

I glanced toward the men's room, then closed my hand over her knee.

"Thanks," I said, and let it slide up her bare thigh and under her shorts until my finger tips touched the edge of her panties. She slowly sucked in air and closed her eyes. Her cheeks reddened.

I leaned to whisper in her ear. "I have a soft spot for bad girls like you. Do you have a soft, wet spot for me?"

She gasped and bit her lip.

"Do you?"

She nodded furiously, but didn't open her eyes.

"Is your pussy dripping for me?"

"Please!" she hissed.

"My cock misses your tight little cunt." I slid a finger inside her panties and twirled the downy hairs it encountered.

"Rick, oh my God."

"Can you sneak out?"

"Please, Rick – I mustn't."

"Tonight, after he's drunk himself to sleep. Come by – I want you to be my slut again."

"Oh, but . . ."

"You want to be my slut, don't you?"

"Yes."

"Say it."

"I want to be your – slut. Oh, please, Rick. Make me do dirty things."

"Tonight."

"Yes."

"Dodie!" It was Walker.

She jumped off the stool and hurried to join him at a table. If looks could kill, she would have dissolved under his glare, but he said nothing to her, or to me.

Bones refilled my glass and grinned. "Must not have much of a dick – if he can't satisfy a little slip of a girl like that."

I chuckled. "It's all about money in the bank, Bones. It makes up for other shortcomings."

Bones grinned and swiped a wet spot on the bar with a rag.

"Bones, what the hell are you doing out on this rock?"

"Like everyone else here, I own a piece of it."

"But – you don't seem – I mean, how did you happen to come by it? These pricks don't sell . . ."

He gave me a look that said I was edging too close to matters best left alone. But, then he smiled. "It was a gift."

It was enough. Bones had done someone a unique favor, and a sliver of island property was his reward.

"Hey, Bones, you've got a boat. How about you give me a lift off this rock? I can pay for the gas."

"Can't – the wife has the boat. She took the in-laws down to Block Island, won't be back for five days."

"Shit. What the hell do you want to go from one freaking island to another for?"

Bones laughed, then as quick as my next breath he resumed his poker face and said, "Watch yourself."

It felt like someone poked a gun barrel into my shoulder. I spun around. It wasn't a gun, just a finger, wielded by Bradley Procter Sloane Whitman. I had to wonder how many family names they could tack on to one handle before it shattered under its own weight of syllables.

Every tribe has its leader, and on this island it was Brad Whitman. He loomed over me, all six feet five inches of him. He was a solid guy, a true sailor. He'd crewed a few America's Cup races and kept himself in excellent shape – a poster boy for good genes. His square jaw was set tight. Just enough gray in the temples to affect that badge of Brahmin nobility. He had feted me at a clambake he'd organized just so the island swells could waste my time discussing real estate they had no intention of selling.

"Hello, Brad. You want to be careful with that thing – it has a nail in it."

He continued to glower. "You're still here – why?"

"You know, I ask myself that same question and I keep coming back to the same answer: I have no way to get off this rock."

"You could try swimming."

"No, thanks. I'll put in here until the ferry arrives."

"You've taken advantage of the goodwill of the fine people of this island. Now that you've been exposed as the agent of a flim-flam artist . . ."

"Whoa, there, Brad. I've been left high and dry by my recent employer. I didn't crash anyone's clambake. And – be honest – I was a momentary diversion in your monotonous routines."

He poked me again in the shoulder. Damn, it hurt. I knew he was trying to goad me into swinging at him, but I wasn't taking the bait. Just one look at him and I knew he could wipe the place up with my ass. He was also an ex-Ivy League boxing champ, a Yalie, Skull & Bones and all that other manly man circle-jerk nonsense.

"Look, Brad, I'm getting off this rock as soon as I can. Let's just agree to stay out of each other's way."

"I don't think so. You take advantage of our hospitality – that's one thing. You interfere with a man's family, that's quite another."

So, that was his beef. I glanced over toward Walker, who sat sneering and safe at his table. Dodie fidgeted beside him with both sets of fingertips pressed to her mouth. I'm not sure what the family connection was, whether Brad was his uncle or a super-cousin. But, Bradley was the one he obviously went running to when he couldn't fix his own mess.

"Brad, I never intrude anywhere I'm not invited."

I could see the blood bubble up into his face and a thick vein bulge at his temple. He wasn't going to wait for me to swing first. Then I sensed something just as solid and dangerous rise up behind me.

"Not in my place, Brad," Bones intoned evenly.

Bradley expelled air through his nostrils like a radiator venting steam. He looked down at me again.

"Trash like you will never understand family values," he fumed.

"Do it for the children," I replied. He looked confused.

"I'm sorry," I said. "I thought we were about to engage in duel of clichés."

"Splendid! What a droll exercise." The voice was unfamiliar to me.

A shiver rattled Bradley. We turned together toward the rail-thin man in the black cape. Long gray hair fell freely over his shoulders. His face was angled toward a sharp chin, and he grinned with small pointy barracuda teeth. If I were to guess his age – maybe sixty, but I suspected he was much younger.

The blonde beside him hadn't said goodbye to her twenties yet. She was tall and Nordic-looking. Her hair was held in a pony tail that fell over one shoulder. She wore short-shorts that enhanced the length of legs that needed no enhancement, and a vest that exposed a flat, tight stomach. The vest hung open, barely covering her breasts that were each just as large as a handful.

Bradley turned his back to me. "Ashton, I thought you were gone from the island for good."

The man answered with a reedy laugh. "Oh, never say never, Yale Brother. Boola-Boola, eh? I've had a yen for fun and games – especially games. We've played such delightful games on this island."

I detected a collective shudder run through the place. Bradley turned toward a table where three other swells stirred uneasily in their seats. They got up and the whole lot walked out of the place without another word, leaving the stranger grinning.

He turned to me and bowed. I lifted my glass to him and let my eyes climb the woman from her toes to her bee-stung lips.

"Come, Gretchen," he said, and they moved to a table in a corner. Everyone else stood and walked out.

*　　*　　*

I left Bones to the stranger and his Valkyrie and made my way to the desolate crop of weathered granite where Wang's house stood. It was a cinder block ranch that looked something like a bomb shelter. It was amazing Wang had acquired it. Someone had broken the trust and sold to an outsider. It had once belonged to an old couple – the kind of folks the swells called "the help".

Domestics and other service types lived through the summer in the shanties of the village. But this pair had been favored with a place of their own, probably after a lifetime of waiting hand-and-foot on their employer. But the island isn't someplace you live year round. I figure the old folks saw their chance, sold to Wang and high-tailed it to Florida or Arizona. They were never spoken of.

It was cozy despite its austere look, with a bed and a bar. Sea breezes kept it cool.

I spotted Dodie a mile away in the bright full moon light. It must have been around 1:30 in the morning. She rode her bike up the furrowed road like a schoolgirl. I greeted her and put her bike behind a wall.

"I'm not wearing any underwear," she said as I hustled her inside. She let her shorts fall to her ankles, and then kicked off her boat shoes. She stood and grinned in a cropped T-shirt.

"Not wasting any time, eh?"

"Oh, Rick. It's so boring here. I hate it when Bink brings me here each summer."

It took me a second to realize "Bink" was her husband.

"Why don't you ask him to take a real vacation? Travel."

"Oh, we do. But, it's more to get away so he can . . ."

I let her silence hang for a moment. "Where he can indulge in his kinks out of sight of the family?"

She shrugged. "You know he likes to – share me."

"Oh, sweetie, and I'm so glad he does," I winked. She grinned, and looked as sweet and disarming as a little girl. Even her pussy was bare.

"Just where has he shared you, my sweet?"

"Oh, can we talk about that later? I've been having such dirty thoughts."

"Plenty of time to play, Cupcake. I'm just curious why a man would lend a sweet little morsel like you out to – who?"

She sat on a lounger and lifted one leg over an armrest. Her pussy was a slick, gleaming slit that she teased with the little finger of her left hand.

"Really, just a few men. He likes to get away, even though we've played games on the island."

"Really? Do you mean the proper wives of Chaukunamaug have swap meets? Why, aren't you all related? That's downright incestuous."

She giggled. "No, nothing like that – except . . ."

"What?"

"You saw the man at the bar this afternoon?"

"The creepy caped dude?"

"Ashton. He used to be a friend of Brad's."

"Used to?"

"Ashton is a writer and an artist. He has some pretty funny ideas – not that I ever read anything of his. But, I guess he met Brad when they went to Yale. That big house at the western end of the island, that belongs to Ashton."

"That ark? It looks like a hotel."

"It used to be. It's huge; it has a lot of rooms. It's been closed up for years, but now that Ashton's back . . ."

"What?"

"Well, Ashton used to have a lot of parties there – kinky parties. He used to hire people from off island, performers, sort of."

"What do you mean, sort of?"

"They used to perform – well – sex."

"Really."

"Yeah, like, one time Ashton staged a little playlet, 'Innocence Betrayed'. A girl played this really sweet, wholesome student. But a bunch of guys kidnap her and take her to an old house. Then they rape her and make her do really wicked and disgusting things."

I could tell by the speed that Dodie's finger flicked her folds that she enjoyed recounting the drama.

"They made her suck all their cocks, and then they took turns, you know, doing her. Then three or four of them did her at once, like, every hole in her body was filled. At the end she begged them to fuck her some more, and do even worse things because she had turned into a total slut."

I thought I detected a wistful sigh escape Dodie's lips.

"Uh-huh. So, what other kind of entertainment did this Ashton provide?"

"Huh? Oh, well, he was famous for his games."

"Games?"

"Yeah, but, that's what got him into trouble too. At least, people stopped going there and after a while he left. He's been gone for years."

"What game in particular?"

"Rick, please, can't you fuck me now? I don't want to talk about . . ."

"C'mon, Sweets, tell me, and then I promise you we'll play games all our own."

"Oh, OK," she pouted. "Well, one night, Ashton had some of us, men and women, go upstairs to the rooms and get naked in bed. The rooms were pitch dark so we couldn't see, and nobody could see us. The idea was that those left downstairs would draw a number and go to that room. Then the woman in bed was supposed to blow the visitor, or if the visitor was a woman, she was to blow the guy in bed. Then later, we were all supposed to write down whose cock we thought we'd sucked. Ashton would never say who, unless we were right."

"Hmm, not too complicated."

"Yeah, but you don't know how cruel Ashton is. After it was all over, he revealed that he had sent a man to a man's room. So, one of the guys ended up getting blown by another guy, but they could never know for sure who. Well, you have to understand the men on this island. For them to think even maybe they'd been sucked off by some gay actor that Ashton snuck over . . . Well, can you imagine? It was such a dirty trick."

The gleam in her eye told me that Dodie got a kick out of the dirty trick despite the effort she put into keeping a straight face.

I did imagine the panic that set in among the bluebloods, who invested such stock in their masculinity – all in the service of siring the next generations, of course.

"Sometimes I ask Bink," she grinned. "He gets all flustered."

"He gets off on watching his wife fuck other men, but an accidental blowjob from a guy gets him crazy, huh?"

"Know what? When he shares me, and a strange man is filling my pussy and making me come, I like to think about Bink sucking the dick of the next man to take me, just to get him ready."

She lifted her T-shirt over her head. I held out my hand and pulled her to her feet, then spun her around and pushed her to her knees as she bent over the recliner.

"OK, you little slut."

She gasped as I reached between her ass cheeks and worked my fingers over her clit. Her buns twisted one way, then the other as she groaned and whimpered.

I quickly accumulated a handful of her gooey juices and smeared them over my cock.

"You wanted to be the girl in the play, didn't you, slut?" She moaned in response. I smeared more of her free-flowing juice over my hardened cock.

"You want it all, don't you? No hole unfucked."

"Please! Fuck my cunt."

"No way. Bitches like you need their asses filled."

"Please, it'll hurt."

I pushed my cockhead, lubed with her pussy fluids, to the ring of her anus. Despite her protests she was trying to relax it enough for me to make entry.

"Don't, please, don't make me be bad."

I pushed past her initial resistance as she exhaled a guttural growl. I kept up the steady penetrating pressure until my cock slid into her bowels and I was buried in her backside up to my balls. I withdrew and plunged again as she began to writhe. Again I withdrew and plunged until I achieved a steady rhythm.

Dodie was crying and squirming. "No, don't make me – don't rape my ass!"

"Yeah, you want it just like the girl in the play. I'll take you off this island, cunt. I'll take you back to New York with me, and make you audition for a pimp, and he'll make you fuck and suck every greasy cock in sight."

"Oh, God, please."

"And, when he's satisfied that you're a filthy fuck bucket I'll sell you to him, and you'll have to fuck for a living, every day, constantly fucked in the ass, fucked in the cunt, fucked in the mouth . . ."

Dodie shrieked and her muscles grabbed my cock like a fist. Jesus, it hurt. Her whole body shuddered as her head thrashed. I tried to pull out but couldn't.

"Christ! Let go!"

Warm liquid ran down our thighs. Dodie relaxed and I drew my cock out of her ass, but the friction did the trick. My dick jerked up like a spring board and spewed jets of come between her ass crack.

"Mother of God," I gasped, and fell backward onto the floor.

Dodie remained slumped against the recliner. Then she stirred.

"Oh, my – I never came so hard or so fast. My poor asshole. You bad, bad man."

I got to my feet, and lifted her to her own. I marched her to the bathroom and we stepped into the shower. I soaped her until I worked up a cloak of suds from her shoulders to her ass. My dick was hard again. I slapped it against her thigh and ordered, "Clean it."

She knelt and began to work her soapy hands around it, occasionally rubbing it against her cheek. Then she began to play with my balls, working up a lather. I leaned into the spray and let it rinse the soap away. She took my cock into her mouth. Her tongue teased the tip, while her fingers skillfully played along its length.

It plopped from her lips just long enough for her to plead, "Come in my mouth. Aren't I a good cocksucker?"

"Oh, yeah, Cupcake. You're the best."

"Tell me," she mewed.

"Cocksucker – dicklicker – come guzzler."

She sucked me with a mission, while her fingers worked her pussy. I was getting close when she began to hum. I launched my load into her throat. Her shoulders shuddered. Then she held me in her mouth until my dick deflated and slipped from her lips.

I turned off the water, toweled her, then myself. Then I carried her into the bedroom. It was early yet; the sky hadn't even begun to lighten.

Dodie was the battery bunny when it came to sex, she just kept going and going . . . And I was getting punchy. Doggie-fucking her, I wove an elaborate gang-rape fantasy for her involving the Fall River City Council. It was time for a break.

I dozed, but she continued to play with my dick. I was content to lie passive and drained.

"Rick – give me a baby."

Jesus! I bolted into a sit. "What?"

"Bink and I have been married almost six years and I'm not pregnant. That's a long time; the family expects children. I'm worried."

I understood. Dodie wasn't saying she was worried either she or Bink weren't capable of producing another generation of Walkers, she was afraid if it didn't happen soon Walker would be under pressure to quietly divorce her. That cut her out of the Walker fortune. Not that she'd starve – Dodie's family was well-off by any normal standards, just nowhere near the Walkers.

"Is there a problem with Bink?"

"No, he just won't let me get off the pill. He doesn't want me to get pregnant by someone else."

I was beginning to understand the depths of Bink's need to farm out his pretty little wife.

"Cupcake, has it ever occurred to either of you how this hobby of his could – backfire?"

"It has."

"Huh? How?"

"A couple of years ago we stayed in Jamaica. Bink offered me to a young man who worked at the resort. He was particularly excited about watching us because – well – he was black, you know."

"Uh-huh."

"He was wonderful," she sighed. "He made me beg him 'till I cried. Then he told Bink to play with his 'Willy' while he fucked me 'proper.' I just love Jamaican accents."

"Uh-huh."

"Anyway, when we were leaving, Ethan told Bink that maybe someday he'd come up to the States and claim me for his whore. I just about wet my panties, but we never gave it much thought, until . . ."

"Don't tell me."

"Yup, about eight months later Bink got a call at home and turned so pale. It was Ethan, he was in New York with his family and he was planning to visit us. Can you imagine? He said he would claim his pretty white whore, or Bink could pay him for me. Can you imagine poor Bink having to buy his own wife?"

"No shit."

"Bink didn't know what to do. What would our neighbors in Weston think if a Jamaican man showed up demanding his white whore?" She giggled.

"So, what happened?"

"Bink ran to Bradley for help. They grew up together, you know. Bink always turned to Bradley like a big brother. Bradley took care of things."

"Did he pay the guy off?"

"No. You know Bones, of course."

"He had Bones talk to the kid?"

"Never bothered us again. I felt kind of badly for Ethan. He had a wonderful cock."

So Bones was still doing favors for them, or paying them back. I was pondering this when I thought I heard the tinkle of ice in a glass. Dodie heard it too and sat up with a start.

"Stay here," I said.

I wrapped a towel around my naked ass and tiptoed to the door, then down the narrow hall to where it opened into the living room. I heard hushed voices.

Then I saw the Valkyrie. She was handing a glass of liquor to Ashton, who was ensconced on the cheap lounger.

"Just make yourself at home."

He raised his glass. "Love what you've done to the place."

"I haven't done anything."

"Hmm, then perhaps your erstwhile employer. I see he maintained the chic décor à la Kmart. It evokes memories of the Daugherty couple – lovely old folks. I knew they'd sell it eventually, and piss off all my distant cousins. Care for a drink? I brought a variety of spirits."

I sat on the recliner. "Sure. Rum and soda."

"Lime?" asked Gretchen.

"Um – yeah."

She held out a bottle of Dark Jamaican as if for my approval. I took it, nodded and handed it back to her. She poured it into a glass filled with cubes.

"Well, sir," Ashton grinned. "I had hoped to return to this pathetic leftover from the Ice Age and cause such appalling consternation among my peers. But, it seems you've already put a bug up this island's rocky ass."

"Hmm, people around here have a tendency to turn on you rather quickly if your fortunes fall."

"Oh, don't they? Bad form, very bad form. But, like the scorpion, it's their nature."

A tiny voice from the bedroom called, "Rick?"

Ashton perked up. "Dorothy? Is that you, darling? How lovely. Come greet your Uncle Ashton."

Dodie peeked around the corner. "Oh, my God. Ashton – please don't tell Bradley."

Ashton cackled. "Bradley? Not your husband? Ah, but I suppose we all understand who the über-wolf is on the island. Not to worry, child. I'll not tell. I'm just delighted to see you. But the gentleman and I need to discuss some business."

Ashton gestured to the Valkyrie. "Gretchen, see to Mrs Walker."

Gretchen nodded and stepped over to Dodie. She towered over her the way Bradley towered over me. She took her arm gently but firmly and turned her back toward the bedroom.

Dodie meekly protested, but went along.

"Gretchen is a treasure," Ashton smirked. "Speaks seven languages, highly intelligent, impeccably educated – the product of an exclusive academy known to only a few of Europe's most privileged."

I nodded. From the bedroom I could hear Dodie. "No, stop – don't do that. Please, I don't want to – I don't – oh, God, stop – please-please-please . . ."

Dodie made a little cry, like an angel dying. Ashton grinned wider, one brow arched as high as his temple.

"Well, then. I'm sure little Dorothy told you about me. Around this accursed ground I am the fucking Antichrist, sir. Ask anyone."

"Pleased to make your acquaintance."

"You will be. You see, sir, I am an artist, a performance artist. I loathe static art. I prefer art that just – happens. And that is what I intend to do, sir, make something happen that will affect all – a shock wave, and I am ground zero."

"Good luck."

"I trust nothing to luck. You are to be my instrument, my catalyst. This will be my farewell performance, and my greatest. Things that are crooked will be put right – or at least made crooked in another fashion."

"Hmm, what do you have in mind? 'Farewell', you said?"

"I am dying, sir. I am told I have mere weeks to live."

"Sorry."

"Why, dying is also a performance, is it not? But, to the point, I have investigated you, sir. You have admirable qualities – loyalty, diligence, and I suspect a sense of justice."

"I'm a hack."

"Quite so – one of the Great Unwashed. Well, I prefer your

type. That is why I have named you as my sole heir and beneficiary.''

I sipped my drink. "Cut the shit."

"It's true. Gretchen will guide you after I've shaken the earthly bonds. She is an excellent attorney."

I sipped my drink again. "I understand you like to play games."

"Ha! Yes, I live for games. But make no mistake, sir. I am deadly serious about my games. I can't think of anything more appalling to these people than if a stranger, a wily predator such as yourself, got hold of a piece of their Eden."

I sat up. "I don't want it. I'm trying to get out of here."

"Come now; sell it if you wish. Just don't sell it to them – better some hotel chain or shady development company run by someone whose name ends in a vowel."

"Why?"

"I was one of them once. I was nurtured on their values. I hate them as I hated myself. Even the Devil needs to do penance."

Behind us, Dodie's cries were coming in quick succession and my cock was tenting my towel.

"No – please – no more-no more-no more – I can't take it!" She cried again.

Ashton stood. "Gretchen, dear, say goodbye to Mrs Walker. Hope to see you again, Dorothy – perhaps you would like to play with Gretchen again."

A long groan of relief echoed from the bedroom as Gretchen emerged. She and Ashton left. Outside the horizon was turning pink.

I returned to the bedroom to find Dodie tangled in the sheets, her thighs glazed. A wan grin of total satisfaction curled her mouth. I didn't think it was possible: Dodie had been orgasmed into exhaustion.

I didn't mind sleeping on the wet spot – it was all wet. I slept until noon, when the sound of the shower running drew me back to consciousness. I stood and stumbled toward the bathroom. The door was locked, but I didn't have the luxury of pondering Dodie's groundless modesty, my bladder was bursting. I went behind the house to take a leak in nature.

"Dodie! Dodie, are you in there? Damn it, come out!"

I walked around to the front to find Walker. Dodie's bike was on the other side of the wall, just out of his sight.

"What's your problem, Walker?"

"Where's my wife?"

"How should I know?"

"God damn you. If she's in there . . ."

"What? A guy who loans his wife out like a lawnmower shouldn't complain when she wanders out of sight."

"I'll – I'll . . ."

"What? Run to Bradley, get him to fix it for you?"

"Dodie!"

"You're pathetic, man. Get the fuck out of here."

He glared, but he didn't try anything. A klaxon blasted from the wharf. It was the ferry.

"Shit!" I ran back into the house. Dodie cowered behind the door. I told her to stay put until Bink was out of sight, then I yanked on some clothes and took off for the village. Walker was already jogging ahead of me. We got to the village at nearly the same time. An SUV with state police markings pulled off the wharf and headed toward the far end of the island.

I bolted into Bones' place. He stood behind the bar talking to a knot of swells. They dummied up and stared at me.

"Bones, why didn't you tell me the ferry was going to pull in?"

"Didn't know – special trip for the ADA."

"What?"

The others drifted over to a corner table, but kept giving me the hairy eyeball.

"What's up?"

"Ashton Bates – the guy who came in here yesterday with the tall blonde – they found him with his head all bashed in over on Cate's Rock."

"But – Jesus, I just talked to him, I . . ." I looked around and decided to shut up.

I went outside and hailed the ferryman, Al Benedict.

"Can you take me over to the Cape today?"

"Can't – Pirelli doesn't want anyone leaving the island."

"Pirelli? Who the hell is that?"

"Cape and Islands ADA. He's investigating the murder. They're flying in a forensics team from Hyannis. Meanwhile, nobody gets on my boat without his OK."

"Fuck!" I stalked back to the tavern.

"Bones, what's the story with that guy Ashton? The fucker just showed up at the house last night – I didn't know him from Ted Williams' grandma."

"Pirelli doesn't want us to talk. He's coming back here to interview everyone."

"Where's the babe – Gretchen?"

"Don't know. They can't find her. They think she might be dead too."

"Screw this."

I headed back to the house. I had a bad feeling.

It was getting near sunset. I stepped out of the shower and pulled on a pair of jeans and a polo shirt and went outside. I could feel the other shoe hurtling through the atmosphere at my head. It arrived in the form of the state police SUV.

A guy about 40 stepped out.

"I'm Glen Pirelli, Cape and Islands District Attorney's office."

I nodded.

He looked over the house. "A little spare for Wang's tastes."

"He never slept here."

"The feds will be locking up this one too."

"When they get around to it."

Pirelli's eyes were black, gleaming pools that fixed on me like a cobra's.

"I understand you entertained Ashton Bates early this morning."

"We entertained each other."

"We'd like to come in."

"Go ahead, it's not my house."

He motioned for me to lead, then he and a sergeant followed me inside. They took a cursory look around.

"What did you and he talk about?"

I decided to let him have it straight. "He said he was going to leave everything he owned to me. He said he was dying."

"You knew him for a long time?"

"I didn't know him from a hole in the wall."

"But he just arrives on your doorstep and announces you're his sole beneficiary. Did you know his personal estate is worth upwards of $30 million?"

"Nope."

Pirelli shook his head. "How are you getting by now that your employer has fled the country?"

"Like everyone else, he screwed me, and left me on this fucking island. I've been trying to get off since."

"Where were you between 8 and 9 a.m.?"

"Here."

"Alone?"

I didn't reply.

He snickered. "Look, I've interviewed everyone on this island, and you know what? Every one of them has someone else who will corroborate their whereabouts when Ashton Bates was killed. Now that's pretty funny, because if you can alibi yourself, I have to start looking for a murderous frogman who climbed onto this rock and killed Bates. So, amuse me – were you alone?"

"No."

"Who was here with you?"

"A married lady."

"I see. And she'll back you up?"

"Maybe, I don't know."

"What did you have to drink last night?"

"I don't remember."

"How about a very expensive and rare Jamaican rum?"

The sergeant held out a paper bag and Pirelli lifted a bottle gingerly by the mouth. It was the bottle Gretchen offered to me. There was dried blood and hair stuck to the bottom.

"Maybe."

"The sergeant here is going to take your fingerprints. You see, this was the murder weapon. The neck, which the killer would have held, has been wiped clean, but not the bottom. What are the chances your prints are on it?"

"If it's the bottle we shared when he came calling, I'd say there was a pretty good chance, along with the prints of his assistant, Gretchen."

"Oh, by the way, what did you do with her?"

"What?"

"Uh, sorry. But, you just gave me a motive, a murder weapon, and opportunity. Your alibi is unreliable."

"How do you see that?"

"I'm projecting here, but you're in tight straits. You're given a chance at getting your hands on millions of dollars. You decide not to wait for him to die; he could change his mind, so you help him along with that bottle. Probably took care of the woman too. As for your married lady, well, I think it's a safe bet she's going to say she was home, snuggled up with her hubby all night. You're affiliated with a known criminal. You're in a world of shit, friend."

"I'd say you had a tough sell. Besides, he was just blowing smoke out his ass, he liked to play games."

"Doesn't make any difference. I just have to convince a jury that you thought he was on the level. In the meantime, we'll be checking his will. So, I have enough right now to bring you over to Barnstable and lock you up, but I think I'll let you stew right here. Hell, you can't go anywhere."

Could things get any more fucked up?

I stayed outside drinking from a bottle of Jack Daniels. Night came and far over the sound the lights glowed on the Vineyard. It was Saturday night and they would be getting ready for some hard partying over there. Beyond the sound the Cape beckoned. But I was stuck on that fucking rock, imprisoned like Dante.

The whine of an engine drew my attention to the Jeep

headlights bouncing toward the house. The vehicle stopped and Bones beckoned to me to get in. A chill ran up my back.

"C'mon," he barked.

I took the bottle with me and climbed in with him. "Where are we going?"

"A place."

"Oh."

We drove on in silence and it began to gnaw at me that Bones might be employed in another errand, paying off another favor. We drove to the edge of the shore until a weather shack loomed in the headlights. They were scattered all around the island. Shelters for hikers.

"Get out," he said.

"How come?"

A woman's voice answered from the darkness. "We have much to discuss."

It was Gretchen. Bones grinned. "Take it easy."

He popped the Jeep into gear and drove off.

Gretchen held an oil lamp and beckoned me to follow her inside the shack. Inside a few dozen candles flickered. She sat on a small wooden bench and motioned to me to join her.

"You set me up," I said. "Why?"

"All will be revealed. Ashton's work is playing out just as he predicted."

"What the hell are you talking about?"

"It's a play, a reality play, if you will. Trust him."

"Trust him? He's dead. Someone cracked his skull with that bottle you handed me."

"All according to plan."

"Lady, you're nuts, and so was your boyfriend."

She frowned. "Everything will fall into place. You will be hearing from Mr Pirelli, no later than tomorrow."

"No shit. He'll be coming for me with a set of handcuffs."

"You are too tense. Drop your trousers."

"What? Jesus, lady, there's a time for fun and then there's . . ."

She pressed one palm against my chest and pushed me back

like I was a rag doll. With her other hand, she deftly unzipped my jeans. I was pushing myself back up when she yanked my pants down to my ankles. Before I could get to my feet she clamped one hand around my cock and the other around my balls. I might as well have been a kitten held by the scruff, I couldn't move.

She wedged her thumb into the hollow at the underside of my cock, and instantly electrical pulses hummed up my rod. She released my balls as the pulses increased in speed and intensity. All at once all I could focus on was the buzz thrumming up my cock.

"There, relax," she soothed.

"Is . . . is this what you did – to Dodie?"

"Something similar. That girl lives on the ends of her nerves. I could have kept her coming until she fell into a coma."

That's where I feared I was headed. I desperately need to come, but I couldn't fire.

"Please!" I hissed.

"Oh, you're going to beg? Good – you're such a good subject."

"I'm going to explode."

"Patience."

"Jesus, please let me . . ."

She slid her thumb down to my balls and my come splat loudly against the wooden walls. Afterward all the tension drained away. Gretchen cradled me in her arms and I passed out.

I stepped into bright sunshine and sucked in two lungsful of ocean air. I didn't even have a hang-over, though I deserved one. Gretchen stood off toward the shore. She turned and smiled.

"Feeling better?"

"I feel great." Then the reality of my situation set in. "Good enough for a guy who's about to take the fall for murder."

"Come," she ordered, like I was a pet dog.

We walked to the village and put in to Bones' Tavern. We'd no sooner sat down when the phone rang.

Bones lifted the receiver. "Yeah, he's here." He held the phone out to me.

"Yeah."

"It's Pirelli. We rushed the autopsy on Bates. He was terminal all right. In another week or two he would have been in agony. Docs confirmed time of death too."

"So what?"

"There is a will. It's filed in Worcester County and it was recently amended."

I could see Pirelli building his case.

"Yeah, and?"

"We would have been searching for weeks before we found it, but we got an anonymous tip last night. But the reason I'm calling you is what happened when we tried to look at it."

"Huh?"

"Justice William Thackeray Ayers tried to have it sealed."

"Why?"

"Someone with some deep juice wants it kept under wraps. We're talking real old school – like back before the Revolution old school."

"No shit."

"You want to get on my bad side – you try to obstruct justice. I don't give a shit who you are; I'm on you like a pit bull."

"I believe you."

"I'll pick you up in 15 minutes."

"Huh?"

"We're taking a helicopter ride."

"Where?"

"Fitchburg – that's where the documents are. I want you there. I have a hunch you'll spot what we're looking for before we do."

Finally, I was off the island, winging over the south coast in a state police chopper. We left Buzzards Bay behind and bee-lined northwest until we passed the turnpike, then due north from Worcester. We landed at the small municipal airport and piled into a couple of cruisers for the ride into Fitchburg.

It was a decaying mill city in Massachusetts' version of Appalachia. It had seen its best days too long ago to remember, and even its worst days hadn't been tallied yet. But in the center of ramshackle buildings and abandoned factories was an oasis, a garden park that lay like a welcoming carpet to the entrance to the Northern Worcester County Registry.

We were met by a big Irish glad-hander with a nose like Bardolph, all flaming and bulbous. "Hi-Hi-Hi! Bernard Shanahan," he greeted us.

"Pirelli, Cape and Islands ADA."

"Good to meet ya, and how's your mother?"

That threw Pirelli off. "Um, she's fine."

"And God bless her."

He shook my hand. "And how's your mother?"

"She died about four years ago."

"And don't we miss her."

He led us into a room, ornately detailed in carved wood. "I laid everything out for you. Mr Bates was good enough to leave an inventory and instructions."

He closed the doors behind him and we went to work. It didn't take long. Ashton's instructions read like a script.

"I got it," I said. It was all there on a bright yellow piece of paper that stuck out like a whore's tits in church.

It was around 11 o'clock and I was alone in Bones' Tavern. I knocked back a slug of Jack and waited.

Bradley blustered through the door and stood like a raging bear in the middle of the room.

"You? Where's Pirelli?"

"He'll be here."

He laughed. "Your hash is in the fire, mister. I knew you were trash, a bag man for a thieving chink."

"But I'm not a murderer."

"Ha! We'll see if a jury says so."

"I'm not a cocksucker, either."

He went as still as a rock. "What?"

"The night of the key party, all you bored bluebloods looking for a little thrill in your gray lives, and here comes Ashton, the gamesman, the jester."

His ears were bright red.

"Draw a key, and get a blow job – or give a blow job – in the dark. Let the sucker guess the suckee – what a hoot."

"You have no business talking about that night. If Walker had the balls to discipline his wife . . ."

"Yeah, Walker and his balls."

I could hear his teeth grinding together.

"You wanted to get your mouth on those balls, didn't you? His dick too, just like when you were kids, experimenting at Camp Bugger-Boy or whatever."

"You prick."

"You knew Ashton at Yale, but you knew him from years before. He was some kind of cousin umpteen times removed. Ashton knew you were in the closet, because he was right in there with you, but he wanted to come out in a big way. You ended up sandbagging him."

"You can't prove any of this."

I ignored him. "When Ashton came to the island with all his wonderful games and diversions, he and you got to talking about Yale, about secrets. Maybe you got drunk and told him how you used to fool around with your younger cousin who looked up to you like some kind of family hero.

"So, Ashton came up with a way for you to taste your cousin's cock and no one would be the wiser. You were the guy he sent to Walker's room. It must have broken your heart that the dumb prick didn't even realize it was you, let alone tell the difference between a man's tongue and a woman's. Of course, by then he was consumed by his current kink – watching Dodie get fucked by other men.

"So, no harm, no foul – until Ashton spilled what he'd done. What a prick, he revealed just enough."

"I'll kill you."

"Like you killed Ashton? He told you he left everything to me – a total stranger – including his piece of this accursed island. That must have driven you crazy."

"Bastard! When they put you away his will will be voided by the courts. Ashton's property will revert to the Chaukunamaug Trust."

"That's what you were counting on. But, maybe with his dying gasp, he told you about a document in his papers that spelled out the whole lurid affair. You see, he was playing a game, and using you like a pawn. He loved games – 'reality dramas' he called them.

"He was dying, within a couple of weeks he'd have to take mega doses of morphine, and he didn't want to linger like that. He engineered his own murder, and he knew you so well, he knew he could goad you into it."

"You can't . . ."

"Yes, we can. Pirelli made it to the papers before your uncle, the Superior Court justice, could order them sealed and locked up for years with motions until they conveniently became lost or damaged. Bag man? I can't hold a candle to you phony bastards."

Bradley tottered toward me like a man suddenly drunk. Pirelli stepped from out of the back room with Bones and Gretchen. Two state troopers came through the door, took Bradley's arms and put him in cuffs.

"Bradley Whitman," Pirelli announced. "You're under arrest for the murder of Ashton Bates."

I bought a loft off Houston Street since returning to New York. Gretchen decorated it real nice. She's been teaching me things: art, languages, cooking, how to hold an orgasm for up to a minute.

When we left the island I insisted on taking the ferry. I handed two five-dollar gold pieces to Al Benedict – fare for the ferryman, with a wish that I'd never ever return.